THE CHANGE UP

ALEXIS BUXTON

Developmental Editor: Running Bookworm
Editor/Proofreader: My Brother's Editor
Cover Designer: Mel D. Designs
Publisher's Name: 419 Publishing, LLC.
Publisher's Address: 1978 Havemann Rd, #161, Celina, OH 45822

Other Titles

CTU Eagles

The Late Hit

The Christmas Scramble

Playlist

"July" Noah Cyrus
"You Broke Me First" Tate McRae
"Rich Flex" Drake ft. 21 Savage
"Your Name Hurts" Hailee Seinfeld
"I Will Not Bow" Breaking Benjamin
"Miss You A Little" Bryce Vine
"I Wanna Be Yours" Arctic Monkey
"It's Not Over" Daughtry
"Dandelions" Ruth B.
"You Belong With Me (Taylor's Version)" Taylor Swift
"What A Time" Julia Michaels & Niall Horan
"Remember That Night?" Sara Keys
"Scared to Start" Michael Marcagi
"Lose Control" Teddy Swims
"Everywhere, Everything" Noah Kahan
"Healing" Fletcher
"Kick Start My Heart" Motley Crue
"Paper Rings" Taylor Swift
"Spin You Around" Morgan Wallan
"Fireman" Lil Wayne
"Slow It Down" Benson Boone
"Flowers in Your Hair" The Lumineers
"Bright" Echosmith
"Hold On" Chord Overstreet
"Always Been You" Jessie Murph
"Lover" Taylor Swift

For the complete soundtrack,
search THE CHANGE UP on Spotify.

Before You Read

This book does feature a few trigger warnings. Please read on with caution as these triggers may be considered spoilers.

This book contains adult material including childhood trauma, psychological abuse, and parental abandonment. The Change Up is an open-door romance with explicit sexual content, strong language, as well as college-aged main characters drinking.

I hope that I've handled these topics in the care that they deserve. Readers, please be advised.

You are enough.

"My light illuminated in his presence because his soul was the one mine had been promised to."—Nicole Fiorina, *Stay With Me*

THE
CHANGE
UP

CHAPTER 1

Chloe

Ave you ever watched the boy you love, love another?

Tonight I'm supposed to be celebrating. It's the Saturday after the football team won the National Championship game. Alcohol is flowing. Music is vibrating from the speakers. Everyone is living their best lives.

Meanwhile, I'm nursing my second beer, which is now piss warm, as I watch the boy I love from afar. He tilts his head back as he lets out a booming laugh. The laugh cuts straight through me as I'm hit with a flood of memories.

Ugh, this is the worst.

My body hasn't moved from this dark corner in what feels like years. It's rooted in place, vines growing up the wall cementing me to this spot. The dark brown-haired boy with the hazel colored eyes is the sun, and I'm the flower stretching to get a hint of its rays. Begging for the slightest bit of attention.

Last semester, my former roommate and I had a huge fight where she basically implied I was a stalker when it came to my feelings for him. Maybe Macy was right. Maybe I do have a problem. But I don't think I do. I'm just a girl who got caught up in the magnetic field of a boy who refuses even to acknowledge her presence. Which is the worst considering he's a vital part of our friend group. The group of people who two years ago formed a bond our freshman year of college and quickly shifted our friendship into some sort of dysfunctional family. But while I'm here begging for a glimpse of the sunny personality he gives everyone else, I'm trapped in the shadow.

We live in opposite spaces.

If he is the entire galaxy, I am only one star.

He doesn't see me. He never does.

Instead, he sees the beautiful bombshell dancing against him. And I can't say I blame him. Monica is your typical sorority girl. Her perfect blonde hair and outfits are always on trend. I don't think I've ever seen her without makeup or her hair out of place, which is great for her, but it feels artificial. Not to mention her high-pitched voice is always too cheery and too excited. Everything in life doesn't require an extra decibel or two. If she didn't try so hard to appear perfect and get the attention of every male on campus, she might not be that bad. But the biggest issue is her personality. She's always dimming his light. She snuffs out his energy. The more that she's in his orbit the more his sunshine starts to hide.

I wonder when she looks at him, does his soul call to hers like it does mine?

I'm sure it does.

Cody Jacobs is a gift. He was handpicked by God himself to touch people's lives. He's imprinted himself in me, only I wish I'd done the same to him.

Internally rolling my eyes as I chastise myself, it sounds like I'm describing the plot from one of the romance novels I love to read.

"Drink up, bitch," my best friend, Brynn, screams over the pulsating music. Her fingers slide under the red plastic cup I'm holding against my chest as she tips the cup toward my face. Scowling at her, I do as she says. Warm liquid slides down my throat as a shiver trails my spine. Chugging the beer down, I don't stop until it's empty. My stomach immediately wants to roll at the awful beer I just inhaled. A drop escapes my mouth and slides down my chin. I use the back of my hand to wipe the stray drop, thankful that I didn't consume all the liquid.

"Thatta girl!" Brynn exclaims, bumping my shoulder with hers.

"Where's your man?" I ask, taking in her appearance. Brynn is pretty in the natural sense of the word. Her long, platinum blonde hair is almost white compared to my warm, honey-blonde. It's curled in loose waves that hang down her back. An oversized, powder-blue CTU Football shirt is the only thing she's wearing. That and a pair of white sneakers. Her style is always casual which she pulls off in an effortless chic manner. I love how she embraces her style and never dresses to impress anyone.

I mean, why would she need to when she scored the hottest football player on campus? Quinton and Brynn hit it off at the beginning of our freshman year, becoming quick besties. I'm so glad they realized they had feelings for each other and finally got together last semester. It only took them until our junior year to wake up, but better late than never. Our circle feels more complete.

I watch as Brynn looks around the room. She shrugs before turning back around to me to answer. "He's around here somewhere with a bottle of whiskey in his hand. These jersey chasers better keep their distance if they know what's good for them."

I roll my eyes. Quinton wouldn't dare look at another girl. Not only is he loyal to her, but Brynn wouldn't think twice about kicking his ass.

Quinton Boyd is a member of the Central Texas University football team—the star running back of the Eagles. This party was well-deserved, but I can't imagine how hard it is to keep the girls away. He had a hard enough time as it was before they won, but ever since the team came home with the trophy, girls have been flocking to him. They act like they have a right to fling themselves on him just because he won a game. It's disgusting. He's still a person and not a trophy to show off.

"Yo, Brynn!" Jeremiah Price, one of the football team's best defensive back shouts from across the room. He might be CTU's favorite defenseman, but to us, he's JP, our favorite goofball. Brynn and I whip our heads in his direction. "I need a partner for pong!"

She nods her head at his request, reaching for my arm. "Come on!"

"I'll be over soon," I say, shaking off her grip.

Truth is, I don't want to leave my corner. My feet are rooted in place, and I don't mind being the fly on the wall.

"Are you sure?" she asks, her eyes boring into me as if she's trying to read my soul.

Pasting on a big fake smile, I nod at her. "Yeah! Now go kick some drunk butt!"

With a quick peck on my cheek, I watch my best friend weave her way through the makeshift dance floor. That's when my eyes wander back to the dark-haired boy who consumes my every thought. Monica has her tongue halfway down his throat, and Cody's hand is skating up the back of her thigh.

I can't watch this anymore.

My feet free from the sticky, beer-soaked floor, and in the next moment, I'm charging through the sea of people. Tilting my head down, I move through the people. But my inner turmoil gets the better of me. As I glance his way one last time, I cringe at the sight of their two bodies fused in a heated make-out session. Drunk bodies bounce off me as I slide and duck my way through the crowd.

Just get to the front door. Once you get through the door, it'll all be better. The fresh air will do you good.

I'm almost through the crowd of sweaty bodies when a guy stumbles into my shoulder. Instantly, I feel a sinking feeling in my stomach. I'm going to face-plant in front of all of these people. But I don't. Instead, I'm tumbling into Cody and Monica. Can I look any crazier? My shoulder bounces off his back, causing them to stumble. I don't stick around to see what happens.

Gaining my balance, I sprint—well, as best as I can in a crowded room—and run out the door. Flicking my wrist, I let the door slam shut behind me. I don't stop walking until I'm on the sidewalk. Mortification courses through me, and I feel the tears welling up in my eyes.

Forget the fresh air. The only thing I want right now is to curl up under my covers with the newest romance book release I downloaded on my Kindle this morning.

If I'm presented with the opportunity to face my troubles head-on or escape reality through the pages of fictional characters, I'm choosing the book every damn time.

Real life sucks.

Give me a broody book boyfriend, someone else's drama, and all the steamy scenes.

CHAPTER 2

CODY

"**D**UDE, THIS PARTY IS SICK," HUDSON, MY teammate, roommate, and best friend, shouts over the music as he tosses his arm around my shoulder. The cup of keg beer sloshes over the rim as he dangles it in front of my chest. I watch as tiny droplets hit the gray T-shirt I'm wearing leaving dark spots behind.

The two of us played together in a summer baseball league outside of Dallas before we even started college. Our summer spent playing ball together bonded us immediately. Both of us have a love for the game and a passion for the next level. Plus, we both like to party.

"Hell yeah!" I respond, gazing around the packed Football House, home to a handful of guys on the team. It's a colonial house that has been passed down through the football team over the past six years. Right now, my buddy Quinton lives here with his brother and two other guys. There was a time when Quinton and I weren't super tight, but that all changed once he started dating one of my best friends, Brynn Wilder.

Drunk people are crammed into every inch of the house. Most of the furniture has been moved out to the garage to create more space. The makeshift dance floor is lined with people ass to elbow. Navigating through the crowd is nearly impossible. It's so crowded people are spilling out of the back door looking for a place to stand where they aren't getting pushed every time someone tries to walk by. If we aren't careful, campus PD will be rolling up and shutting this shit down.

And none of us need that.

Especially those of us on the baseball team.

Baseball season kicks off in a few short weeks. This is supposed to be our year. The year we bring home the hardware just like the football team did. Central Texas University will be the place to come for athletics if that happens. Scratch that, when that happens.

While this university is known for always producing epic sports teams, it seems the teams always manage to come up short in the eleventh hour.

But not this year. This year the baseball program is ready.

I'm ready.

We've been waiting for this opportunity for years. Not to mention our coach is celebrating his tenth season with the team, which is practically unheard of in college sports. Especially for never winning a championship game. Everyone has their eyes on us, which means the team has to be extra careful not to get into any trouble, especially the underclassmen. My eyes scan the room, and I quickly find seven underclassmen all with red Solo cups in their hands.

Hopefully, since the football team just brought home Central Texas's first championship trophy, the campus police will be more willing to turn a blind eye to all the noise. It seems like just about everyone is at the Football House. At least we aren't the only place with too much noise tonight. Some of the fraternities are also hosting parties to celebrate the team's success as if they contributed to the winning season. And I'm not complaining. There's nothing I enjoy more than partying.

Except baseball.

Baseball will always be my first—and only—love.

Being here, witnessing this celebration has made my desire to bring home the hardware for the baseball team grow even stronger. I'm almost desperate at this point. I'll do whatever it takes to get the team ready. And prove to my dad that I do, in fact, have what it takes. But fuck him, he's not taking me out of this moment.

"Bro, tell me why the fuck you ended things with Monica," Ty groans, coming up to meet us and interrupting the whirlwind my brain was spinning. I follow his gaze to the dance floor.

Girls are dressed in skimpy clothes, grinding on each other and hoping to bring home a jock. I'm not stupid. I know the girls on campus are only after one thing.

Skimming the crowd, my eyes land on honey-blonde hair and eyes bluer than the sky on a cloudless day. She tries desperately to blend into the wall, avoiding the crowd completely.

The only problem is I see her. I've always seen her. No matter how hard she tries to melt into her surroundings, those bright eyes call to me like a siren singing her song to lure me into her depths. Those bright eyes beg me to dive head-first into her soul.

Only they're not the blue eyes attached to the girl Ty is talking about. They're not the eyes of the girl who had been working her way into my bed over the last couple of weeks.

Nope, this girl.

This girl is completely off-limits.

"Earth to Jacobs." Hudson nudges. It's then that I realize his arm is still dangling off my shoulders. Shrugging out from under his touch, I take a long gulp of the beer in my hands. I don't stop drinking until the cup is empty.

I need another one.

"Seriously, dude. Monica is a total catch." Ty continues. His eyes peruse her as she makes her way over to us. I watch as he takes in her low-cut dress which has her large tits on display. One wrong move, and she's going to have quite the wardrobe malfunction. But knowing Monica, she'd welcome the attention.

Monica and I ended things a few weeks ago. It was fun while it lasted, but the two of us had an arrangement. She was a distraction, someone to let me work my stress out on. Nothing more, nothing less. A means to an end.

"Cody," she chimes, throwing her arms around my neck. Her pink plumped lips find mine. Monica seems to have forgotten that our little arrangement is over and that I don't do public displays of affection. But maybe I can let things slide one more time. We always have a good time together. The girl knows her way around the bedroom. And the season doesn't start for a few more weeks.

Monica's lips are still planted on mine, and I give her a small kiss back. It's not at the intensity she's after, but it's enough to satisfy her for now. Hudson is still grinning like a cat who ate the canary, knowing I'm going to allow her back in my bed one last time.

Reaching up, I lightly circle Monica's wrists before pulling them down. Ending our kiss, I step away giving us a little more space.

"I'll be back." I don't give her any room to object before I brush past her and head toward the kitchen. But I see the slow smirk that spreads across her lips.

I need another drink.

Pushing my way through the crowd, I don't even flinch

when my shoulders bump into others. Nothing is getting in my way from getting another drink and getting me back to the girl who is going to distract me one last time from the one girl I can't have.

"Cody!" A platinum blond pops in front of me flinging her arms around my neck. I guess I was wrong. There's only one person I'd let get in my way. Scratch that, there are two, but only one who would actually make the move.

I can't fight the smile that breaks free. She releases me before stepping—stumbling—away from me. I reach out and grab her by the crook of her elbow, steadying her. "You a little drunk, B?"

The mischievous smile that spreads across her face is answer enough. "Maybe." She slurs, eyes full of happiness, and a slight glaze.

Happy looks good on her.

Brynn Wilder has been through a lot. But you wouldn't know it. Her stubborn ass kept it buried deep inside her. Hell, I considered her my best friend, and she never once let on that she's had to deal with insurmountable guilt and grief at such a young age. Once she finally let us all in, so much of her wild behavior began to make sense.

The endless cycle of men. The spontaneity. The weed and alcohol. The wild nights of endless partying. I mean, it's college, and we all love to party, but B took it further than most. It all clicked into place when she decided to be real and share the nitty-gritty details that made up her fucked up childhood. She was living to forget, to escape the past. And no one could fault her.

But since falling in love with Quinton, she's always happy. Happy in a real sense of the word, not the fake happy bullshit so many of us put on as a front.

"Having fun, Cody?" Brynn's eyes bounce to mine as she tries to get a read on me.

"I'm having more fun now that you're here."

"Aw, Cody," Brynn slurs. "You know I'm always down to have some fun with you."

Out of the corner of my eye, I see Quinton staring as he makes his way closer to us. One of my favorite things to do in life is rile Q up. I like to see how far I can push him with my flirting before he steps in with his alpha-possessive ego. It's fun and innocent because those feelings just aren't there for Brynn and me. There were two seconds where I thought I had feelings for Brynn, but those feelings quickly faded away. She's my best friend, and that's it.

"You wanna get out of here?" My voice carries over the music. She must see him approaching too because she turns up the charm and fights the laugh that's desperate to break free.

"The fuck you two will," a voice shouts. I watch as two muscled black arms wrap around Brynn's waist. I can't fight the booming cackle that erupts from me.

"Wassup, Q?"

"What's up is I come to check on my girl and find your punk ass propositioning her." Q's eyes narrow into slits, his chest huffing and puffing as he stares me down. Quinton has an inch, maybe two on me. But where I'm built like a baseball pitcher, Quinton is built like a brick shit house. I have no doubt that he would pummel my ass into the ground in a heartbeat. I mean, I'd still manage to get one, maybe two, good shots in, but he'd have me destroyed in no time.

Brynn stands there, resting her weight in Quinton's arms, and watches as her boyfriend tries to intimidate me. Keeping a straight face, I stare right back. I'm not one to back down from a challenge. A few minutes pass—okay, a few seconds—before my eyes flick down to meet Brynn's gaze. Our eye connection has Q tightening his grip. In the next breath, the two of us erupt, Brynn clutching onto Quinton's arm as her body shakes in hysterics. No longer able to keep up the charade, I stick my fist out for Q to bump.

"Jesus, bro. Take that alpha-male bullshit, and get the fuck out." My grin takes over my face, and I can't help but laugh harder when I watch the serious expression melt off his face into pure confusion.

"You're such a pain in my ass, Jacobs," Q grates, finally hitting my fist with his.

I watch as Brynn turns her body in his arms. She glides her hands up his arms, over his chest, before finally resting them behind Q's head. "Relax, Q. You know I've only got eyes for you."

His lips find hers and suddenly the room feels a bit too small for the three of us. Clearing my throat, I glance around the room before mumbling, "I'm just gonna..." I let the words trail off as I point over my shoulder. Leaving the two love birds alone, I continue my search for the booze.

I found the booze. Oh, did I find it. I am drunk, working my way to wasted.

The alcohol has spread through my veins leaving me in a state of blissful intoxication. Music is pumping from the speakers, the beat flowing through me. I don't know if my heart is beating from the alcohol, the music, or the adrenaline, but my blood is flowing.

The party isn't showing any signs of ending. The crowd has thrown the 'E-A-G! L-E-S! Eagles! Eagles! Eagles!' chant out only a hundred thousand times. This campus was desperate for a championship trophy, and we are fully embracing the celebrations.

A few of the more popular football players—Quinton; Tyler Harris, the quarterback; Jeremiah Prince, dubbed JP, one of the defensive backs; Crew Riggsby, a tight end; and a few others—all participated in their best touchdown celebration dances.

It helps that Monica has found her way back in my grip. At this point in the night, it's welcomed. We both know how we are ending this party.

The music changes to a Drake and 21 Savage song. The beat is sick, and Monica must feel it too. She's backing her ass up against my dick and moving her hips to the beat. Goddamn, this girl can move. It's one of the reasons why I slept with her the first night. She knows what to do in bed. That might make me sound like a douche, but I don't even care. It's the truth. Even if, for me, it's all she's good for.

Gripping her hips tighter, I pull her in closer, driving my hardening cock into her ass. I feel the moan reverberate through her body.

Leaning forward, I brush my lips against her ear. "One more night?"

She nods her response. Spinning her, I grab her wrists, gliding them up until they are wrapped around my neck erasing the space between us. She moves and grinds her hips to my front.

Heated eyes find mine, no doubt covered in a glassy film from all of the alcohol I've consumed. "You know how to work your body."

With that praise, she's pulling my face to hers. Our lips find each other, only this time it's in a welcomed kiss. With a flick of my tongue against the seam of her lips, I prompt her to open for me. My tongue dives into her mouth, and I don't fight the groan that escapes. One of her arms slowly slips from around my neck, gliding across my chest, and brushing the zipper of my pants. My cock twitches at the contact.

Tongues tangling, I welcome the very public, very graphic display of affection. Getting lost in the moment, I skate my hands from her hips and grip her round globes, pulling her harder to me.

A minute later, Monica is stumbling into me. Breaking our kiss to catch us both from falling over, I'm just about to turn and have words with the dick who bumped into us only to see golden hair flying through the door. The smell invades my senses.

Lilies.
Sandalwood.
Wildflowers.
Her.

CHAPTER 3

Chloe

A MORE MIA.”

“Hi, Dad!” I greet, using my dough-covered fingers to place the call on speaker.

“How’s my favorite daughter?”

A soft chuckle escapes my lips. “Dad,” I groan. “I’m your only daughter.”

“Therefore my favorite.” I shake my head. This is such a dad joke, and mine uses it all the time. “What are you doing this morning?”

“I’m currently wrist-deep in pizza dough for girls’ night tonight.” My eyes glance around the kitchen of the townhouse I share with Brynn as I take in the mess before me. This morning I was in the mood to do some major baking which means now the white granite counters are scattered with baking ingredients and dirty dishes.

Being in the kitchen is my favorite form of self-care. It’s a way for me to shut my brain off, embrace the chaos, and make something beautiful. The kitchen is my source of solace. I know

I'm an anomaly, and you won't find many college-aged people in the kitchen making homemade pasta and baking loaves of bread, but it's what I enjoy.

It allows me to connect with my dad. Growing up, I was always in the kitchen helping him. I loved being his sous chef, and by helping him I, too, grew to love cooking and baking. My mind flashes to a memory I had long forgotten. I was seven, standing on a step stool, missing two front teeth, and my hair was piled high in uneven pigtails because my dad hadn't gotten the hang of doing them. Flour coated my face as he taught me how to make scones. The recipe came from his mom—my nana—as the two of us were needing something comforting.

Over the years, he's given up and lost a lot along the way, but one thing that never wavered was his hard work and dedication. It's admirable to see how hard he's worked to be where he is in his career by the age of forty.

When I was twelve, Dad got his big break. He won a food competition which earned him the award of becoming a sous chef at a top restaurant in Dallas. Between a food critic and journalist at the local paper, he was featured in a few articles talking about the next up-and-coming chef to hit Dallas. This was the gateway to the biggest career break he could have asked for. Now Scott Mariano is a Michelin-star chef and one of the country's top chefs. He owns two restaurants—an Italian restaurant in Dallas called Amore and Mariano's Prime Chophouse in Boston.

We owe a lot to the journalists who wrote dozens of articles on Dad. Seeing how crucial featured pieces are to newcomers in the food industry, it really inspired me to pursue a degree in journalism. I want to meet and highlight local chefs and help someone get their big break. Ideally, I'd love to get a job working for *Bon Appétit* magazine or even writing articles for Food Network's website.

My dad hums in response. "What's my little sous chef baking?"

"Oh you know, a little bit of everything. Vanilla bean scones, chocolate chip cookies, and pizza dough. Brynn and I are having a girls' night, and pizza sounded good.

"CTU's very own patisserie. I'm proud of you, Amore Mia."

A smile breaks free while my body heats with a warm and fuzzy feeling over my dad's compliment. "Thanks, Dad. I did learn from the best."

Using my flour-covered hands, I continue kneading the dough working the flour in. Pushing and pulling the dough until it starts to form the correct consistency.

"Speaking of the best," he begins with a mischievous tone. "I've been asked to open a new restaurant in Arizona. It happens to be at a beautiful spa, and I'm arranging for you and your friends to stay there to celebrate the end of your junior year. Which I'm still in denial about."

My hands freeze and sink in the dough. My stomach flutters with excitement.

"Are you serious?" My voice breaks in a squeal. A little happy dance breaks free, and I'm prancing my feet up and down. Giddiness rolls through me.

Growing up, Dad and I didn't have a lot. It was just the two of us after my mom up and left us when I was six. Dad and I have always made do with what we had. We lived in a two-bedroom apartment that some days felt no bigger than a shoe box, especially when Dad was trying out new recipes in the kitchen. Pots and pans littered every available space, the dirty ones often ended up on the floor to make room for more cooking.

It was a sacrifice.

But we never went without the essentials. I was clothed, fed—probably better than most kids since my dad knew how to work the kitchen—and showered with unconditional love.

And while some days the love felt a little overwhelming, I know my dad was making up for my mom's abandonment. Making sure I knew how special I was. After all, I was his Amore Mia.

"Yes, beautiful girl. You and your friends deserve a little trip away from campus and what better way to celebrate the end of the school year than with your best friends…at a spa."

"Daddy, you're the best!" It was a good thing the phone was on speaker and not pressed to my ear, or my dad would have lost hearing with the high-pitched squeals that escaped. His chuckle fills the space, warming my heart, and it's at this moment I miss being home with him. Dad's job keeps him glued to the restaurant, and when he's not there, he's making special appearances on a very popular food network. Now with the new restaurant opening, I'll probably see him even less.

It's getting harder and harder to find time to see him now. My class schedule isn't forgiving, and his life revolves around his business. It'll become even more chaotic as he travels back and forth from Dallas to Arizona. My heart hurts that our relationship is changing, but I'm so proud of him. I'll never let him see me sweat our relationship, not when he's sacrificed so much while giving me the world.

But I can't fault him, he's found his passion in life. And after sacrificing for years while raising me, he deserves his moment. Plus, he's never too busy to give me a call and catch up, so I'll cherish everyone I get.

"I love you, Amore Mia." Voices come from his end of the phone, and I know that our time is ending. "I have to run. I'll have Kimmy email you all the details. I'm so proud of you, baby girl."

"I love you too, Dad," I start to say, but the line is cut off. Kimmy is my dad's assistant, and she's practically part of the family. If it wasn't for her keeping my dad in line, he'd live in the restaurant—or his car outside one of the restaurants.

Pushing my phone aside, I turn my attention to the dough that needs rolling out. Using the rolling pin, I press it into the soft mixture before I roll it away from me and then toward me. Keeping the movement going until the dough is the right thickness. Setting the pizza dough aside, I reach for the dough for the scones before grabbing the cutter as I begin cutting the mixture into triangles.

Sweets are my favorite food. There isn't one I prefer over the other. Give me some sort of carb, and I'm one happy girl. Except I'm one of the only girls who will be declining chocolate pastries. Give me the warm tastes, caramel, vanilla, cinnamon, and I'll be your bestie for life.

With the spatula, I lift each triangle and place them on the wax paper-lined baking sheet before placing them in the oven to cook.

Clicking the buttons to set the timer, I turn to make my way over to the kitchen sink and begin filling it with water and soap. It's time to tackle this disaster before Brynn comes home. It wouldn't be the first time she's come home to an explosion in our kitchen. Never once has she complained about the mess. She knows not to bite the hand that keeps her fed. If it was up to Brynn Wilder, she'd live off fast food burgers and milkshakes.

"Chloe!" Brynn yells from the front door, arriving at the perfect time. "I've got the beer, do you have the pizza?"

Nodding my head, I remove the pizza from the oven. "Of course. I wouldn't leave you in charge of the food."

"Hey, I take offense to that." Brynn strides into the kitchen with a six-pack of Shiner bottles before plopping down on a bar stool. Removing my oven mitt, I grab the magnetic bottle opener that rests on the side of the fridge. Walking back toward Brynn,

I pass the opener across the granite. With a quick flick, she has two beers open and is sliding one toward me.

Catching the bottle, I bring it to my lips for a quick pull. Thirst has set in from all of the baking I did today, and even though beer isn't my first drink of choice, I'm too thirsty to care. I know that lifting weights should be on everyone's radar, but rolling out dough is as exhausting. Or maybe I'm just severely out of shape. I'm a runner, not a lifter.

Brynn's eyes flit around the kitchen. I watch her drool over the waiting pizzas that just came out of the oven. A pepperoni and pineapple pizza—yes, pineapple goes on pizza—and a supreme with all the toppings. Her eyes find the scones placed under a domed tray which are waiting by the coffee maker.

"What all did you bake today?"

"Vanilla scones, chocolate chip cookies, and the dough for the pizza."

"That's all?"

With an eye roll, I answer, "Yes, that's all."

She nods in response as she takes another drink. To some that may seem like a lot, but I've been known to bake six or seven different things depending on my mood. While I love to bake just because, it's also one of my biggest stress relievers. When life gets a bit too overwhelming, I've been known to hole up in the kitchen for hours baking and baking until my body nearly collapses from exhaustion.

Is it healthy? No. Is it therapeutic? Absolutely.

Taking the pizza cutter out of the drawer, I slice it into triangles—the superior pizza shape—while Brynn fills me in on her day. The two of us always seem to have our schedules opposite each other. I have classes from early morning to evening on Monday, Wednesday, and Friday while hers are from early morning to evening on Tuesday and Thursday. We may live together, but we rarely see each other. Her evening class was canceled tonight which is how we managed to both be free.

Sliding a slice of each pizza on our plates, I pass Brynn her plate before reaching to grab my beer. The two of us make our way into the living room.

"What's on tonight?" Brynn asks, taking her spot on the far end of the couch.

"It's Tuesday," I pause, trying to remember the TV schedule. "Oh shit, it's the first episode of the new season of *Vanderpump Rules*!"

"Dude! This season is going to be fucking crazy!"

"Absolutely crazy," I respond around a mouthful of food. Flipping through the channels, I surf until I find Bravo. They're playing last season's finale.

Turning until my back is to the armrest, and my knees are folded, I settle into the cushions, letting them envelop me like a giant bear hug. My attention finds Brynn, and I chuckle as I watch her shovel a mouthful of pepperoni and pineapple pizza into her mouth. She moans around the bite.

"Chloe, this pizza is amazing! Like can you just drop out and open a pizzeria? You'd be a millionaire in no time. Seriously, every person on campus would be keeping you in business, especially after parties."

"Thanks, B, but my dad is the chef, not me."

"Whatever." She takes another large bite of her pizza.

"So how's Q?"

"Ohemgee! I swear he's spent the last two weeks partying his ass off. From college parties to parties at The Eagles Nest. Hell, he's even gone to other bars. Everyone wants to party with the CTU Eagles."

Chewing around a mouthful of food, I take a second to swallow. "I mean it is a big deal."

"Obviously," she says. "But this week he's paying for it. He's like a hungover zombie right now. I saw him last night, and he was laying in bed with his blackout blinds shut trying to sleep off a two-week-long bender."

I laugh, shrugging. "What else is the top running back in the country supposed to do after bringing home CTU's first championship?"

"Please, the boy doesn't need any more ego going to his head. The other day we were having sex, and he paused right in the middle, looked me dead in the eye, and said 'call me Mr. MVP.'" I burst out laughing, choking on the beer I had just attempted to swallow. "I'm not kidding. Motherfucker literally said that. Like I'll call you Daddy before Mr. MVP." She made a gagging noise, and the laughter kept pouring from me.

"Was he joking?"

"Thank God he was. He said he was waiting for my reaction." Her eyes roll. "I told him I was waiting for my orgasms, and he owed me three after that bullshit."

The two of us laugh. I watch as Brynn goes from hysterics to her face dropping, as her features turn serious.

"What's wrong, B?" I ask, my voice softening as I watch my friend wage a war in her mind.

"He's leaving."

Giving her a tight-lipped smile, I reach for her. Brynn sets her plate on the table before putting her hand in mine. I pull her toward me as she slides across the couch. She doesn't stop until the two of us are wrapped together under my blanket.

"Babe, deep down we've always known that Quinton was going to enter the draft and leave school early. He's been talking about his plan since we've known him."

"I know, but like now it's *really* happening."

"Brynn, Quinton Boyd is in love with you. Madly. Deeply. Whole-heartedly. He's not going anywhere."

Her body shimmies before her head rests against my

shoulder. I pull her in tighter to me, wrapping my arm around her shoulders. "I know, but shit, I thought the jersey chasers in college were bad. What's it going to be like when he's in the NFL? Women are going to be throwing themselves at him even more."

"It's for one year. One year apart. Once you graduate next spring, the two of you can be together again. And let me remind you, he loves you!"

"You sound like Cody."

I tense at the mention of his name, hoping Brynn didn't catch the way I stiffened.

She noticed. Sitting up and slipping out from our little cocoon, Brynn turns slightly to face me. "What was that?"

"What was what?"

Her eyes narrow into slits as she stares me down. "You stiffened when I mentioned his name."

"No, I didn't." Lie.

"Yes, you did. Did he do something to you?"

"No." Yes.

She stares me down. This time I had luck on my side, and the TV starts with the intro to the new season of *Vanderpump*. Thank God.

"This isn't over," Brynn says as she settles in next to me, situating herself so the two of us are cuddled together.

Reaching beside her, I watch as she grabs her phone. Swiping open the camera app, she situates the lens until the two of us are at the angle she wants in the frame. Snapping a picture of us, she heads to Instagram before posting it with the caption 'Beers, Bitches, and Vanderpump #noboysallowed.'

"Oh!" I shout during the next commercial break. "My dad called today. He is arranging for us to have a girls' weekend at this spa where he's opening a new restaurant."

"Dude, your dad is freaking awesome," Brynn says with a sigh. "Can he adopt me?"

"Have you finally let the crush on my dad go?"

"Hell no. He's still a Daddy."

"Oh my gosh, Brynn!"

"Whatever, you know your dad is hot."

I roll my eyes before scrolling through my emails. There's a lot riding on this semester. This is my fifth semester on the campus newspaper staff, and it's the one class that I really love. All of my classes are great, but there's just something about getting the hands-on experience of writing for an actual newspaper. The assignments for the semester are supposed to be emailed out any day now which has my phone glued to my hand.

"What's got you so focused on your phone?"

"I'm waiting on an email from the professor of the newspaper staff."

"An email with your assignment for the semester?" she asks, curiosity painting her face.

I blow a deep breath out and toss my phone aside. "Yeah. I'm really hoping I get assigned the lead on the lifestyle beat. It'd be the closest to getting more in-depth practice for post-college."

Brynn pauses the TV before shifting her entire focus to me.

"You've got this, babe. Seriously, you're insanely talented. I mean you are obsessed with words. You're the biggest bookworm I know. Not to mention, I love reading everything you write, and you know I don't like to read. You have a passion for the written word. Every article you write puts the reader in the scene."

"Thanks, Brynn Brynn."

"Anytime, Chlo Chlo. Now can we please get back to the Tom and Katie drama?"

Brynn's right, I've got this.

This is my semester.

My year.

CHAPTER 4

CODY

THERE'S A CRISP AROMA IN THE AIR.

It's the smell of freshly mowed grass, raked clay, and worn-in leather.

It's the smell of determination, hard work, and passion.

Spring baseball season is officially here. But baseball never sleeps, especially with fall ball league and winter conditioning.

This weekend is our first tournament which means The Spring Showcase is upon us. This tournament is the first chance we get to show everyone that Central Texas University means business this season. Any motherfucker that gets in our way better watch out.

"Jacobs!" Coach Callan Weber yells as he makes his way up the steps of the dugout. Tilting my head from side to side, I enjoy the creaks and cracks the bones make. It's a warm day for January. Even though Texas doesn't get much break for the winter, it's still unseasonably warm.

With a nod, I address him. "Yes, Coach?"

"Elbow still treating you good?" His eyes are hidden behind

reflective lenses, but I can feel them boring into me, reading me, looking for any hints that I'm lying. Lucky for me, my elbow has been feeling great.

"It's feeling great, sir. Ready for this weekend."

"Good, I'm glad to hear. Keep an eye on it. I don't need you going all tough guy on us this season. Jacobs, we know you're resilient, but I'm going to need you one hundred percent. If it starts to bother you, get it checked out."

I nod my head in response. At the end of last season, I was pitching one of our last games and felt a sharp pain shoot through my arm. I thought it was the famous "Tommy John" injury, most often a tear to the ulnar collateral ligament. Thankfully, it was just a slight tear in the ligament and wasn't anything that a minor surgery and some physical therapy couldn't fix. But the scare has everyone on high alert, making sure that it's not a full Tommy John injury.

"Throw a few." Coach Weber directs me. Standing on the dirt mound, I get into position on the rubber. My body goes into auto-drive as I follow the same routine I do before every pitch. I kick my left foot back and forth in the dirt until I have it smoothed out where I want it to be. I lean my body forward, bending at my hips, bringing my gloved hand up to cover my mouth. Squinting to read the hand signal Nolan—my catcher— gives me. I shake my head—one, two, three times—before nodding in agreement.

Standing, I bring my arms to my front. With my hand gripping the ball, I feel the laces. The scratchy material grazes over my fingers until I've settled my digits in the correct position for the pitch.

In fluid movements, I reach back and cock my arm before slinging it forward. The ball sails through the air in the perfect curveball, the sound of the ball hitting the leather ricocheting through the field. It's the best sound in the world.

"Hell yeah, Cody!" Hudson yells from the outfield where a few of the guys are running through drills.

Coach claps a hand on my shoulder. "Nice, Jacobs."

And with that, the man of few words walks away.

Coach Callan Weber has been one of my favorite coaches I've had the privilege of working with. He has a tough exterior that hides his charismatic ways.

Weber was the youngest coach in our conference to be hired on as a head baseball coach at the ripe age of twenty-six. He helped his college team win two National Championships before he played three years in the major leagues where his team was a runner-up in his last season.

During the off-season, he suffered a career-ending knee injury on a ski trip with some buddies. Coach Weber encourages us to go out and have fun because *you never know what's going to happen next*—his exact words. But while he wants us to have fun, he still rules with an iron fist to make sure we are keeping our heads in the game and focused on what's at stake.

Reaching into the bucket at my feet, I grab another ball before going through the exact same motions I did when Coach was standing next to me. Even though he's not beside me observing, I take it just as seriously. Like Coach, I have that passion, that love for the game, that drive to win. I'm eager to bring home the hardware, and I refuse to be distracted. It's why I don't fuck around like the rest of the guys do during practices.

When we step between those painted-on lines, it's time to get serious. No talk of girls or partying.

I want to win. I want to be better than my dad. I want to strive to be the best and accomplish my dreams. But if that doesn't happen, I don't want to live my life knocking others down like my father. I'll support my teammates from the sidelines.

He had his chance, but arrogance got in his way. When he was in college, Dad thought he was the best thing to grace his university. While playing—the few games he played—his cocky, holier-than-thou attitude got him nowhere. He made enemies with his teammates, his coaches viewed him as problematic, and he wasn't playing enough to gain the attention of scouts. This was all before his career-ending injury.

A long time ago, I vowed to walk the fine line between cocky and arrogant.

And to be better than him.

And dammit, I will be.

The clinking sound of weights hitting the racks fills the space as I walk through the state-of-the-art weight room doors. Practice was quick since we are hitting the road for our first tournament this weekend. Coach wanted everyone to get some reps in before a mandatory gym session to get some light lifting in. Everyone is feeling the buzz in the air.

Ty's music is linked up to the room's Bluetooth speaker. I watch the jackass attempt to bust out some trendy moves he probably saw on social media. Ty Billings is an excellent baseball player, but the dude has no dance moves. He's one of the only guys on the team who will do anything the CTU Athletics social media team asks him to do, including viral goofy dances.

I make my way over to my favorite bench that the guys leave open for me. They know I'm a superstitious fuck. If I don't follow my routine, I'm fucked for the week.

It's ridiculous, but it's how my brain ticks.

"Clear the way for King Jacobs as he makes his way to his precious throne." Ty hollers, taking a break from the dancing. I flip him off over my shoulder as I keep striding to my spot. Reaching up, I pull my Bluetooth headphones up over my head, drowning out the distractions around me. There's no way I'm listening to trendy pop music right now, not when I need harder music to get me in the zone.

Taking a seat, I lay back under the bar just as Drowning Pool's 'Bodies' starts to float in through my headphones. Hard rock will always be the best weightlifting playlist, and that's a bet I'm willing to take.

Reaching up, my fingers grip the cold metal bar as I begin to lift it from its position when Hudson appears out of fucking nowhere, almost causing me to drop the damn bar.

"Fuck," I hiss. The motherfucker just laughs. Hud always helps spot me, but I didn't see him in the weight room when I walked in. Since I'm just doing light reps, I didn't think about a spotter.

Bending my elbows, I let the bar drop before I power it back up.

Bend. Press.

Repeat.

Bend. Press.

Repeat.

Lifting is such a repetitive action, but it's my favorite way to calm my nerves. There's nothing like a good weightlifting session to drown out the noise.

The guys and I wrap up our reps in the weight room before we all make our way into the locker room. CTU received multiple donations to revamp the locker rooms for all major programs. This is our first year using the improved space. Not only was our locker room renovated, but CTU's entire baseball facility was revamped in a multi-million dollar project.

There have been so many changes starting with the exterior and moving throughout the entire building. But the hallway that leads to our locker room is one of my favorites. Lining the walls are photos throughout the entire CTU baseball history stretched to be the wallpaper. At the opening of the hallway, on one side are older photos from the beginning of the program which get newer as you continue down the corridor. The last photo on the wall is from last season, supposedly the photos will change every year. The opposite wall is a minimalistic design of the CTU Eagles logo throughout the years.

But it's what's at the end of the hallway that always catches my eye.

At the end of the hall, on the wall facing the hallway is a large photo with the word "OMAHA" written above it.

Omaha is home to the College World Series and it serves as a constant reminder of what our end goal is: win a National Title.

Turning right, past the Omaha wall, is another hallway. This space is lined with jerseys from CTU players who have made it to the majors. Inside a large, glass frame their rookie jersey is displayed with their baseball card attached below with a plaque that includes their name, years at CTU, and the date and team name of their debut in the league. It doesn't matter if that person played an inning, day, month, or year, their jersey is on display.

It's great motivation for me to work hard because one day I want to come back here and see my jersey on this wall.

Moving past the wall, I enter double doors that lead to the locker room. As I enter, I take a glance at the bulletin board which is always updated with information that the coaching staff or university wants us to know. There's usually information for away games: what time the bus leaves, where we are staying, how we are getting there—plane or bus, what we need to wear or pack, and any other pertinent information.

Attached is also a photo of how the locker room is supposed to look which acts as our guide to keeping the place in top shape. The university offers paid stadium and facility tours so it's crucial our locker room always looks showroom ready. Coach rotates assigning players to do certain tasks during the week such as dusting and vacuuming. It's his way of teaching additional responsibility and reminding us that it's an honor to play for this program.

Each player has their own locker—a huge upgrade from what we were used to in high school. Our lockers are open, wooden spaces which look more like a display than a typical storage compartment.

I remember one time when I was really young, maybe five or six, I got to go on a stadium tour with my dad to see inside the Atlanta Braves locker room. Since that day, I've dreamed of having my own "special" locker.

In the center of the wooden locker is a large opening where we keep jerseys, CTU windbreakers, and pants all in a variety of CTU color combinations. Keeping everything hung to the left side of the opening, it allows coaches to make sure we are keeping our locker clean and we have a place to sit.

Above and below the opening are smaller cubbies where we store uniform-issued hats and each player's bats, storage drawers for storing undershirts, belts, cups, or anything else that is needed, and lastly, a drawer where a variety of cleats are stored and where we can put our day shoes to keep the clutter off the floor. Everything has to be folded and organized.

"Boys, grab a seat," Coach Weber says as he emerges from his office with some of the other coaches. We do as we're told, finding seats in our assigned lockers. "The games we face this weekend will be challenging. We are facing some great teams who are going to give us a run for our money. They want to win as desperately as we do, which means I need heads in the game. Don't be picking fights with your girlfriends this week or whatever drama you boys find yourselves in usually. This is our opportunity to show the league we are here to win."

Heads nod as we listen to Coach give us the talk. It's the same he gives us before each game. Tried and true. And one we know we better follow or the consequences won't be fun. "Check the board for details as it'll be updated by Wednesday with the final plan for traveling. Oh, and we'll be having a new reporter from the Eagles Gazette trailing us this year. I don't have any additional details, but treat them with respect and help answer any questions they have. And for goodness' sake don't make yourself look stupid. You all have the right to not comment on something if you're uncomfortable."

And with that Coach dismisses us. I reach for the small bag of toiletries I keep in my drawer before stripping out of my athletic shorts and tight-fitting workout shirt. Ignoring everyone around me, I head to the bathroom to grab a quick shower before breakfast and class.

I stand under the hot spray for a few minutes—just letting the water trail down my body—before reaching for my soap. I'm so ready for the season to start. To feel the dirt under my cleats as I mentally prepare to throw pitch after pitch. Baseball is a mental game, and I've got to keep my head straight. Rinsing the soap off, I reach for the towel on the ledge. Quickly drying off, I wrap the towel around my waist and head back to the main room.

Hudson, Nolan, and I get done at the same time so the three of us head to the breakfast room. Coach doesn't allow the use of cell phones in the locker room or breakfast room. It's his way of making sure we not only stay focused but make the effort to talk to each other.

"Think this newspaper reporter will be as wild as the ones who covered the football team?" Hudson asks from beside me.

"Dude, I don't think anyone will be like those two," Nolan adds with a chuckle.

Last year the two reporters who traveled with the football team were fired for misconduct. No one knows the specifics, but the rumors have been circulating since. I've heard anything and everything from secret sex parties with hookers to ragers with massive amounts of illegal drugs to even underground poker games where people would bet on the outcome of the football game. The university has been trying to keep the full story under wraps.

"I heard they were getting expelled from CTU."

"Hookers and blow will do that." We chuckle at the blatant comment from Hudson.

"I don't really give a shit who it is. Hopefully, it's someone who isn't an idiot and knows what the hell they're doing. We don't need someone who is in the way and pulling away our focus," I say as I open the door to the breakfast room.

The dining room isn't nearly as big as a dining hall on campus, but it's large enough to fit two round tables with chairs, a long bar with CTU logo barstools under a TV, and lower cabinets that run the length of two connecting walls.

Buffet trays are set up with scrambled eggs, sausage and bacon, hash brown patties, and trays of fresh fruit, while inside the fridge are a variety of bottled drinks and yogurt. While we always have a team breakfast when we are in season and a team meal before any home game, the room is for us to keep whatever food we want—as long as it's labeled.

"I'm sure the paper and coaches won't let a rookie reporter join us. They won't want the distraction," Nolan adds as he fills his plate.

"I hope you're right," I grumble.

I have no room for drama and distractions.

CHAPTER 5

Chloe

THERE'S A BITTER CHILL IN THE AIR DESPITE THE VERY spring-like weather we were having earlier in the week. It's the type of chill that seeps through your clothes and goes straight to your bones. I'm a Texan through and through. I don't do cold weather. How anyone lives in the north will forever blow my mind. Frigid temps and snow on the ground? Hard pass.

A new romance novel just hit my Kindle, and I'm dying to curl up in an oversized sweater while getting lost in a romantic suspense Mafia book.

Who doesn't want to read about a morally gray brother's best friend falling for the daughter of one of the most feared men in the Mafia who is supposed to be marrying someone else? I'm all about a Mafia baddie.

And to make matters worse, I'm not even supposed to be on campus today. Thursdays are one of my days off from classes. The only reason why I'm stepping foot on campus is because our professor set up a mandatory meeting to discuss our beat assignments for the campus newspaper, The Eagles Gazette. The email

I was waiting for the other night came, but inside was not what I was expecting. Instead of our assignments, we were all notified to meet in person for a formal discussion involving the new assignments. The beat assignments are assigned to every member of the staff to inform us which genre of events we will be covering, such as arts, sports, politics, lifestyle, and so on.

The Eagles Gazette is a club organization on campus where a few members of the staff are offered paid positions while others are hired on an intern-like basis. Each semester beats get reassigned to some degree. Our professors and editors want everyone to get experience writing about different topics to help make us well-rounded journalists. While I think the idea is great, I want to write about the things I'm passionate about.

Students' views on current political topics? Hard pass.

The latest local food establishment whipping up new sandwich creations that are geared toward the late-night munchies? Gimme!

This semester my eyes are on the feature beat, though. I've worked hard the last two years to really home in on my skills and perfect my writing. I feel like I've finally earned the chance to be the lead, even though the feature isn't generally something in my wheelhouse. I know I've got the skills to write an epic article.

However, the rumor around the newsroom is that the feature is going to be all about the new festival coming to Central Texas University this spring. It's a two-day food, drink, and music event. That is exactly what I've been put on this earth to cover.

Walking through the quad is a breeze today, taking me no time. Typically the cobblestone sidewalks are jammed packed with students making their way to the different brick buildings that line the campus. Everyone must've been smart and decided to skip today to not have to deal with this unusually cold Thursday in mid-January.

Why couldn't my professor just cancel and email us our assignments?

Climbing up the few steps to the front entrance of the Union—the building that is home to the basement newsroom—I feel my phone buzz in my purse. The incessant vibrating alerts me that it's an incoming call and not a text.

Who calls anymore?

Stepping aside, I move to the outside corner of the building to get out of the wind as I thumb off my gloves. Grabbing the ringing phone, "Dad" flashes across the screen.

"Two calls in less than forty-eight hours. Does my dad miss me?"

"I always miss my Amore Mia," he answers. I can hear the smile he no doubt has spread across his face. "But that's not why I'm calling."

"Dad, that's not ominous at all." A forced chuckle leaves my lips as worry slides down my spine. "Is everything okay?"

"Well," he starts as I notice the noise of the restaurant disappears which means he's just closed himself inside his office for privacy, the action not easing any of the creeping anxiety.

"Dad..." I prompt.

"Sorry, Chloe. It's chaotic today. A shipment is delayed, and everyone is in a panic. But that's not why I'm calling. Have you checked the weather?"

The weather? Of course I don't check the weather. I live in Texas. What could I possibly be worried about?

"No. I don't even think I have the weather app on my phone. I had to delete a few apps when my storage was running low."

Dad grumbles something indecipherable in Italian.

"First thing, download the app. It's irresponsible not to have an application notifying you of weather alerts."

I roll my eyes as his lecture continues about responsibility and being an adult. My eyes drift back to the quad as I watch a handful of students jog into nearby buildings.

"...ice storm," he says, and my attention clues back into the conversation.

"Wait, what did you just say?"

He sighs. "You tuned out everything I just said, didn't you?"

"Sure did. My brain is freezing. I'm standing outside waiting to go into class."

"Dammit, why didn't you say something? There's an ice storm coming this weekend. You need to prepare," he repeats, grumbling something else I can't make out. He really needs to work on his whole grumbling under his breath. "I'll text you a list of items you should have. If you can't get something, let me know. Get inside." He pauses. "Oh, stay safe, and I love you, Chloe."

I smile. How he can go from rough and gruff to overprotective in a single conversation just amazes me. "I love you too, Dad."

Tossing my phone into my purse, I reach for the handle and swing the door open. The blast of hot air hits me, and I sigh at the warmth, even though it almost takes my breath away.

I hate the cold.

So much for me going home to read. Instead, I'm going to have to fight all the unprepared Texans at the store.

An ice storm? What the hell?

This is Texas. We don't do ice.

Rushing down the stairs, I enter the newsroom and make my way over to the last empty desk. I still beat the professor so I'm not technically late, but I'm definitely tardy by my standard.

The room is filled with desks which would resemble an office space with cubicles, only our desks aren't separated by walls. It's an open space that can be chaotic when people are in a rush to get their articles in on time, but I love the chaos. I thrive on the noise. The sound of fingers hitting keys. Of phones ringing. And our editor demanding assignments. It all thrills me.

Flopping down in my desk chair, I start unbuttoning my trench coat and removing the multiple layers I have on. Abby, one of the other staff members, gives me a quick nod as she smiles over at me in a way of greeting. She handles more of the political beats. I don't envy her.

Professor Weaver enters the room as she slams the door closed behind her. Everyone, including me, jumps at the loud noise. "I did not mean to do that," she says, cringing at the noise. "Okay, today is going to be quick. In case you hadn't heard, there's an ice storm heading this way, and I want you all out of here as soon as possible."

She is now the second person to bring up this potential storm. Maybe my dad wasn't overreacting for once. Shit, I really shouldn't have deleted the weather app off my phone. But we aren't supposed to get harsh winter weather in Texas. It's why I love living here, well, part of the reason. There was no way I was moving out of state and away from my dad.

Tossing her coat on her desk, she quickly types in her login for her computer. The projector flicks on, and we take in the screen before us.

"Now, this semester is not going to be what anyone was expecting. It's taken a couple of weeks to sort out assignments given the circumstances the newspaper organization has found themselves in with the university."

What does she mean? This is supposed to be my year. My turn to showcase how much my writing has improved. If I don't get to cover the festival, I'm going to be devastated. This is my chance to break out from the pack. To show other magazines and newspapers that I have what it takes. Dread courses through my veins, and I'm really questioning my decision to even get out of bed.

"As you all know, we had quite the drama with our sports beat team. Joe and David have been removed from our staff and are facing further disciplinary action from the university."

Murmurs fill the room as everyone whispers over the rumors that caused CTU to expel two students on the staff. Rumors have been flying throughout campus, but no one has gotten the entire truth told to them. Supposedly, the two were engaging in illegal drugs and sex parties at the hotels the school was paying for. Not sure of all the details, but no matter what, it wasn't good.

Professor Weaver clears her throat, gaining everyone's attention before continuing. "With that being said, we now need to shuffle veteran staff members around to make sure that an experienced writer is covering the Sports A Team, especially with it being Coach Weber's honorary year."

Please don't let it be me. Please don't let it be me.

"Chloe Mariano, you will be assisting in the sports coverage this semester. You'll be the lead with a focus on the baseball program and the featured article on Coach Weber." And my stomach sinks. "Abby Taylor, you'll be shifting focus and covering the Red, White, and Brew festival."

Sports? This is not how this semester was supposed to go. I was supposed to be the lead and write the most epic article that was going to be my big break. It would've been the perfect article to submit for any upcoming internships, which I need to start applying for this semester.

"Professor Weaver." I force myself to speak up.

But before I have a chance to continue, she interrupts me. "Chloe, I understand this isn't what you were wanting. Truthfully, none of us wanted this outcome. However, we are all doing what we have to do given the situation. You're not only one of our strongest writers, but you're someone I can trust to take traveling seriously and not participate in any behavior that would embarrass the newspaper. I know that you'll do a fantastic job covering sports. At this time, either take the position or see yourself out."

The harsh tone and words cut through me, and I'm taken back at the forceful nature Professor Weaver speaks.

With a forced, tight smile, I nod in acceptance.

"Great. Now that that's settled, the rest of you will be covering your usual assignments. Politics will be discussed at a later time as we work to create a joint task force." She pauses, and her eyes sweep over the room where some of the underclassmen are sitting. "Sports B Team, while I know this is also not the news you wanted, as no one is being promoted to lead, please know it's not because I don't think you're talented. It's because we need a veteran on this story. You'll be splitting up the coverage of the remaining spring sports. That's all for today. Look forward to more details coming in your email. In the meantime, get out of here and start prepping for the ice storm. Stay safe everyone."

While Weaver is busy closing out her tabs, I quickly stand and start dressing with all of the warm layers that I had on. I never should've taken them off considering we were only in here for a few minutes. I understand she didn't want to deliver this news in an email, but it was seriously a waste of everyone's time to venture in here today.

Grabbing my purse, I turn to leave and ignore Abby calling my name.

Not only did she steal my opportunity, but now I'm going to be forced to spend the entire semester with Cody Jacobs.

Tears burn the corner of my eyes as I fight like hell to keep the moisture from sliding down my cheeks. I'm not going to let my fellow team see me as weak. But dammit, the disappointment is strong.

Climbing up the stairs, I turn down the nearest hallway that I know has a public restroom. I just need to make it to the stall, and I can let myself be weak.

Pushing through the doors, I find the room vacant as I make my way to the last stall and flip the lock behind me. Ripping off a piece of toilet paper, I hold it in my hand to use while placing the seat down for me to sit on. As soon as I sit, the tears flood my vision.

With my face in my hands, I just let myself have a moment to react.

To feel all the feels.

Anger and disappointment for not hitting my goal for the semester.

Anxiety and nerves about having to cover a new topic.

Then, on the other hand, a small part of me feels excited about having to push myself to write a new topic.

Dread for having to spend my semester traveling with the baseball team—and Cody Jacobs.

Moisture is escaping my eyes like a waterfall, and I fight to keep the sob from erupting as it builds pressure in my chest. I can feel the mascara streaking my cheeks, and I know I'm going to have to do some major damage control before I leave this bathroom.

But at this moment, I don't even care.

I'm Chloe Mariano, I always have it together. The girl who always has the shoulder for her friends to cry on. But right now, I just want to curl up in a ball and mope. I want to be the hot mess. The girl who doesn't have it all figured out and gets to fly by the seat of her pants.

Voices filter in the space as I quietly grab a handful of tissue paper to start erasing the black streaks that have no doubt wiped away all of my foundation. Remind me to never skip the waterproof mascara.

After a few minutes of listening to the girls and their gossip, footsteps begin to retreat and I hear the door open with their exit.

I could have gone out there, but I didn't want to see the look of judgment over my mascara-streaked face.

Sticking my head out, I take a quick peek around to make sure the coast is clear. Seeing that I'm the only one in the bathroom I rush through the process of washing my hands. Digging through my purse, I find my emergency supply of makeup remover wipes and begin fixing my streaked mascara.

Finally, at a point where I feel ready to face the few students on campus, I exit the bathroom to begin my journey to the student parking lot.

I guess I'll be putting my book on hold for a little while longer. And on top of that, I can't even properly sulk because there's an ice storm coming. Pulling up the text from my dad, I scan over the list of supplies he sent me. Time to pull up my big girl panties and embark on the madness of winter storm preparation shopping.

This is not how this morning was supposed to go.

CHAPTER 6

CODY

CAN THIS DAY GET ANY FUCKING WORSE?

I swear there's nothing like Mother Nature to fuck up your plans. Jesus, this is Texas, why is an ice storm even happening?

Right now the team should be on a bus heading for Arlington for the Showdown Tournament. Instead, we're busy preparing for a damn ice storm.

Thank God the university and our landlord value athletics because they've been dropping off supplies to the Baseball House all afternoon since we were supposed to be gone all weekend. A few grocery bags of food, two cases of water, a large space heater, and a cell phone bank were delivered. Hudson went out and found a generator and filled up a large can of gasoline. He said if he was getting iced in, there was no way he was going to not be playing video games. Nerd.

Is the team spoiled? Maybe. But here's the thing, I don't care. I'll take advantage of all the handouts because *why not*?

"Jacobs, wanna go grab a pizza before we're stuck in this

fucking house for the weekend?" Hudson asks from where we're chilling in our living room. We've been playing Xbox for the last hour.

Tossing my controller on the coffee table, I stretch my arms over my head. "Yeah, man. Wanna order Cousin Jimmy's?"

Cousin Jimmy's is a CTU staple. This place is the only take-out on campus that stays open until four in the morning. They have the greasiest pizza that is the shit for late-night munchies or hangovers. And they're cheap as hell. You can get an extra-large pizza, ten breadsticks, and two large drinks for ten dollars. Who the hell can pass that up?

"You order, I've got to take a shit," Hudson says as he gets up from his spot on the sectional.

"Less information, Hud."

Glancing around, I can't find my phone. Standing, I start searching the floor and the cushions. This couch swallows everything. Tossing the cushions on the floor, I finally find my phone tucked in the back corner.

I close out of the million alerts from the weather app letting me know that there's an ice storm approaching. No shit, I get it. I don't need a reminder every fifteen minutes.

Pulling up the Cousin Jimmy's app, I type out our pizza order. Three Cousin Jimmy's specials for the whole house. The four of us will crush this order in no time.

"Twenty minutes," I shout, hoping Hudson can hear me. I should send him a message, no doubt he's on his phone using it as his newspaper like everyone else.

When Hudson and I make it back to the house, Niko and Ty are both home sprawled on the couch waiting for us. Carrying the food straight into the living room, I set the boxes down on the coffee table. Tossing the guys a few napkins, we sit around and eat our food like heathens. All of us are depressed over the shitty circumstances we found ourselves in today.

All week we've been hyping ourselves up because baseball was officially supposed to be back, and now we are left with shitty weather and a major adrenaline crash. I watch as Hudson and Ty duel it out in *Call of Duty* in between slices of pizza they are inhaling. Maybe I should have ordered another special? I didn't realize the guys would scarf down the food like savages.

My phone vibrates in my pocket pulling me from another zombie being slayed.

Brynn: Sorry to hear about the tournament.

Me: It's all good. Fucking sucks, but I'll live.

Brynn: You will! Look at it this way, now you have a chance to think about your perfect girl and let your bestie know all the traits you're looking for so I can find you the perfect woman.

Me: Baseball is the only thing I need. What's with you trying to constantly set me up?

Brynn: I want someone to double date with!

Me: Bored with Q already?

Brynn: Never. Look I know this is going to be your year, but don't forget to have some fun. There's more to life than baseball. Why not try and find a girl to actually date?

Me: Not gonna happen, B. Stay warm this weekend.

Brynn: Don't worry, Q will keep me warm.

Me: Gross. Chloe go home?

Brynn: No, she's at the townhouse, but I haven't been able to get a hold of her.

Locking my phone screen, I tap it against my thigh as I let Brynn's words replay in my head. Knowing Chloe, she's got her nose in a book and is completely ignoring the world around her.

But what if she's not okay?

What if she let her battery drain and now she's stuck at home, alone, in the middle of an ice storm? If it were my sister stuck alone in an ice storm, I would want someone checking in on her. As much as I want to stay inside and avoid the shitty weather, I can't sit here and worry about her all night. Which I know I will, even though my mind shouldn't be on Chloe Mariano.

CHAPTER 7

Chloe

THIS HAS BEEN THE LONGEST AFTERNOON EVER.
After receiving the worst news of the semester, I spent the last two hours fighting with every Texan as we all prepped for the ice storm that is supposed to arrive sometime this evening. I'm exhausted, frustrated, and completely spent.

So what am I currently doing? Casually doing some baking and cooking because the store was completely out of bread.

Why is it that when a natural disaster threatens, everyone stocks up on bread? Nonetheless, I didn't want to be left out, and thankfully the store had plenty of ingredients to make my own loaf at home.

For the past hour, I've been listening to my romantic suspense Mafia audiobook while preparing food in case we lose power. And let's face it, I'm blowing off some steam. While my dough has been rising, I made a pot of vegetable soup that is simmering on the stove. All I want right now is a bowl of soup and crunchy bread. Comfort food and cold nights just go hand and hand.

Wind beats against the windows and our glass patio doors. The first sound of ice hits the glass, and I jump. I'm so glad I made it through the store when I did. There's no reason for anyone to be out in this mess. Ice is no joke, especially for a Texan, and you won't catch me out until this weather passes through.

While I was at the store I received a text from our landlord letting me know that he was entering our apartment to do a few storm preparations. He dropped off a small box of supplies: flashlights with extra batteries, a battery-operated radio, and a first aid kit. It wasn't a lot, but it was helpful.

Since Brynn is staying at Quinton's, she told me to pull her comforter off her bed for an extra layer for me. My dad offered to bring me a generator, but I told him to not even think about getting on the road. While he was concerned that I wouldn't have power, I convinced him that I would be fine without electricity, but I wouldn't be fine if something happened to him. He finally agreed. With it being just the two of us, it doesn't take too much convincing—for either one of us—to always take precautions.

I've gathered all of my candles and spread them throughout the apartment. I've never been more thankful for my obsession. And the fact I only like a handful of scents is a blessing in disguise so when they're all lit, I won't have scent overload.

The timer on my phone goes off, startling me since I've been lost in the words the narrator has been speaking, and I reach for the covered bowl the dough has been rising in. Digging the mixture out of the bowl, I plop it onto the flour-covered counter. Kneading the mixture, I work the flour until I have the right consistency. Just as I reach for the olive oil dispenser, the power cuts out.

Tonight was not the night to listen to a suspenseful audiobook.

Complete darkness takes over the entire apartment. I'm left

standing with dough and flour-covered hands. Slowly I inhale a deep breath before a long exhale.

This is fine. The stove is gas, and I can still finish everything as planned. Only I didn't think about lighting any candles ahead of time. Tapping my hand across the counter, I seek out my phone to turn on the flashlight. The light filters into the kitchen, allowing me to see just enough to ignite the stove. Quickly, I oil the cast iron before placing the dough inside. Placing the lid on, I set the Dutch oven on the burner to bake.

I'm halfway through washing the sticky dough off my fingers when there's a knock on the front door.

This is a scene out of every horror movie. A girl is home alone. The power suddenly goes out. The girl goes searching for the breaker. Then *bam* someone attacks said girl. While I know my situation is a little different, I can't help but notice the timing is impeccable.

And I have no idea who could be coming by the apartment in the middle of an ice storm.

I dry my hands off on the towel before making my way over to the front door with just the light from my phone's flashlight.

It's okay, Chloe. No murderer is out in an ice storm to attack you. It's probably Brynn and Quinton coming back to keep you company.

Although I hope not because I really don't want to listen to the two of them go at it all night.

Standing on my tiptoes, I look through the peephole. Duh, you idiot, it's dark outside.

"Uh, who is it?" I ask, hesitant because I want to know, but also what if it's someone I don't know, and now they know I'm home?

"It's Cody."

Cody.

Why is he here?

"Chloe, let me in. It's freezing out here."

Snapping out of my thoughts, I rush to unlock the door knowing that he's right. It's freezing out there, and ice pellets are coming down.

Cody reaches down to pick something up before he comes inside.

"What are you doing here?" I ask, helping him inside.

He doesn't answer. Instead, he sets a black box down at my feet and slides off his backpack before reaching back outside to grab a bag. "I came to check on you."

"Ohh-kay," I draw out, completely confused as to why he's here. "Brynn's not here."

"I know. I came to check on *you*." He repeats, stepping further inside and taking off his tennis shoes. "She said you were home alone and wouldn't answer. I wanted to make sure you were okay. Do you not have anything else for light?"

"The power literally just went out, and I haven't had a chance to light candles. If you're going to be a jerk, you can just leave."

I don't need him here, and I don't want him here. We aren't friends, he's made that clear. I'm perfectly capable of taking care of myself. I still haven't had a chance to curl up with my dark motorcycle romance that was released this morning. That's how I plan on spending my night, not entertaining Cody Jacobs.

He sighs as he takes out his phone and turns on the flashlight. He places it in the front pocket of his jacket which is shallow enough to allow the light to stay out. He reaches down, unzipping his backpack before pulling out a rectangular box.

"Uh, what's that?" I ask, staring at the metal shape in his hands.

"It's a DVD player. I stole it out of Hudson's room with a few DVDs. They're all comedies but like the good, classic comedies."

My brows knit together. I'm utterly confused. But before

I have a chance to question anything else, Cody grabs the black box at his feet and carries it into the living room. He places it down near the TV stand and walks back toward the front door.

And like a puppy, I'm right on his heels.

"You don't have to follow me around." Cody slips his tennis shoes back on and before I know it, he's walking out the front door, but he doesn't close it all the way behind him.

What is going on?

His back pushes the door open again, and in his arms is another box. This one is much larger and looks heavier. Cody kicks the door shut and slips his shoes off again before he makes his way toward the kitchen. I follow as he heads into the laundry room, and I cringe knowing that I have lace bras hanging all over the place.

I watch as he pauses at the entrance, no doubt the light of his phone has hit the delicates. But he doesn't seem to mind. I'm pretty sure I saw him smirk as he walked over to the corner and set the box down. After a few minutes, I hear something running and the power clicks back on.

"There," he says, walking into the kitchen where I'm leaning against the counter in shock. "Give me a minute, and I'll have the space heater turned on. The generator isn't very big, and we need to conserve gas, but I thought we could at least turn on one breaker to get some heat going. We'll turn it on and off to keep the chill out."

This has been the craziest day, but nowhere would I have predicted that Cody Jacobs would drive over, in an ice storm, to bring me a generator, a space heater, and a random DVD player.

"What smells so good?"

I just stare at the boy in front of me. "I-I-I made vegetable soup, and there's a loaf of bread baking."

He makes himself at home by removing his jacket and hanging it on the back of a bar stool. With a few strides, Cody is standing at the stove, removing the lid of the soup and stirring the tomato-based mixture.

What the hell is happening? Did I fall and bump my head somewhere along the way today?

Placing the lid back on the pot, I watch as Cody turns and finally takes in my appearance in the little light we have. His eyes start at my head where my long, blonde hair is pulled up in a claw clip. They trail down my makeup-free face and continue down my body. He stares at the white satin pajamas with tiny purple flowers detailed along the edges. Even in the low light, I can still make out his eyes darken.

And that's when I remember that I'm not wearing a bra.

Quickly I fold my arms over my chest attempting to cover my hardening nipples.

A light chuckle escapes him as a smirk spreads across his lips as he whispers, "You and your purple."

I try to keep my heart from doing a little pitter-patter at the realization that Cody remembers that purple is my favorite color.

He walks toward me, and my heart stops. Like it legit stops beating in my chest. I don't know what Cody is about to do. But him reaching out and twirling the loose pieces of hair around his finger before tucking it behind my ear was not what I predicted. My breath stutters at the contact. That smirk appears on his face as he looks down at me, skimming his finger across my cheek. Goosebumps spread across my body as he brushes past me and heads into the living room.

What is going on?

I did not have being iced in with Cody Jacobs on my BINGO card this winter. Not only is he stuck inside with me, but it has been the most awkward three hours in the history of being forced together. Even with *Step Brothers* playing on the TV.

Since that little incident in the kitchen where he touched me—which cannot happen again—the two of us have barely spoken to each other.

We even ate our soup and bread in silence. Cody mumbling the occasional compliment was the only sound filling the room. As grateful as I am that he came with a generator and space heater, I wish I was here alone.

I've been engrossed in my Kindle while Cody has been playing around on his phone since the one-and-only movie ended.

"Do you have a book I can read?" he asks, interrupting my thoughts.

Glancing over, I find him watching me and realize he is being completely serious. "Um, I'm not sure that you would like any of the books I read."

"Try me."

Chewing my bottom lip, I try to think of a book I have that Cody Jacobs—star pitcher for the CTU Eagles—would enjoy.

Do I give him something full of angst?

Something sports-related?

Or maybe he'd like an all-out smutty book?

Eh, forget the all-out smutty. Iced in reading smut sounds like a scene from a book, and I'm not about that life right now.

"Do you mind reading on my iPad?"

He shakes his head in response. Tossing my Kindle aside, I rush out of the room and climb the steps to my room. I'm so glad I thought to charge all of my electronics when I got home from the store. Making my way back downstairs, I thumb through my ebooks on my iPad and find the one I'm looking for.

"Okay," I start, handing Cody the device. "This is a MMA romance that I think you're going to love."

"We'll see if I *love* it." He smirks and wiggles his body into the armchair to get comfortable.

Now my entire being is uncomfortable knowing that he is reading one of my books. I try to settle back into my single-dad motorcycle romance.

Finally, back in the zone, I'm interrupted again. Only this time it isn't Cody but my phone vibrating. Sighing, I reach for it on the table.

Brynn: You doing okay?

Me: Yep. Did you send Cody over?

Brynn: No? Why is Cody there?

Me: He brought a generator and a space heater. Then the weather got too bad, and now he's stuck here.

Brynn: Ooooo, sounds like something out of one of your romance novels. Don't be afraid to use each other to stay warm.

Me: Yeah, that's NEVER going to happen.

The couch moves next to me, and I glance up, cheeks heating, as Cody is now sitting right next to me. I hit the close button on my phone before he has a chance to see the screen.

"Why are some of these lines highlighted?"

"Oh, those are from me. They're lines that I enjoyed and wanted to remember."

He nods his hand in understanding. "I'm going to get a glimpse inside Chloe Mariano's head."

"Believe me, it's not all that interesting."

His body presses into mine as Cody tries to grab my Kindle from where it's resting on my lap. I'm at a particularly spicy scene, and I don't need him seeing the things that I have highlighted on this page. Both of us shuffle trying to grab the device. In what seems like slow motion, Cody slips, and when I look up, both of our faces are within inches of each other.

My cheeks flame as I watch his eyes bounce from my eyes to my lips. We're too close. Is Cody about to kiss me?

"Cody," I rasp out as he continues his descent toward my mouth. A small part of me is giddy while the other is questioning everything that's going on today. It's like we got stranded together and all of our common sense just disappeared.

What if we just let things happen? What if for one night we forget who we are?

But Cody forgot about me a long time ago.

My hand shoots out and pushes against his chest, shoving him away.

"Shit," he breathes out as he runs his hands through his hair.

I stand from the couch and start backing out of the room. "Look, you can sleep on the couch. There are plenty of blankets in the storage baskets. I'm going to bed."

"Chloe..." Cody starts, but I put my hand up stopping him.

"Don't, Cody. You don't get to come in here and act like a knight in shining armor. Don't you dare come into my house and make this any more awkward than it has to be."

I don't give him a chance to respond, I turn and hightail it to my room.

After the day I've had, all I wanted to do was mope alone with my book. Instead I've been forced to spend an uncomfortable evening alone with Cody. I've had plenty of opportunities to tell him I'll be covering his baseball season, but instead I chose to be petty. He can be the one who is surprised and uncomfortable.

Am I being childish? Yes.

Do I care? Nope.

Screw this day. Screw this storm. Screw this night.

CHAPTER 8

CODY

I'M STANDING AT THE COUNTER MONDAY MORNING chopping up fresh vegetables for the egg bites I prep for the week. While the school provides breakfast for the team after practice, there are some days when I need a little extra protein, which is why I keep a batch in the fridge. Typically I do all my meal prepping on Sundays, ebut the weather had different plans this week.

Sometime Thursday night, our bathroom pipe froze and busted. Thank God Ty was up and heard the clanking of metal and burst of water. He was able to get to the shut-off valve before there was too much damage. Our landlord has had crews in all weekend getting the repairs made before the team leaves for our first road trip of the regular season on Wednesday.

I can't believe it's been three days since I snuck out of Chloe's house.

After our almost kiss—what the hell was I thinking—I waited a couple of hours before I went upstairs to check on her. I felt horrible that she went upstairs while I slept on her couch in the only room that had heat. If I wasn't such a self-absorbed douche, I would've fought her harder on sleeping in the living room. Instead, I sat there with my hands in my hair and watched her storm out of the room to her bedroom.

When I finally got the balls to man up, I went up to her room to make sure she was warm enough. I had never been in Chloe's room, but let's just say it's everything that I would've imagined Chloe's room to look like. When I peeked my head in, I found her curled up with a mountain of blankets surrounding her body. Warm blond hair was spread across her pillows. I should've stopped when I noticed that she had plenty of blankets to keep her warm.

But curiosity is a motherfucker.

Using my flashlight, I did a quick scan of her space. Creamy white walls filled the room. A light pink velvet headboard was met with more white bedding. Two white bookcases lined the wall opposite her door. The shelves were crammed with books, decorative pieces, and picture frames.

As I stepped further into her room—feeling like the biggest creep ever—there was this feeling I can't quite describe that told me to keep looking around. Next to the bookcases was a long cream dresser with a jewelry box, a small television, and more picture frames.

Reaching for one of the frames, I took in a young Chloe with her dad. She was wearing one of his chef hats inside a kitchen. Curly-haired Chloe with a missing front tooth. I smile at the image as I put it back in its place.

Turning, I notice that there isn't any type of desk in the room. Knowing Chloe, that completely surprises me. I never took her as a do-homework-in-the-living-room type of girl. But she never fails to surprise me.

And that's when my eyes catch on the top shelf of her bookcase.

There's no freaking way.

Carefully, I walk toward the bookcase. My fingers trail over the spines of books before I grab the purple rabbit. Flipping it over in my hand, the soft fur grazes my fingers as memories flood my vision.

I can't believe she kept it.

The next morning I left as soon as I got the chance. The door of my car was frozen, but I was able to thaw it out with a pitcher of lukewarm water. While I waited for the car to defrost, I stole a croissant and a cinnamon roll that was sitting on the girls' counter, knowing who it was that baked the delicious treats, and it wasn't my best friend. The drive back to my house might've taken forty-five minutes, but I couldn't stay at that townhouse any longer.

Once upon a time, I wanted a girl like Chloe. The sweet, caring, nurturing bookworm. The kind of girl who would prioritize your relationship and would always be faithful. But along the way, everything changed.

Now the only priority I have is baseball.

Brynn told me to think about finding a good girl to settle down with, the only problem is I found her a long time ago and fucked it all up.

Now it's just me and the love of the game.

Vibrating pulls me from my thoughts, and I fish out my phone from my front pocket. A long sigh leaves my lips as I see 'dad' flash across the screen. Dread and frustration pool in my stomach as I internally prep myself for how this conversation is going to go.

"Hello?" I greet setting my knife to the side. Handling sharp objects while on the phone with my dad is never a good idea.

"Are you ready for Wednesday? I saw you'll be the starting pitcher. Their center fielder is their home run hitter, and he loves a curveball."

"No worries, Dad, I survived the ice storm. We only had one pipe burst in our house. Oh, and I'm doing great. How's the family?"

"Lose the smart-ass comments. I don't have time for it. You need to be focusing on your first game since you couldn't play this weekend."

I step away from the counter and rest my body against the opposite counter before running my hand down my face. Frustration seeps from my body.

"It's not like I chose not to play this weekend. You know Texas was blanketed by a freak storm system."

I watch as Hudson enters the kitchen and goes straight to the fridge. He pulls out a bottle of orange juice and sits across from me on a barstool. Twisting the top off, he gives me a questioning look as he takes a long pull of his drink.

My dad continues to berate me on how I need to be focusing, how weak I've become since moving to Texas if I can't handle a little ice, and what I need to be doing to make sure that I'm ready to pitch in my first game this season, even though we've had numerous scrimmages this winter.

The oven chimes that it's reached its temperature. Unfortunately, Dad hears that too. "Did you find a woman to prepare your meals for the week? You always were distracted by a pretty face. Or are you wasting your time in the kitchen? I knew you weren't focused on the game. We all know how easy it is for an injury to occur and your career be over."

I fight to keep the groan from escaping. "No, Dad. I don't have 'some girl' to make my food for me. I'm perfectly capable of making my *own* meals. But listen, I've got to go. We have practice in an hour," I lie about that last fact. Practice isn't until this evening, but he doesn't need to know that.

He continues giving me his advice, which ends up being backhanded comments. Yeah, he had an injury his freshman year of college, but there was no way he was going to make it in the pros. He never had the talent or the discipline it takes.

Instead, he calls me daily with updates on how I should be preparing or criticizing how much I sucked at whatever he saw on one of the taped replays of my game. The conversations between the two of us have gotten so one-sided that I'm surprised he even knows what my voice sounds like. The only reason I continue to answer is so that he keeps his focus on me and not my sister, Leah.

I don't even wait for him to be done, I find a lull in the conversation and end the call before tossing my phone on the counter.

"Your dad?" Hudson asks.

"Who else would it be? We have a game in two days." Walking back over to where I was cutting vegetables. I grab the chopped peppers, mushrooms, and spinach and toss them into the mixing bowl of scrambled eggs. Taking a ladle, I scoop the mixture into reusable silicone liners and pop the pan in the oven.

"You could just quit answering his calls."

"You know I can't do that."

"How much longer until Leah's out of that house?"

"Too long." Leah is my younger sister. She's a senior this year, but any time left in that house is too long. I've tried my best to keep the attention off her and focused on me, but it's hard when my dad is a massive control freak.

Niko and Ty both come walking into the kitchen. The four of us get along great, but we're all so different. I think that's why we can live together. None of us are slobs. Although Ty is the worst at picking up after himself, he's not as bad as it could be. Niko just transferred in this year. He's a moody sonuvabitch who keeps to himself. When he does talk, it's usually something important. Otherwise, Niko is the quiet one who sits around listening and observing everyone.

Ty grabs two sports drinks and tosses one to Niko. The two sit next to Hudson at the bar while I wash my dishes.

"The vibe is all off in here," Ty says. I shake my head at his words. He's all about the vibes and harmony. That peace and love bullshit.

Niko stares me down. "Are we going to talk about the elephant in the room?"

My eyes bounce around my roommates. They all stare me down. No one has mentioned my sudden disappearance Thursday night. We've all been busy dealing with the aftermath of the burst pipe and being pieces of shits who don't move from in front of the Xbox. And I've been busy reliving my night at Chloe's and the things I discovered.

Not only did seeing that purple rabbit surprise me, but I kept reading that MMA romance she gave me way later than I should have. When I left Friday morning, I kept her iPad and finished reading. I was going to just buy the ebook, but I was enjoying reading the story along with the parts she highlighted.

What really surprised me was all the steamy scenes she had annotated. Is she into all the things she highlights in her books? Has she done these things before?

My mind immediately flashes to one of the scenes I just read. A girl on her knees in the bedroom. Waiting on the main guy to return. Submitting to him.

The things he said and the things they did have me quickly picturing Chloe in that same situation, and I feel the blood start to rush south. Before I have a chance to really enjoy the thought of Chloe on her knees before me, I hear Niko's voice interrupting.

"What elephant?" I ask, playing dumb.

Niko's eyes shrink into slivers as he glares at me while Hudson shakes his head.

"Where'd you disappear to Thursday?" Ty prompts.

"Don't worry about it," I answer, shrugging.

Hudson has his famous shit-eating grin on his face. I swear he can read my every move. "Were you at a pretty blonde's house?"

The timer on the oven goes off. Slipping on a pair of oven mitts, I reach inside and pull out the pan of egg bites, setting them on a cooling rack. Turning toward him, I glare back at him, but it only spurs the guys on. "Monica's? You two back to fucking?" Ty asks.

"Hell no. That ship has sailed. Baseball season is here, and I don't need any distractions."

"Brynn's?" Ty guesses again. Technically, he isn't wrong. I nod, ending the line of questions. No one will think anything of it since it's not uncommon for me to stop by her house. And for all they know Quinton was there too.

Niko eyes me skeptically. He's always observing everything and keeping his comments to himself. No doubt he knows I'm full of shit, but he won't say anything.

"Oh, that's not unusual. So why's the energy off in here?" Ty questions, leaning back in his chair.

Reaching for the glass storage container, I quickly toss the egg bites inside. Placing the lid on top, I walk them over to the fridge and place them on an empty shelf. I don't even care that there will be condensation on inside.

"My dad called and started shit. What else is new? But I'm done talking about it. See you guys at practice." And with that, I grab my water bottle and leave the guys sitting at the counter.

"Listen up!" Coach Weber shouts across the indoor facility. "No one could have predicted we'd be canceling our first tournament with an ice storm. But we head on the road in two days, and we need to get focused."

We spent most of the practice running drills to make sure

everyone was loose and ready for the game. Once drills were over, the training staff walked us through deep stretching exercises. My body has never felt as loose as it does now. Coach can do this after every practice, and I'd be down for it.

"As I previously mentioned, this season we will have a new reporter from the newspaper staff traveling with us. Answer her questions, don't give her any shit, and if I find out anyone is treating her with any less respect than you'd give one of us coaches, you'll have me to deal with."

"Who do you think it is?" Hud asks from beside me. All of us are resting on one knee in a semi-circle while Coach talks to us.

Shrugging, I keep my attention trained on Weber. I watch as Coach's attention focuses past where the team is gathered in front of him. Hudson turns to follow Coach's gaze, while I couldn't care less about who is joining the staff. I'll do what I'm told and not make a big deal about it.

"Holy shit," Hudson whispers, but not quietly enough, as Weber glares at him while I laugh under my breath. Heads whip to the right as murmurs spark and elbows nudge others. Curiosity finally gets the best of me, and my eyes follow the direction that everyone is staring.

Chloe Mariano stands in front of the team dressed in skin-colored tights, a soft cream and beige plaid tweed dress, white boots that sit over her knee, and a pink wool coat. She looks as feminine and elegant as ever. Damn, why is she wearing that in front of all these guys?

"Damn, who is that?" one of the guys whispers.

"She's fine," someone else adds.

I know she can hear the whispers, but she's not showing any sign of caring.

Instead, she's focusing on me. And the daggers she's throwing my way say she's not too happy to see me right now. *Fuck.*

"Team, this is Chloe Mariano. Chloe comes to us from the

newspaper staff. She will be traveling with us and attending home games to cover the season. I expect Chloe to be treated with respect, while I expect Ms. Mariano to respect your boundaries as well. Let's all work together, keep the drama off the field, and make this a season we won't forget."

Chloe gives everyone a tight smile that seems forced. She lifts her hand in a small wave, and it's then I notice that she's not as tough as she is pretending to be. There's a slight tremor in her hand exposing her nerves.

Did she ask to cover our season? What kind of game is she playing? How long has she known? This is definitely information that should've been shared while we were forced to spend the night together.

This season is shaping up to be one of the weirdest seasons I've faced.

And it better come with a trophy at the end.

CHAPTER 9

Chloe

" I HAVE NO IDEA WHAT THE HELL I'M DOING."

Today is the first road game. It's been three weeks since the dreadful day when I was assigned sports. After a lot of thought and a lot of self-pity, I've accepted this new challenge.

It's fine. Everything is fine.

This is a new journey. It's a plot twist in the story that no one saw coming.

Am I being forced to spend time with a boy who never leaves my mind? Yes, but that's okay. I won't let him distract me. Especially when he and I will never work out.

And I mean never.

The only boyfriend I want can be read in black ink, found between the pages, and is fictional.

I'm Chloe Mariano, and I've been faced with nothing but challenges since I was six years old.

I spent way too much time last night going through my closet weeding out outfit after outfit. I have no idea what I'm supposed to pack, what I'm supposed to wear, and where I'm supposed to be during the game.

Am I going to be in the locker room? A press box? Or in the stands? Each scenario called for a different outfit.

Finally at a quarter till midnight, I grabbed my laptop and typed out an email to my professor hoping that she would be able to give me insight on what is expected of a sports reporter. When I cover lifestyle or interview restaurateurs I never have to worry about these things. I show up in a dress or skirt that is professional but still my style while interviewing the band, the chef, or whatever the assignment calls for. I never have to second guess myself like I am right now.

There was a reply in my inbox when I woke up this morning. It simply said that I'll need to touch base with the coach and see what he prefers. So here I am at seven-thirty, showered in a silk robe and staring at a mess of clothes and a semi-empty suitcase.

At least I can pack my pajamas. Three pairs line my suitcase. One white lace short and tank top set, one lilac linen long-sleeve and pant set, and one light pink and white pinstripe shorts and button-up short-sleeve top set.

"What happened?" Brynn gasps from the doorway.

Turning her way, I pull my bottom lip between my teeth while shrugging. I let my arms drop with a smacking noise against my thighs. Moisture gathers in my eyes, and I feel the need to start crying.

Brynn's expression softens and her shoulders relax as she strides into my room with two mugs of coffee. "Chlo, what's wrong?"

"I have no idea what to pack. I have no idea what I'm doing. Maybe I should just drop the class. I have enough credit hours... who needs the newspaper experience for a resume?"

"Take a drink." She thrusts the mug of coffee toward me, and I take it from her, bringing the warm liquid to my mouth. Blowing on it a few times, I take a sip. Rich coffee greets my taste buds which is followed by an overwhelming taste of vanilla, chocolate, and the fruitiness of Irish Whiskey.

Swallowing, I turn my attention back to my roommate, who's sitting cross-legged on my bed with a smile as big as the Cheshire Cat. "Baileys?"

She shrugs. "Figured you could use some before your trip."

I laugh and take another long drink of the hot deliciousness.

"Okay so since you avoided my questions, I guess it's safe to assume you are not doing well, but we'll come back to that. For now let's solve one problem and figure out what you're wearing."

"That's the thing. I don't know where to start because I don't know where I'll need to be to cover this assignment."

"Just tell Coach Weber what you need. Where do you want to be?"

"In the dugout. I want to get a feel for the game. I want to feel the energy that radiates off the players and buzzes from the field. I want to listen to the guys and watch how Weber coaches."

Standing from my bed, I watch as Brynn heads to my closet. Girl is on a mission as she slides hanger after hanger searching for a particular item. Too bad Macy doesn't live here anymore. Having a fashion major in the townhouse made outfit decisions so much easier. "If you'd tell me what you're looking for, I can help you find it faster."

She ignores me and continues her search. While she's looking for whatever it is, I carry my mug across the hall to my bathroom. Brynn is the only one who has an attached bathroom. I used to share a bathroom with Macy, our old roommate. She abruptly moved out, and we ended with an explosive fight. It was a mixture of both of us being wrong and taking things out on each other that never should have happened. Needless to say, our friendship is severely rocky.

The dynamic in our townhouse since Macy moved out and

Brynn started dating Quinton is off. It's weird. I'm beyond happy for my friends, but I miss the days of just being the three of us.

As I set my mug down on the counter, I pull out my toothbrush, toothpaste, and face wash. After I'm done brushing and washing, I rummage through my drawers to gather all my makeup and start my daily process. Fifteen minutes later, I'm making my way back into my room and hoping that Brynn figured out a game plan.

Brynn stands over my light yellow hardshell suitcase as she zips it close. I stare at her wide-eyed because not only did she get me packed in fifteen minutes, but she didn't even try to get my approval on the clothes she packed. I mean, there's honestly nothing in my closet that I would be against. Throughout the years, I've really homed in on my style, and I've been very conservative with each piece I bring into my wardrobe. Whatever Brynn chooses will have to do. Tapping my phone screen, I glance down at the time. And whatever Brynn picked will really have to do because I've got to be out of the house and on the bus in forty-five minutes.

"There's still a variety in here, and you'll like them all, but there's no reason to stress about what you wear. Chlo, you are the best-dressed girl on campus. You always dress cute with your flowy dresses and skirts. Own that. Don't change who you are just because you are covering sports. If you feel like the straps make the dress too revealing, throw on one of your cardigans."

She stops and makes her way over to me. Reaching up, she grips my shoulders, gaining my entire attention. "Just don't stop being you, babe. I know this is out of your comfort zone, and we both know how much you hate being out of your happy place, but don't let this change you. You're going to fucking crush it."

Blinking rapidly, I try to keep the moisture from escaping my eyes. Leave it to Brynn to go all hype girl as I try to keep my makeup from running. She really is the best friend ever. I wish it was possible to get just a small percentage of her boldness.

It's not that I'm not confident. I carry myself well. I know who I am and what I like. I dress with confidence, especially since my style of clothing isn't typical. When it comes to clothes, I'm all about dresses and skirts. There's nothing better to me than having my legs free and not being confined in pants. I mean I obviously wear jeans, shorts, and leggings, but they aren't my go-to. I'm a girl who loves flowy, feminine, floral pieces. Give me a flared-out dress that hits above my knees, sneakers, and a cardigan or jean jacket, and I'll rock that look all day every day.

But when it comes to my internal thoughts, yeah, I struggle with being confident. I've never been the girl who is chosen first. There's always someone better. A prettier girl, one who's easier, one who's smarter.

In grade school, I wasn't the girl who was chosen first in gym class. I wasn't popular, I wasn't part of a clique of girls, I wasn't anything special. Instead, I was the girl who walked the halls with eyes and whispers pointed at her, the little girl who just wanted to belong and make friends, but while everyone was playing together, I was sitting alone. I was the little girl labeled the "cooties" girl.

Kids were cruel and instead of being sensitive and comforting, they made fun of me because my mom left. The unlovable little girl who lived in the "dirty" apartments who couldn't even keep her mom around.

And that's when I turned to books. Each time I was left out of an activity at school, each time I wasn't invited to a birthday party, each time a school dance would come around and I wasn't asked, I turned to the love stories that filled the pages. Books were my escape, and to this day, I would much rather get lost in a book than face reality. But life doesn't work that way. I keep my books close, but I've also been trying to work on myself. To gain the confidence that I've been lacking for so long.

And Brynn knows my story. She keeps me going when I want to curl in on myself. Her pep talks are her way of reminding me that I'm enough. I'm who I'm meant to be, and I need to stop letting others dictate who I am.

Of course, it's easier said than done. Especially when the only boy that you've ever wanted never gives you the time of day. You're just the girl who hides in the corner—he doesn't see me.

Dammit, Chloe. Stop with him.

Pulling Brynn in, I wrap my arms around her giving her a tight hug. "Love you, B."

"Aw, I love you too," she pulls away and plants a quick kiss on my cheek. "Now get dressed. I can take you to the complex so you don't have to catch an Uber."

"Thanks." I watch as she leaves before striding over to my closet. I grab a black midi dress with mini yellow flowers printed throughout the entire dress. Removing the hanger, I let my robe fall free and slide the dress over my head. Fluffing my hair out of the back of my dress, I adjust the bubble sleeves that hit at my elbow. This dress is the perfect combination of sweet and casual. It'll be comfortable on the long bus ride to Louisiana, but still gives the essence that I'm here for business and not to mess around with the team.

Slipping on a pair of white sneakers, I quickly plait my honey-blond hair in a single loose braid. I pop in a pair of white floral stud earrings before I do a final scan of my outfit. Hair and makeup, simple. Dress and shoes, cute and casual. With one last nod, I grab the handle of my suitcase and my brown cross-body.

Phone and charger. Check.

Toiletries. Check.

Clothes packed by me—make that Brynn. Check.
Kindle and AirPods. Check and check.
It's time to stop procrastinating, Chloe Girl.

"Coach Weber."

The tall, very attractive baseball coach turns to me. He's wearing navy sweatpants, a CTU Baseball long-sleeve shirt with a CTU Baseball cap, and aviator sunglasses covering his eyes. Coach's attire is a lot more casual than I was expecting. He takes a moment before responding, and with his dark lens, I'm not sure if he's appraising my appearance or if he's struggling to remember who I am.

Assuming he can't remember who I am, I reintroduce myself. "Chloe Mariano from the newspaper. I'll be joining you this season." My voice wavers in my introduction over concern that he doesn't remember me and concern that he's going to be frustrated that I'm standing before him.

"Of course," he begins. "I remember, Ms. Mariano. I'm just surprised to see you this dressed up for an almost seven-hour bus ride."

"Oh," I falter. "I wasn't exactly sure what I should show up in so I went with my usual outfit. Is-is this okay?"

"There's no dress code here. Feel free to dress in whatever makes you comfortable. If anyone ever gives you any hassle don't hesitate to come to me or one of the other coaches on staff. We have a few other women on the training staff, and all the guys are to treat you with the same respect as anyone else."

I smile. Coach Weber's response was not one that I was expecting. In high school, the girls were forced to abide by archaic dress codes in order to keep the pervy high school boys from getting too excited in class. Shoulders covered, shorts past our fingertips, and absolutely no low-cut shirts because heaven for-bid, girls were a distraction.

"Thank you, Coach. And please call me Chloe." He shakes his head in acknowledgment. "Sorry, I'm new to all of this. Where would you like me to put my bag?"

"You can take it to the side of the bus and the equipment team will make sure it is loaded in the storage compartment. Feel free to sit wherever you want on the bus. When we get to the hotel, the coaches will all gather for a debrief in the conference room. Please join us, and we'll go over all the details."

I nod and begin walking in the direction Coach instructed me to take my suitcase. I don't make it very far before Coach Weber calls my name. "Chloe," he starts as I turn my head over my shoulder. "I forgot one thing. Have fun. But not as much fun as the last two guys did."

A wide smile stretches across my face. "You've got it, Coach."

"Oh, and you can call me Callan."

"Yeah, that's not going to happen, Coach." He chuckles, and we both go about our way.

Maybe this isn't going to be so bad after all. I thought for sure Coach Callan Weber was going to be a hard ass who took every-thing seriously. I mean, isn't that how all the coaches in movies are? They're gruff, never smile, don't take any crap, and are all about being focused. Callan is not what I would've pictured at all.

Handing off my bag, I climb the stairs and enter the charter bus, and my feet stall when I reach the top stair.

Holy smokes. This is nice.

Definitely not any old-school bus. I've never been on a charter bus, and this is not what I was picturing. Inside are rows of black leather seats that look insanely comfortable like mini recliners. Each row has four seats: two on each side separated by the aisle. Above the seats are temperature vents and gauges, individual lights, and TVs in the back of the headrests. If it were possible, my jaw would be on the ground like in cartoons.

There are a handful of guys on the bus. Toward the front, there appear to be a few members of the coaching staff while some of the seats toward the back are occupied with players staring at me. And that niggling of self-doubt is crawling up my spine. Forcing the thoughts that are fighting to break free, I put one foot in front of the other and began walking toward an empty seat.

A few of the coaches turn my way, and we give the typical tight-lipped smiles and head nod greetings. Ignoring the eyes coming from the back of the bus, I leave a few rows open before sliding to a window seat on the opposite side of where people are dropping off their bags.

I am so out of my element.

Anxiety starts to creep in, inviting that element of self-doubt that I'm not good enough to be covering sports. Not to mention, the idea of seeing Cody after our awkward night together. Is he going to be angry that I didn't tell him I would be along for the season? I was really hoping I could convince my professors to find someone else. But karma wasn't on my side.

Deciding on being anti-social, I take a few minutes to make myself comfortable. Reaching inside my cross-body, I pull out AirPods and my Kindle before depositing my purse on the floor at my feet. I'm stuck between wanting someone to sit beside me and wanting the seat next to me to be open.

Scrolling through my phone, I click Spotify and find my go-to reading playlist: Noah Kahan Radio, which is filled with a mixture of genres ranging from alt-country, indie, and folk played by some of my favorite artists. Their voices are so sooth-ing and their songs are good, but the beat never pulls me out of my reading, which is hard to find.

Switching on my Kindle, I open the latest novel by Elsie Silver. I'm back in my small town era, and I couldn't be more excited to spend this bus ride devouring her words. I've been dying to read Jasper and Sloan's story since I started the Chestnut Springs series. Who doesn't want to read about a damaged hockey god who ends up on a road trip with his childhood crush?

Players start to file onto the bus, but I keep my head down and focus on the words in front of me. The idea of making uncomfortable eye contact as we do the weird smile/nod combination makes me cringe. I'd rather come off as completely standoffish than awkward.

I'm only a few pages into my book when the notion of looking up completely encompasses me. It's like I physically feel him before I even see him. My eyes find him immediately. Only the beautiful golden hazel eyes are staring back at me completely cold. His eyes pin me with anger and frustration while his facial expression is completely blank. Cody Jacobs stares back at me with zero emotion, and I feel myself shrink in my seat. He brings a paper cup to his mouth, and I watch his sharp jaw and Adam's apple bounce as he swallows. Cody passes me with no acknowledgment that I'm even sitting on this bus.

Hurt courses through my body. I'm not naive enough to think that our night spent together during the ice storm would change our relationship. It was just Cody being Cody. He can't help but insert himself into being the hero in every girl's story.

A light touch on my shoulder startles me to the point I jump about a foot out of my chair dropping my Kindle on the ground in the process. Grabbing my heart, I rip an AirPod out of my ear with my other hand.

"Oh my gosh," I say breathlessly.

"Shit, Chloe. I thought you heard me." I hadn't realized Ty Billings slid into the seat next to me. "Mind if I sit with you?"

I just stare at him confused as to why he is choosing to sit with me out of all the empty seats on the bus. Ty and I have been in the same room together many times. He frequents Sunday dinners at the house, and of course, we all party together, but I can count on one hand the times we've talked one-on-one.

"Uh, sure."

"Thanks." He plops down in the seat next to me, a huge grin stretched across his face. "Oh, this is for you."

A paper to-go cup is put in front of me, and I smile at the gesture. "Thanks, but I'm really particular about my coffee."

"It's a honey lavender latte."

My eyes open wide as I stare at him in complete shock. Honey lavender lattes are my favorite, and I have no idea how Ty would know that.

Taking the cup from his outstretched hand, I gesture it toward him. "Thanks."

While Ty sits in the vacant seat next to me, I watch him get situated in his seat. The warmth seeps through the sides of the cup instantly warming my hand, and I smile. I'm such a coffee snob, and I only like certain flavors. The fact I have my favorite drink and a new book is making this day much better.

Ty pulls his phone from his front pocket while removing his AirPods from the opposite pocket. His fingers fly over the screen of his phone, and I try not to be a creep and read over his shoulder. People who do that to others who are sitting next to them are the worst. The two of us get situated as the bus starts moving.

I'm taking this as a sign. A sign that I'm going to be okay.

CHAPTER 10

CODY

THE MELODIC SOUND OF HER LAUGHTER FILLED THE bus for the majority of our ride. And dumbass Billings is the cause of her happiness. I hate it. Anger has been coursing through my bloodstream, and my gaze has been shooting him daggers in the back of his head this entire ride.

My mind is supposed to be getting focused on the games ahead, but instead, it's been focusing on the soft melody of her voice. Thank god she finally fell asleep half an hour ago, but not before she had to get up and walk down the aisle to the on-board bathroom. The smell of lilies, sandalwood, and wildflowers evaded my senses. The smell is contagious. It's addicting. It brings me back to hot summer days, lounging under a shade tree next to the lake, and fresh gelato.

Fuck me.

"Bro." Hudson nudges my shoulder, breaking me from my stare down with the back of Billings's head. "You're going to bore a hole in the back of his head."

"Why is she here?" I grumble under my breath.

"Is this going to be a problem? Because if it's going to be a problem, then I'm going to Weber to get her off this bus. We don't need a distraction in the dugout this season."

There's a small part of me that wants him to go to Coach. To alleviate the problem. But I couldn't do that to her. I've done enough to her.

The bus driver hits a pothole as he turns down a tight road causing everyone to grumble at the jerky motion. After a few more turns, he guides us through the overhang of the hotel we'll be calling home for the next two nights. Once we're parked, all the guys stand in our seats and stretch out our stiff muscles.

Today was a travel day which means no game, but we'll still head to the field for a short practice. Coach will have us go through some light drills, stretching, batting practice, and I'll do some throwing to make sure my arm is ready for the game.

I'm ready to hit the field. To feel the dirt under my cleats. To feel the way the laces graze against my calloused hands. To focus on nothing but my catcher's glove in front of me. For nine innings, I can completely shut the world out and focus on pitch after pitch.

No thoughts of my dad.

No thoughts of my future.

No thoughts of the blonde-haired, blue-eyed girl who smells like wildflowers.

Reaching for my backpack, I sling it over my shoulder as I follow Hudson down the aisle. I will myself not to seek out Chloe, but apparently I'm weak when it comes to her. My eyes cast down, and that's when I see her head resting on Billings's shoulder, the two of them looking awfully comfortable together. My hands fist at my side as I grind down on my molars, and I swear I can hear one of them crack. I feel my eyes narrow into slits as I glare down at my roommate, teammate, and friend, and if looks could kill, there'd be a heap of dirt where Billings sat.

Get a fucking grip.

This isn't me. I'm not the jealous type. Hell, I don't even want a girlfriend. Baseball is my only love, but I can't explain this feeling. Why am I feeling so possessive over her?

Stepping off the bus, I head straight for the hotel lobby to get my room assignment. The equipment team will make sure that all of our bags get distributed to the correct rooms. Our room assignments are always the same—selected based on alphabetical order by last name. Which means Hud and I are always placed together. We both have our quirks and pregame rituals that we both respect.

For this trip, we are staying at an above-average hotel. The lobby is bright and welcoming. There is a sea of people wearing powder blue and red—a mixture of the team and fans starting to trickle in.

That's one thing I love about playing for Central Texas, we always run into fans no matter where we play.

Two dark wood reception counters contrast against the bright white ceiling and bright orange and black walls. Past the reception area is a common area with small leather couches and chairs. A few TVs are scattered throughout the space. Next to the seating area is the hotel restaurant with a coffee area, bar, and dining tables.

Making my way through the crowd, heads start to whip in my direction. I wouldn't say I am the most popular player on the team, but as far as pitchers go, I'm pretty well-known. Which means I'm recognized pretty often. Today I'm not in the mood to deal with fans and cleat chasers, though. Unfortunately, I spotted the group of girls in their cutoff denim shorts and their skin-tight CTU tees which means my chances of slipping by the crowd are slim to none.

But just as I'm about to jump in line to get my key card, I hear my name called in a familiar voice. Turning, I spot Hudson over the crowd. He gives me a head nod as he holds up a white envelope.

Our key cards. *Thank fuck.*

Bypassing everyone, I sneak off to the elevators.

"This is getting insane," I grumble to Hudson. The elevator chimes, and the door slides open. The two of us step inside. Hudson hits the 'five' and the 'door close' button at the same time. Neither one of us wants to be stuck in the elevator with cleat chasers, not before the game at least.

I feel my phone buzz in my pocket as we step out onto our floor. But I ignore it. I have an inkling that it's my dad, and he's the last person I want to talk to right now. He'll keep calling, and I'll deal with it later. Right now, I just want to get settled in our room until practice.

I need time to get a sleeping blonde out of my head.

And get rid of the green monster who wishes it was my shoulder she was leaning on.

This evening's practice was about two hours. Enough time for us to review our game plan for tomorrow. Louisiana State is a big team to play against this early in the season. This means we need to come out with our bats swinging, and I need to be ready to throw strikes.

Hudson hits the shower first while I order food for us. Technically, we are supposed to be on a strict diet, but we've managed to talk Coach into letting us have our pregame dinner of pepperoni, sausage, and mushroom pizza with a salad—of course—per Coach's instruction. During our time together playing summer ball before our freshman year, Hud and I started eating this before games, and it's become a ritual. The one time we didn't get pizza we both had the shittiest games of our careers. Since that game, Coach has made an exception for us.

What can I say? Baseball players are a superstitious bunch, and we each have our weird rituals we do before games.

Twenty minutes later, I'm freshly showered and answering the door to the pizza delivery guy. Hudson set up his Xbox on the hotel TV, and the two of us are about to bash on some pizza while killing zombies.

The warm pizza smells amazing and immediately my mouth is watering. Grabbing a slice, I plop down on my bed where my controller waits for me.

"Did you order two pizzas?" Hud asks, lifting the lid and pulling out a slice.

"Nope, must've been a mistake."

"Wanna see who's next door? Maybe they want it."

Jumping up from my spot, I head over to the door of the adjoining room. Rapping my knuckles gently on the wood, I wait for one of the guys to answer. After a minute without an answer, I knock louder.

Within a couple of seconds, I hear the lock flip, and the door swings open. And I'm struck speechless with my jaw on the floor.

Chloe stands across from me toweling her wet hair. Her face is wild and crazed, frustration laces her flawless, makeup-free face.

God, she's perfect.

I don't miss how her eyes travel over my body taking in my near-naked body as I stand before her. I watch her breath hitch as she realizes I'm not wearing much clothing, just a pair of loose boxers. If I'm not careful, I'll be sporting a boner that will really make our situation that much more uncomfortable.

I can't help my eyes from roaming over her, taking in the white tank top with tiny flowers scattered across the material. Down to her exposed petite, yet athletic, legs. And her shorts are barely covering her perfectly round ass.

Bringing my eyes up, I can't help but notice her nipples are pebbled, and fighting this boner is getting harder and harder.

Stop thinking about things getting harder.

Her voice clears, and my attention snaps to her stoic face. "If you're done ogling me, can you tell me what you needed so badly?"

Hudson chuckles from behind me, and I glance over my shoulder to find him sitting on the edge of his bed, taking a bite of pizza, enjoying the awkward show in front of us.

"I thought you were one of the guys."

"Clearly, not." She snarls. "Coach said he assigns rooms in alphabetical order, and lucky me, I get a room to myself that will always be next to yours."

I quirk a brow, and her eyes roll. I'd love to give her a better reason to have her rolling her eyes.

"Jacobs. Larsen. Mariano. You really should pay more attention in classes, Jacobs."

"So we're on a last name basis?"

She doesn't answer, just stares me down, and I want to melt under her stare. Chloe isn't going to make this easy on anyone.

"We aren't friends, remember?" Chloe folds her arms across her chest, and I can't help but follow her movement.

"Well, I was going to offer you the extra pizza that was delivered with ours and to see if you wanted to hang out, but if we aren't friends, fucking forget it."

She scoffs and shakes her head as she goes to close the door in my face.

"Chloe, wait," Hudson interjects. I'm going to kill him. "Take the pizza."

She smiles at him, and it's a real, genuine smile. The kind I never get and desperately crave. "Thanks, but I already ate."

He gives her a warm smile and understanding nod; she

returns the gesture with a tight-lipped smile before shutting the door in my face.

"Do you always have to be such a dick to her?"

"Fuck off," I grumble and return to my spot. "Listen, I've made a mess out of things with Chloe, and I don't know how to fix it. So it's best that we just steer clear of each other."

"Have you tried talking to her?"

Taking a large bite, I chew the pizza as I think of how I could possibly explain what happened with her without it sounding like an excuse. It's been so long that, at this point, she has no reason to ever listen to what comes out of my mouth.

"I almost kissed her."

He chokes on the water he's drinking. Coughing, he tries to work the water free. "When?"

"During the ice storm."

"That's terrible timing. Did y'all talk, or did you just try to take advantage of the situation?"

"There was no taking advantage. It was just a moment we both had, and I thought it was okay."

"Clearly, you were wrong." I glare at him before he continues. "Dude, you're so fucked."

"Thanks, Captain Obvious." Before he has a chance to say anything else, I hit the play button for the game.

He's right. I'm so fucked. In more ways than one. I swear I can still smell her wildflower scent.

Later that night, I'm tossing and turning waiting for sleep to take me under. After our pizza and a few games of *Call of Duty*, I finally decided to answer my dad's call.

I knew I shouldn't have. I knew I should have just let it go to voicemail so I could just delete the message instead of trying to answer it. But clearly, I'm a glutton for punishment and need the punishment that his calls bring.

Hell, maybe that's part of my pregame ritual. Answering a call from my dad as he berates me about how much I suck and how much better the team we are playing is.

While most dads call to go over the game you played and give you constructive critiques on what you did wrong, I've never had that. Instead, my dad decides to tear down my game. He's planted a seed of doubt which only grows and increases the inner demons that I battle daily. These demons remind me that I'm not good enough. That I'm never going to make it to the big league. That I'm going to wash up and be useless just like my old man.

He couldn't hack it in college, and while most dads would encourage their son to be better than them, he wants me to be worse.

I know I should stop the cycle, but I'm afraid that if he doesn't have me to punish, he's going to find a reason to punish Leah. I can't have that. She's been through enough and doesn't need any more of his attention on her. Until she's out from under his roof, I'll be the punching bag he chooses to hit over and over again. In a weird sense, maybe I need the hits. Maybe they make me tougher, stronger.

Rolling over, I practice a few breathing techniques we've been doing in our yoga sessions as I try to shut my brain down and get a few hours of sleep. But before I have a chance to drift off, a noise sounds from the hallway.

As captain, it's my job to make sure that all of the guys abide by Coach's lights-out policy. Tossing off the covers, I make my way over to the door and try to peer out of the peephole.

That's when I see her.

Blonde hair piled on top of her head. Black tight shorts and sports bra. And no shirt. *Fuck*.

Chloe gets to wear whatever she wants, but I don't like her walking around a hotel in the middle of the night alone. Guys would take advantage of the situation and blame it on her because *she's asking for it. Hell no.*

She hits the button to call the elevator, and I know there's no way I'm going to make it out in time to ask her where she's going. So like a creep, I continue to watch to see what floor she lands on.

Floor two.

With a deep sigh, I quickly toss on a pair of athletic shorts, CTU T-shirt, socks, and running shoes. I glance at the alarm clock on the table between Hudson and me, one forty-five. Swiping my phone and keycard off the table, I hurry to the elevator, closing the door quietly behind me.

I guess I'm heading to the gym.

CHAPTER 11

Chloe

I CAN'T CATCH A BREAK.

Seriously. Not only am I forced to be with the baseball team all semester, but now I'm forced to be next-door neighbors with him every road trip.

Why must Coach go in alphabetical order? Why can't he just exclude me and stick me on the end? Or I'll even take another floor like the rest of the coaching staff, trainers, and equipment team.

I must've done something in my past life to warrant such awful karma. Is it because I used to wish the kids growing up would get lice or have explosive diarrhea in school? I used to wish awful things on the bullies, especially in elementary school right after my mom left us.

Karma really is a bitch.

And why did he have to stand in front of me in nothing but a pair of boxers? Isn't that a weird thing to be wearing when you're sharing a room?

Of course, he just had to bang on the door as soon as I got

out of the shower. The bathroom was full of steam after my long, hot shower, and I didn't want to leave the room. It seriously felt like a sauna and after this weird travel day where I fell asleep on Ty Billings—ugh, don't even go there Chloe—I just wanted to enjoy a little self-care.

But typical me, I forgot to adjust the temperature in the room. I think the staff set it to the Antarctica setting because I swear I could see my breath. The extreme temperature change had my body reacting with nips so hard they could cut glass.

Whatever you have to tell yourself, Chloe Mariano. The hard nips had nothing to do with the Adonis standing in front of you.

Sighing, I hit play on my Spotify playlist and up the tempo of the treadmill. I tried so hard to fall asleep tonight, but sleep kept evading me. Every time I was about to drift off into a sleepless state, images kept popping into my head.

First, it was the dreadful 'show-up-naked-in -front-of-everyone dream.' You know, the one where you're running late, so you rush through your routine only to be caught standing in the nude in front of your peers. Or for me, it was arriving at the baseball game and walking into the dugout in front of the entire baseball team...naked.

That is the worst dream and completely unlikely to ever happen.

As if that wasn't bad enough, images of Cody standing before me captured my thoughts. Only this time, he appeared in the doorway separating our rooms, but he swapped his boxers for a towel hung low across his hips. That perfectly defined 'V' led straight to the Promised Land. His tall, lean, chiseled body was on full display. Abs cut so deep that I wanted to drop to my knees and run my tongue over the edges.

The Promised Land? Get a grip, Chloe.

I couldn't get the image of him taking in my body out of my head. His eyes darkened from his usual hazel color to dark forest green with specks of gold that heated as his arousal ignited. The way his eyes kept trailing my body had me wanting to damn it all to hell and jump the man. It has been so long since I'd been touched by someone other than myself. But tonight, with Hudson watching us like we were his own personal soap opera, was not the time.

My body turned warm as images of him hovering over me, naked, tangled up in the sheets, were starring in their own movie in my brain. I felt the slickness start to coat the inside of my thighs as the ache grew in my center. As badly as I wanted to slide my hands underneath the satin material of my panties, I was not going to get off on the idea of Cody.

Even as I attempted to read my latest romance novel, I kept picturing the main character as him, despite the character not being described as anything like Cody. He was taking over my whole damn mind, and I needed it to stop.

In the end, I decided to go work out my frustration on the treadmill. This brings me to where I am now, continuing to up the speed to past five as "Power" by Kanye West blares in my AirPods. I need the distraction. If I run a couple of miles, I'll hopefully be exhausted enough to finally get a few hours of sleep.

I watch my body in the mirror in front of me as I assess my form. I'm a runner. I love the high that comes with pushing my body. My only problem is the more I run, the more my form starts to deteriorate, the more my body closes in on itself. I'm still perfecting my form, and as I watch myself, I keep an eye on how I'm positioned so I don't lose my form. I usually prefer to be outside, but hitting the treadmill is a nice change of pace. I can also really watch my form and figure out at what point I start to close myself off instead of running tall and relaxed.

Mile one is within reach, and that's when I notice I'm no longer alone.

Cody freaking Jacobs is standing in the doorway of the hotel gym in the middle of the night.

I can't catch a break.

Instead of stopping, I hit the increase speed button again, pushing myself to a tempo I don't typically run unless I'm in a road race. Try as I might, my eyes can't help but follow him as he enters the gym. He's still behind me and instead of climbing onto a machine, Cody grabs two free weights and makes his way to the edge of the bench.

He sits and begins to curl the weights that are gripped tightly in his hands. His jaw is set tight, and I know it's not from the weight. He can lift a lot more than what he is right now, but considering there's a game tomorrow, he must not want to tire his muscles too much.

The two of us continue our workouts without a word passing between us. Quite frankly, I have nothing to say to him. The whole point of me coming down here was to escape him and the thoughts of him. Instead, I try not to watch him in the mirror as his corded muscles tighten and the oh-so-sexy veins protrude in his arm.

I'm lost, shimming my shoulders and bopping my head to 'Super Freaky Girl' as I approach the halfway mark of mile three. Pushing myself, I continue to focus on clearing my mind and making sure I'm maintaining good form. I haven't spared a glance at Cody since he came in. But my willpower is slipping, and I hope to take a quick glance, just one more image to get stuck in my brain of his bulging muscles.

But when my eyes flashed to him in the mirror, I found him already watching me. Our eyes meet, and an explosion sets off in my brain as his intense gaze sears straight into my soul. My breath hitches, and I feel my toes catch on the moving belt.

In one instance, I witness my life flash before my eyes and

my inevitable collapse on the moving surface. Squeezing my eyes shut, I wait for impact.

Only impact doesn't come.

Strong arms wrap across my waist. Cody grips my hip with one arm while his other hand grips the handle of the treadmill keeping me from a very painful fall.

Adjusting his stance, he brings both of us to a standing position, his grip never leaving my hip forcing our bodies to be pressed against each other. My breath comes in fast pants causing my sports bra-clad chest to brush up against him. He groans at our contact, but neither one of us moves away.

"Shit, Wildflower," he says, concern lacing his voice.

Breathlessly, I stare up at him. "Thank you."

He nods. The hand not clasping my hip moves to brush a spare piece of hair from my face. My heart stutters at the contact. Cody's eyes move from mine as they run over my body, and suddenly I feel like I'm standing in front of him stripped bare. He's looking for any injury, but there isn't one. Thanks to him.

"Are you okay?" he asks, his eyes finding mine.

With a small smile, I nod. "I am. How did you catch me so fast?"

"I don't even know. I saw your foot catch on the belt, and I just knew what was coming next. I practically dove to make sure that you didn't hurt yourself."

My smile falls as the realization of what he just said hits me. "But you could've hurt yourself."

"Would've been worth it." That cocky smirk is back on his face, and it causes me to wobble a little.

I watch his eyes bounce from my eyes to my lips and back like he's asking for permission. He must see something on my face because before I know it, his head is dropping, and his lips are a whisper from mine. Reality comes slamming back into me, and I push my hand to his chest.

"I need to go to bed," I blurt the words out in a rush needing this moment to stop. Needing space from the one who seems to be everywhere all of a sudden.

A frustrated sigh escapes him and the hand gripping me releases my hip as he brings it to run through his hair. Slowly, he steps away from me, but his gaze never leaves mine.

"When are you going to forgive me?"

A frustrated laugh leaves my lips. "Forgive you?"

"Yeah, forgive me."

"Maybe when you give me an explanation. Or hell, I'd even take an actual apology. How am I supposed to forgive you when you can't even be honest with me?"

"Chloe..." He starts, but I'm quick to put my palm up interrupting him.

"Don't, Cody. Look, I'm here to do a job just like you have a job to do on the field. Stop pretending like the two of us have anything to do with each other. Let's leave the past in the past and move on. I don't want to be here as much as you don't want me here."

Turning from him, I storm out of the gym. Suddenly, I'm ready to sleep and forget this night ever happened. Pushing through the door, I'm rounding the corner when I hear a frustrated curse come from behind me.

I don't turn around.

And I don't stop until I'm safely behind my door. A place where Cody can't randomly show up.

I don't bother to shower either. I just toss my phone and AirPods on my nightstand before crawling into bed.

I run my hand through my ponytail as I take in my reflection in the mirror. My eyes look tired. They're bloodshot with blue bags underneath them. No amount of eye patches or concealer is going to make me look like a human today.

After last night's run and gym debacle, I was able to fall asleep immediately, which surprised me. But it still wasn't long before my alarm was going off.

Today the baseball team has a noon game, but there's a lot that has to be done beforehand, and I'm on the same schedule as the team if I want a ride to the stadium. I could tell Coach I will catch an Uber, but this is my first game, and I need to make a good impression. I want to see the ins and outs that go into a game day.

Reaching for my lipstick, I'm about to apply the pink-ish-nude shade when there's a knock on the door. Thankfully, I'm fully dressed, and the knock is coming from the main door, not the connecting door. We won't be having a repeat of yesterday.

With a quick glance in the peephole, I notice it's a member of the hotel staff.

"Hi there."

"Good morning, ma'am," the young concierge greets. "I'm sorry to bother you this morning, but we got your request for a honey lavender latte."

Accepting the coffee from his outstretched hand, confusion must line my face as he's quick to explain. "We received a call this morning that the occupant of 513 would require a honey laven-der latte. Was this not the correct drink?"

"No, no. It's correct. Thank you."

With a smile and a head nod, the concierge leaves me stand-ing there with another cup of my favorite latte.

Is this Ty's doing? I wonder as I shut the door to my room. He showed up to the bus yesterday with a drink and now this morning. I really hope this isn't a sign that Ty has feelings for me. As much as I think he's a great guy, I don't want the drama. Especially since he's Cody's teammate and roommate.

Can we say awkward?

Taking a sip of the delicious drink, I savor the warmth as it spreads through my body. I'm a ho for a good latte. The added honey just makes it even better.

After another drink, I quickly line my lips and apply the lipstick. With one last glance in the full-length mirror, I take in the outfit that Brynn picked out for me.

For the first game, I went with a simple spaghetti strapped, red and white micro-stripe dress—that is tight in the bodice and slightly flares out at the hip—a light wash denim jacket, and white Converse. My hair is curled but pulled up in a long ponytail, and I have a small backpack purse that will hold my camera and notepad, along with my other essentials.

"You can do this," I tell my reflection. With one last deep breath, I head out the door to meet the team in the lobby.

The hallway is bustling with guys from the team. I follow a group of them, whom I'm unfamiliar with, to the lobby.

"Honey lavender latte?" Ty asks, nudging my shoulder as he steps up beside me. The two of us enter the elevator together. The space is tight. Ty gently touches my hip and adjusts me so that my back is to his front. It's a little awkward, but I'd rather be pressed up against Ty than someone I don't know.

"It is," I finally answer his question. "Did you get…"

My question is cut off as a strong hand grabs the closing door, pushing it open. I know those hands. I had that hand on my hip last night. My cheeks heat as the memory of us pressed against each other flashes through my mind.

Cody steps on, and everyone makes space for him which causes me to press even further into Ty's front. His grip tightens in the same place Cody's did last night.

I watch as Cody's eyes track Ty's movement. His eyes narrow into slits, and his jaw ticks.

Aw, is someone jealous?

The ride down is awkward and silent. No one talks. It's like everyone can feel the tension in the air. As soon as the doors open, everyone takes Cody's lead, darting out to meet the rest of the team. Ty and I step out together, but before we get too far I turn over my shoulder and give him a tight-lipped smile.

"Good luck, today."

"Thanks, Chloe. Have fun today."

And with that, we both go our separate ways.

Game time is quickly approaching. We've been at the field for almost two hours, and the guys have been busy warming up. Some guys are practicing fielding grounders while others are taking part in batting practice.

Coach Weber instructed me that I had full reign to come and go inside the dugout as I needed. If there was ever a game I didn't want to sit inside the dugout, he would make sure that I had seats available to me. He really is a great guy, and at the end of the day, I'm really excited to be covering his story. I only wish a certain someone wasn't on the team, or that Weber was a coach for a different team.

I've been walking the stadium for thirty minutes, taking it all in and watching different players do their own warm-up routines. Somehow I've managed to walk the dirt path that leads to the outfield where the pitchers are warming up with catchers.

I find a spot against the fence, one that's out of the way and won't be a distraction. I've noticed the lingering glances some of the players have thrown my way. Each time I find their eyes on me, that annoying blush creeps up my neck and warms my cheeks. I don't do well being the center of attention of any guy, let alone a whole team. And I don't want to be the cause for anyone's focus to shift.

After only a few minutes, a shadowed figure stands beside me. My first instinct is it's Ty since the two of us keep finding ourselves in the same situations. But with a quick look out of the corner of my eye, I realize I'm way off. I'm thankful for the sunglasses I'm wearing, hoping that they hide the surprise in my eyes.

Niko Vega is standing beside me.

"So what's the story between you two?" Niko asks, startling me from where I've been not so subtly watching Cody throw pitches.

"Wh-what do you mean?" I stumble the words out, embarrassed that I was caught watching him. I was really hoping the sunglasses would help shield my eyes better.

He chuckles. "C'mon. Don't bullshit me."

"Excuse me?" My eyes widen at this blatant comment.

"You watch him a lot, yeah? You might try to hide it and keep up this hatred facade, but you suck at it. Because you don't stare at him like most girls stare at him."

Turning toward him, I steel my shoulders and put on my battle face. "What's that supposed to mean? How exactly do I stare at him, Niko?"

"You stare at him like there's a story to tell. Other girls watch him because they want him to give them attention, hoping to get him in their beds. You look at him, like...like..."

"Like he hurt me?" Shock laces Niko's eyes at my own admission. He wasn't expecting me to say that. I imagine Niko was waiting for me to admit my love for Cody Jacobs just like every other girl on this campus. There might've been a time when I would've loved him, but the first cut is the deepest, and I won't be forgetting what he did to me.

"Because he did, Niko. Then I had to sit back and watch

him develop a flirty, brotherly, whatever friendship with my best friend. I thought things would start to change and that he wouldn't constantly be in my presence, but life said 'watch this' as my professor assigned me the task of covering the baseball team this semester when I shouldn't even be covering sports. I can't fucking escape him."

I watch as Niko's eyes widen—no doubt because I said fuck—but I was swept up in the heat of things.

"Shit, Chloe, I had no idea it was that deep."

"No one does." I sigh, feeling the moisture gather in my eyes. I will myself not to start crying right here on the baseball field. "Everyone thinks I have this infatuation with him, when sure, maybe at one time I did, but there's so much more than that."

Niko watches me, and I feel his eyes bore into me, like he's reading my soul. I want to cringe under his assessment, but I don't. I straighten my shoulders and walk past him. When I think he's going to let me pass, I feel his arm reach out and his hand lightly wrap around my wrist. I glance over his shoulder and see that we've garnered the attention of some of the guys throwing in the outfield—Cody being one of them.

"Does he know how you feel about him?"

I shake my head. "There's nothing to tell. Our story is over, and I just want to get through this semester."

CHAPTER 12

CODY

WE WRAPPED UP OUR THREE GAMES AT LSU bringing home three wins. There's nothing I love better than to sweep a series. It's such an accomplishment against a damn good team.

But then we came home and swept another series against a team from New York. I love the early season games because we don't have to travel too much or too far away. Whoever is in charge of the schedule tries to make teams from the north travel to us so we don't have to play in the snow. That shit sucks, especially when we aren't used to the frigid temps.

At least tomorrow we head to College Station to take on Texas A&M for a Wednesday night game. It's a late one which means we'll do a short overnight trip and leave early Thursday morning.

Now we are getting to the point where we will have one game during the week before a three-game series against a different team. Once the season is in full swing, it becomes a lot.

Early morning practices, classes all day, traveling, meetings with the media or the team in the mix. I love it, and I wouldn't change it, but damn it's exhausting.

"You look like actual shit. Do you even sleep?" Brynn—my oh-so-honest friend—says from beside me. Narrowing my eyes into slits, I just glare at her. "Okayyy, we are not in the mood. Good thing I'm the freaking best and brought you this."

She brings the arm I didn't realize was behind her back to her front, and in her hand is a large coffee.

"Have I told you lately how much I love you?"

"Not lately."

"Well, I do." Taking a sip of the coffee, a smile spreads across my face. "You're the best."

She quirks her eyebrows letting me know she knows she's the best. "How's the season going?"

"Not bad at all. We look pretty good. It's just getting used to the schedule. It always takes me a couple of weeks to adjust."

She lets out a soft chuckle. "Yeah, Chloe has been walking around looking like a zombie."

"I'm sure she's a cute zombie," I mumble, not quietly enough, though, because Brynn's eyebrows hit her hairline, and she stares me down.

"What was that?"

"Nothing."

I watch as Professor Peters enters our psychology class. I'm not a big fan of the guy, I never have been, but especially not after he tried to make some creepy moves on Brynn last semester. He knows he fucked up because he never looks at our corner of the lecture hall. Maybe he knows I'll kick his ass and turn him in. You don't just get away with insinuating your student is a whore and will have sex with you. That's abuse of power, and it makes me fucking sick. Not only is Brynn not a whore, but she's not the type of girl to sleep with a professor. Yeah, it's taboo and shit, and her moral compass is a little skewed, but she's not that type of girl.

"You and Chloe need to work your shit out. I know something is going on between the two of you, even if you both never act like it. But now that you both are spending time together, maybe it's time to work your issues out. Or bang the tension out?"

I roll my eyes as Peters begins the lecture. As much as I hate the prick, I need the class to graduate since psychology is my major and everything.

Two hours later, Brynn and I are walking side by side as we exit the class. I refuse to let her be alone in his presence. Is it a bit of a caveman? Yes. Do I care? Nope.

"Are you heading to the Union?" Brynn asks as she pulls her cell phone from the pocket of her leggings. "Quinton and some of the guys from the football team are there already."

"Uhh," I start, and I'm about to agree to it when Brynn's previous words sink in. You and Chloe need to work your shit out. She's right, of course she is. But how do we work it out? It feels like too much time has passed us for us to have an awkward conversation. "I'll catch you next time."

She pauses. "Cody?"

"I'm good, B. You're right. I've got to figure out a way to work my shit out with Chloe. It's gone on long enough."

"What's gone on long enough?"

I stare at her with a puzzled look on my face. How has Chloe never told Brynn about our history? I mean, I guess it makes sense. Brynn has never shown any signs she knows that Chloe and I have a rocky relationship. If she would've known, there's no way she would've let this bullshit fester the way that it has.

Shaking my head, I ignore her question. Instead, I pull her in for a quick hug goodbye. Eyes are on both of us. I can feel them boring into my back. It's hard to be a normal college student—for both of us.

Everyone is waiting for Brynn—or Quinton—to screw up and step out of their relationship. Which they never will. Those two are endgame, and the people who don't believe it are blind.

I mean, I'm not looking for love in college, but if it were to fall in my lap like it has them, I wouldn't say no.

Wait, shit, yes I would.

I'm not here for relationships. I'm here to graduate and make it to the major league. Freaking Brynn seeps love like an infectious disease, and here I am eating that shit up.

"See ya, B."

Back at the house, it's a quiet Tuesday evening. Hudson is at the library studying. Ty is holed up in his room working on a paper. And Niko is standing in the kitchen cooking.

"It smells good in here," I muse, sliding my keys into my pocket and tossing my bag at the bottom of the stairs for me to take up when I make it that far.

"Cheesy rice and steak. I made enough for everyone." Niko moves around the kitchen, slicing the steak into thin strips. Steam floats from the pan on the stove. Niko is from Southern California and embraces the Mexican culture he was surrounded by, including the amazing cuisine. Whenever he gets the urge to cook, he always fixes us the best Mexican food I've ever tasted—I'm talking some of the tastiest street tacos and guacamole around. I've watched him make the guac, and it's rather simple to make, but it never tastes the same as when he makes it.

"Thanks, man," I say, grabbing a bottle of water from the fridge.

"Actually, I'm glad you're here."

"What's up?"

Niko scrapes the steak from the cutting board into a hot pan. The sizzling sound fills the kitchen as the smell hits the air, and my mouth waters. "I talked to Chloe while we were at LSU."

Immediately, my hackles are up. I remember watching the two of them have a strange, semi-heated conversation before the game had started. He doesn't know her well, and what could the two of them possibly talk about to have him needing to have a follow-up conversation with me?

"What about?"

I watch as he moves the steak through the oiled pan. With how thin the steaks are, it shouldn't take them long to be done. Then maybe he can turn his full attention onto the conversation we are having instead of the dramatic build-up shit.

"She told me you two have a past and that you hurt her. Want to elaborate?"

"Not particularly," I mumble. What gives him the right to act like her protective big brother? He doesn't even know her. Is he trying to imply that I hurt her physically? If he is, did she let him believe that shit is really going to hit the fan?

"Well, here's how I see it."

"Yes, please enlighten me on the past that you know nothing about."

Flipping off the stove with more force than necessary, Niko turns, and his full six-foot-five attention is on me. With his shoulders back and the serious expression he wears, I should be shrinking. He might have an inch or two on me, but I'm not backing down. I deal with a bully on the daily—my dad—and I'm not scared of Niko Vega.

"If I find out that you've hurt her—mentally or physically—I'm going to kick your ass. She doesn't deserve the bullshit she's been dealt."

I stare at Niko because I can't figure out why he's so

protective of her. He's genuinely a good guy and definitely doesn't put up with talk about women in any degrading way, including some of the typical locker room talk.

I know he was raised by a single mom, so I get why he wouldn't put up with that shit. I can't say I agree with it either.

But he's starting to piss me off. He doesn't know anything about Chloe and my past. And I would never be one to hurt a girl on purpose. I've been living with someone who instills mental abuse on the regular, and I could never imagine doing that to someone.

"Fuck off, Niko. Don't come into this house, insert yourself in our drama, and act all high and mighty. Yeah, Chloe and I have a past, but fuck you for thinking that I've hurt her physically. That'd be the last goddamn thing I would ever do to her or any girl. Yeah, I hurt her. I fucked up, but believe me when I say it was for the better."

"What the hell did I interrupt?" Hudson says entering the tension-filled kitchen.

Niko and I stare each other down, neither one of us answering him right away. I see Hudson sit at the stool next to me out of the corner of my eye.

"Wow, who are y'all fightin' over?" Ty adds from the doorway.

"Chloe," I grit out, not taking my eyes off Niko. But as I say her name, Niko's eyes widen as he stares over my head. Taking a deep breath, I close my eyes because I immediately know she's standing right there. Call it intuition, or hell, maybe my nose can constantly sniff out her floral scent like it's some kind of bloodhound, but turning to look over my shoulder, I see her standing there right beside Billings.

"I-I," she starts to say something, her eyes finding mine before turning to look up at Ty with a familiar smile I once used to see on her face. "I'm going to head home. See you guys tomorrow."

And with that, she turns and practically runs out of the house.

"Are you two fucking?" I grit the words out.

"Not that it's any of your business, but no we aren't. We both have the same communications class and decided to work on this week's reading together."

Dragging both my hands down my face, I rest my head on them and prop my elbows on the counter. I can feel Hudson's eyes on me while I have an internal meltdown.

For so long, I've acted like Chloe Mariano doesn't exist. I've been friendly with her when I'm in social settings where she's attended, but I've avoided being alone with her. And here she is, in my house, in my space, hanging out with my friends.

Seeing her with Ty almost gutted me. The thought of the two of them together, fucking on the other side of the wall that Ty and I share, I can't think of it.

Hudson's the first to speak. "Look, I think there's a lot of history that hasn't been talked about. And while I'm not one to want drama, I think it's time the four of us got on the same page. Niko wants to kill Cody because he thinks he's hurt Chloe," Hudson pauses as he points to each of us as he speaks so no one gets confused about the 'he' Hud's referring to.

I watch Ty's eyes narrow at me as he wonders if what Niko thinks is true. I shake my head hoping he gets the hint before Hudson continues. "Cody wants to kill Ty because he thinks Ty is developing feelings for Chloe. And I want to kill the three of you for acting like chicks and getting your panties in a wad instead of just saying what's on your mind."

Hudson pauses again as he takes in a long, deep breath. "I want this season to be our season. We've been busting our asses for two years to get where we are today, and I'm not going to sit by and let a girl ruin our chances. So either the three of you work your shit out and then, Cody, you work your shit out with Chloe, or I'm going to Coach and getting her reassigned. We don't need the distraction."

And with that declaration, Hudson stands from where he's sitting and marches out of the room, flipping us off in the process.

Nobody moves. The three of us all watch each other waiting to see who caves first.

"Chloe and I have a history that was never resolved. Yes, I hurt her." I look at Niko as I continue. "but it's not what you think."

And there I sat on a Tuesday evening before a road game, spilling the secret I've kept about the girl who's stolen my thoughts.

CHAPTER 13

CODY

"Undefeated!" Billings shouts as we pile into the elevator after our third game in College Station. We all cheer in celebration as excitement seeps from our pores. March is here, and baseball is in full swing.

I can't fight the beaming grin that lights up my face.

Reaching in front of me, I put my hands on Hudson's shoulder, squeezing him. He turns and wraps his arm around my shoulder. "And we have this motherfucker to thank!"

My eyes find Chloe's in the sea of my teammates trying to fit in this elevator car. The smile on her face has me grinning wider than I thought I could.

"Showers, and we are hitting the bar tonight," Niko says from behind me. "You good with that, Cap?"

"Hell yeah," I respond. I'll never get tired of being referred to as captain. I've worked my ass off to earn that title, even though my dad thinks otherwise. I'm sure I'll be getting a phone call any minute now for my performance review on how much I sucked and how I should've thrown different pitches. But I'm not answering tonight. Tonight I'm going out to celebrate.

"You wanna come with us?" Ty directs the question to Chloe, and I can't help but turn and wait for her response. She must feel me watching her because her eyes find mine immediately.

"Not tonight. I've got a date." My heart hammers in my chest at the news of her date. Is it one of the guys on the team? Does she know someone from College Station? Chloe digs inside her purse for something as she avoids the stares coming from the guys. She pulls out the white device that she always has. "With my Kindle."

The air returns to my lungs, and I can freaking breathe again. Hudson nudges me as his laughter fills my ears. The fucker.

"Ah c'mon, Mariano. Leave the romance novel at home and come have some fun with us," Niko tries to persuade her.

"Maybe next time, boys." We all watch as she strides out of the elevator with a confidence she wasn't wearing when she first started with the team.

The truth is we all have enjoyed having her around. No matter how hard she tries to hide away from us and pretend to be the wallflower she wants to be, her personality is like sunshine, and we all crave her rays.

The walk on the way back to the hotel is a little challenging. While none of us set out with the intention of getting drunk, we did indeed have a few beers and a couple of shots. Everyone needs to unwind from the pressure and celebrate the undefeated season.

With the promise that no one was getting hammered, the guys convinced me to be cool with everyone having a few beers. To celebrate my decision, I was awarded with some kind of specialty shot. One shot led to another, which led to another, and here we all are stumbling along the sidewalk.

"Do you think she'll ever come out with us?" Ty slurs the question as he slings his arm over my shoulder causing both of us to sway. He doesn't need to explain who the 'she' is in his question. Ty and Chloe have bonded, and I hate that she feels like she can't come out with us.

"I hope she does," Niko chimes in.

Hudson gives me a look before adding, "Cody can talk her into it."

I stare at him. Why would he think I'd be the one who could talk her into going out? She hasn't wanted anything to do with me. There's still a lot of groveling that needs to be done on my part before Chloe trusts anything that comes out of my mouth. If anyone could talk her into going out, it'd be Billings.

Stopping outside the hotel entrance, I turn toward the group of rowdy guys behind me. "Okay," I start, a slight slur to my words. "We need to be really quiet when we go in there. Coach cannot get any complaints about us."

"Aye aye, Captain," comes from a wiseass in the back. I narrow my eyes, but can't figure out which one said it as some of their faces blur together.

Putting on sober faces, we make our way through the empty lobby. Coach didn't give us a lights-out curfew tonight since we don't have a game tomorrow. We just need to be ready for the bus at seven thirty a.m. to head back to CTU.

I hear a noise behind me—probably someone stumbling—and it's not long before drunken laughter fills the space. Turning over my shoulder, I bring my finger up to my lips, shushing the team.

It takes two trips to get everyone up to our floor, and I wait outside our room until everyone is accounted for. No one brought back a girl this time. It was a night out with the team.

It's not something we do enough, but it needs to be done more often. A winning season means we need to be a strong team.

Watching the last of the guys filter into their rooms, I turn and swipe the key card, waiting for the magnetic strip to turn the light green. Hudson's already in the shower, so I make my way over to my bed, plugging my phone into the charger resting on the table between the two full-size beds.

Sitting on the edge of my bed, the internal debate begins—to shower off the bar or just climb straight into bed. I'm one of the only guys at the house who doesn't have to shower after a night out. And since we cleaned up before bed, I decided to wait until morning.

With my elbows bent and resting on my thighs, I stare at the wall that separates us from Chloe. Is she still up? What is she wearing? Is it something like that white set I saw her in?

Will she ever forgive me? Can there ever be an us?

"Did all that alcohol give you x-ray vision?" Hudson muses as he slips on his boxers underneath his towel.

My eyes don't leave the wall, and I don't answer him. I watch out of my peripheral vision as Hud places his phone on his charger before climbing into bed.

Before we went out tonight, Hudson knocked on the adjoining door and practically begged her to come out.

Since we've been on the road and sharing the same wall, the three of us have made the most of it. There's always an invitation to join us for our pregame pizza and video game night. She doesn't always accept, but every once in a while, she'll come over for a slice of pizza and a Coke. While we play *Call of Duty*, Chloe will sit in a chair and watch for a little while. I think it's her way of not coming across as being rude for eating and leaving. I'd never think that of her, but I know that's how she is.

I stand as I make my way to the bathroom to brush my teeth when I hear something strange. Quirking my brows, I glance at

Hud. He's settled in bed, covers up to his waist, texting away on his phone. He sees me pause and gives me a quizzical look.

"Do you hear that?"

Both of us stop and listen to the noise again. It's not the TV, we never turned that on. Straining my head, I hear a muffled groan—yelp—something that doesn't sound normal coming from Chloe's room.

"What is that?" Hud questions. Shrugging, I stand there listening.

And that's when I heard a scream come from her room. Without a thought, I move toward the connecting door praying that she didn't lock it earlier this evening. Plowing through the door, my feet stop short at the sight in front of me.

The only light in the room comes from the soft glow of the bathroom light which illuminates a sprawled-out Chloe. She's writhing on her bed in nothing but a lace nightgown—one I can only imagine is soft to the touch. Rose gold headphones sit on her head as her hand kneads her breast before she tweaks a nipple while the other hand uses a—oh god, is that a vibrator?

Oh fuck. Fuck. Fuck. Fuck.

"Is she—"

Hudson starts but I quickly turn and push him from getting a view of Chloe. I need to hightail it out of here before she sees me.

A shriek fills the air as movement flashes from behind me. "Cody!" I catch something purple in the air as I hear the loud thump of something hitting the ground. I'm pretty sure Chloe just chucked the vibrator she had pressed up against her pussy at me.

Fuck. Me.

"What the hell are you doing in here? Don't you knock?"

I risk a peek over my shoulder and see Chloe has covered her near-naked body with her sheets. Her chest rises and falls as her already pink cheeks flame brighter.

"I thought you were in trouble."

"Trouble?!" She shrieks.

"We heard you scream. I-I-I don't know what I thought, but I was worried and—"

"You just barged in here?" She runs her hand through her mussed-up hair, and I'm instantly wishing it was from me. I remember how soft the tendrils felt as they slid through my fingers.

Shit, forget replacing her hand, I want to be the one making her scream loud enough it alerts the neighbors. I want to feel her tight heat and bring her to the brink of orgasm.

"Wait? Did you just say you heard me?" Her eyes widen as mortification spreads over her blushed cheeks.

Scraping my hand down my face, I nod. "I was walking by and heard you scream. I thought you were in trouble."

Her eyes close tight as if she's trying to erase this moment. Truth be told, I'd like to erase it too. The reasons for Chloe to hate me keep stacking up.

"I'm sorry," I say as I turn on my heels and leave the room, closing both doors.

"Was she just doing what I think she was just doing?" Hudson asks as he tries not to let the laugh slip free.

"We aren't ever talking about this again."

Climbing into bed, I lay there as sleep never comes.

The image of Chloe burned fresh in my brain.

My Wildflower is perfect.

CHAPTER 14

Chloe

Me: Cody walked in on me having a *moment* to myself.

Brynn: Like a self-care night?

Me: I mean...kind of.

Brynn: OHHHHH! Hahahahaha like you were giving yourself some self-care *wink*

Me: How much do you think an Uber will cost to get back to CTU from College Station?

Brynn: OMG stop!

Brynn: How did it even happen?

Me: Noise-canceling headphones + a spicy book.

Me: Oh, and I forgot to lock the connecting door. Apparently, Cody thought I needed help.

Brynn: Needed help getting that O.

Brynn: I'm sorry. It must've been mortifying. Q is staring at me like I've grown two heads because I'm laughing so hard.

Me: DON'T YOU DARE TELL HIM!

Brynn: ...too late.

Me: FML

Mortification still courses through my body as last night keeps replaying in my head. I still can't believe I was loud enough for Cody to burst through the door.

On one hand, it was really sweet of him to want to protect me. Over the last couple of weeks, we've found some kind of common ground with our friendship. Actually, I'm not even sure friend is the right word for him—maybe peer. Or acquaintance? Either way, we are acting civilly toward one another. I mean we are going to be stuck together for the foreseeable future, so it's in both of our interests to get along, especially for those around us.

But on the other hand, he caught me wrist cramped, back arched, and mid-orgasm as my vibrator hit the right spot when the male narrator whispered those filthy words in my ear.

Yep, definitely mortifying.

Thank God he made sure Hudson didn't walk through the door too. I can't imagine the two of them standing there watching me come. Well, I guess I could imagine that. I am a romance reader after all.

Not the point, Chloe.

The bus back to campus is going to leave in ten minutes, and I've been sitting in this dark corner of the lobby waiting for the hotel to fall into a sinkhole and take me with it. But life doesn't work that way, and I really don't want to draw more attention to myself by being late and pissing Coach Weber off.

Slipping my round, tortoiseshell sunglasses down from the top of my head. In my mind, I imagine that no one can see me because the frames take up most of my face. Reaching for my suitcase, I adjust my cross-body over my chest as I make my way to the bus.

Please don't let me run into anyone. Please don't let me run into anyone.

Turning the corner, I glance up and, of course, make eye contact with none other than Hudson Larsen.

Hello, death. It's me, Chloe.

My cheeks heat at the contact, and immediately I duck my head, trying to appear invisible and waiting for the earth to swallow me whole. Hudson quickly averts his eyes as I dart toward the door. The quicker I get out of the hotel and onto the bus, the quicker I can get my headphones on and stare out the window.

What if Cody told the guys what he saw? I mean, isn't that the kind of stuff guys talk about in the locker room?

The bus is mostly empty when I step on it. I head to the same seat in the same section as I normally sit. Only this time, I put my bag in the seat next to me giving the universal sign that this whole row is taken.

Only a few minutes pass before the hair on the back of my neck rises and a warm feeling runs through my body. I know that if I look up right now, Cody Jacobs will be making his way down the aisle.

After a couple of seconds pass, I take a risk and glance up. Ty Billings is heading toward me with his signature wide-mouth grin. He doesn't appear to know what happened last night, and for that, I'm thankful Cody didn't open his mouth...at least not yet.

"Good morning, Chloe," Ty greets warmly.

"Hey, Ty." I return his smile with a wary one. I've really enjoyed getting to know Ty better this semester. I knew that we had similar majors, and we've had a few classes together over the years, but this is the first time we've had the chance to actually get to know each other. The two of us have bonded and typically sit together, but today I just want to be alone.

It's like he can read me like a book. Instead of trying to sit next to me, he reaches forward with a paper cup in his hand. "Here you go."

Sighing, my shoulders fall, and a tight-lipped smile slides across my lips. Guilt swarms my belly. He's been supplying my honey lavender latte addiction regularly, and here I am giving him the cold shoulder.

"Thanks, Ty. You know you don't have to keep doing this."

His smile falters, barely, but it's enough for me to notice. "Noted," he responds, and I watch his expression go from happy-go-lucky to a little distant. "I'm gonna sit in the back today."

"Ty—"

"It's all good, Chlo."

I watch as he retreats, and I feel like the world's biggest asshole.

Sighing, I slide my headphones over my head and return my gaze out the window as I watch the tree-lined streets pass us by on our way back to campus.

You've screwed up again, Chloe.

And just like all the other times, I'm not enough.

I'm switching over the last load of my laundry into the dryer when Brynn bursts through the front door scaring me enough to make me jump.

"Are you being chased?" Carrying my laundry to the kitchen table, I start folding. Being on the road is really screwing up my routine, and I'm running low on clean underwear.

"What? No." Brynn shakes her head as she walks toward the kitchen. She pulls out a Shiner Bock. Popping the top, she takes a drink before hopping up to sit on the counter.

"I've just never seen you run so fast."

"Oh shut up." She tosses her cap at me, laughing. For how fit Brynn stays, she's not huge on exercise. She has the best metabolism I've ever known, which I'm super jealous of. Unlike Brynn, I have to work on maintaining my body, and even at that, I'm a little soft around the edges.

"I've been dying to hear the full story, and it's killed me that you've been at home all day, and I've had to actually be in class today." Bringing the bottle up to her lips, she takes another long pull. "Spill the deets, babe!"

Groaning, I fold the nightgown I was wearing last night when it happened. Blushing at the memory, I toss the garment aside. "It was mortifying, B."

She scoffs. "Oh whatever, I bet he thought it was so hot. Q loves to watch—"

"Brynn!"

"What? I'm just saying there is absolutely nothing wrong with a little self-care."

I roll my eyes and inhale deeply. "Look, I know there's nothing wrong with *masturbation*," I say, whispering the word.

"Jesus, Chloe, own it." Brynn pauses before yelling. "MASTURBATION! Guys do it all the time, why can't we, as girls, express that we have needs too?"

"Hey, I read romance books for fun. Sure, I love the stories and getting to escape reality, but I also love the smut. I'm not a prude, but I'm private. What's wrong with that?"

"Babe, absolutely nothing. But I hate seeing you beat

yourself up over it. I mean, I think it's sweet that Cody came bursting through your door. That's the kind of guy he is. He's caring and protective over his friends. That's what makes him so great."

It's my turn to scoff before mumbling, "Except he's not."

"What do you mean?" Brynn's eyebrows quirk as she stares at me. I feel that stare penetrate the layers I've been building for two years.

"We have a past." I blurt the words out without meaning to. I've gone this long without anyone knowing my whole truth. I'm not about to spill any more secrets in the middle of this kitchen after we were just talking about masturbating. Tugging my laundry basket toward me, I grip the handles and storm out of the room, leaving a confused Brynn sitting on the counter.

A few hours later, I'm nose-deep in a book, forever grateful I used today to write my sports article recapping last night's game, working ahead on assignments, and catching up on the typical household chores—laundry, meal prep, and some light cleaning.

My mind is spiraling. I've caught myself reading the same paragraph over and over, unable to shut off the conversation from earlier.

Brynn and Cody have this unique bond. And while I'm so happy they have their relationship, I'm tired of feeling like an outsider. To Brynn, Cody is incredible. He's there to root her on, make her laugh, give her an ego boost with his flirty texts, and he'll defend her till the end.

But he's not the perfect guy everyone thinks he is.

To me, he's pain, he's sleepless nights, he's self-doubt.

In my almost twenty-one years of life, I've battled with self-doubt more times than not. The feeling of not being enough constantly consumes me. When I stand in front of a mirror, I look back at the girl staring at me and pick apart every inch of her.

I don't feel pretty enough. I don't feel smart enough. I don't feel like I'm ever good enough to get the guy. I want so desperately to be the girl picked first. The girl who gets the fairytale story, the happily ever after.

It doesn't help that I live my life through the pages of romance novels. I always see the girl get the boy. But life isn't a romance novel, and I'm stuck on the outskirts watching all the girls get the boys.

Maybe it's my fault? Maybe I'm broken?

Maybe God made me the girl who stands on the sidelines rooting for her friends. I'm the girl who's there to give pep talks and be a shoulder to cry on.

One day, maybe there will be more to life than being the girl every guy passes over. Until then, I'm stuck being the spectator, the cheerleader, the type of girl no guy wants.

A knock on the door interrupts my endless spiral of unworthiness.

"Come in."

Brynn peeks her head in the doorway with her hand covering her eyes. "Is it safe to enter? All vibrators put away?"

Shaking my head, I can't help but laugh. "Yes, it's put up and on the charger."

"Thatta girl," she says, laughing. "I made dinner if you want to come down."

My eyebrows furrow. "You made dinner?"

"Okay, no, but I did order from DoorDash."

Brynn is a lot of things, but being a good cook is not one of them. Quinton better make good money when he makes it to the NFL because he's going to need to hire a home chef, or he'll be stuck eating cereal for breakfast, lunch, and dinner.

Once we're downstairs, I follow Brynn as she leads us into the kitchen. I pause in the doorway to check out the spread before me. The light-stained, round table that sits in our small nook is set with our neutral, jute placemats, off-white stoneware plates, gold flatware, and wine glasses. Platters of food from my favorite local Italian restaurant sit next to the bouquet of fresh flowers I placed there this morning.

On my drive home from the baseball center, I stopped at my favorite local flower shop—something I usually do on Thursdays since I don't have class. The owner, a sweet widower who lost her husband three years ago, is always excited to see me.

Today she had a couple of arrangements ready in case I stopped by. One was a mixture of blush-colored daisies with a yellow center and eucalyptus sprigs. Very simple but so elegant. The other bouquet was a variety of ranunculus, daisies, greenery, and garden roses in shades of pinks, greens, and yellows.

What can I say, I'm a simple girl—give me flowers, a book, and good food, and I'm happy.

And that's exactly what I had planned—to curl up with my book, light my favorite clean-scented candle, put on my favorite reading playlist, and spend the evening relaxing in my room before another busy weekend full of baseball.

Luckily the team is home this weekend so I won't have to miss classes, and I can sleep in my bed.

"Everything looks great, but this feels a bit like a date." I wink at Brynn, letting her know that I'm just joking around.

Pulling out her chair and taking a seat, Brynn quickly adds, "Oh you know, just trying to wine, dine, and sixty—"

"Don't even finish that," I say through a laugh. "Save that for Q."

She smirks before reaching for the bottle of Pinot Grigio chilling on the table. The two of us fill our plates with salad, calamari, and fettuccine weesie. While no Italian restaurant is as good as my dad's—and yes, I'm totally biased, and I don't even care—the local Italian restaurant is a good alternative for the days when I don't feel like trying to cook one of my dad's meals.

Twirling the noodles on my fork, I take a very unladylike

bite. The rich, creamy mixture hits my tongue, instantly causing me to moan around my fork.

"This is so fucking good," Brynn says around a mouthful of food. I groan in appreciation as the two of us continue to shovel the most unflattering bites into our mouths. Apparently, I was starving and didn't get the memo.

"I'm sorry about earlier."

Setting her fork on her plate, Brynn turns her full attention on me. "You have nothing to apologize for. I took things too far. Clearly, there's more that you haven't shared with me, and that's fine. We all have our secrets, but just know...I'm always here for you."

"Thanks, B."

Her phone buzzes on the table and interrupts our conversation. She flips it over, chewing on her lip, before typing out a response. My eyes narrow as I take in the shift in her body language. Scooting her chair out from under her, she stands and rushes over to the sink.

"What—" I'm interrupted by asking her what's going on when there's a knock at the front door.

"Can you get that? I-I-I need to wash my hands." Brynn flips the handle of the faucet before lathering—and I mean lathering—her hands with soap. She looks like she's about to wash an entire kitchen's worth of dishes rather than her hands.

My eyebrows furrow, and I know I have very large creases spreading across my forehead. "Sure."

Hesitantly, I walk to the front door before glancing through the peephole. His back is to the door, but I would be able to recognize the tall, muscular body that makes up the man consuming my every thought in a crowd of people. Scanning him from head to toe, I take in the way that his jeans hug his lean waist and make his ass fantastic. The long-sleeve he's wearing clings to his back, stretching across the lats he's clearly been working on. Oh for fuck's sake, of course. Of course, he's wearing his powder blue hat with CTU stitched in red across the front.

Why does the sight of a guy in a backward hat make me want to drop to my knees?

Ugh, I've been spending too much time with Brynn.

Resting my forehead against the door, I take a second to give myself a mental pep talk. He's probably here for Brynn. He's not going to bring up last night. And if he does, I don't have to take it.

Taking a deep breath, I turn the knob and face the boy who keeps finding ways to crush me. He slowly turns his body to face me, and my breath catches in my throat.

The carefree boy with a wild spark in his eyes stands before me completely, utterly deflated. His eyes are downcast as he struggles to meet mine. The happy-go-lucky energy that normally radiates off him in ways that feel contagious is long gone.

"Hey, Chlo. Think we can talk?"

Nodding my head as words won't form, I open the door wider to welcome him inside. I have no idea what the hell is going on, and his mood has my guard on high alert.

Cody steps through the door, his frame erasing the space between us causing me to take a step back.

Brynn flies from the kitchen and heads toward the steps. "I'll be upstairs FaceTiming Q. Don't kill each other. I really don't want to have to deal with keeping any more secrets."

Cody nods his head at her and silence falls over the room as we watch her run up the stairs, her bright blond hair flying behind her in her wake.

I bring my bottom lip in between my teeth and turn my attention back to Cody, but when I look back at him, he's already looking down at me causing my breath to stutter. It seems he has a way of doing that.

"Want to go into the living room?"

"Yeah, that works."

"I'm going to grab my wine. Want some?" I gesture my thumb over my shoulder toward the kitchen table where the mess from dinner is still sitting, but it looks like Brynn put any leftovers away. She moved quickly. With a glance at the stairs, I narrowed my eyes as a sinking suspicion that the text Brynn got while we were eating was from the boy at my side.

"Nah, I'm good."

"Beer? Water?"

"Just came here to talk, Chlo."

Nodding my head, I quickly rush into the dining area as Cody turns and walks into the living room. Grabbing the wine bottle, I refill my glass with a hefty pour before following the steps Cody took.

He's sitting on one side of the couch, leaving the other side open for me. My mind quickly flashes to a couple of weeks ago when we were both stuck at the house together. And the look in his eyes before he tried to kiss me. Looking at him today, you never would have guessed it was the same person.

Leaning forward, I watch him try to find a comfortable position. He settles on bending his elbows and resting his body on his thighs. Keeping his body facing straight ahead, his head turns before finding my eyes.

What he says next shocks me.

"I'm sorry for fucking everything up."

CHAPTER 15

Chloe

THEN

"HEY HON, CAN YOU TAKE MY TABLE IN THE BACK *for me?"* Marnie, *the owner of Marnie's Diner, asked me.*

Placing the rag I was using to wipe down the counter in the bucket on the shelf, I make my way over to take a new order. I've been working at Marnie's Diner since I was a freshman in high school. I started out clearing tables and being a dishwasher, until halfway through my sophomore year when Marnie moved me to waitress. She works with my school schedule to make sure that I'm getting enough hours while still maintaining my grades.

Now I'm two months away from moving from Dallas for the first time and starting my first year at Central Texas University. While my dad could pull strings and get me a job anywhere or at any restaurant in the city—including his—he wanted me to learn the industry by starting at the bottom. Not that Marnie's is the bottom, because the diner does incredibly well. It's a staple in the neighborhood and has recently been featured in a few travel magazines for its unique 1950s flare and incredible home-style recipes.

Even though at fourteen, and after years of spending my free time in my dad's upscale restaurants, I always pictured that my first job would be working alongside my dad, I didn't realize how privileged that dream was. But at eighteen, I'm really glad I was able to experience working in the diner. It's been a lot of fun, and it's not as high pressure as my dad's restaurant. And the people I work alongside have inspired me to pursue my journalism degree. Each one of my coworkers has a story. They've struggled to make ends meet, they have a love of cooking, and they are paving their own path in the restaurant industry. Not everyone starts out and goes straight to the Food Network level.

Reaching into my pocket, I pull out my purple-covered notepad and pen to take the newcomers' order. Glancing up, my feet falter at the two guys sitting at the table. Both are gorgeous with their messy, damp hair, and muscles on full display thanks to their cutoff shirts, but it's the one sitting facing me who causes me to lose my footing.

He's stunning.

Warm hazel eyes are the perfect mixture of green, blue, yellow, and brown, with flecks of gold that shine even in the fluorescent lighting of the diner. His dark-brown hair is messy as if he's been running his hands through it all morning. But it's his smile that makes me weak in the knees. Straight, white teeth surrounded by full lips that have me wanting to know how they would feel pressed against mine.

I watch as he tilts his head back, exposing the long column of his throat, and watch his sharp Adam's apple bob up and down. His hazel eyes find mine, and I swear I melt right there on the spot from the contact.

Stopping at the edge of their table, I try to clear my throat and form words. The two guys are hot, and I quickly find myself unable to speak. I've never seen either of them before, and I know I would've definitely remembered them, especially hazel eyes.

"H-hi, I'm Chloe, and I'll be your waitress this morning."

"Hi, Chloe," the boy sitting across from hazel eyes greets. I look down with a smile and notice that he has a stunning shade of icy blue eyes.

"What can I get you guys to drink?"

They each list off their drink order: Blue Eyes orders a black coffee with cream, and Hazel Eyes orders a black coffee and water.

I go to tuck my notepad back in my apron and find those hazel eyes still staring at me. Chewing on my bottom lip, I give a small smile and let them know I'll be back with their drinks.

Reaching for the coffee pot, Marnie slides up beside me. "I thought you'd appreciate that table a little more than me."

"Marnie!"

"What?" she asks, amusement lacing her words. "They're cute and way too young for my fifty-year-old self."

I shake my head as I go back to getting their drinks.

The rest of their dining experience is spent with me fumbling over words, avoiding eye contact, blushing whenever my avoidance of eye contact failed me, and feeling like the biggest virgin ever. Of course, I was, but I didn't need to constantly act like it. It felt like there was a neon sign pointing down on me flashing brightly, letting everyone in the diner know that I've never been touched.

Hazel Eyes tracks my path back to deliver their drinks. Under his watchful gaze, I feel my body start to heat and shake.

Please don't let me drop this tray. Please don't let me make a fool of myself.

With a small smile, I set the drinks down in front of the guys.

"Dude, I'm glad Coach moved our practice to the field down the road. This place is sweet," Blue Eyes says, glancing around the diner. "It's like we walked back in time. I can dig it."

I watch as Hazel Eyes runs his hand over the back of the shiny, red leather seat. "Yeah, it's pretty awesome."

My eyes find his as he turns his attention back to me, and I feel the heat creep up my cheeks. Running my hands down my peach-colored uniform, I clear my throat and reach for my notepad.

"Do you guys need a minute, or are you ready to order?"

Blue Eyes skims the menu before closing it. "I'll do the southwest omelet, wheat toast, a side of fruit, and a side of bacon."

I jot down his order and turn my attention to Hazel Eyes. "Can I get the same, but add a cinnamon roll on the side?"

"Sure. Would you like the cinnamon roll out now while you wait?"

"Yeah, that'd be awesome."

With a quick nod and a tight smile, I head back to the kitchen to put their order in.

A few minutes after I've dropped off their fruit and Hazel Eye's cinnamon roll, the bell chimes notifying me their order is up. The guys dig in immediately after I place their plates in front of them, and I leave the bill for them to pay whenever they are done.

I'm so busy with the morning rush—taking orders and wiping down tables—that I don't see the guys leave. Disappointment floods my lower belly, and I internally curse myself for the feeling. I don't know these guys, and they don't know me. Blue Eyes mentioned that their coach moved practice, and since I've never seen them before, I assume they are part of the college baseball summer league. Every May through August, guys from all over the country come to our little suburb and play for the local baseball team.

Striding over to their empty table with a mixture of relief and sadness, I quickly begin clearing the empty dishes. Piling the plates together—I'm amazed at how much these two ate—I swipe the check off the table with the cash they left behind. There's writing underneath the signature that catches my eye.

You have a beautiful smile.

Pulling my lip between my teeth, I nibble as a bashful grin pulls at my lips. If only I knew which one of the two wrote the note.

For the next week, Blue Eyes and Hazel Eyes show up for breakfast where they order the same thing each morning.

And one of them leaves me a sweet message at the bottom of their receipt.

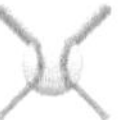

You have a beautiful smile.
You pour a mean cup of coffee.
You're sunshine on a rainy day.
Wildflowers. That's what your scent reminds me of.
The blue of your uniform makes your eyes shine bright.
I love the ribbons you wear in your hair.
Rough practices are worth it when I get to see you after.

On the eighth day in a row, only Hazel Eyes shows up to the diner.

"H-hi." Running my hand down my dress, I glance up at him. The nerves pour off me like a rainstorm. The two made me nervous together, but now that only one of them is here, I feel intimidated, when I shouldn't, but I haven't been able to get hazel eyes and dark hair out of my head the entire week that I've waited on them.

"Morning." Hazel Eyes closes his menu—I don't know why he bothers to even open it—and leans forward until he's resting his weight on his elbows. "I'll take my usual, please."

With a smile and a nod, I turn to walk away. There's no need to write down his order, I have it memorized.

Later when I drop off his order, I grow a backbone and decide to make conversation. "So I haven't noticed you before. Are you just in town from the summer?"

He nods his head in response. "Yeah, I'm from Georgia. This is my first summer playing summer collegiate ball."

"That's really cool. I've never been to a baseball game."

His jaw drops. "Never?"

"Never. Um, I'm not much of a sports girl. I'm more of a homebody who would rather stay in and read."

Shaking his head, I watch as he runs his fingers through his messy dark hair. "You have to come to one game."

"We'll see," I respond with a smile.

"Chloe," Chef Steve calls from the kitchen. "Order up!"

Glancing over my shoulder, I watch as the chef places plates on the silver tray.

"I've got to grab that. Let me know if you need anything."

Turning on my toes, I make my way back to the kitchen. As much as I enjoy the company of Hazel Eyes, he always comes at the peak breakfast rush. Once again, I'm too busy to make it back to his table. Out of the corner of my eyes, I watch him slip out the door. Sighing, I head to clear his table.

Just like all the other times, there's a note underneath his signature.

Go on a date with me? I'll be waiting for your answer.

I read over the note five times, and when I look out the window, I catch Hazel Eyes watching me as he gets in his car. He tosses me a wink and a flirty smirk that has me warming from the inside out.

I'm a flustered mess for the rest of my shift. Marnie eventually sent me home early after my third mistake. Climbing into my beat-up Honda, I drive home ,and it's on that drive home I start to worry about going on a date.

I've never been on a date. Hell, I've never had a guy give me any type of attention. My entire time in school I was ignored by the opposite sex unless they were making a joke at my expense. And now I've been asked out on a date by a guy who is entirely out of my league.

What do I wear? How do I act?

It's not like I have a mom to ask these questions of or even any girlfriends. I guess I could ask Marnie, but she doesn't date.

Why him? Out of all the guys in the universe, does it have to be the hot baseball guy?

He's the hot jock who gets the popular girl, and I'm the girl who waits on them at the diner after they've had the most glorious night together.

I'm not the girl that gets the guy.

And now I'm beginning to wonder if this is some kind of bet Hazel Eyes and Blue Eyes have with each other.

Is that why he was by himself today?

I couldn't sleep last night. Hours of endless tossing and turning. I heard my dad come home from the restaurant at two o'clock, and I waited until he went to bed before turning on my table lamp and pulling out the current paperback I was devouring. I knew if I would've turned my light on before he went to sleep, he'd be in right away to lecture me on how I needed sleep, or he'd be asking me twenty questions to find out why I wasn't sleeping.

My dad took the worried parent role on as soon as my mom left. He fusses over everything, and if I would've said I got asked out by a boy in town for the summer, he would have immediately told me to shut it down. Or he'd invite the guy over for an interrogation meal, and I was not about to have that happen.

When my alarm went off at a quarter after four, I jumped out of bed and went straight to the shower. Exhaustion weighed heavily on me as I only slept for maybe an hour. Typically, I put zero effort into my appearance. I work at a diner and end up smelling like fried food after every shift. But knowing that Hazel Eyes would be waiting for a response to his question had me flustered.

I spent extra time curling my honey-blond hair, I added minimal makeup with extra coats of mascara before swiping on a long-lasting pink lip color. Staring at myself in the mirror I looked like a different girl. Sure I was still Chloe Mariano, but a prettier, more put-together version.

Whistles greeted me as I entered the kitchen of Marnie's. My cheeks flamed, and I instantly wondered if I was overdoing it.

"Hey, Marnie, who's the new girl?" Chef Steve called out. Marnie stepped out of her office, and her smile lit up her face.

"Oh, Chloe, girl, you look beautiful. Does your new look have anything to do with the two hotties who keep coming and requesting a table in your section?"

Blushing, I cut Marnie a glare as I tried to relay to her that she was embarrassing me in front of the whole crew. "I couldn't sleep last night so I had extra time to get ready this morning."

"Uh-huh." Marnie heads back to her office as she hums a tune that I can't place, but if I had to guess, it is something romantic. Marnie has been without her husband for nine years, but that hasn't deterred her from love.

The hours seem to fly by as I spend the first few hours of my shift going from table to table taking orders, cleaning tables, and rolling silverware into napkins. At 8:45, I'm ringing a to-go order when the bell above the door chimes. Instantly, I can feel his gaze land on me. My blood starts pumping through my body, and my cheeks flame, no doubt with a pink hue that the customer in front of me can clearly see.

Glancing up, I watch Blue Eyes and Hazel Eyes follow Marnie to their booth in the back—the same one they sit in every day. As he's following Marnie, Hazel Eyes turns, and his eyes lock onto mine. He flashes me the briefest smirk that would have my panties combusting if I were that type of girl. Clearing my throat, I tuck a loose strand of hair behind my ears and finish ringing out a dozen cinnamon rolls and a box of coffee.

As my customer leaves the front counter, I rush through the kitchen doors. Finding the tiny mirror Marnie had installed on the wall, I take in my appearance. Not bad after three hours of work. With an internal pep talk, I run my damp palms down the front of my white apron.

You can do this. You can talk to hot guys. You can say yes to a date. You deserve this, Chloe Mariano.

Pushing my way through the door, I let my feet carry me to the corner booth where Hazel Eyes is watching my every move. Nerves swim through my system.

"Good morning." My voice comes out way more chirpier than it normally does and instantly Hazel Eyes lights up.

"Morning, Chloe." His bright white smile takes over his face, and I can't help the smile that follows across mine. The two of us lock eyes and silence falls over the booth. It feels like hours are spent as we both try to decipher the other.

Blue Eyes clears his throat, and I turn my attention to him. "Sorry about that. Would you like your usual?"

"That'd be great." Blue Eyes hands me his menu, and he turns his attention to his friend.

Hazel Eyes assesses me, and I swear it's like I'm standing in front of him naked. "I'll take the usual as well."

"Great, I'll go put that in for you both." I take the menus that Blue Eyes has extended and go to turn on my heels. Hazel Eyes stops me before I have a chance to walk away.

"Chloe, um..." He pauses, and a boyish grin takes over his face. "Have you had a chance to think about that date?"

Heat flares from my head to toe, and I imagine I'm about as red as our seats. Of course, I've thought about a date. It's the only thing I've been thinking about for the past twenty-four hours.

"I have given it much thought. Unfortunately, I don't feel comfortable going on a date with a boy I've just met and whose name I don't know."

I take my opening to walk away as I hear Blue Eyes scold Hazel Eyes about how he could ask for a date without offering their names.

"It's Cody, Cody Jacobs, and he's Hudson Larsen." Cody introduces himself in front of the busy rush inside Marnie's Diner.

I pause before I have a chance to get to the counter, turning slowly.

"I'm sorry I haven't introduced myself sooner. Truth is, you're beautiful, and it's intimidating. I just couldn't help but come here every day for the past week and a half because it means I get to see you."

Placing one foot in front of the other, Cody erases the space between us until he's standing right before me. He's tall, a lot taller than I would've guessed, with seven or eight inches on me. His navy Atlanta Braves T-shirt hugs his tight athletic build. I can only imagine the muscles and ridges that are hidden beneath the cotton.

"Hi, Cody." The words come out in a breathless whisper as we've officially garnered the attention of the entire restaurant. Customers have abandoned their meals and are enjoying the show between the two of us.

"Hi." That boyish grin is back on his face, and it's contagious, causing a smile to spread across my lips. Instead of messy hair, a navy Braves hat sits on his dark locks. Cody reaches up, removing his hat before running his fingers through his unruly hair. Instead of returning his hat forward facing, Cody spins it around and rests it backward.

I swear my knees go weak. There's just something about a man with a backward ball cap.

Leaning forward, he lowers his voice before asking, "Now that you know my name, would you like to go out with me?"

Nibbling on my lower lip, I take in the man in front of me. "Yes."

"Really?" Shock replaces the boyish grin as I nod assuring him that I'm serious about the date. "What time do you get off?"

"12:30!" Marnie shouts from somewhere behind me. My eyes widen as I look over my shoulder and find Marnie behind the counter with her hip perched against the metal material watching our entire conversation.

"Perfect, I can pick you up then."

"I'll need to shower after this," I say before dropping my voice for only Cody to hear. "I'll smell like the fryer."

He nods with a pondering expression. "I'll let you get back to it."

"Thanks. I'll get your order in."

We both turn, but not before we both glance back over our shoulders with silly grins pasted on our faces. I hurry to input their order before scurrying off through the swinging doors that lead into the kitchen. Marnie is hot on my heels as I lead the way to her office. She shuts the door behind her, and I let out a girlish squeal.

"Oh, my sweet girl, I'm so happy for you." Marnie squeezes me in her arms.

Since working for Marnie, she's quickly become a stand-in mom. There have been many times I've come to her for advice, a shoulder to cry on, and to talk about lady issues that I didn't want to talk to my dad about.

"Cut out early. I'll cover your section, and the tips are yours."

"Marn, I can't do that."

"Yes, baby girl. You can, and you will."

The bell in the kitchen chimes, and I hear Chef Steve call out my name.

I walk like I'm floating on a cloud for the rest of my shift. Marnie kicks me out thirty minutes before my shift is over. Cody and I exchanged numbers, and he texted me the details of our date.

For the next seven weeks, my days start with a 'good morning' text from Cody. Hudson and he have the same breakfast every morning—unless they are traveling—and the rest of my days and nights are spent with Cody Jacobs.

It was a summer when we were inseparable.

It was a summer where we didn't talk about what came next.

It was a summer where we lived in the present with no talks of the future.

Day dates, baseball games, breakfast at the diner, a weekend trip to Galveston, and everything in between.

It was the summer of Chloe and Cody...

Until it wasn't

5:05 AM

Me: Good Morning :)

10: 22 AM

Me: Missed you at the diner this morning. See you after my shift?

12:05 PM

Me: Cody? Are we still meeting?

4:43 PM

Me: Is everything okay? I'm sorry for calling so many times, but I'm worried.

The next day.

4:12 AM

Me: Did I do something?

Three days later...

8:35 AM

Me: So I'm not even good enough for a response?

One week later...

10:02 PM

Me: Screw you, Cody Jacobs.

CHAPTER 16

CODY

I’M SORRY FOR FUCKING EVERYTHING UP.”

Hanging my head between my arms, I glance over and find Chloe staring at me. Eyes squinted, mouth slightly ajar, her glare never leaves my face. I know I’m coming out of left field, but this apology is a long time coming.

“Is this about last night?” She whispers the question, embarrassment pinking her cheeks.

“No, it’s about everything. It’s about our summer and every encounter since, and me constantly fucking everything up.”

She scoffs as she presses her palms into the cushion as if she’s about to get up. Without thought, I reach across the couch and clutch her thigh. Her eyes snap to mine and down to where my hand is resting on her leg. “Please, Chloe.”

Brushing my hand off her, she stands and begins pacing back and forth in the open space between the coffee table and their TV stand. Every few seconds she glances up at me with an expression I can’t quite read. I want to know what’s going through her head. I want to know what she’s feeling, but she’s clammed up like a goddamn locked box, and I'm stuck sitting here watching her process. Or short circuit. I can't quite tell.

"Chlo—"

Her eyes snap to mine. "Don't."

Pursing my lips together, I lean back into the cushion and wait. An awkward silence falls over the room as her pacing continues.

"You've had two years to apologize, and you haven't said anything. Why now?" Her pacing stops, and her hands find her hips as she stares me down.

"I don't know why now, but I never should have let it get to this point."

She scoffs. "You think? You ghosted me."

Chloe practically screams "ghosted," and I sure hope Brynn is busy on the phone with Quinton because all of our dirty laundry is about to be shared right here, right now.

"For weeks you ate in my diner. You were supposed to pick me up from my shift. But instead, you left me unanswered for a week. A week I spent trying to figure out what I did. How I wasn't good enough for you. Wondering if something had happened to you."

The air vibrates around us, and I don't know what to say. I can't form words because I don't know why I did things the way that I did.

"I went to the field. After the fourth day of not hearing a word from you, I went to the field to get answers, and you want to know what happened?"

I didn't want to hear what happened. Hudson later told me what went down at the field, and I'm not proud of that either.

Shaking my head, I hope that prevents her from continuing. A menacing laugh escapes her lips and has me snapping my eyes to her. She looks maniacal.

"You weren't there, and every single one of those guys

ignored me. Hudson told me nothing was going on between us and that it was never serious. NEVER SERIOUS! I felt duped. You were the first guy to give me any attention that didn't revolve around making fun of me. You were my first everything—date, kiss, more. But it was never serious. I guess all of those late-night confessions were a joke. I guess I read way more into the situation than you ever did."

Sighing, I remove my hat and run my fingers through my hair. "Hudson told me what he said, and I'm sorry for that, too. In some twisted way, it was his way of making sure you moved on. That you knew that I wasn't coming back for the summer. There was so much happening at home, but I wanted to keep you away from that part of my life. I was embarrassed. I just wanted one summer to get away and have fun. Falling for you wasn't something I ever could've predicted."

Her shoulders slump, and her body relaxes as she slides down to the floor. She sits there with her legs crossed in front of her. "You could've talked to me." Her voice is broken.

"I know, but I was embarrassed." My voice dropped as I tried to get her to look at me, to really see that I was in fact, upset over everything. Chloe's eyes cast up and lock onto mine. "I never would've imagined we'd end up in the same place, but when I saw you on campus with Brynn, I couldn't believe it. It felt like fate was giving me a second chance, but then you acted like you didn't know who I was. So I kept up with the facade that we didn't know each other. But I never forgot you."

"But why just disappear?"

"I got a phone call in the middle of the night that my dad had a heart attack. Leah called me sobbing on the phone." Chloe gasps at my admission. "I didn't think. I just wanted to get to my sister."

"Did you think that I would be mad that you went home to your family?"

"Of course not. I didn't think we'd ever see each other again. We never talked about college or what was next. I knew there was no way I could've made a long-distance relationship work, not with school and baseball."

"So you decided to just ghost me? Cool."

"I thought it was best at the time. Look, my dad is an asshole. I wanted to protect you from him, from my fucked up relationship with him. And I've been living with the decision to ignore you for two years, and I know that it was wrong. I should have at least texted you back that I was fine."

Her eyes bug out, and her jaw drops in shock. "The least you could've done? No, the least you could've done was be man enough to let me know that you had to go home for an emergency and that our time together was more than just nothing."

"Dammit, Chloe. I know. If I could go back, I'd do it all over. But I was young and dumb and a chicken shit."

"Pretty much," she mumbles as she runs her hands up and down her crossed arms.

Sighing, I lean forward and place my elbows on my knees. "I didn't come here to fight with you."

"Did you think you'd just come here and say sorry and that everything would go back to normal? We'd go back to endless days together, and I'd just forget about everything that happened?"

Honestly, I did think that's how things would go, but based on the look on her face, there's no way I was going to admit that now.

"Uh, no?" Her eyebrow quirks as she hears the question in my voice.

Standing, she starts walking out of the room. I jump to my feet and follow her. She stops at the front door before reaching for the handle to open it.

"Thanks for finally giving me the apology I've deserved for two years, but I think you need to go."

"Chloe, please," I beg, hoping she hears that sincerity in my voice. I didn't want to come here and fight with her.

"Go, Cody. I need to think."

With a terse nod, I slip my shoes on and walk out her front door.

This was not how I saw things going.

"We're going out tonight." I bark the words out as I enter the house I share with my three teammates.

Ty is the first to turn his head from the couch the guys are sitting on playing some MLB video game.

"Bro, it's the night before a game." He quirks an eyebrow at me as he tries to get a read on my mood.

Tossing my keys on the table that sits inside the front door, I storm up the stairs but not before calling out over my shoulder. "And I don't give a fuck. I'm leaving in twenty."

I hear controllers hit the table from behind, and I have no doubt the guys are staring at each other in confusion.

Rarely do I go out the night before a game, and if I do, it's usually to get food and celebrate while we are on the road. I know how wild the parties are at CTU, and I try to avoid them at all costs. There's nothing worse than being the only sober one at a rager. But tonight, tonight I don't give a shit. Consequences be damned.

Twenty-five minutes later, I'm on a mission to get to the bar as soon as I push open the doors to the Eagle's Nest, the local campus staple. They're known for their fun theme nights, cheap wings, and cold beer. Tonight is their weekly 'Thirsty Thursday' night with their five-dollar pitchers and two-dollar bomb shots. And bombed is in fact what I plan to be.

"Jacobs, you good?" Niko stands in front of me blocking me from my trip to the bar.

Gritting my teeth, I narrow my eyes at him. "I will be as soon as you move out of the way."

"I've got him," Hudson reassures Niko. I don't need him to be worried about me. Instead of waiting for Niko to move out of my way, I shoulder past him.

Tonight I just want to forget. I want to forget ever meeting Chloe. I want to forget the hurt I caused her. I want to forget the pain I saw on her face tonight. Everything is a mess between us, and now we are forced to spend our days together. It's awkward, and it's affecting my game. Tonight I just need to forget. Even if it's just for a few hours.

"Jacobs!" Coach Weber yells my name from across the field. I'm currently head down in a trash can emptying the contents of my stomach. Niko forced me to drink a disgusting hangover cure drink, and it was starting to help, until Hudson decided to hit every goddamn pothole from our house to the stadium. It was a five-minute drive, and I swear he was making it a point to rattle my brains.

I know Hudson's disappointed. I'm the captain of the team, I'm supposed to be the leader, and getting wasted the night before a game is not how I should be leading the team.

I thought I was making the right decision. I thought that by going out I'd forget the look of pain etched on Chloe's beautiful face. But I woke up this morning and still saw it.

I'm tired of fucking everything up.

Reaching for the water bottle that I propped against the trash can, I squirt a solid stream into my mouth before rinsing and spitting it back out in the trash can. Sweat runs from my pores as I continue to sweat out the liquor from last night.

The guys toss me pitying looks as I make my way over to where Coach is standing on the third base line. Dread pools in my stomach at the conversation that awaits me. The disappointment is settled on his face as well as the anger that is radiating off his body.

"What the fuck is your problem today?"

I stand tall, even though his eyes make me want to cower like a child being scolded by their parent. "It won't happen again, Coach."

"No, it won't happen again unless you want to ride the pine the rest of the season. Get your head out of your ass. Get rested up. And get ready to play your heart out. Now get the hell off my field and out of my sight. You're dismissed."

Never have I ever been kicked out of practice. But I can't say that today's decision wasn't warranted.

Head down, I make my way over to our dugout where I quickly gather up my gear before walking through the door that leads underneath the stadium where our locker rooms are located. I don't stop walking until I exit the stadium. Since the guys are still practicing, I start the fifteen-minute walk back to the house.

If I don't get my act together, I'm going to end up being the lousy player my dad keeps reminding me that I am.

Enough with the distractions. I need to get my head back in the game.

CHAPTER 17

Chloe

THIS GAME IS A JOKE.

Standing in the back of the dugout, I try to make myself the invisible wallflower I am because the boys, especially Cody, are stinking up the place. After going down four to nothing after the second inning, Coach pulled Cody from the mound, and he's been sulking on the bench since. His bad attitude has leached into the rest of the team, and no one can get their bats working.

Now at the bottom of the eighth, the Eagles are down seven to one with no sign that a comeback is going to happen.

The energy in the dugout is toxic. I've never seen Coach Weber so frustrated with the team. Granted, I've never seen the team play this badly before, and I'm lucky enough to get a front-row seat at the chaos. Hudson won't even look at Cody, let alone talk to him, and I have a sinking suspicion that the gossip on campus was correct. Cody was at the Eagle's Nest last night and got obliterated.

And I can't help but feel that it's my fault.

To be completely honest, I was shocked that he came over last night. After two years of avoiding each other, the day after he caught me with my hands down my pants—literally—he wanted to make nice. Years of not mattering, of feeling like a spot on the wall, now he wanted to apologize.

And to find out he ghosted me because his dad was sick, and he figured we'd never see each other again. Like who does that? Even if we never would've seen each other again, doesn't common courtesy say you should at least text back and let the other person know you are, in fact, still alive?

The sound of a ball connecting with a bat interrupts my thoughts as I watch the other team land another hit to left centerfield.

Hudson and Luke Danners take off after the ball, but Hudson beats him to it. Scooping it up, he throws the ball to Ty at third base who is able to catch it and save a run from scoring. It's too little, too late, but at least it's not another scoring play.

Reaching into my cross-body—this is where I curse myself for not liking pants because I always have to carry my phone in a purse—I pull out my phone and quickly type out a message to Brynn.

> Me: Are you still at the game?

> Brynn: Unfortunately...I was just thinking about bailing.

> Me: Can I bail with you?

> Brynn: See you out front in five.

Closing the message and locking my phone, I place it back in my bag before turning to head toward the door that leads inside the stadium. My feet falter as I realize I'm going to have to walk past a pissed-off Cody in the process. Keeping my head down,

I rip the band-aid off and go for it. I'm about to pass him when my subconscious decides it's a good time to look up.

Our eyes meet, and I give a tight-lipped smile as I head out.

"Giving up?" Cody asks, causing me to pause.

My eyes find the scoreboard before I turn back to him. With a shrug, I let that be my answer and continue out the door.

So much for things not being awkward this season.

Walking through the underground tunnel, I make my way to the hallway that leads to the stairs to climb to the main level. My feet hitting the metal stairs are the only sound in the space, and I enjoy the few minutes to myself.

Emerging from the stairwell, I find Brynn and Quinton waiting for me. Brynn's dressed in a pair of ripped jeans, a baseball jersey, and a powder blue CTU hat. I'm surprised Q let her wear a jersey that wasn't his. They both have this alpha-possessive vibe, but it works for them.

"Dugout that bad?" Brynn asks as she steps into place beside me.

I stare at her with wide eyes and nod my head. "So bad. I'm supposed to meet with Ty to work on a project, but I'm going to rain check. I need a night in."

Brynn and I follow Quinton through the crowd of fans exiting the stadium. It looks like we aren't the only CTU fans ready to get out of this stadium and erase this disastrous night from our memories. Q's body has a way of cutting through the masses like Moses parting the Red Sea which makes it easy for us to exit the stadium in no time. He leads us up through the parking lot to his Tesla, waiting in a reserved spot.

"So all we need to do is win a national championship, and we'll end up with a reserved spot?" I muse as he unlocks the car and opens the passenger door for us.

"Nah, you just gotta be the hottest guy on campus." Brynn responds for him as she presses her body against him. These two and their PDA. If I didn't love other people's love, I would be constantly nauseous around them.

Maybe someday I'll have something like that.

You could have something like that if you would forgive Cody and hear him out.

Where did that thought come from?

Shaking my head, I lean it against the window and let Quinton drive us home. Only he doesn't take us straight home, instead he pulls into a Shake Shack. Brynn and Q share a knowing look, and I know that tonight Brynn is going to enjoy her special stash.

She turns in her seat, her bubbly personality radiating off her. "Wanna get high and watch Friday with us?"

I laugh and shake my head. I'm not much of a pot smoker. I'm barely a get-drunk kind of girl. "No, that's okay. I think I'm just going to have a self-care night and try to check in with my dad."

"Ohhh, one of your 'self-care' nights," Brynn says with a wink and air quotes. My cheeks heat, and my eyes dart to Quinton where the two of us make eye contact in the mirror.

"Brynn!"

She cracks up laughing. "Oh please we all know when you are having one of your moments. You aren't the quietest."

My eyes widen at her comment. I thought the noise-canceling headphones were my problem last time, but apparently, I'm louder than I thought. Placing my face in my hands, I mumble, "Oh god," before sinking in my seat. I really did mean that I wanted a night in to pamper myself with a face mask and manicure.

Clearing his throat, Q drives us forward until we are in front of the speaker. "What do you guys want?"

"Strawberry milkshake, double shack burger, fries with

cheese and bacon," Brynn answers as she leans over the center console to look at the menu.

"Chlo?"

"Vanilla milkshake, chicken shack sandwich, bacon and cheddar fries, please?"

Quinton repeats our order while tacking on his order—two double shack burgers—but instead of individual fries, he orders a box of cheddar and bacon fries. Brynn eyes him, and he just shrugs his shoulders. These two will clean out the house when they're high. It's quite comical to watch because the next morning they feel like shit from all the junk food, so they spend hours at the gym working it off.

Once our order is placed, I pull out my phone and find the blue money-sharing app. I thumb out a quick payment to Q, even though he's going to object to the idea of me buying my own meal.

There's a notification from the university's Twitter account.

Central Texas Eagles baseball suffered a frustrating 9-1 home loss to Lafayette. Eagles are back in action tomorrow at 1:00.

Yikes. The team managed to give up two more runs after we left.

I let my eyes drift shut as I rest my head against the window. The drive home isn't long, but I'm not in the mood to listen to Brynn & Quinton's verbal foreplay. So I let my mind drift away to a summer sunset on the beach and a cute boy's arms wrapped around me.

"Thatta baby!" I hear Ty cheer from beside me as Hudson smacks a hit resulting in a triple. We are halfway through Saturday's day game, and the boys look so much better than they did last night.

The energy inside the dirt-floored dugout is vibrating. I can't keep the smile off my face from the guys whooping and cheering each other on. Coach Weber is even dancing. I'm so glad I didn't talk myself into skipping today's game.

The Eagles are up five to one in the fifth inning. Even though Cody won't be pitching today, Coach is punishing him for yesterday's shitty game, his vibe is motivating the team to be better than yesterday.

My eyes keep drifting from the turf and dirt field in front of me to the dugout where a boyish grin keeps calling to me. He's light and vibrant, joking around with his teammates.

And damn, does his baseball cap do things to my insides. Not to mention the way those baseball pants mold around his muscular legs.

Today the guys are wearing my favorite uniform color combination: powder blue pants with a red belt, a matching powder blue shirt with Eagles in red script writing, and a red flat bill baseball cap with CTU across the front. The red hat makes the green and gold flecks of Cody's hazel eyes pop, and I keep finding myself in a trance watching him high-five his teammates.

Maybe I can find it inside to forgive him.

Luke Danners steps up to the plate, and after the third pitch, he nails a line drive blooper in between Lafayette's second baseman and center fielder. The hit results in Hudson scoring, putting us up by another run. I watch as Hudson practically skips down the stairs as he enters the dugout doling out high fives. There's been tension between Hudson and Cody, I could feel it all day yesterday, but as Hud tries to bypass Cody, Cody slaps him on the ass causing both of them to crack up. A huge smile breaks free as I watch the two go through the same celebratory handshake I've been watching them do since the summer before we started college.

I can't help the laugh that escapes my lips. I try to keep quiet so I'm not a distraction to the team, but I fail because Cody's eyes seek me out immediately. Chills break through my body, and a pit settles in my stomach.

As we stare at each other, I watch his lips curve at the ends. My lips mirror his, and I feel a blush rise in my cheeks.

Cheering from the crowd interrupts our stare down, and both of our heads snap to the field as Nolan, who is the team's catcher, launches a bomb out over the left fielder's head. The ball continues to sail until it lands over the fence resulting in a three-run homer.

The dugout clears as the guys rush out to home plate to wait for Nolan to round the bases. While the guys are all out on the field, I climb the steps and position myself with my camera to capture the celebration.

Arms fly and cheers erupt as Nolan steps on home plate. I click away at the camera as I capture the celly dances, high fives, and rowdy energy the team exudes. Heads turn my way as the guys start their journey back to the dugout. I don't stop clicking the camera, wanting to catch it all.

Bringing the camera down from my face, I let it hang around my neck when some of the guys start coming toward me. With their hands in the air, they wait for me to slap them. Another smile breaks free as the overwhelming feeling of belonging warms my soul. I feel like a part of the team.

"Yeah, boys!" I yell as my body breaks out in a little shimmy.

"Chloe!" Coach Weber calls from behind me as dread pools in my stomach. Turning on my toes, I find Coach standing at the top of the stairs high-fiving the guys as they come back in. "Did you just do a little dance?"

Making my way over to him, a laugh breaks free. "Yeah, I did."

He points his finger at me. "Every out-of-the-park home run, you do a little dance!"

"You hear that boys?" Ty yells. "Chlo's going to dance for every out-of-the-park homer."

Cheers and claps fill the air as embarrassment paints my skin pink.

"I'm glad you're a part of the team," Weber says as I hop down the stairs.

I return to my spot at the end of the dugout when Ty sidles up next to me. He runs a finger down my arm where my skin is exposed thanks to the sundress I'm wearing today. "Sorry if I embarrassed you."

"It's all good, Ty. Just remember, payback is a bitch." I bump my shoulder with his as his eyes widen.

"Do you have any plans after the game?"

"I have a hot date with a leather-clad biker who runs an MC." I fight to keep the cackle from escaping as I watch Ty's eyes widen as bewilderment takes over his expression. I really did try, but I can't help the loud outburst that garners everyone's attention. I look past Ty and give the guys a quick apology. "I'm kidding, Ty. I need to type up my notes recapping today's game, and I need to do the reading we have for Mass Media. What's up?"

"Oh my god, Chloe. I'm not one to yuck someone's yum, because believe me I'm for all the kinky shit, but you had me going for a second."

My eyes bulge at Ty's comments about kinky shit. I'm no virgin, but I'm extremely inexperienced in the bedroom department. I've read about plenty of kinks in my books, but I can't imagine ever acting on them.

"You wanna come over, and we can work on the reading and assignment together?"

"Yeah, that sounds good. I didn't bring anything with me so I'll need to rideshare home and to your place. My car is in the shop."

The dugout breaks out in chaos as guys rush around grabbing their gloves and heading back out to the field.

"You can ride with me." Before I have a chance to object, Ty is grabbing his glove and marching out onto the field to take his position at third base.

The game ends with us winning ten to one in a much-needed redemption battle. Coach Weber was quick with his post-game speech telling the guys how proud he was of how hard they worked, and while he knows there will be some celebrating, no one better show up hungover tomorrow. His eyes glared daggers into Cody.

Ty drove Niko and me to my townhouse where I quickly ran in, changed out of my dress into a lounge set, and grabbed my backpack before we took off to the guys' house. Once we got to their house, all the guys took off to their rooms to shower. Which means I was left alone to wander.

As much as I wanted to snoop, I made my way into their kitchen in search of something to drink. Opening the fridge, I dug around glass containers full of food and found a hard seltzer in the back. Reading the label, I smiled to myself that the only seltzer was my favorite flavor: blackberry.

Popping the top, I make my way over to the brown leather sectional. I'm grateful that the couch is leather because I'm not sure if I'd sit on it if it was cloth. I've been witness to way too many things happening on this couch at parties. Getting comfortable, I settle into the cushions while pulling up my Kindle app on my phone.

Never would I have imagined that I would be chilling on the couch inside the Baseball House. Not after my past with Cody.

As frustrated as I was with not getting the feature beat for the campus newspaper, I'm quickly learning things happen for a reason. Over the last few months, I've had to step way outside my comfort zone. I've actually had to live and not live vicariously through my romance novels.

"Chlo, what kind of pizza do you like?" Ty asks from where he's making his way down the stairs, dressed in navy sweatpants, a long-sleeve with his high school written across the chest, and his hair still damp from his shower.

"Pepperoni and pineapple."

He comes to a complete standstill as he eyes me warily.

"Bro, don't even try to argue with her that pineapple doesn't go on pizza. It's a lost cause." Cody appears from the stairs, typing away on his phone. He doesn't even glance up, just adds his two cents and moves on.

Ty walks around the sectional and plops down on the opposite end. His long legs land on the coffee table as he grabs the remote from where it's sitting on the couch. Turning on the TV, he thumbs through the channels before landing on ESPN.

"Whatcha reading?"

"Just finishing this chapter about the hottie in a MC."

"Ah, the hot date."

Nodding, I go back to the words on my phone while a hockey game plays in the background.

"Running to grab the pizza," Cody shouts as he heads out of the house.

"That was quick."

"He had it ordered before I even asked you what you liked."

Noted that Cody Jacobs still remembers how I like my pizza, and he knew there was no chance I'd be changing my order up.

Hudson and Niko emerge from their upstairs bedrooms—both in comfy clothes and damp hair. Seriously, these guys could all be models in a sports magazine. I imagine they might get their chance someday if they keep playing the way they are and make it to the big leagues.

Placing my phone on the coffee table, I grab my seltzer and

follow the guys into the kitchen. Ty is right behind me, and the four of us start getting things ready for dinner.

"I see you're making yourself at home, Mariano." Hudson's eyes land on the skinny can I'm holding.

"I didn't take you for a hard seltzer kind of guy, Larsen." I quirk my eyebrow at him.

"Touché." Hudson reaches up into the cabinet and grabs a stack of paper plates while Niko sits on a barstool. I sidle up beside him and watch as Ty grabs ingredients for a salad out of the fridge.

"Let me help." I start to rise out of my chair as Ty's eyes lock on mine.

"Not a chance, Chlo. You cook for us all the time." Over the last couple of years, Brynn, Macy, and I would host "family dinners" for our group of friends on Sunday nights. It was our way of having a home-cooked meal and seeing our friends. With baseball season taking up so much of our time, we haven't had a chance to host a dinner this season. Popping the top off a few containers, I watch as Ty dumps the contents of the first container into a larger bowl. "Besides, most of the vegetables are already cut up."

"You guys are so domesticated."

Niko lets out a snort laugh from beside me, and my head whips in his direction. "Fuckers are showing off because you're here."

"Is that so?"

Hudson and Ty both look at me with boyish grins on their faces. Rolling my eyes, I lean back in my seat and bring my seltzer to my lips. Taking a long pull, I bring the can away and shake the liquid to gauge how much is left.

The guys all share some kind of look like they're in on something, and I immediately wonder if there's something on my face.

"Have you started the reading yet?" Ty asks as he chops up

some fresh tomatoes. Only the lettuce, peppers, and carrots were cut up for the salad.

I shake my head as I watch his lack of knife skills which has me sitting on my hands in order to keep them busy before I jump up and take over. Ty says he has it handled, and I really hope so because I don't want to deal with a severed finger tonight.

"Do you mind grabbing my baseball bag for me? It's the one sitting by the front door."

I slide off my barstool and make my way over to the front door where I spot a black and white baseball backpack. Picking up the heavy bag, I carry it back into the kitchen and set it down on the barstool I was just occupying.

"Inside is my textbook where I've worked on highlighting a few items that I think will help us with the study guide. Do you mind taking a second look while I finish here?"

"Okay, random," I chuckle as the room around me falls silent as I unzip the large part of the bag. Even Ty's chopping has stopped.

Sliding the zipper open, I open the large compartment and my breath catches in my throat as a small gasp escapes my lips.

Hands trembling, I bring a hand up to my mouth while I reach inside the bag with the other. Letting my fingers trail the lilac ribbon that's secured with a safety pin.

As shocked as I am to see the ribbon secured to the bag, I'm even more shocked to see the paper that it's clipped to. If I were to open it up all the way, I'd see a receipt from Marnie's Diner for a cup of coffee, a southwest omelet, wheat toast, a side of fruit, a side of bacon, and a cinnamon roll.

"What the hell is this?" My tear-brimmed eyes snap up as I find all three guys watching me. "H-how did you get this, Ty?"

"Dude, that's not your bag, it's Cody's." I bring my attention to Hudson as he watches me with a small smirk on his face.

He knew this was Cody's bag. My eyes go from guy to guy and realize this was part of their plan. These meddling jackasses.

I can't keep the tremble out of my hands as I go back to tracing the ribbon.

The summer we spent together, Cody loved to tug out my ribbons. He would run them through his fingers and play with the ends before tugging them out.

Clearly, he kept one.

And clearly, he never forgot about that summer.

As I try to wrap my mind around my latest discovery, I hear Cody come into the kitchen. He starts to say something, but his words trail off. Turning toward him, I watch his eyes move down to the bag that's sitting in front of me. He sets the food on the table and puts his hands up like one would defend against a wild animal.

"Wildflower, I can explain."

I don't give him the chance.

In three strides, I'm erasing the space between us, not stopping until I'm standing in front of him. My hands fly around his neck as I bring his head closer to me while pressing up on my tip toes.

My smooth lips find his soft ones. He doesn't react right away, and I instantly feel rejected. Before I have a chance to step away, his arms wrap around my back in a tight grip as he presses his lips harder into mine.

A small gasp escapes my lips, and he takes that as an invitation to slip his tongue inside my mouth. The boys cheer in the background, and as our tongues brush each other, a small moan escapes my lips as reality comes crashing down.

I'm kissing Cody Jacobs.

And it's even better than I remember.

CHAPTER 18

CODY

CHLOE MARIANO IS KISSING ME.

Holy shit. Chloe is kissing me.

After everything that has happened, I never would have imagined that I would get the chance to kiss her again. To feel her soft, pillow-like lips.

I smile into our kiss and slowly start to break apart our connection. As much as I never want to stop kissing her, I'm reminded that we aren't alone as I hear the guys start to cheer.

Chloe pulls away as I take in her flushed cheeks and swollen lips. Her hands come to her face, and she starts to hide from us.

Reaching up, I gently encircle her wrists and tug her hands away. "Don't hide, Wildflower."

At the mention of the nickname I gave her, her eyes pop to mine. "You've been giving me hints all this time, and I've never wanted to believe it. I thought you just threw that name in to rile me."

"I mean a small part of me wanted a reaction," I say with a

shrug, still holding onto her wrists that have now settled in between us. "But not in the way you were thinking."

She shakes her head at my words before I continue. "I've been playing your game. It's my job to read signs, and I've been reading you, Wildflower. You might not have wanted anyone to know about us, but I never forgot about us."

Her face flushes as her lips find mine again.

Clearing his throat, I glance up to glare at Hudson for the interruption. "Not that we aren't all happy you two decided to make out in front of us, but food's getting cold."

Shaking my head, I reluctantly release Chloe's wrists while reaching for a chair. Pulling it out, I gesture for her to sit as the guys make their way over to the table. Niko waltzes over with three yellow, an orange, and a blue bottle of sports drink. Ty carries the wooden salad bowl to the table while Hudson brings over a pile of paper plates and a handful of forks. We're nothing if not classy.

Hands fly as pizza boxes are flung open. Everyone is starving after today's game, which was a massacre in our favor. We needed this win after yesterday's shit show that I caused. Seriously, what the hell was I thinking? Going out the night before and getting completely shit-faced? I know better, and I opened myself up to my dad's awful text messages.

After every bad pitch I gave up, I had a new text waiting from him. Luckily I had the bright idea to delete the entire text thread instead of reading each text; otherwise, I would've ended up chucking my phone against the wall. I might not have been able to throw a fastball yesterday, but after I read the first text from my dad, I had no doubt I'd be able to land a fastball against the wall.

Chloe is the first to reach for the salad bowl. I watch her pile a mountain of the green leaf mixture on her plate before she's reaching for the pizza. She grabs the biggest triangle of pizza in the box. I watch as she brings the slice to her mouth before taking a large bite. I smile at how she's not shy about eating in front of us. You'd be surprised how many girls have an issue with consuming food in the presence of guys. And that's exactly why I like Chloe—a lot actually—because she's not afraid to be herself.

Once she's happy with her plate, I watch as she lolls her head to the side, staring daggers at Ty.

"So, Billings," she starts as an icy tone laces her words. Ty's shocked expression finds hers. "Did you orchestrate this whole night, or did you really want to work on that study guide together?"

Niko chuckles, and I bounce my eyes between all the guys as I take a large bite of pepperoni and pineapple pizza.

Ty reaches up and strokes his face, eyes bouncing from Niko to Hudson. "Well, I mean I definitely wanted to work on our study guide together since midterms are next week, but then the opportunity kind of presented itself."

"And I came up with the idea," Hud adds. "I kind of screwed things up between you two. I'm sorry, by the way, for how I treated you and handled the situation that summer. I feel guilty" He winces at his confession.

Chloe nods her head at his admission and turns back to her plate. Silence falls over the table.

Hesitantly, I reach over and place my hand on her forearm. She startles from the contact, and I'm about to pull away when she looks over at me from under long black lashes and smiles. I rub my thumb across her smooth skin.

Damn, that smile of hers.

I could just get lost in it. She exudes sunshine even though she constantly wants to shy away from the attention. If only she saw herself the way I see her. But now that we are moving forward with fixing our past and righting all my wrongs, I'm going to make sure that Chloe Mariano sees herself the way I do. She's going to be walking around campus with her head held high.

And everyone is going to know she's mine.

Pushing my plate away, I stand and gather my trash as Chloe finishes her food. "Not to rain on your parade, Billings, but I've got my girl back, and I'm not about to share her with you tonight."

Chloe turns, brow quirked as she stares me down. "Your girl back?"

"Yeah, Wildflower. It's long overdue." I give her a wink back and watch her cheeks turn pink. Goddamn, I love making her blush.

I told myself baseball was my only love, and I'm not saying I love Chloe—at least not yet—but there's something about her that calls to me. And as excited as I am to have her wanting me, to have her forgive me, I can't let her become a distraction. Friday is a big reminder of what happens when I let my emotions dictate my decisions. I can't afford to have problems off the field.

Walking around the island, I stand behind Chloe, resting my hands on her shoulders and running my thumbs in soothing motions. She relaxes against my touch, and I can't help but notice how responsive she is to my touch.

I wonder how she would respond if I touched her in different places.

Lifting her head, her eyes find mine, and her lips curl up. "Wanna go watch a movie?"

Nodding my head, I take her hand and lead her out of the room.

"Don't worry, we'll clean the mess," Hudson shouts from behind us.

I practically pull her up the stairs and into my room where she pauses at the doorway. I watch her take in the room, and I'm curious about what she's thinking. Chloe's never been in my room, and while she doesn't know that I've been in hers, I give her the time to snoop through my things.

Stepping further into the room, I make my way over to my bed where I sit and wait for her. Glancing around, I try to see the room through her eyes. I'm not a clean freak, but I'm not the typical douche whose room is absolute chaos.

The walls are painted a pale gray with white trim. A queen-sized bed with a dark gray upholstered headboard sits centered against the wall under a large window. As much as I wanted a king bed, the space would have been tight, and I wanted a room where I felt comfortable spending an extended amount of time... studying.

The beige comforter is pulled up to cover my pillows, while not a perfectly made bed, at least the sheets aren't sitting haphazardly. A warm brown rustic nightstand is placed beside my bed where an empty coffee mug and water bottle sit. Opposite the nightstand is a matching dresser home to a large TV and a few odds and ends items. My brown desk matches the rest of the furniture and sits on the same wall as the door. There's a neat stack of textbooks and notebooks next to my laptop where I left them.

A few scattered articles of dirty laundry are draped near the hamper, and I realize now I'm fitting the typical guy stereotype of getting my clothes near the basket. Across from my desk is the attached bathroom which isn't huge. It's large enough for a single sink vanity, shower stall, and toilet of course.

As she continues her perusal of my room, my palms sweat with anticipation of what's to come. My heart hammers in my chest with nerves as I finally have the girl who has consumed my mind alone in my room. I hope I don't fuck it up this time. I doubt Chloe will give me another chance.

Chloe walks toward my desk and runs her fingers over the smooth surface. She leafs through some of the notebooks I have sitting there, and I smile at how bold she is, before continuing to my dresser. There are a few framed photos on each side of the TV. Chloe grabs the frame holding a photo of me and my sister.

"Leah?"

"Yeah, that's Leah from a couple of years ago."

"She's so pretty." I hear the smile in her voice and a burst of pride runs through me. I adore my sister and being this far from her is always tough. In the summer, I rarely go home and visit. I try to keep the toxicity out of the house, and it comes out in full force when I'm staying at the house, causing extra stress on everyone. "I bet she's glad that you aren't home to ward off the boys."

A groan erupts from my chest. "Don't remind me about my sister dating. She's going to be eighteen next weekend."

She sets the frame back in its place, and I watch her look at the framed photo of me and my buddies from high school before moving on to the other side of the TV. There's a framed photo from our freshman year at a party. All my favorite CTU crew is in it—Hudson, Ty, Brynn, Macy, Chloe, Quinton, Grant Campbell, and Tyler Harris. Niko wasn't in the picture since he hadn't transferred in yet.

I suck in a breath and wait to see if she inspects the photo closer. If she does, then she's going to see that I'm looking at her and not at the camera. I remember that night. It was a night where I was getting quite buzzed while my thoughts kept drifting to her and our summer spent together. We were lining up for the picture when I caught a whiff of her infamous scent.

Wildflowers erupted in my nose, and I was thrown back into the past.

Of hot summer days lying in the shade. I'd skim articles on ESPN while she'd read.

It was simple, but it was perfect.

Thankfully, she doesn't say anything as she turns her body toward me. Her lounge wear hugs her body. It's in her favorite color purple, something that makes me smile because Chloe is nothing if not predictable. She loves light pastel colors, and I can't say I blame her. The shades look perfect against her creamy white skin and honey-blond hair.

Bringing her lip between her teeth, she starts to chew on it. I can feel the nervous energy radiating off her, and I'd love nothing more than to soothe her worry away, but she's like an injured animal. Smooth, slow movements, or else she'll bare her teeth and run.

Fuck it. I can't take it slow with Chloe, not when I finally have her alone in my room. Searching her face for any cues, I watch as a flame ignites in her eyes, sparking that passion between us that runs deep to our roots. My hands cup the side of her face as I bring my lips to hers. Sparks detonate at our contact, and our bodies relax. I take the opportunity to trail my hands down her back, soft and slowly, before I'm rounding the curve of her ass. The ass I can't help but let distract me while she's in the dugout during games. Unable to fight the impulse, I squeeze her cheeks between my fingers.

"I'm not having sex with you," she blurts, turning her face away from mine, which causes me to choke on air because I was not expecting that. "I'm not a virgin anymore, you missed the chance to own that, but that doesn't mean I'm just going to have sex with you."

Hitting my chest, I sit up as I try to catch my breath. Reaching my hand out, I keep it lifted in the air as I wait for her to take it. Her eyes bounce back and forth like it's a weapon and not my hand. She reaches out and takes it as I pull her to sit beside me.

"Shit, Wildflower." I shake my head as I continue to regulate my breathing. "Listen, I'm in this for more than sex. It's never been about that. Our relationship that summer wasn't about sex, and I'm not going to pressure you into anything that you're not ready for. If I could go back and change things, I would, but I can't, and I hope you will forgive me. You, me, us, it's been a long time coming, and now that I have you back, I want you. Your mind, your heart, your body, all of it, but you set the pace. And I'm gonna need the name of the fucker who took your virginity."

'Alpha-Cody' was making an appearance, and based on the book I read of hers during the ice storm, I'm hoping she doesn't mind it. I mean she had so many lines highlighted from Christian/Tristan, whatever his name was.

"I-I didn't think you wanted to have sex, but I wanted to make sure we were on the same page."

"Now wait a second, I never said I didn't want to have sex. I've been dreaming about that for two years, and after catching you fuck your toy, it's all I've been able to think about." Her face flames as I remind her that I caught her servicing herself. "But that's not what I had in mind for tonight. I've waited this long. I can wait a little longer."

She nods her head as she plays with her hands in her lap.

"But, Wildflower, you can use me." Her eyebrows come together causing cute wrinkles on her forehead. Jesus, did I just say her confused wrinkles were cute? "I'm available anytime you want to get off. I promise I can do it better than your toy. Hell, maybe we can do a combination of the two."

I flash her my devilish smirk and watch as her eyes darken with desire.

Clearing her throat, she shuffles from where she's sitting up the bed, coming to rest with her back against the headboard. I take it we are done talking about that situation.

Grabbing the remote from the nightstand, I gently toss it on her lap. "You pick the movie."

"Any movie?"

"Any movie, Wildflower." I know I'm going to regret my words as soon as she gives me a mischievous grin. But I don't even care if she puts on the cheesiest chick flick, I just want to spend the night with her.

"Close your eyes," she says as she flips through the apps on the TV. I close my eyes and feel my lips curl up.

Rustling comes from beside me as my senses are heightened. Her body moves as the WB theme song fills the speakers. She nestles her side against mine as instrumental music begins.

"Once upon a time," the female narrator begins as Chloe settles her body against me. Without thought, I bring my arm around her and pull her tight to me.

Tilting my head, I open my eyes and find her watching me. Leaning forward, I bring my lips to her forehead. "God, I missed you, Chloe."

She snuggles closer into me. One of her arms is bent between us while the one furthest away rests against my stomach. Slowly, she traces the lines of my abs, and I try not to focus on how good it feels. If I focus on her touch, a third member will be joining us for this very chill, very non-sexual, movie night.

Tonight I'm watching *A Cinderella Story* with the girl I haven't been able to get off my mind in two years.

I can't help the smile that spreads across my face as I lean down and kiss the top of her head.

This is my year.

This is the team's year.

But maybe it could be our year, too.

CHAPTER 19

Chloe

I WOKE UP THIS MORNING WRAPPED IN MY COMFORTER and wishing I was back in Cody's arms. I did not expect last evening to happen. The two of us laid in his bed watching *A Cinderella Story* and talking about this, that, and everything. It felt like we were those two teenagers who spent the summer chasing sunsets and never wanting the days to get shorter. Shorter days meant fall was approaching.

Tossing off my covers, I'm hit with the sudden urge to get my body moving. As much as I love running, I don't feel like I've been able to prioritize getting outside to run. I've mostly been hitting up hotel gyms for any type of exercise. Even though I know I'm more than likely safe, running on an unfamiliar campus gives me anxiety.

But there's nothing like running outside.

Feeling the pavement crunch under my shoes. Inhaling the fresh air. Seeing spring come alive in Texas.

Central Texas University has been around for one hundred and fifty years. The sidewalks are lined with mature trees that flourish in the warm months. Even though our townhouse is considered off-campus, if I run toward the back of our complex and cross another parking lot, I'm able to get to the brick-lined streets that make up CTU. I love the unique features CTU was built on and that they have kept updated all of these years.

Snapping on my silver belt bag, I double check that my phone, keys, and student ID are secured in the bag before I pop in my AirPods. Today's goal is an easy five miles around campus and back. My Mass Media Law class was canceled this morning, which means I don't have to be on campus until noon for my newspaper class, which is optional, but I try to make it as much as possible. I love writing in the newsroom, even if I don't have an assignment, the chaos is soothing.

I let my legs take over as I glide across the sidewalk keeping my head up but constantly looking ahead to make sure there aren't any high spots in the pavement. Running at this point is second nature. I could completely shut my brain off, and my limbs would know what to do. My feet would know to slide across the pavement, not pound. My legs have learned to push off the pavement in long strides. My arms have learned to stay bent, but relaxed, while my back stays straight.

Running and cooking are the two things that allow me to mentally shut out what's going on around me and focus on the task at hand.

Well, running typically allows me the luxury. This morning I'm still thinking about waking up in Cody Jacobs's bed yesterday.

I still can't believe I made the first move. But when I opened up that bag and saw my ribbon and note, everything escaped my brain. It was the sign I needed to realize Cody viewed our summer together as something; it wasn't nothing.

And when my lips met his...it was like the stars aligned,

fireworks went off, and a bright neon sign was flashing saying this is it. This is everything I've been waiting for.

I smile at the memory.

But then cringe at my admission that I wasn't a virgin anymore. Why I felt the need to blurt that out, I have no idea. Maybe a small part of me wanted him to know I didn't sit around waiting for him. That while he was hooking up with half the campus, I wasn't still pining for him to take my virginity.

As a teenager and even a young adult, I never viewed my virginity as something super special. For me, it felt like I was walking around screaming about how inexperienced and unlikable I was in high school. I wasn't the girl who got the boy. I was the outcast no one wanted.

The summer Cody and I spent together, we spent a lot of time exploring each other's bodies, but it never escalated to more. I thought we had more time.

There's still a lot we need to work through. I can tell he's hiding parts away from me, and if we are going to really give things a go, we need to lay it all out there. But Saturday night, we both wanted to soak in each other's company.

Chuckling, I still can't believe he laid beside me and watched me quote *A Cinderella Story*. I thought for sure he'd immediately reject the super cheesy, early 2000s teen movie. But he didn't. He let me snuggle into his side and watch the movie while rubbing tiny circles on my back.

Through my AirPods, the sound of my phone alerts me that I have a new email. I internally debate whether I should ignore it, but within a second I do the responsible thing and step off the sidewalk. Resting my hands on my head, I take a few deep breaths before pulling out my phone.

Clicking on the new email I skim the message from my professor who leads the university's newspaper. She's requesting I stop by her office as soon as possible. Assessing my running apparel of light gray running shorts with the mini bike shorts underneath and a coral sports bra, I decide I'll reroute my run so that I'm finishing up on campus. I can quickly pop into her office and run home when we're finished.

Shrugging, I pop my music back on and continue my run through campus to the Union.

"Chloe!"

Stopping in my tracks, I search the sea of people for who called my name. A large smile breaks across my face when I spot dark brown hair hidden beneath a CTU Baseball cap and hazel eyes coming straight for me. Only he isn't returning my smile. His face is dark and furrowed. I can feel the anger seeping from him the closer he gets.

Not in the mood to deal with him, I turn and head inside the Union. He can come and find me. Weaving through students, I get in line at the little coffee shop that is right inside the door. Eyes track my movement from people around me. Normally I'd shy away from the stares and curl in on myself, but I somehow woke with a boost of confidence that I hadn't had before.

Cody comes up behind me, and I can feel his breath on my neck. Reaching inside my belt bag, I pull out my student ID which is loaded with money as I approach the counter.

The tall male barista eyes my attire causing a growl from behind me. "Uh-uh, what can I get you?"

"Hi, can I get one of your chocolate protein smoothies?" Looking over my shoulder, I find Cody glaring daggers at the barista who won't take his eyes off me. If I were Mr. Barista Man, I'd be avoiding pissing Cody off. His molars grind as I ask him, "Want anything?"

Cody's eyes find mine, and I give him a warm smile. "No thanks."

I swipe my Student ID as the Barista starts making my smoothie.

Stepping aside, Cody follows me, and the two of us debate back and forth on what is acceptable behavior in a crowd. I look around the space and notice every eye in this section of the Union is on us.

"Why do you look like you just got done working out?"

"It's because I did. I was on a run when I got an email that I needed to meet Professor Weaver as soon as possible."

"And you didn't think about changing?"

"No, Cody. I didn't think about changing. I was almost here anyway so I headed over as is."

He grits his teeth, and I chuckle. "Your alpha is showing, Cody Jacobs."

"I don't like the idea of you walking around like that."

Quirking a brow, I eye him down as he starts rummaging through his bag. "I appreciate your concern, but I can handle myself. It's not like I wear this all the time."

He steps even closer than I thought was possible as he reaches up to my face. Running a finger down my cheek, I lean into our embrace. "People are staring at you."

"No, Wildflower, they're staring at you."

I roll my eyes because no one is staring at me. They're watching the hot baseball pitcher interact with a nobody and wondering why he's talking to me.

Leaning down, he ever so slowly brushes his lips against mine. Gasps come from around us as I reach up and wrap my hand around his nape. He deepens the kiss, and I know I should pull away, but I can't bring myself to do so.

The barista calls out my name and with much reluctance, Cody pulls away. But he doesn't give me space like I assumed he would. Instead, he wraps his arm over my shoulder, and I wrinkle my nose at the thought that he's touching my sweaty body which is now dry.

"Cody, I stink."

He guides me over to the counter where I grab my smoothie, nodding at the guy behind the counter as thanks. "Nah, you always smell like flowers to me."

"And roses really smell like poo-poo-ooh." I sing the lyrics to "Roses" by Outkast causing Cody to shake his head.

The two of us make our way over to the steps where we descend to the basement which is where the newsroom is located.

"How was practice?" The words come out quietly in the empty hallway.

"It wasn't too bad. We had a few running drills to do, but I loved the yoga afterward. Who would've known?"

I scoff. "I've seen your yoga instructor. I'm sure you all are enjoying the yoga."

"I only have eyes for you, Wildflower. I always have. Those other girls were just a distraction."

My cheeks turn pink as we approach the newsroom door. "This is me."

Cody removes his arm, and I instantly feel the loss of his body heat. The basement is chillier than normal, and I'm going to be showing everyone how cold I am. He's rummaging through his bag and pulls out a white shirt before handing it to me.

"Here. It's clean, don't worry. But this way you're warm."

"I'm not cold." But my body takes that moment to betray me as I shiver, exposing a major case of hard nips. Shit.

His eyes find the tight buds immediately. Clearing his throat, he brings his attention back to my face. "Uh-huh."

"Fine." I take the white long-sleeved shirt and slip it over my head. Cody's intoxicating scent floods my senses, and I smile. The shirt lands at the hem of my shorts and to look like I have pants on, I take the front hem and tuck it under my sports bra to give it a faux-cropped look.

His eyes rake over my form as he assesses how it fits on my body. The long-sleeve is long on my body. But I love that I'm wearing a shirt with his last name and number on my back. It might feel like his way of marking his territory, letting everyone know I'm his, but surprisingly, I don't mind the gesture.

"Fuck," he rasps. "My shirt looks damn good on you, Wildflower."

Leaning in closer, I reach up and find his ear. "I bet it looks even better on your bedroom floor."

I swear I hear him audibly gasp as his jaw drops to the floor. "Shit, Chlo. You need to get into your meeting, or I'm throwing you over my shoulder and testing your theory."

"Bye, Cody." I start to walk away before I feel his hand tug at my fingers. He pulls me toward him where his lips find mine in a searing kiss. A moan fills the space, and I couldn't tell you whose voice it came from. I feel the kiss melt into my center leaving me with damp panties.

Ending the kiss, he steps away as his feet carry him backward. His eyes never leave mine. "When can I see you again?"

Deciding to be coy, I give him a one-shoulder shrug as I enter the newsroom. My skin is hot, and I have a moment where I debate on turning on my heels and running out the door after him. I want to know if he'll make good on his promise to throw me over his shoulder.

Or if he'll come to his senses that I'm not good enough for him.

I don't have much time to think about that issue, even though the thought has been rattling around in my head all weekend. At some point, Cody is going to wake up and realize that there are better girls out there for him. I'm no one's first choice.

"Hey, Chloe!" Abby shouts from where she is sitting at one

of the circular tables in the center of the room. Heads pop up from computer screens as everyone watches me enter the room.

With a quick wave to Abby, I head into Professor Weaver's office. Technically, this isn't her office, as she has her own office like the rest of the professors in a separate hallway. This is just the adviser's office for the university paper. The walls are decorated with framed special editions of The Eagle Gazette. Other than that, it's very generic.

Professor Weaver sits behind a monitor, her long brown hair piled on top of her head in a messy bun. She's in her late thirties, and while she is the picture of professionalism, there are days where she looks a bit like a hot mess. Today is one of those hot mess days. With minimal makeup, her outfit is very casual with a loose pair of boyfriend jeans and a basic black tee.

"Knock knock," I announce my entrance while knocking on the door frame. She glances up and sighs in relief.

"Oh thank god it's you."

I continue into her office before sitting down on the chair opposite her. I don't miss how she takes in my appearance.

"I was on a run when I got your email."

She chuckles. "You could have gone home. It wasn't anything serious."

"It's okay. My run was taking me to campus anyway."

She nods, but she takes in my shirt again. I want to shrink under her assessment. Pursing her lips together, she leans back in her chair. "How is everything going with the baseball team? Running into any troubles?"

"Everything is going great. There haven't been any issues that I'm aware of."

"That's great. With your schedule, we haven't been able to be in the same place at the same time. I wanted to reiterate how important it is that while you are covering all of the baseball games, you get some one-on-one time with Coach Weber. The main article on him will run in our last issue before school is out for the semester. I will send you a list of items that you will need to ask him about. These questions range from fun to personal to baseball-related. Feel free to pull him aside throughout the next couple of weeks. He'll be more relaxed in a casual setting."

Nodding my head, I take in all the information she is throwing my way while my phone is blowing up in my belt bag. "Thank you for sending me the questions to ask. I've been reading articles written by other reporters on coaches, as well as researching what I should be asking him. This will be much more helpful."

"Of course. I should have taken you to the side rather than dropping the bomb in front of the whole class. To be honest, I was quite overwhelmed with some personal items and trying to figure out the coverage that—as unprofessional as this might be to admit—I was spiraling and not thinking."

"Honestly, I felt blindsided." I pause trying to read Professor Weaver's expression as my phone vibrates for the millionth time. "But it has been a great experience, and I've enjoyed the opportunity to try something new."

She eyes me warily, and I want to hide. "I'm sure you've had plenty of opportunities to try new things. But I want to remind you that you are there to do a job."

Staring at her in bewilderment, Professor Weaver must realize I have no idea what she's implying. I watch as she takes a deep inhale. "A photo of you was just posted on the CTU Gossip Gazette lip locked in the middle of the Union with a very popular baseball player, and while I realize fashion has gotten quite lax with the amount of skin that is shown, as a member of the Eagles Gazette, please be more mindful of your appearance."

Humiliation floods my system as my face flames. I fight the urge to cover my face and cower in my seat. The whole campus is aware of Cody and my recent development, and I was caught in a photo with nothing on but a sports bra.

The CTU Gossip Gazette is the worst. Even though its name is similar to the newspaper, it has nothing to do with it. Instead, the Gossip Gazette is a social media account run by a group of students who rely on gossip tips from other students to fuel their content. Anyone can submit photos or leads about other students. The admins make sure that nothing damaging is posted or said that could be considered bullying or hate speech, but some things get posted out of context.

For the past two and a half years, I've managed to avoid anything being submitted about me. Within forty-eight hours of Cody and me being, well, whatever we are, I managed to get posted.

Straightening my shoulders, I look Professor Weaver in the eyes and nod.

"I understand, and I was not aware a photo was being taken. I planned to come straight here in my workout clothes, which I understand might not have been the best idea, but I was afraid I'd get shaky without fueling up. Running into Cody wasn't part of the plan, but at least he had an extra shirt." The words tumble out of my lips as the fear of being fired takes shape. "I won't let it happen again."

With a tight-lipped smile, she nods her head. "I believe you, and I understand. You're an excellent student and asset to this paper, Chloe. I was a college student once...a while ago, but I had my fair share of indiscretions. Please just be mindful as the paper is under a lot of pressure and scrutiny this semester."

"I understand."

"Great. I'll send you the email with some talking points for Coach Weber. I can't wait to read your next article recapping the baseball game. Keep up the great work, Chloe."

I get to my feet and exit the office, making my way over to the table Abby is still sitting at. I pull out a chair and plop down across from her.

"Whew, girl, you're all over the internet," Abby says before I even have a chance to make myself comfortable in my chair.

Finally able to, I bury my head in my hands while letting out a very unladylike groan.

"How bad is it?" My voice is muffled from behind my hands, my phone vibrates again.

Giving up on ignoring it, I unzip the silver polyester bag and pull out my phone. The screen lights up with more notifications than I have received in two months.

"Chloe, you okay?" Abby asks concern all over her face. "You look a little pale."

I imagine I could be a ghost's twin right now as the overwhelming urge to pass out hits me.

Ignoring Abby's question, I scroll through the notifications staring at the Instagram mentions first.

Opening the app, the first thing I see is a picture of me standing in the café wearing my gray running shorts, coral sports bra, and silver belt bag across my hips while my arms are wrapped around Cody's neck, our lips locked in a searing kiss on a gossip account.

The photo looks hot and looks far more inappropriate than the actual moment.

I pause to stare at the photo before clicking the notifications tab which keeps flashing with more mentions.

@pastel_princess is that you?

I'm pretty sure that's @pastel_princess

Ew what's @jacobs_cody doing with that weirdo @pastel_princess? I promise I'm more fun than she is.

@pastel_princess trying hard enough?

@pastel_princess why not just show up naked?

After the fifth comment I read where some mean girl is making it a point to mention how bad I look, how trashy my outfit is, or how much better Cody could do all while propositioning him, I close out of the app and power off my phone.

The insecurity I've been working so hard to keep locked away starts to rear its nasty head. It's one thing to wake up every morning and hear those negative thoughts as I stare at myself in the mirror, but it's entirely different to read them from a stranger. A stranger who doesn't know me, doesn't know my story, or hasn't even been in the same room as me. They just view me as a threat, someone between them and Cody, and choose to tear me down to make themselves feel better.

Not only am I reading the hateful words, but so are others who feel the need to chip in with more hurtful comments.

Realizing that I'm sitting in a room full of people, I glance around and find eyes bouncing away from me.

"Do you have anything that needs editing?" Deciding I'm not leaving this room anytime soon, I ask Abby for some work that will keep me occupied for the next few hours. There's no way I can walk across campus, not with this post everywhere. Thankfully, Ty is in my last class of the day, and I'll get notes from him.

Shuffling through papers, Abby hands me a small stack of notes. "I can always use some help. Do you mind reading through these notes and comparing them to my article? I want to make sure I have the story portrayed accurately."

"Of course. I'll email you with any notes."

Popping my AirPods in, I find an open desk and log into the system with my school information.

And this is where I stay for the next five hours before I call a rideshare to take me home.

CHAPTER 20

CODY

WHEN I WOKE UP THIS MORNING I HAD NO intention of seeing Chloe.

Not because I didn't want to because after waking up Sunday morning with her in my bed, I want to say fuck it all and spend every waking moment with her. She looked like she belonged in my bed. The way her honey-colored hair sprawled across my pillow as she slept soundly had me resisting the urge to wake her. Soft snores came from her slightly parted, kissed swollen pink lips. Chloe looked like a dream. But life doesn't work that way. And the idea of wanting to say fuck it all made me realize I need to keep my eyes on the goal ahead of me.

Baseball comes first. It has to. I've got to make it into the major league to prove my dad wrong. He doesn't think I have the willpower to play at the next level. Too bad for him because I have more determination than he ever did. And each time he sends me a text message trying to tear me down, it only adds fuel to the fire.

I was storming as I walked through the quad heading to grab

a water since I left mine at the stadium. As I reached the Union, piercing blue eyes caught my attention. Even from a distance, I knew it was Chloe. I watched her put her hands on her head as she took long deep breaths. Her chest rose and fell, and my gaze tracked her movement, lower and lower, until her shirt ended and her perfect stomach was on full display. I saw red as I looked around the quad and noticed all the guys eyeing her.

My feet took off after her before I even knew what was happening. I'm all for girls wearing whatever they want, but my immediate caveman behavior was to make sure she was safe in a sea of douchebag college guys.

To add on to the list of things I didn't plan on doing this morning, kissing Chloe in the middle of the Union was not one of them.

Of course, every time I'm near her, I want to kiss her, to touch her, to feel her near me. But I didn't plan on acting on that temptation. I'm going to blame Coach Weber for my lapse in judgment. When I told Chloe practice wasn't too bad, I might have been telling a white lie. Practice was excruciating, my brain was fried, and it was all my fault. After our disastrous loss Friday night, Coach made sure to punish us big time this morning.

And he promised to make tomorrow's practice just as difficult since we don't have a game until the weekend.

It was like hell week all over again as he made us go through conditioning drills. Practice was inside the indoor facility where he had cones set up for running drills. All of us were lined up for burpees which led to sprints which turned into ab workouts. The punishment was hard and this type of workout isn't something we do during the season, but we deserved the pain.

After leaving Chloe outside the newsroom, I went home to shower. The shower ended with me crashing on my bed. Clearly, my body was exhausted.

"Dude!" Ty shouts as he bursts through my closed door. "Have you checked your phone?"

Groaning, I roll over and find Ty standing inside my room. "No, I crashed after practice."

"You created a shit storm on campus today."

I quickly rack my thoughts about what happened earlier. My nap knocked me out so hard that I woke up a little disoriented. Like getting hit in the face, flashes of this morning came rushing back to me. Seeing Chloe. Kissing Chloe. Chloe in a sports bra. Us in the middle of the Union.

Reaching for my phone, I flip the 'sleep mode' off and watch as the notifications pour in. Mentions on Instagram and X. Missed calls and a couple of voicemails, which means something must really be wrong because who leaves a voicemail, let alone calls? Text message after text message pour in.

Holy shit. Who died?

"What the hell happened?" Running my hand through my messy bedhead, I swipe left to clear out all of the social media notifications.

Ty lets out an exasperated chuckle. "Someone caught you and Chloe at the Union and sent it into CTU Gossip Gazette."

I hate the CTU Gossip Gazette. Their entire feed is full of rumors and bullshit that only fuels drama around campus.

"This is bad."

"You think?" Ignoring his smart-ass comment, I scroll through the—does that say seventy-five?—text messages. I don't have that many close friends. It looks like anyone who had my number decided to blow me up. Typing Chloe's name in the search bar at the top of the messaging app, I don't see anything recent from her. I have half a dozen texts from Leah, but it's the all-caps, 'WHAT WERE YOU THINKING?' from Brynn that has me opening up her messages thread.

There's only one recent message so I quickly type out a reply.

> Me: I wasn't thinking. How is she?

Brynn's response is immediate like she's been sitting around waiting for my response.

> Brynn: I have no idea. I can't find her or get a hold of her.

> Me: What do you mean?

> Brynn: I mean she's turned her phone off, and I can't reach her.

"Shit!" I loudly groaned, jumping to my feet and bending down where I tossed my clothes haphazardly before my nap. I can't sleep in pants or a shirt, no matter if it's for the night or a nap, I need to be down to my boxers.

"Have you heard from Chloe?" I direct my question at Ty as I toss on a baseball cap while grabbing my phone, wallet, and keys. Brushing past him, he's hot on my heels as I head down the stairs.

"No, her phone's off. Where are you going?"

"I have no idea. I'm going to walk campus until I fucking find her." I caused this. I made the move in the middle of campus without thinking of the repercussions.

Even though we aren't professional athletes, we are under a lot of scrutiny as if we were. Fans want to meet us and aren't afraid of how they come off. The media is always watching, waiting for us to screw up.

"You didn't cause this." Ty says from behind me as if he's reading my mind. "That gossip site is bullshit."

"It may be, but there's nothing we can do about it." Opening the front door, I go to step out before calling over my shoulder. "Let me know if you hear from her."

Taking off in a brisk walk, I head down the sidewalk toward campus. The path isn't too crowded, but I do catch a few eyes pop in my direction.

My phone chimes from my pocket, and I pull it out, fumbling it in the process. I save it from tumbling to the hard pavement and swipe it open.

Brynn: She just walked in the door.

Thank god. But now I'm in the opposite direction of her townhouse. Closing out of Brynn's message, I find Ty's name and type out a quick message asking him to pick me up at the location I just sent him.

Popping my head up, I look around for a place I can wait. A large shade tree sits at the end of a driveway. Walking toward it, I lean my back against the trunk hoping to avoid being seen. While I wait, I scroll through the notifications on various social media platforms.

The comments about Chloe are horrible. I will never understand how people can say such cruel things about others who they've never even met. I love technology, and I love social media. It allows me to stay in touch with my sister and my friends from high school and travel baseball. But everyone hides behind their screens and feels they have a right to express their opinion.

Whether it's bullying someone, making someone feel invalid for having a differing opinion, or a community of people objectifying professional athletes as if they don't have their own lives. Even if I wasn't with Chloe, reading these hateful comments about her from other girls on campus while they proposition me would never have me choosing them.

My dad's name flashes across the screen as I read the millionth comment about how Chloe Mariano isn't good enough to breathe the same air as me. Deciding to rip the band-aid off, I answer the phone.

"Hello."

"Ah, you do know how to answer your phone." He says from the other end of the phone. I can hear a sports broadcast blaring in the background, which means Dad is sitting in his leather arm-chair in his office as he enjoys a bourbon. It's his evening habit. I don't know how my mom stays with such a worthless being.

He's cruel with his words as he constantly spews hatred. Never has he been the type of dad to encourage me. Instead, he finds faults in everything. If I got an A- on a paper, he'd tell me I wasn't smart enough. If I didn't make varsity, he'd tell me I wasn't talented enough. It's been a constant cycle for as long as I can remember.

I thought by moving away, I'd escape him. But technology allows him to stay in constant contact with me whether it be through calls or text messages. He's even resorted to sending me articles from critics whose job is to critique my game.

"This *really* isn't a great time for your bullshit."

"Don't give me that tone, boy. You might be the king of Texas, but I'll still show you who's boss." I roll my eyes at his threats which are laced with slurred words.

"I'm sorry, sir."

He grumbles on the other line as I hear the ice clink against his glass. "I knew you would never amount to anything. You walk around like you're some baseball god, but you're nothing. Too weak. Undisciplined. Always choosing to get your dick wet over baseball. Now look at you, kissing half-naked girls on campus. You might as well have just whipped it out and given everyone the entire show."

I zone out as his words continue. It's always the same thing, with just different reasons for why I'm undisciplined, weak, and overrated. I've always wondered if things would have been differ-ent if he had made it to the major league. Even if it were just for a year or two. Would he have been a better dad? Would he have supported me instead of being my harshest critic? If Mom never would've gotten pregnant with Leah, would she have stayed?

I cringe at that last thought because I would never wish for a life without Leah. The two of us have been each other's rock since day one. But the drinking got worse after Mom had Leah. A small part of me wonders if he would've shown his true colors sooner, would she have found someone else to have a family with?

"Are you listening to me, boy?" He grumbles a shout on the other end of the phone pulling me out of my thoughts.

"Of course."

"We'll see you at the game in South Carolina in a few weeks. Try not to be worthless." He hangs up the phone before I can respond. This is how the calls always go. He calls, I answer. He bitches, I take it. He hangs up on me, I stare at the blank screen wondering why he keeps this up.

Ty pulls up to the curb, and I pull open the door, rushing inside before he even has a chance to put the car in park.

Ten minutes later, he's dropping me off in front of the townhouse Chloe and Brynn share. Racing up to the door, I knock rapidly until Brynn whips the door open. Quinton isn't far behind her, and the two glare at me.

"She's in her room. She won't let me in."

Brushing past her, I take the steps two at a time. With a light knock, I don't wait for Chloe to respond before I push through her door. I find her curled up in a ball under her covers. Used tissues lay on her pillow surrounding her.

"Wildflower." The word leaves my lips in a whisper, and I feel broken at the sight before me.

Toeing off my shoes, I lift the edge of the covers and slide in behind her. Sliding my arm around her middle to pull her closer, I feel my skin graze her bare skin. I roll my eyes to the ceiling and take a long deep inhale praying my dick doesn't get excited. This is not the time.

"Cody," she mumbles. "What are you doing here?"

"I came to check on my girl. I'm sorry I didn't come sooner. Practice was harder than I let on, and I crashed when I got back to the house." Brushing the hair off her shoulder, I lean in and press my lips to the spot between her neck and shoulder.

Her back straightens, but I see her soft inhale as she tries to fight how she feels. "I can't believe I let that happen."

"You didn't let anything happen, Chloe. What happened earlier wasn't your fault. If anything it was mine. I wasn't thinking. I couldn't go another minute without feeling those lips on mine. I should have been more aware of where we were. Drama seems to follow me around. Especially when it comes to the Gazette. They love writing shit about my life."

She lets out a frustrated groan. "That's not what I'm talking about, Cody."

"I'm not following, Wildflower."

Chloe sits up, and I watch the covers fall from her shoulders down her almost bare body. She catches them at her chest, crossing her arms, which does nothing but press her bra-covered boobs higher.

Of course, she's wearing a sexy lace bra. The pale green color looks perfect on her body. This girl has no clue how beautiful she looks. I could just sit and stare at her for hours. But I won't because that'd be creepy as fuck.

Sliding off her bed, I reach my hand out. "Get up," I demand, harsher than I intended, but there's something we need to do right now.

"Wh-what?" she stammers, confusion lining her face.

"I said, 'get up.'" Pushing my hand toward her, waiting for her to grab it.

Tentatively she places her hand in mind. Pulling her off the bed, I lead her toward the full-length mirror hanging on the wall. Stopping a few feet away, I rest my hands against her curvy hips as I position her body so that she is standing directly in front of the mirror, her back to my front.

Pausing, I take a few moments to appreciate the beautiful

woman in front of me. Her ocean blue eyes stare back at me as she watches my eyes skate over her pale green lace bra, down her slender stomach, and down to her matching pale green lace boy-short panties. Panties that hug her lean hips where her hip bones protrude slightly. My eyes wander down her petite, yet strong, athletic legs made from all the miles she runs. Bringing my eyes back to hers, I watch her cheeks tinge pink from my blatant perusal of her features.

I see the moment she wants to hide herself flick across her face, but she doesn't. Instead, she slowly straightens her back and holds her head high. It takes her a minute to do so, but she does it nonetheless.

"When you look in the mirror, tell me what you see." Shock and confusion flash across her face. "Tell me what you see, Wildflower."

Clearing her throat, I watch as she takes in her reflection. Chest heaving, she chews on the inside of her cheek as she skims her body. Her head tilts from side to side as I patiently wait for her to answer. Just when I think she's going to avoid the question, her mouth opens.

"I see a girl who let the freshman fifteen get the best of her," she finally replies.

"Weird," I say, taking her hand that's resting at her side. With a squeeze, I continue. "I see a strong, beautiful woman with perfect curves. A woman who values her health by working out and taking care of the body."

A blush spreads across her cheeks, while I prompt her to add more. "What else do you see?"

"A wallflower."

"I see an observer who doesn't like the spotlight." Slowly, I trace her arm with my free hand. Running my palm down until it's back resting on her hip. "Come on, Wildflower, dig deeper. What do you really see when you look in the mirror?"

There's a long pause after I ask the hard question. As I watch her take in her appearance, I see the moment she breaks. Tears well in her eyes. As the moisture breaks over her lash line, tears streak her flawless face, and as much as I hate seeing them fall, I know this moment is what we need. A chance to be vulnerable with each other. To work through all the barriers we keep in place guarding our hearts.

At this moment, I'm going to see the real Chloe Mariano. The beautifully sweet, damaged girl she keeps hidden behind locked doors.

Finally breaking down as the tears stream down her face, her eyes find mine in the mirror. She wants me to see how she feels at this moment. "I see a six-year-old girl who isn't good enough. I see the little girl who wasn't even good enough for her mom to stay."

Sobs rack through her body as her knees weaken. Pulling her tight to my body, she collapses her weight in my arms as the sobbing continues. "You are enough. You are more than enough, Wildflower."

"I wasn't enough for you two years ago," she says in between sobs. My chest breaks as I realize all the damage I did to her over my selfish behavior.

For years she's battled the feeling of not being enough and the abandonment by her mom, and here I did the same damn thing.

CHAPTER 21

Chloe

Then

"**N**O, SHE'S NOT ENOUGH!"

"*Quiet, Camilla,*" my dad hisses from the living room. "*She's going to hear you.*"

"*I don't care, Scott. You told me—no, you promised me—it would get better. It's been seven years. We are still in the same rundown apartment.*"

I watch as my dad puts his hands on his head, shoulders dropping as he looks so sad. My parents are having another one of their fights. They have been having them more often. The fighting always begins after Daddy tucks me into bed, and he reads me a bedtime story. Right now we are reading The Wizard of Oz. *It's a thicker chapter book so Daddy only reads one chapter a night.*

It's becoming one of my favorite books. I was really sad when the bad storm came to the farm, but I'm glad Dorothy had her dog, Toto. At least she isn't alone on her journey to find the wizard who can help her get home. I told my Daddy I wanted a pair of red glitter heels just like she wears.

"It won't be long, Camilla. I promise."

Mom huffs out a breath. "That's what you keep saying, Scott. I'm done putting my life on hold waiting for you to make something of yourself. You're just a line cook. That's all you've been for the past five years."

Daddy and Mama think I'm in bed, only I've found the perfect hiding place between our beige fabric couch and the end table Daddy and I found on our way home from school. We stopped at a garage sale, and I picked this one up. It was my fault we had to get a new table. I was playing too rough with my dolls, and I accidentally knocked it over causing the leg to break.

"Just a line cook? Is that all you think of me, Camilla?"

"Yes, Scott. You were only supposed to be one night after a party. Too bad for me that my one wild night in college resulted in a broken condom and a baby. You promised you'd always take care of us. You promised me the world. This isn't the world."

"So leave, Cam. That little girl is the world. How can you stand here and say we aren't enough?" My Daddy looks so sad, and I just want to hug him, but I can't leave my hiding place, or Mama will get mad I'm out of bed.

"I never wanted this. I never wanted to be a mom at nineteen. She might be your whole world, but she isn't enough to make me stay. Take care, Scott."

From my spot, I watched my Mama reach for her purse and two suitcases as she walked out the door leaving us behind.

My Daddy crumpled to his knees crying so hard he shook.

As quietly as I could, I went back to my room. I didn't think Daddy wanted me to go to him.

Laying in bed, I couldn't help the tears that started pouring from my eyes. My mama didn't want me. She didn't love me. I wasn't enough to make her stay.

Sometime later when I had fallen asleep, I felt my Daddy climb into bed next to me. He pulled me close and whispered how much he loved me and that I was his world. His Amore Mia.
But all I could think about was how I wasn't enough.
What if someday I'm not enough for my Daddy?

CHAPTER 22

Chloe

"YOU ARE ENOUGH. YOU ARE MORE THAN ENOUGH, Wildflower."

His words keep replaying in my head while I sniff. There's no doubt snot is pouring from my nose. I'm a hot mess in my underwear.

If only the vicious trolls could see me now. Imagine all the material I would be giving them.

Smooth, gentle touches glide down my back as Cody tries to calm my cries. I should be embarrassed to be pouring my literal feelings out, but I can't find it in myself to care.

This is the first time in a long time I've let myself feel.

"Wildflower. Look at me."

I shake my head because ew, snot.

"I don't care what you look like right now." It's like he can hear my thoughts. "I promise you don't need to be put together all the time. You are perfect just the way you are."

Wiping my face, I gather as much moisture as I can before

wiping the wetness on my bare legs. Slowly, I bring my head up, and our gazes find each other.

His hands gather on either side of my face as his thumbs wipe the tears from under my eyes. "What happened two years ago was not your fault."

"It." He punctuates the word with a kiss on my left cheek.

"Was." Right cheek.

"Not." Forehead.

"Your." Nose.

"Fault." Lips.

I don't know where to go from here. Words fail me. I can write article after article, but right now my mind is going, what's a word? What's a sentence?

"I have a lot to make up to you and a lot to explain to you, but right now, you're my priority. You are the only thing that matters to me."

I scoff. "What about baseball?"

"Baseball can wait." My eyes widen at his admission. Cody Jacobs has never put anything over baseball, and this is something that everyone knows.

Shaking my head, I push out of his embrace. Pacing the small walkway in my room, I continue staring at him while moving my head back and forth. He starts coming toward me, but I raise my hand stopping him from coming closer. "Don't say that."

"Say what?"

"Say that I matter more than baseball. We're just getting started."

"Oh baby, we're just picking back up where we left off. You're already my Wildflower. And I've been yours since our mornings at Marnie's Diner."

"Cody, we've changed since then."

"Yeah, but that's something we'll learn as we go. But you're still the same Chloe. Some of our journey has changed, but I still know what makes you Chloe Mariano. You still love to go on runs and spend your free time in the kitchen." Slowly, he steps one foot in front of the other and starts erasing the gap.

"Your nose is always in a book, and if it ain't romance, you don't want it."

We both smile at that line. I had a sticker on the back of my Kindle the summer we were together that said something similar.

"Your favorite color is purple, but in a pastel or lilac shade. If you're not wearing a dress or skirt, it's a matching loungewear set. You prefer sneakers with your dresses. You love pineapple on pizza. Your favorite coffee is a honey lavender latte. Hmm, what else am I missing?"

"Wait?" I stop him, and he quirks an eyebrow at me. "You remembered honey lavender is my favorite latte?"

He flashes me his famous boyish smirk, and with a wink, says, "Who do you think was making sure you got a honey lavender latte every morning before a bus ride or at the hotel?"

My jaw drops because no way. There's no way Cody has been the one organizing my morning coffee delivery.

He kept my ribbon. My note. Remembered all the little details that make me, me. Had my favorite coffee delivered to me regularly. I wonder if he remembers... My thoughts trails off as I find the stuffed purple rabbit that has been sitting on my shelf since I moved to college.

"The purple rabbit," I whisper the words as Cody's lips twitch in a knowing smirk.

"I can't believe you kept it for all of these years." His voice has a hint of nostalgia. "That was the best money I've ever spent."

"That carny had no idea who you were." I chuckle at the memory.

"Best fifty bucks and stuffed animal I've ever won."

Bringing my bottom lip between my teeth, I run a million scenarios in my head.

Just go for it, Chloe.

In two quick strides, I eat up the space between us as I throw my arms around his neck. Grasping the nape of his neck, I pull his head down to meet his lips with mine. Cody's arms wrap around my back, and a shiver runs through me as I realize that I'm not wearing any clothes.

Sliding his hands down my bare back, his grip tightens on the back of my legs just below my butt. Before I know what's happening, he's hoisting me in the air. My legs wrap around his waist on instinct, and as I gasp at the sudden change of position, Cody takes the opportunity to deepen the kiss.

Tongues melting, my body has a mind of its own and starts sliding against his. My almost bare center grinds against his jean-clad cock. I moan as the friction hits my clit causing a tingling sensation to burn through my body. Desire pools in my gut as the anticipation of what's to come ignites. My back bows as my chest presses against his, and I'm hungry for more.

It's been so long since I've been touched by someone other than myself, and I've been craving Cody's touch for years. I might have told Cody I wasn't a virgin, but not by much. Halfway through my freshman year, I was tired of being reminded of Cody. Brynn and I were at a party, and I found a nice enough guy to get the job done. It was not a great experience, but I left with no virginity—also no orgasm.

Cody pulls away, and his eyes find mine. "Where'd you go?"

"Nowhere. I'm right here," I lean in and find his lips again. His hand finds the back of my head as he presses me to him. I moan against his lips as my body starts writhing on him.

He starts walking me backward, never breaking our kiss. Gently he lays me down onto the top of my bed before he's settling on top of me. His lips leave mine as he starts trailing open-mouth kisses along my jaw, down my neck where he pauses to suck the skin in between his teeth, before continuing down the front of my collarbone.

"Fuck, Wildflower." Cody groans as he sits up on his knees and peers down on my almost naked body.

Feeling self-conscious under his perusal, I start to bring my arms up to cover my exposed stomach. His hands encircle my wrist, stopping my movement. My eyes find him, but the shiny gold flecks that surround his hazel eyes are darkened with desire.

"Don't cover yourself from me. I love this body." His eyes trail over my body, and I feel my skin turn pink.

Leaning down he kisses my forehead. "I love this head of yours. Even though it likes to work overtime to tell you lies. I love how brilliant you are.

"I love these eyes of yours. They give me a glimpse into your soul. They also allow you to read your filthy smut. I've also been dying to know more about those highlighted words in your books. Since the ice storm when I read that book of yours, I need to know if you're into those kinks I read about." I gasp as he grazes his lips over my eyes. "But we'll come back to that later. I'm not done."

"Now this mouth." He groans as he plants a kiss that smacks across my lips. "This mouth gives you your voice that I love so much."

His hands cup my breasts as he squeezes them gently while I let out a moan. Releasing one of my boobs, he slides his hand up over my heart and rests it against my collarbone. "These tits are the perfect handful, and they drive me wild. Especially when you wear these lace-covered bras. But the thing I love most is your heart."

He nibbles little kisses over my flesh, and my nipples pebble into hard peaks. His eyes don't miss it as he pulls the hard bud into his mouth. "Your heart is pure. It loves hard, and it's so kind."

Writhing under his words, my panties are drenched. Clearly, Cody has unlocked a praise kink that I was unaware I had.

"Would you like me to continue? Or do you finally understand how I see you?"

"I-I-I understand. But for the love of god, fucking touch me, Cody."

His hands start kneading my breasts while our lips clash. My pussy seeks him out as I writhe beneath him craving the friction we had earlier while he held me in his arms. I run my hands up his chest gathering the fabric of his shirt as I bring my hands higher. We break the kiss while I tug the shirt over his head.

"You have entirely too many clothes on." I pant, running my hands back down his now bare chest.

It's my turn to explore. Kissing my way from his mouth, down his sharp jawline, to his neck. Sucking his skin into my mouth, I nibble on his neck. He groans as he runs a single finger from my chest, down my stomach, and dips below my panty line. Pausing, he looks up, searching my eyes for confirmation. I nod my head, and it's all he needs before he runs his finger down, taking my panties with him.

Tossing them behind us, he grabs my arms and lifts them above my head. Holding my wrist, I nip and kiss his bicep. My eyes catch on a small spot of black ink I've never noticed before.

It's tiny, and I guess I wouldn't have seen it if I wasn't this close.

"Wait." He pauses, releasing my arms immediately as his eyes drop to mine, laced with concern.

"Did I hurt you?"

"No. Not at all. But what's this?" I use my finger and touch the tiny tattoo that's only about an inch long if that.

That boyish grin curls his lips, but it's the hesitancy in his gaze that has me even more curious. Sitting up on his knees, he straightens his arm and pulls the inside of his elbow toward me.

Leaning up on my elbows, I move his arm until I have a better look.

My eyes snap to his. On the inside of his bicep toward the back of his arm is a tiny drawing I've never noticed before. It's a single-line flower tattoo.

"Cody?" I prompt.

Did he get this tattoo for me?

"I never forgot about you, Wildflower," his eyes sear into me, and I feel the words. "You've always been with me."

I wrap my arms around his neck as my lips crash against his. A moan escapes, and I have no idea which one of us makes the noise. Curling my fingers into the dark locks at his nape, I force our lips tighter together. Our tongues tangle and duel, which elicits a rush to my core.

His hands are back on my body as he uses enough force to lower my body back onto the soft mattress. I relish in his weight as it lands on top of me like a boulder grounding me to the earth. There's just something so sexy about having a guy's weight on you. He keeps one elbow bent to help support himself.

Cody's lips leave mine, and before I have a chance to object, I feel the soft nip of his teeth along my jawline. He continues down the column of my neck as he licks and sucks the soft flesh at the same time his fingers swirling around my already erect nipple. Cody sucks my skin into his mouth at the same time he pinches my pebbled peak.

The sensation floods my body, and I can feel the sticky, wetness between my thighs where I rub my legs together in hopes of some relief. I cry out the pleasure, and I realize that I'm so close to coming from this alone. I didn't think it was possible to come like this, but maybe I was wrong.

He trails open-mouthed kisses down the valley between my breasts and over the planes of my stomach.

As I watch his dark hair descend, I can't help the bout of

anxiety that racks my body. I've never had a guy go down on me. Granted my sexual history is almost nonexistent, but the idea of him touching me there with his mouth is too much.

Reaching for his arm, I halt his movement as I try to pull him back up my body.

"Yo-you don't have to do that." Embarrassment floods my cheeks, and I try to avoid any eye contact between us.

Cody rests his weight on his elbows and tries to find my eyes. "I'll stop if you want me to, but I've been fantasizing about tasting this pretty pussy, and I'm starving for it."

My eyes widen at the words that come out of his mouth. He's fantasized about what I taste like?

He must sense my hesitancy because he sits up, and I watch as his fingers trail down my face. "Hey, we won't do anything you aren't ready for. Trust me?"

I nod, chewing on my lower lip. I decide that it's time to be vulnerable. Pushing my fears aside, I choose to be honest. "I've never had anyone do that before. So if you don't want to, I'm fine with that."

Shock flickers across his face, and I feel like this whole night keeps getting ruined.

"Oh, I want to Wildflower. Can I taste you?" Closing my eyes, I pop them open and see the dark desire in his eyes. I nod my head, and with one quick kiss, Cody dives back down my body.

Oh, god. I've lived this moment a hundred times through the lines of my romance novels, and now I'm about to find out if it's as euphoric as it's been described.

I watch as he positions his body between my legs, pushing my thighs to spread me wider before his mouth covers my mound. His tongue licks my slit, and I moan at the contact.

"Mmm." He pops his head up and smirks at me. "I knew you'd taste like my favorite dessert. So sweet. So perfect."

He's like a starved man as he sucks my clit into his mouth

with a slight nibble as he plunges two fingers inside me. I writhe and wither at the contact.

"Oh oh oh. Yes!"

He curls his fingers up against my inner wall, and I feel the tight sensation in my lower body. It feels like a million tiny flowers blooming all at once between the peaks and valleys of the sun. His tongue melts over my center again, sending an ethereal shock wave through my system.

"I-I-I think I'm going to come."

"Come for me, Chlo. I want to feel you come apart on my lips." Cody licks and flicks my bundle of nerves as he quickens his pace. I clench against his fingers as he bites down on my clit as my orgasm rips through my body, the experience more blinding than the sun. I cry out and don't care if the entire complex hears me. I have never come so hard in my life. Not even with my plastic, vibrating friend.

Panting, my chest heaves as I come down from the toe-curling orgasm that ripped through my body. Cody kisses a trail up my body until his lips find mine. I taste myself on his lips. Trailing my hand across his hard stomach, I find his thick erection pressing against his pants. I let my fingers trail his waistband before I start to slide inside it to release him.

"Not tonight," Cody whispers against my lips. "Tonight was about you. You're special to me, Wildflower, and anyone who doesn't see how perfect you are can fuck right off. You're enough for me."

Moisture gathers in the corner of my eyes. For so long I've just wanted to be enough for someone.

And here I am, lying in bed after the best orgasm of my life with the boy who broke my heart but never forgot about me.

CHAPTER 23

CODY

"**H**EY, JACOBS! I PAID GOOD MONEY TO GET ON A flight to see you throw strikes!"

I hear the voice shout from the stands, and my eyes start raking over the crowd. I'm with some of the guys in the outfield as we warm up for our only game this weekend.

My eyes snag on the brunette who is wearing a CTU Baseball jersey and cutoff denim shorts while leaning over the right side railing. Her face is half hidden behind the baseball cap she's wearing, but I'd recognize that smirk anywhere.

Raising a finger to my catcher, I gesture for him to hold the ball before I take off in a jog to the stands. With a nod toward the security guard, I wait for him to open the gate before I climb the couple of stairs that lead to the seat. She races toward me, and I catch her as she jumps into my arms.

"Leah! What the hell are you doing here?"

"What? Can't a girl surprise her big brother?" I set her back down on her feet and take in my baby sister standing in front of me.

"Of course you can, but you should have told me you were coming. I would've made sure you had a ride from the airport."

She rolls her eyes, and I smile. God, I missed my sister.

"Don't worry. I got a ride with some guy I met at the airport."

My eyes widen, and my jaw drops. "Leah, you cannot—"

Her laugh fills the space between us. "Relax, big brother. I took an Uber and then stalked your friends on Instagram to get some details."

I glance past her and find Brynn and Quinton in the stands with some more of our friends. Looking past them, I watch as Chloe descends the steps behind them, her eyes watching me talk to Leah. There's a flash of jealousy in her eyes, and I have to say, green looks good on my girl.

Brushing past my sister, I reach down and grab her hand in mine, pulling her behind me. "What the hell, Cody?" she asks, but I'm too busy trying to get to the girl who stole my heart.

We both pause as our eyes lock on each other—her halfway down the stairs and me at the bottom. I rake my hand over my face as I take in Chloe's outfit.

Damn, my Wildflower is pretty.

Standing before me, she's not in her typical outfit of a dress or skirt. Instead, she's dressed more casually in a pair of black leggings that hug her body deliciously and a red baseball jersey that's left unbuttoned exposing a white T-shirt knotted in the front revealing a sliver of her toned stomach. But that's not what steals my breath away. No, it's the gray baseball cap with a longhorn across the front. Because I know that if she were to turn around, my last name would be embroidered on the back.

I can't believe she still has the hat I wore during the summer league.

Her eyes bounce from mine to Leah standing behind me before recognition crosses her face. I chuckle as I watch her body physically relax. We both start closing the distance between us, and I grip her face between my hands before crushing my lips to hers.

She pulls away, her eyes widening at the very public display. Granted there's still time before the game starts, but that doesn't mean the stands haven't started filling up.

"Wildflower, I want you to meet my sister." I turn toward my sister and watch a giddy Leah climb the stairs.

"Oh my gosh, this is her?!" Leah squeals, pushing past me and wrapping Chloe up in her arms.

Chloe's eyes widen, the gesture catching her off guard. Leah pulls back and holds Chloe at arm's distance. "I've heard so much about you."

"Jacobs!" I turn to find Hudson standing on the field with his arms thrown out in a 'what the fuck' manner.

I turn toward my sister and give her one more hug. "Have fun and behave."

"Don't lose." I shake my head before leaning down and giving Chloe another kiss. "Are you coming down today?"

"You should sit with me!" Leah chimes in. The idea of my two favorite ladies sitting together warms my heart and scares the shit out of me at the same time. Leah isn't afraid to share all kinds of embarrassing stories about me.

A wide smile stretches Chloe's lips, and I know the decision before she even says anything. "I guess I could cover the game from the stands. Maybe work on an angle from the fans' standpoint."

"Have fun, you two."

"Good luck," Chloe says. Giving her a wink, I turn and jog down the steps and back out onto the field.

Nolan tosses me a ball as he squats back down in his catcher's stance. Rotating my shoulders, I tip my head from side to side letting the tension ease as I get my game-day face on.

"You good?" Hud asks, coming up to stand beside me.

"Did you know Leah was coming?" I glance out of the corner of my eye, and I can't read his expression. "She messaged me to make sure she could crash at our house."

I nod before I throw the ball to Nolan.

Fifteen minutes later we are walking out onto the field to line up for the playing of the national anthem. With a glance over my shoulder, I wink at my girl who is watching me before she throws her head back in a laugh, no doubt over something Leah said. It feels good to see my sister relaxed and having fun.

Turning my attention back to the mound, I shut my mind off and get focused on the game ahead of us. A guy with a TV camera is coming down our line, but I don't pay him any attention.

As the anthem ends, we all clap before turning back to the dugout where we jog to get our gloves.

It's time to play ball.

With a deep breath, I head out to the dirt-covered mound. My gaze snaps to each one of my teammates who take their spots behind me. This is it. We are in the top of the ninth inning up five to nothing as I get ready to pitch in the last inning of the game. We are three outs away from me pitching the best game of my career with the chance to end this game with a no-hitter. Typically at this point in the game, I'd be pulled out with our closer in, but Coach must feel the same thing I do.

This is my game to break records.

The section in the right-center field has boards of backward Ks attached to the wall, and I cannot believe how well this game is going.

Nolan jogs from his position behind home plate to where I'm standing on the mound, kicking the dirt just how I like it.

"You've got this, bro. It's just me and you behind the plate." I give him a tight nod as he taps my shoulder with his glove before heading back to his spot.

The crowd is loud as claps and cheers ring out in the stadium as the first batter steps up to the plate. We are back to the top of Loganville's batting order, which means their top hitters are looking to get a hit off to end the streak and my chances of a no-hitter.

Adjusting my hat, I look ahead and wait for the batter to get into position and quit his whole pre-hit ritual. Resting my gloved hand on my chin, there's only a small gap between it and my hat, but it's enough for me to narrow my eyes and wait for Nolan to give the pitch call.

The music cuts out as the batter takes his stance. I watch the bat go up and down as he awaits the pitch. With one last inhale, I start the pitching process. Digging my foot in the dirt, powering through the step, and letting the ball fly out of my fingers, the last thing I feel is the rough texture of the stitching.

I watch the bat come around and miss the ball. The loud "thwack" of the ball hitting Nolan's leather causes the crowd to erupt.

The next two pitches go the same. One out, two to go. I turn my back to the plate and take a few slow strides away from the mound while I wait for the next batter. Turning I walk back to the mound, bouncing my shoulders up and down. My adrenaline is pumping, and I can hardly stand still.

But I have to.

I have to focus on the next pitch. Eyeing Nolan down, I watch him move his fingers in a sequence to call out the pitch. He calls for a slider, and I shake my head. He taps the side of his leg before giving a new sequence. Curveball inside? I nod.

The pitch is in the air, and I wait, unable to breathe, as I watch the batter step forward and swing. Somehow the ball grazes right over the metal bat just missing a connection.

Tipping my head to the side, I let out a long exhale as I crack my neck. Nolan tosses me the ball back, and I resume my position.

These are the moments where all of the hard work and dedication pay off. All the long days throwing in the backyard. The years of traveling to play endless games.

Throwing up a hand, the batter calls for time as he steps out of the box to talk to his third base coach. I take the moment to step off the mound, and without thought, my eyes find Chloe in the stands. She's standing in between Brynn and my sister with her hands folded under her chin where her head rests. Her lips are moving, but I can't make out what she's saying. I opt to give her a wink. She catches the movement and smiles before sending a wink back to me.

Damn, I love that girl.

Love? Yeah, it's safe to say I love Chloe Mariano. I have since our summer together.

Since I'd pick her up after her shift at the diner, and we'd spend all day together before she'd come to my games. Chloe would look so pretty in the stands in her infamous sundresses, hair braided down her back, or in pigtails with my hat perched on top of her head. For some games, she'd sit with rapt attention watching pitch after pitch while some days she'd sit with her nose stuck between the pages of her latest book. It never bothered me when she would rather pay more attention to her novels than to my game. There was a comfort that would wash over me when I'd look up and find her in the stands.

It's the same comfort I feel right now.

I shake the thoughts from my head, reining in my inner

thoughts and focusing on the job at hand. Bending at the waist, I wait for my pitch call.

Standing, I go through my motions and fire a fastball right down the center causing the batter to whiff. The next pitch has the same result. And just like that, I'm one batter away from pitching the game of my life.

A no-hitter.

But the next guy to step up to the plate has the hair rising on my arms as dread pools in my stomach.

Mark Daniels is one of the top hitters in the league. The weight of this game lies solely on his shoulders. He's a tough competitor, one I've been facing since high school where he played on the rival team. Throughout our years, we've had quite the duel between us. I've learned his quirks, but he's also learned my cues.

He lines up at the plate, his eyes staring me down. I don't let him see that I'm worried. I'm not, but I'm also not *not* worried.

Nolan gives me the sign, and I deliver the pitch as a crack pierces the air. I whip my head in the direction of the outfield and watch the ball in the air.

Go foul. Go foul. Go *fucking* foul.

"Foul," the outfield umpire shouts, and I could drop to my knees with relief. Fuck that was a close one.

Coach steps out from the dugout, calling time as he makes his way to the mound. He better not be pulling me out of this game.

"Jacobs, you doing okay?" Coach asks, standing in front of me while the rest of the infield circles around us. The circle gives us a little bit of privacy.

Nodding my head, "Yeah, Coach, I'm good. I've got this."

"I know you do. Just wanted to come out here and calm you down. We've got your back, Jacobs."

"We got you," the guys say as they swat me with their gloves.

Everyone jogs back to their positions, including Coach who

stops at the steps of the dugout. The stadium starts clapping as everyone shows their support before quieting down as Daniels and I get into our positions.

Ripping the ball through the air, it's low, but not low enough to be called a ball.

"One more to go, baby!" Billings shouts from third base.

One more.

Nolan gives a sign, and I shake my head.

He gives another sign. I give him a tight-lipped expression and shake my head.

Nolan's eyes go over to Coach who is giving him a sign that he translates into our sign. A small smirk finds my lips, and I nod.

Powering off the mound, the ball flies through the air. I watch as Daniels steps forward, rotating his hips. He's swinging, but the ball changes up speed and dies down. Daniels misses the ball as Nolan catches it in his mitt.

"Strike three!"

The crowd erupts as the guys race toward the mound.

Holy shit. I just pitched a no-hitter.

I can't keep the smile from erupting across my face as the guys start jumping on me, and if I'm not careful, we're going to end up in a dog pile, and I'll be underneath them.

"Hell yeah, man!" Nolan says first.

"Dude, you called the pitches."

"Yeah, but you threw them, fucker!"

Hudson chimes in next. "You fucking did it!"

Yeah, I fucking did it!

I turn to head toward the dugout, but my feet plant like I'm stuck in cement as my girl stands just outside the dugout. She's holding a camera to her face as she clicks away, her wide smile shines from behind the lens. My heart stops as I take her in.

I love watching her in her element. I know this isn't the assignment she was hoping to have, but she's crushing it. I'm in awe of her talent. Not only does Chloe have a way with words, but she has an eye for photography. I'm also selfishly glad she got assigned to cover our team. It was the push we both needed to mend our shattered past.

Before I have a chance to go to Chloe, my sister is flinging herself at me. I'm able to catch her before she tackles me.

"Bub! I'm so damn proud of you!" Leah screams as she wraps her arms around my neck. I squeeze her back.

"Thanks, sister!" I set her back down on her feet as I wrap my arm over her shoulders. The two of us make our way over to Chloe.

"Now let's go celebrate my birthday." She tosses the words out so casually over her shoulder. Spinning around, she gives me a wink before adding, "Oh, and I guess we can celebrate the best game of your career."

Chloe sidles up next to me, and I bend down wrapping my arms around her waist and lifting her off her feet. Our lips find each other for a brief moment before she pulls me back. "Put me down, Cody."

Rolling my eyes, I do as I'm told. "I'm so proud of you. That game was insane."

"Thanks, Wildflower. I saw you up there freaking out."

She scoffs. "I wasn't freaking out. I was just praying to the baseball gods to let this be your big game."

"Well, it paid off."

"It sure did." She bumps my shoulder as I step down into the dugout.

"I'm taking your sister with me to the house, and then we'll head to your place."

"Be careful."

"I'm always careful."

Leaning down, I can't resist the urge to kiss her one more

time. "I know you are, but Leah is...well she's a troublemaker who isn't under my dad's roof this weekend."

She smirks before turning and walking away from me.

Some of the guys stop her at the top of the dugout. They say something that makes her head tilt back in laughter and a pang of jealousy runs through my veins.

She must sense it too because she finds me watching her and gives me a wink.

With a wink back, I turn to make my way through the door that leads to the hallway where our locker room is.

It's time to celebrate.

CHAPTER 24

Chloe

"Y**OU SHOULD WEAR THIS DRESS.**"

Quinton drove Brynn, Leah, and me back to our townhouse where we'd spent the last thirty minutes going through clothes trying to figure out what I should wear to-night. Apparently, one of my floral minidresses isn't good enough.

We've now made our way into Brynn's room where she and Leah are going through some of Brynn's party dresses.

"Pass." I veto the super short, blue bodycon dress that has more cutouts than connected fabric.

"Fine, but I'm the birthday girl, so what I say goes," Leah says.

"Okay, but why do I feel like that will be the start of a very epic night if we have to do what Leah says, kind of like 'Simon says,' all night long?" Brynn chimes in from the spot in front of her mirror where she's applying a sharp cat eye.

Leah turns with a gasp. "Yes! Let's do that!"

"No, no, no," I say with a shake of my head. "We are not letting the just barely legal eighteen-year-old dictate our night."

"Boo!" both girls yell at me.

But I don't even care. Cody's only shared bits and pieces of his life at home, and if Leah is under any of the same pressures that Cody has been under, she's going to be ready to break free. Which means we could have a very crazy night on our hands. As much as I think it would be fun, I feel like someone needs to be the responsible one.

"Here," Leah says, handing me a fuchsia satin mini dress with a halter neckline that flares in an A-line hem. The back is completely exposed, and a sly grin spreads across my face. Cody is going to lose it when he sees me in this dress.

"Bitch, I know that look!" Brynn laughs as we make eye contact through the mirror. "It's like the night I wore my leather mini skirt, black see-through mesh shirt over the top of a black bra, with my sky-high heels, and we ended up breaking Q's table. You're going to walk into that party, and jaws will drop."

"With a lead-up like that, I know you girls are going to make tonight the best birthday celebration."

I smile at Leah from across the room. "It's going to be a good night."

An hour later, the four of us are walking up the sidewalk that leads to the Baseball House in mini dresses and high heels. Quinton stuck around while us girls got ready. He's a saint for waiting. The three of us took way too long to figure out what we were going to wear. Cody was blowing up my phone for the last half hour wondering what was taking us so long and curious if his sister was causing trouble.

After spending a few hours with Leah, I see similarities between her and Brynn. And now I know why Cody and Brynn became best friends. Both are just trying to find their way in a world where they've been forgotten. Leah might not have suffered the same heartbreaking childhood as Brynn, but she's suffered at the hands of her father who has placed such high pressures on his children. Not only does he expect the world from them, but he constantly finds ways to knock them down.

I also found that Leah was accepted to CTU, but she's holding out on accepting until she hears back from West Coast schools. She hasn't told her brother this, and I promised I wouldn't tell him. I hate keeping secrets from Cody, especially since we're just now getting to a good place. Secrets kept us apart once, and I don't want a repeat. But I'm hoping that once Leah gets her acceptance letters, she'll open up to him.

Quinton leads us up the walkway that has students piling out over the yard. The thumping from the music can be heard from outside. Q pushes open the front door, and we are met with chaos.

Loud music blasts from the speakers. Bodies are grinding against each other on the makeshift dance floor in the living room. A few couples are making out on the outskirts of the room, most half-naked or in the midst of ripping one another's clothes off. The party has barely started, but I can already tell it's going to be quite the night of debauchery.

Moving past the living room, I find a set of familiar faces, a group of guys both from the baseball and football teams lined up around the dining room table where beer pong has been set up. Scanning the line of guys, my eyes catch on hazel eyes that are already staring back at me. Cody's eyes skim my body, and I swear I can already feel his touch. A cocky smirk moves across his lips.

I send him a wink before pulling Leah by her hand to the dance floor. The DJ is playing the hit "Baby Boy" by Sean Paul—an oldie but goodie—and the beat has our hips shaking as soon as we find a space in between bodies. Leah's lithe body moves seductively, and I can only imagine how Cody is feeling right now. He's so protective of his sister, but it's her birthday weekend, and she deserves to have some fun.

Brynn and Quinton disappeared when we got here. I assume they're off to make out in the corner. The two of them can never keep their hands off each other.

It's crazy to think that at the beginning of the semester, I was the one on the outskirts, the wallflower hiding in the shadows. Now I'm in the midst of the chaos in a dress that barely covers my body dancing with Cody Jacobs's sister.

All the cyberbullying from the photo on the Gossip Gazette has started to die down. Cody went crazy in the comment section threatening anyone who looked at me the wrong way or said one more nasty thing about me. I appreciated it especially after he came to the townhouse and made me feel seen. That night shifted everything between us.

Leah and I are dancing through our fifth song when I feel a warm body sidle up behind me. It's the first guy to come up and approach us, which surprises me considering Leah's dance moves. I wonder if Cody threatened everyone who walked in here that his sister was going to be here tonight and is off limits. If that's the case, she's going to be pissed.

While we were getting ready, Leah was telling Brynn and me how she ended things with a guy she was casually seeing. It wasn't anything serious since she refused to get tied down with anyone from her hometown since she wanted to move across the country. But that meant she was a free woman who was now a legal adult looking for fun.

"Damn, girl. This dress is sexy," his voice comes from behind me, and I feel his fingers graze my exposed skin. "Gotta boyfriend?"

Leaning back into his touch, my ass meets his front. "Nope. No boyfriend."

He growls before leaning his head closer to my ear. "What the hell, Wildflower?"

Spinning in his grip, I find dark, broody eyes staring down on me. It'd be intimidating on anyone else, especially since he towers over me by a few inches even in my heels. But I know Cody would never do anything to hurt me.

I quirk my brow at him. We've never had the "talk," but it's pretty clear as day that both of us are together in a very much exclusive manner. I just love to find ways to get under his skin.

In one swift motion, his hand flies to my neck where he grips it tightly, tilting my chin up to meet his steely gaze. His grip is tight enough to make me gasp as wetness pools in my barely there panties. A soft moan escapes from between my lips.

"You're fucking mine, Wildflower." The words leave his mouth in a growl as his lips find mine. His tongue dips inside, and the kiss quickly turns heated as his fingers, still wrapped around my neck, tighten. I didn't take myself to be someone who liked to be choked, but damn, I can get behind this.

The way he's dominating my mouth with his tongue has me wanting to drop to my knees and worship him. Right here. In front of the whole damn party. Being with Cody brings out a side of me that I didn't know I was hiding. She's dark and sexy. A devil dressed like an angel.

My body is turning into a puddle, and my knees are about to give out on me just as Cody's opposite hand grips me tighter, and he pulls my body closer to him. I can feel his hard length pressing into my stomach, and I wish it was pumping inside of me. We still haven't even had sex yet, but I can't stop thinking about the two of us together. Him tossing me around the bedroom as I'm wet and needy.

"Get a room!" Leah shouts from behind us, and I feel a devilish smile spread across Cody's face.

He pulls back and brushes his thumb against my swollen lips. "You look beautiful tonight, Wildflower."

Heat floods my cheeks as I bite my lower lip. I run my hand

down his Henley-clad chest. "You clean up pretty well. You had a great game today, Cody. I'm proud of you."

I watch his eyes fill with heat, and before I know it, I'm grabbing his hand and pushing our way through the masses. I hear Leah's booming laugh as she yells, "I didn't mean right now!"

Making our way into the kitchen and toward the back hallway where the half bath is located, we pass Brynn and Quinton where they are gathered with some of the guys from the football team. Brynn is sitting on the counter, a bottle of tequila in her hand as she pours the silver liquid into shot glasses.

"Keep an eye on her," Cody calls over his shoulder as I move us through the kitchen. I'm not sure who he's pointing the command to, but Brynn and Quinton both know who he's talking about. Catcalls follow us as we move past the line of people waiting for the bathroom.

The timing couldn't be better as a girl is exiting the bathroom as we come to the doorway. I push Cody inside before anyone else has a chance to yell at us for cutting the line. Too bad for them, this is Cody's house, and he does what he wants...therefore I do what I want.

"Damn, what's gotten into you?" Cody's puzzled expression eyes me with confusion. Instead of answering him, I reach up to the halter neckline. Fingering the buttons, I finally unclasp them and let the pink silky material fall to my feet.

Cody follows the motion as I watch his eyes widen and desire darkens his hazel eyes into a deep brown. "Fuuuck," he rasps out as I lower myself to my knees.

Nibbling on my lower lip, I take a second before looking up at him. His chest heaves as he takes all of me in from my ivory skin, to my hand-full-sized breasts, to my pebbled nipples, and down to where my hands are resting between my damp thighs.

"I-I've never done this. I, um, I might not be good at it, but I want to do this for you. I want to know what it's like. Teach me?" My cheeks are warm from the admission, but it's true. Since the night in my room where he ate me out, I've been desperate to return the favor and feel him on my tongue.

"You've got this, Wildflower." Cody encourages, swiping a loose hair that's fallen out of my high ponytail.

Reaching up, I undo the buckle of his leather belt. The rattling of the metal fills the space along with the heavy bass from the party going on outside our doors. I make quick work unbuttoning his jeans and sliding the zipper down exposing his large—very large—bulge hidden behind the pair of black boxer briefs. I slip my fingers behind the band and hear him let out a small hiss as my fingers brush the skin of his lower stomach. Sliding the material down, his cock springs free, and I inhale a startled breath at the size of him.

How the hell am I supposed to fit all of that in my mouth?

He chuckles at my wide-eyed expression as he sweeps the back of his fingers down my cheek. "You can take it, baby."

Dear god those words do things to me. Skating my hands up his thighs, I reach for him as the weight settles in my hand. I pump once, twice, before leaning forward and licking the bead of precum from the tip of his dick. The saltiness hits my tongue as an involuntary hum leaves my lips.

My tongue continues its perusal as I lick him from root to tip, twirling my tongue around his crown, before repeating the process. I know what I need to do. I'm not completely clueless. I read a lot of romance books where giving head is constantly brought up. I know there's licking involved. And sucking.

Thank God I read books because I don't want to be the girl down on her knees literally blowing on a cock that's in my face.

"Fuck, Chlo, you're killing me."

With one last swipe around his tip, I slide his cock inside my mouth, my lips meeting my hand that's fisted around him—well, as much as I can. He's so long and thick, I can't get my fingers to touch. Suctioning my lips around him, I begin moving my head up and down at the same pace I move my fist. Slow motions at first, but those motions quickly turn faster as I pull him farther into my mouth. He groans in appreciation as he wraps my ponytail around his fist.

"You're doing such a great job, babe."

I moan around his dick at the praise as my wetness continues to coat the inside of my thighs. As much as I want to take the time and truly explore this Adonis in front of me, time is not our friend as the pounding on the bathroom door begins.

Sucking him further in my mouth, he hits the back of my throat, and I fight the small gag that wants to escape. The hand which is wrapped around my hair begins to pump my head faster. Reaching up, I pull on his balls, and he lets out an appreciative moan.

"I'm going to come." He groans the words, which only encourages me more.

Sliding my tongue up his shaft, I lick around his crown before sucking him harder. I feel him tense before his pumps turn shaky. His hot, salty seed hits the back of my throat, and I take all of him.

Swallowing, he slides out of my mouth with a pop as I lean back on my knees, swiping the side of my lips.

His heavy pants fill the room. "You've never done that before?" he questions as I shake my head.

"No, but I read a lot of romance books."

He chuckles. "I'm never giving you shit again for having your nose in a book."

I smile up at him as the pounding intensifies.

"We better go." I stand to my feet, reaching down to pull my dress up while Cody tucks himself back in his jeans. Leaning over me, he brings his thumb and finger to my chin, tilting my head toward him. His lips find mine, and I smile around the kiss.

"I cannot wait to get you out of this dress, again."

Cody reaches for the handle to unlock the door, he doesn't have a chance to open it before I drop a bomb on his mood. "Except your sister is staying with you, so no action tonight."

His head hits the back of the door, and he lets out a frustrated groan. I can't help the laugh that escapes. He opens the door, and we are met with angry stares. Cody smirks at them as he takes my hand in his, leading us to the kitchen.

We step in the kitchen and find the guys, Brynn, and Leah gathered around the kitchen island. Cheers and claps erupt as we enter.

"Damn, dude!" Hudson shouts as he continues clapping. My face feels like it's on fire. Cody isn't bothered at all, and why would he be? He's used to being in the spotlight, and he's definitely not shy with his previous conquests.

"I could've gone without knowing what you two were doing in the bathroom," Leah says from where she's sipping from a red plastic cup.

Cody slides his arm around my shoulders and pulls me in closer to him. "Oh, I just needed Chloe's help with—um—"

"Getting off?" Brynn mumbles, and the guys crack up.

"Ew," Leah says, reaching for the tequila. "Shots?"

"Yes!" I shout, thankful for the topic change. Cody stares his sister down, and she quirks her eyebrow.

Grabbing a glass from Leah, I hold it in the air. "Happy birthday, Leah!"

Sounds of 'happy birthday' echo in our space as we all down our drinks.

CHAPTER 25

CODY

I woke up Sunday morning on the plush couch in our attic. There was no way I was having my little sister or girlfriend sleep up here in a room without a door. Not that they wouldn't be safe, but it still gave me peace of mind knowing they weren't sleeping out in the open.

There was also no way I was sharing a bed with my little sister. When we were younger, no big deal, but not today. Plus, she snores, and I need my beauty rest.

Coach canceled all practices and workouts for today, and I couldn't be more thankful. I think the whole team could use a lazy Sunday after we've had weeks of endless baseball.

Making my way down the stairs, I take in the calmness of the house. It's completely different from the chaos that surrounded the house when I went to bed sometime around two this morning. Leah and Chloe went to bed around midnight, both of them heavily intoxicated. Chloe isn't a big drinker, so it didn't take her long to reach her limit, and my sister surprised me with how much she could put away. It seems that she's been living quite the double life back home.

The house is trashed, plastic cups and cans litter the floor and counters. Furniture is still piled in corners, but it doesn't matter. It can all be cleaned. Yesterday I pitched the best game of my career, and nothing, and I mean nothing, was stopping me from celebrating.

Not even a text from my dad who told me I shouldn't have let Daniels get a hit off.

His texts are getting easier to just swipe to delete, especially since Leah was under my roof and not his. Only a few more months, and I'll be able to get her out of there for good. She hasn't talked to me much about her plans post-high school, but whatever they are, I'm ready to move her into the house until the fall. And then it's time to cut all contact with my parents. I hate this for my mom, but what has she done to stop my dad's lashings for me and Leah?

Reaching for the coffee grounds, I go to open the coffee maker and find that a pot of coffee awaits. Turning on my heels, I spot a lone figure sitting at the dining room table, her dark hair—the same shade as mine—gathered in a messy bun on the top of her head. Her head rests on her arms which are resting on her bent knees. Leah looks so much like the little girl I grew up with.

"Morning, Big Bro."

Smiling, I finish pouring myself a cup of coffee and head to the empty seat next to her. "Morning, Bug. How'd you sleep?"

"Did you know your girlfriend is a cuddler?"

I chuckle because of course I know that, but also because Chloe is the clingiest sleeper. It's like she's slept alone for so long that now that I'm finally in her bed, she refuses to let me go again.

"She cling to you all night?"

"Oh my gosh, all freaking night. It was super cute but also super gross because I'm not you. She's a good one, brother."

"She really is." Bringing my mug to my lips, I let the rich, nutty coffee slide down my throat. There really is nothing better than coffee when hungover.

"You're an idiot for what you did that summer. But I get why you did it."

"How are things at home?" I watch as she starts to spin the wheels in her head to make the truth sound better than it actually is. "The truth, Bug."

An exasperated chuckle leaves her lips as she shakes her head. "It's always the same, Cody. He's miserable. I swear Mom stays medicated so she doesn't have to deal with him. It makes her complacent—she does whatever he asks. I've been staying with friends more than normal and blaming it on senior year exams. They seem to buy it. There's only a few more months to go, and I can get out of there."

"Speaking of getting out of there. I want you to come and stay with me for the summer. We can get you packed and moved out after graduation. I've talked to the guys, and they all agree we'll give you the attic as your own space. I just need you out of there, Bug. I don't know how much more of Dad's wrath I can take."

Leah reaches over, wrapping her hand around mine and squeezes. "Thank you."

My brows furrow as I stare at my sister. "What for?"

"For everything, Cody. For taking the brunt of Dad's abuse, for showing me how to be brave, and for offering me a place to stay after graduation."

"Leah, I would do anything for you."

"I know that. I also think you should know that I've applied to some colleges that are further away."

"How far away? Did you not hear back from CTU?"

I watch as Leah avoids my eyes as she stares holes into the wood table. I have a feeling I'm not going to like what she's about to say, but no matter the news, I'll find a way to be happy for her. She deserves the opportunity to go out on her own and live her own life.

"I heard from CTU and I got in—" She stops me mid-breath from congratulating her. "But I'm waiting to hear back from the University of Washington."

My jaw nearly hits the table because the state of Washington is far away. Like clear across the country. Her bottom lip starts to tremble, and at that sight, I'm up and dropping to my knees in front of her. Pulling her into me as she wraps her arms around my shoulders. "I'm so sorry, Cody. I know how bad you wanted me here with you, but it's just too close."

"Bug, you deserve this. I'm so fucking proud of you."

She sniffles in my neck as she mumbles, "You're not mad at me?"

"I could never be mad at you. This gives me a chance to visit. Hell, I might even try to have the Mariners come scout my games."

Leah pushes back and stares at me. "Dude, that'd be awesome."

We both smile, and everything is right in the world.

"Am I interrupting? Baby Jacobs, he better not be making you cry," Hudson says as he makes his way over to the coffeemaker.

The smile she gives to Hudson has me quirking a brow. Does my little sister have a crush on my best friend?

Clearing my throat, I watch her eyes widen and a nervous look replaces the love-struck expression on her face. I ask her a silent question with a look, and she shakes her head, but her worrying at her bottom lip doesn't ease my mind.

My best friend and sister? Nope, not even going to touch on that today.

"So what's for lunch?" Hudson asks. "Am I ordering Cousin Jimmy's?"

"Lunch? It's—" Pulling out my phone I check the screen and see that it's 12:45 in the afternoon. "Oh shit, we slept the whole morning away."

Hudson sits in the empty seat across from me, which happens to be the other empty beside Leah. "I think I crashed around three."

"Was there anyone left?"

"Just a few people. Niko was manning the house."

"Of course he was."

"Did you enjoy your first CTU party?"

Leah perks up and turns her full attention to Hudson. I watch both of them to make sure there aren't any hidden messages behind their words. I love Hudson like a brother, but he better not have let his lips touch my sister. "It was fun. I think the parties back home are wilder, but I had a good time."

"Last night was tame since we are in season. You'll have to come for a football game, well, you'll get the chance next fall if you get into CTU."

"I'm actually waiting to hear back from the University of Washington."

Hud's eyes widen, and he glances over at me. "Well, shit, little sis, I hear the parties out there are crazy. You'll get in, there's no doubt."

"Thanks, Hudson. It'll be your turn to come visit me."

The sound of soft feet padding against the floor interrupts our conversation, and I look over my shoulder to find my Wildflower—looking like an absolute hot mess. Her blond hair is all over the place, creases mar her forehead where she's squinting from the light, and her body sags as if she's in pain.

"Good morning, princess," Hudson greets Chloe with a chuckle.

"You look like shit," Leah adds.

Chloe tosses her middle finger over her shoulder as she bee-lines straight to the coffee. Getting up from my chair, I follow her.

Wrapping my arms around her, I pull her to my front and trail soft kisses down her neck. "Morning, beautiful."

She groans at my greeting, and I chuckle. Chloe Mariano is not a drinker, and she definitely doesn't do hangovers. Stepping out of my embrace, she makes her way over to the table, plops in a chair, and rests her head on the table. Hudson and Leah both laugh at her pain.

"What time is your flight?" I ask my sister as I take my seat again.

"Four. I have an Uber scheduled to pick me up at two."

"I can take you."

She shakes her head. "Nope, I've got this. We can say our awkward goodbye here and not at the airport. Plus, you can't even go back with me."

I nod, resigned to the fact that she's right.

"I'm going to go grab a shower in your room," she says, standing and patting me on the shoulder as she heads past me. She stops and kisses Chloe on her head. "Feel better, my cuddle bug."

My heart warms at the gesture and the words that come out of her mouth. Those are the same words I would whisper to my sister when she wasn't feeling good.

I don't think there's anything better in the world than seeing your sister and girlfriend get along so seamlessly.

Chloe and I have been wrapped up under the covers in my bed for over an hour since my sister left. She's dozed on and off since taking pain relievers and electrolyte drinks while I've watched highlights on ESPN.

I've been checking my phone sporadically as I wait for my sister's text letting me know she's boarding her flight.

Fingers trace my stomach causing a chill to spread through my body. Glancing down, I meet Chloe's gaze as she stares up at me.

"I can't believe you're mine again," I murmur against the top of her head as her lips find my side.

"Why didn't you ever tell me about your dad?" My body freezes at his mention because I've wanted to keep her away from thoughts of him. He hasn't earned the right to meet this sweet, caring, incredible girl.

"And before you panic," Chloe continues, "Leah filled me in on how problematic he is. Cody, he verbally abuses you and threatens you with our future. Is that why you never answered my texts?"

Leah and her big mouth, but in her defense, these are conversations I should've been having with Chloe. I just didn't want her to feel guilty.

"Yes, he's part of the reason." Sitting up, I lean my back against my headboard as Chloe shifts so that we are both facing each other. "I honestly thought we'd never see each other again, but while he was in the hospital he saw my phone and your name flash. He used you to twist things in my head telling me that I'd never amount to anything, that I'd always let you be a distraction, that I couldn't have you and have a future in baseball.

"Was it absolutely bullshit to listen to a word he said? Abso-fucking-lutely, but I was eighteen years old and thought he was still looking out for me. I thought that if I chose you, I couldn't have baseball. But it was just his way of twisting the truth in his form of fun. He loves playing mind games, and once he feels he's planted an inkling of doubt, he uses it and manipulates the situation."

Taking a breath, I find her watching me. She doesn't say anything, and I'm afraid I'm losing her all over again. "I realized what he was doing halfway through my freshman year here when the texts started rolling in after every game. I could pitch the best game, but he'd always find a way to criticize me. Things as little as how I chose the wrong pitch. One time he called to recite statistics of opposing hitters, just so he could get in my head by psyching me out on how good the batters I would be facing were. It was then I realized he wanted me to fail. He couldn't make it so he didn't want me to make it. I'm his son, and he's jealous of me. He wants me to fail like he did."

"I'm sorry, Cody. I'm sorry you've had to live with this." She leans forward and flings her arms around me as she crawls into my lap. "But it's time to let him go. You are incredible. You are going to do great things. The pros are looking at you, and that's something to be proud of. You did it. He had nothing to do with where you are today."

"I just need to keep taking it until Leah is out."

"I'm really glad I got to meet her," Chloe says, a smile spreading across her face.

Leaning forward, I gently brush my lips against hers. "I'm glad you two got to meet. I loved having both of my girls in the stands watching me play."

Chloe slides off my lap, and I fight the groan that wants to escape. "Speaking of baseball," she starts, and I can sense her energy change. "What's your-um-your future look like with baseball?"

Her question lands like a punch to the gut, knocking the air out of me. What does my future look like? I just got my girl back, am I about to have to leave her again? Baseball right now is so up in the air that I don't know what direction I want to take.

There's a part of me that wants to stick around for my last

year at CTU to finish my degree and play one last time under Coach Weber.

On the other hand, I'm nervous that I could be missing a chance to further my career if I turn down any offers.

"I honestly have no idea." My head hits the headboard as I run my fingers through my hair. "Ideally, I stick around for senior year and get drafted, but who knows? Weber has been handling a lot of the communication for me."

She nods her head as her phone vibrates on the table. I watch as she reads the message, her body language stiffening before she hops off the bed.

"I need to go home."

Chloe gathers the pink material of the dress she wore last night. "Here," I start, jumping off the bed and heading for a drawer. "I picked up a couple of things for you."

Reaching into the drawer, I pull out a pair of black leggings, panties, and a sports bra before opening another drawer and grabbing one of my T-shirts.

"You bought me clothes?" she asks, taking the items from my outstretched hand and dropping the blanket she's been wrapped up in most of the day. Last night she slept in an old tee and a pair of my boxers, but since we've been lounging around all day she opted for naked cuddles.

"It's no biggie, just wanted to make sure you were taken care of." She tosses her arms around me for a quick hug before she backs away and slides the clothes on.

While she's getting dressed, I grab my phone, wallet, and keys. "I'll drive you."

"You don't have to. I can grab an Uber."

Squinting my eyes, I just stare at her before she relents. "Fine."

The two of us make our way to my car that's parked in the driveway and a few minutes later I'm pulling into her parking lot. I've barely shifted the car to park when Chloe's jumping out of the passenger side. Turning off the ignition, I'm right on her heels.

"Wildflower—" I start, but when I glance up, I see why she was in such a hurry to get to the house.

CHAPTER 26

Chloe

O UT OF ALL THE POTENTIAL TEXT MESSAGES I COULD have received today, I was not expecting the one I received while at Cody's house.

It's a message I've been waiting on for months.

"Macy?" I call out as I walk up the sidewalk. She's sitting on the front stoop, her brunette hair pulled up in a ponytail, and I can feel the nervous energy radiating off her.

Good. She should be nervous.

Her head pops up but before she has a chance to say anything, Cody is reaching for my hand. I watch as her gaze tracks the movement. "Wildflower—" he starts but doesn't finish.

Glancing over my shoulder, I find Cody staring at Macy while his jaw tightens. Turning into him, I reach up and kiss him. He pulls me into him and plants a longer kiss on my lips. "I'm good, Cody. Thanks for giving me a ride home."

He flicks his gaze over my shoulder and stares Macy down. "Call me later, babe."

Nodding my head, my lips find his cheek before I step away

and start the much-needed conversation between my former roommate and close friend.

"I'm sorry for interrupting your Sunday, but I think it's time we hash things out. I really miss having you in my life Chloe."

I scoff, sliding past her and twisting the knob of our front door. Thankfully, it's unlocked as I push my way inside, Macy on my heels.

Brynn peeks her head out from the kitchen, and she smiles. "Hey, girl!" she greets Macy.

The two of them had a bit of a strained relationship, but somehow along the way the two of them have worked out their differences leaving me in the dark. But at the end of the day, Macy didn't screw over her friendship with Brynn the way she did with me.

My mind immediately flashes back to the last time the three of us were in the same room together.

"What's going on with you two?" Brynn asks from her spot on the couch.

My shoulders deflate at Brynn's question. My gaze leaves the TV, as I glance over at Brynn before finding Macy's eyes.

"We're just agreeing to disagree."

I watch Brynn's eyebrows form a V as confusion laces her face. "About?" she draws out.

"I have feelings for Cody," I rush out. "Macy knows. She's figured it out from watching me."

Brynn's face morphs into shock. I can only imagine how she's processing this news. It's not something I have ever openly broadcast with my friends. And hell, I don't even know if it's a crush. Macy can think whatever she wants, but it doesn't make it true. Maybe it's not a crush. Maybe the feeling I'm feeling is hatred.

I watch as Brynn is hesitant in her response, "Chloe, that's great. But I'm having trouble figuring out why you're mad at Macy?"

Shaking my head, I go to tell Brynn that it isn't what they think, but I don't have a chance before Macy interrupts me.

"She's mad at the way I called her out on it. I mean, it's so freaking obvious," Macy responds to the question before I have the chance. Standing from her spot, Macy turns to give me her entire attention. I can't help the feeling I want to cower under her glare. But I won't. I won't give her the satisfaction when she doesn't know the truth. "You stare at him like he hung the moon, but you're too childish to say anything. You act like a lost puppy. Either man up and tell him, or get over it."

"How about you just worry about your relationship with Gregg and stop worrying about me?" I snap, and anger courses through my body.

"Just go pack," I yell, dismissing Macy. "I'm done with you acting like you're so much better than me because you're in a relationship."

Macy plants her hands on her hips, chest heaving, as she stares me down. It's intimidating and reminds me of how a parent would scold a child. But I refuse to let her get to me.

She doesn't get to come into the house that we share, drop the bomb that she's moving out to take care of some guy she barely knows, and treat me like the dirt on the bottom of her shoes.

"Whatever, Chloe. Keep standing on the sidelines looking like a psycho stalker. I'm not the only one that's noticed." As those words leave her mouth, Macy storms out of the room while I sink onto the couch.

Screw her and screw this friendship. If she wants to act like a child, she can leave. I'm used to people turning their backs on me.

"I was going to make some lunch, but I can go upstairs to give you girls some privacy." My eyes widen as they snap to Brynn, her words interrupting my thoughts from the last time the three of us were in the same room. She meets my stare and gives a small shrug. "Or I can stay?"

"Yeah, that'd be great." The three of us gather around the kitchen table as silence fills the space.

"I miss this. I miss our friendship. I miss you—," Macy starts before pointing the last word at me. "Chloe."

Tracing the lines on the table, I don't look up when Macy stops talking. "I didn't cause this, Macy. You did."

"And I'm sorry for it." She reaches across the table resting her hand on mine which causes me to flinch. "You're right, and you have every right to be angry with me. I freaked out on you. It was all misplaced frustration, and unfortunately, you were the first one I saw."

"But I don't understand why you couldn't have taken five minutes to explain to me—to us"—I point my finger between me and Brynn—"what was going on? Instead, you turned on me. You used my feelings for Cody as an excuse to attack me."

I lean back in my chair and watch her process the words. Like Macy, I miss our friendship. Out of the three of us, Macy and I were the closest. Maybe that's why she poured her frustrations out on me because she thought I could take it. And I probably could have if she hadn't used Cody against me. It wasn't necessarily her fault. She didn't know my dark past with Cody, but it's still not an excuse. I'm valid to have feelings and frustrations toward her.

"It looks like things have worked out between the two of you, though," she muses. "I've been keeping up with you on Instagram."

My palm meets the table. "You don't get to take credit for that!"

Macy's hands rise as Brynn flinches. "Cody and I had a past. A past that we never resolved or acknowledged. We've been skirting around our past for two and a half years. While I don't think you meant to attack me, you attacked something that I've been fighting hard to avoid the whole time we've been here."

Macy apologizes again as tears fill her eyes. She's always been the most emotional out of the three of us. I mean, I'm not far from her on the crying scale.

"What happened?" she asks, swiping the loose tear away.

I spend the next fifteen minutes catching them up on our past, on parts of Cody's past, and our reasons for why we didn't broach the topic any sooner.

"Now I feel even more like the biggest asshole in the house."

"Well, I mean..." Brynn trails off with a shrug.

"I still don't understand why you did it. I mean I think I've assumed why, but I want to hear it from you. I thought we were closer than that."

"I was scared. I was scared shitless actually. My entire world had flipped on its axis. I had spent weeks fighting my attraction to Gregg because I was afraid of getting hurt again. But in the process of fighting those feelings, I still got hurt. When I got the phone call he was in the hospital, it was like someone had ripped my heart out of my chest. In a second, my life flashed to a life without him. A life where I never had the chance to tell him that he was more to me. Honestly, and this is going to sound like an excuse, but you were the first one I saw, and I took that frustration out on you. I'd watched you and Cody parade around each other, and it made me so angry because it's obvious you both had some kind of attraction, but neither one of you would act on it. At that moment, I was seeing how short life is, how quickly things could change. I was getting my second chance, a chance to move in with Gregg and help him with his recovery. I hadn't slept, and the stress was so insurmountable that I erupted on you."

The explanation that Macy just gave me is one I've been waiting for. Deep down I knew I wasn't the initial target, but it didn't ease the pain. Growing up, I didn't have friends. I don't know how to handle these tough situations.

"It's taken me a minute to realize that you weren't actually trying to attack me, Macy. I sat and cried on the phone with my dad, but he knew. He knew that you were hurting, and I was the unfortunate punching bag. It didn't ease the hurt. I knew you were hurting, but you took your pain out on me."

"I did, and if I could go back, I think I would change it. To be honest, I was such a basket case that I would like to say I wouldn't act that way again, but the truth of the matter is, I was selfish and hateful with my words." Macy pauses and stares at me. It's in her stare that I feel her sincerity. I feel her apology, and it's where I feel that the words she spoke weren't said in malice. "At the end of the day, I can't change the past, but I can fix things. You're one of my very best friends. I grew up with brothers, but you and Brynn are like the sisters I never had. Please know from the bottom of my heart that I'm sorry. I love you, Chlo."

The room is blanketed in silence as I work to process everything I've heard tonight. I think a part of me has forgiven Macy a long time ago. The distance has done wonders for our relationship. It's allowed us the time to process and to focus on ourselves. Not to mention our relationships. From what Brynn has told me, Gregg and Macy have progressed at a super fast pace—which never surprised me, those two were bound to end up together.

Brynn is the first to break the silence. "Chinese and romcoms?"

Macy looks at me from the corner of her eyes. She's waiting for me to make the decision.

"Look, I appreciate you coming over..." Macy's face falls at my words. "...and I appreciate your apology. Right now, we aren't the same. Things aren't just going to go back to how they were before you moved out. But I miss you too. We only have another year left together before who knows where we all end up. Brynn will end up wherever Quinton gets drafted, I'll probably end up back in Dallas, and you'll end up wherever the fashion industry takes you."

"Bitch, please, you'll go wherever Cody goes," Brynn chimes in with a smirk.

"Hopefully, New York," Macy mumbles. Our heads snap in her direction. "I have a fashion design competition, and the winner goes to New York for an internship."

"Macy, that's incredible!" I shout, and I really am happy for her. "See this is the point I'm trying to make. We don't know where our futures are going to take us, and I'd rather focus on making the most of our time together. No more secrets, okay?"

Everyone's eyes bounce to each other, and we all give a nod. "Macy, you pick the movie. Chloe, you figure out the cocktails. I'll order Chinese."

"You know I had no desire to ever be a cheerleader, but there's just something about watching these *Bring It On* movies that makes me want to fling pompoms in the air." Brynn points her fork toward the TV where *Bring It On: Again* is playing.

"I couldn't agree more." I nestle into my pillows from my spot on the couch.

"Chloe, I could totally picture you being on the cheer team. You just ooze pep, and all your feminine energy would be perfect for a squad," Macy says from where she's lounging on the opposite end of the couch.

"Not popular, remember?"

"Yeah, yeah, yeah," Brynn muses. "Speaking of, how's hot Daddy Scott?"

I can't help the gagging noise that flies out of my mouth as I toss a pillow at my bestie. "Oh my god, Brynn!"

She shrugs. "What? He's hot, and he hasn't been by in like forever."

"I miss Scott's cooking." Macy practically has drool sliding down her face.

"You guys are pathetic. I actually haven't had much time to talk to him. We send more texts back and forth, but he's busy with the restaurants. Did I tell you he's opening a new one in Arizona?"

"Uhh—no!" Brynn shouts, spinning around from her spot on the floor to face us. "Does that mean we get to go on a trip?"

Her hopeful expression has me breaking out in a wide smile.

"He invited us out for an end-of-the-school-year vacation, but..." My words drift off.

How do I tell them that I haven't said anything because of Macy?

The idea of going away made me physically ill because my closest friend and I weren't speaking. I didn't feel like celebrating when a relationship I held near and dear to my heart felt like it had ended. I knew going away with Brynn would've been a great time, but it wouldn't have been the same. Nothing has been the same without Macy in our house, much less in my life.

As I sit here in our living room, sipping on cocktails, and watching our favorite cheesy 2000s rom coms, I'm beyond happy. Will I easily forget what caused our fall out? No, but I so don't think that Macy meant to hurt me. I was just in the wrong place at the wrong time. I can't imagine the emotional tornado she was experiencing, and while it isn't an excuse, I can understand her pain.

When my mom left, I shut down. I was faced with insurmountable bullying when I was at a pivotal age. Instead of defending myself, I sat alone and let the bullies win. As I got older, I never defended myself. I let people think I was the 'dirty' kid who lived in the low-income housing with her crazy dad. Meanwhile,

I might not have lived in the nicest place or had a dad with a normal job, but what they didn't know was how much love our apartment held. It was just the two of us, and we never took each other for granted. Dad created masterpieces for dinner in our tiny apartment. He sang while he cooked, showered me with affection by reading to me every night before bed, and instilled in me the importance of a strong work ethic to achieve what we are passionate about.

I could have let the bullies win, but I never did. Every day I would show up at school with my prettiest dress on and the brightest smile. They could make fun of me all that they wanted, but at the end of the day, I was in control of my emotions.

We all handle our struggles differently. Macy needed to react, and as much as it hurt me to take the brunt of her emotions, after some time, I knew it was just her way of projecting. She was scared and felt like a trapped lion, and I was the zookeeper in her path.

I'm not going to punish her anymore.

"Honestly, I kind of forgot that he had mentioned it. A lot has happened this semester, but if you guys don't have any plans mid-May, we have a suite at the fancy spa resort where he's opening the restaurant."

Macy's posture stiffens at the sound of my voice. Worry lines lace her flawless face, and I want to erase them.

"Macy, I want you to come with us. Seriously, the last couple of months have been hell. I miss you, and it's time to just put the past behind us."

"Do you mean that?"

"Of course I mean it. Dad made the reservation for three, and I can't imagine celebrating my birthday without you."

Without a moment of hesitation, Macy flings her body across the couch and envelops me in a hug. Her arms are wrapped around my neck as she pulls me in tight against her. "I've missed you so much." Her words are muffled in the side of my neck.

"I've missed you too."

Brynn jumps to her feet, her body flying through the air and landing on top of where Macy and I are embraced. "It's about time you bitches worked your shit out!"

We laugh because it's so true.

A vibration goes through us from my cell phone just as there's a knock on the door. "Come in!" Brynn shouts from our pile.

"Brynn! You can't just tell anyone to come in. What if it's a killer?"

"It's probably Q."

"Probably?!" I shriek as footsteps, as in multiple, sound from the doorway.

"What the hell am I interrupting? And can I get in between?" JP asks from above us as Quinton chuckles. JP is a beast of a defensive back on the football team. He's also one of Quinton's closest friends—the two are practically attached at the hip.

Brynn slowly climbs off the pile and finds her feet before she makes her way to her boyfriend. Macy is next to climb off me, only she finds her spot on the couch again.

"Sorry, JP, you missed all the fun," Macy purrs seductively. Us girls chuckle. JP is such a horn dog and is always insinuating that the three of us are closer than just friends. He's ridiculous.

"Damn, man. I told you we didn't need to stop for milkshakes." JP pouts as he squeezes his thick thighs in between me and Macy.

Quinton sits in the recliner as Brynn crawls up on his lap. He looks over at us and gives a small smile. "I missed seeing you girls together."

"Thanks, Q. We missed being together." He and I share a knowing smile. I'm beyond happy for him and Brynn. Since the two of them have been dating, it's allowed Quinton and I to get to know each other better. Over the last couple of months, we've had many late-night chats when Brynn was asleep, and I was up for a late-night snack. He knows a lot of my history—my struggles with my mom's abandonment, part of my past with Cody, and how much the rift between Macy and I affected me.

Quinton Boyd is one of the good ones, and I'm glad to call him my friend.

"So what are you watching?" JP muses, digging into the couch and lifting his feet to rest on the coffee table as he pulls some of my blankets off me.

"*Bring It On: Again*. And please take more of my covers." My eyes roll as he does in fact take more of my covers, but I don't mind.

"Oh hell yeah, is it cold in here?"

"No, bro, there's no Toros in the atmosphere."

"Fuck the Toros, give me the Comets. Goddamn, that Gabrielle Union is fine."

I shake my head at JP's attempt at a joke and pull my phone out from the crack of the couch. There's an unread message from Cody. He's checked on me a few times since dropping me off, but I haven't really filled him in.

Cody: How's it going, Wildflower?

Me: Great, actually. Macy and I worked our shit out.

Cody: I'm glad.

Me: Me too.

Cody: I wish you were here though. My pillow smells like you, and I'm missing my girl. It's not fair you got to sleep in my bed without me last night.

Me: It was weird sleeping without you.

Cody: Must not have been that weird, you cuddled my sister.

I shriek at his response, and everyone's heads snap in my direction. My eyes meet theirs, and I shake my head as heat warms my cheeks.

Me: Shut up! I did not!

Cody: You did. Leah gave you shit, but it's all good, babe. I love your cuddles.

Me: *homer Simpson hiding in a bush* GIF

Cody: *laughing emoji* What are you girls getting up to tonight?

Me: Chinese, cocktails, and cheesy 2000s rom coms. We're watching Bring It On: Again. JP & Q just crashed the party, but they brought milkshakes.

Cody: Gabrielle Union is so hot.

Me: *eye rolling emoji*

Cody: Have fun, Wildflower. Call me tomorrow.

Me: Sweet dreams.

CHAPTER 27

CODY

April is here in Texas. The weather is heating up and so is the CTU Eagles baseball team. It's been a remarkable season with a good chance that we will go far in the postseason.

I'm so ready to get to Omaha where the collegiate tournament is held. If we keep dominating the field the way we have been, there's no doubt in my mind we'll be playing through June.

Standing in front of the bathroom mirror, I tousle my hair until it's the perfect messy look. It's early Saturday morning, the team bus leaves in a few hours for a local away game weekend. For the last two weeks, while I've been balancing attending classes, practices, and games, and my time with my girl, I've also been planning out ways to honor the best national holiday—April Fools' Day.

Now luckily for most of my friends, I don't do this every year. The last time I dished out epic pranks was freshman year, and only Hud and Brynn were around to remember that. I'm hoping since I skipped last year that they both were lulled into a false state of security.

Tossing a few outfits into my overnight bag, I run through all my baseball items to make sure I haven't forgotten anything. It's still early enough that I should be the only one who's up in the house. Digging through my closet, I find the hidden bag in the back which is full of my supplies.

Tiptoeing out of my room, I pause for a second, listening for any movement from the guys. When nothing sounds out of the ordinary, I head to the shared bathroom the rest of the guys share.

The bathroom is a moderate-sized space with a combination tub and shower, a single sink with a mirrored vanity above the basin, and of course, the toilet. Reaching inside the shower, I pull out Hudson's shampoo. Bringing the container to the sink, I reach inside my bag for what I'm looking for. Switching out his shampoo, he'll never know what's coming.

Once the bottle is returned to the exact spot he had left it in, I pull out the next item and get to work setting up the next prank. Ten minutes go by, and Niko and Hudson's pranks are set up. Ty's was a little challenging, but I was able to sneak into his room last night to get his set up.

Closing everything in the bathroom and making sure I've left nothing behind, I enter stealth mode as I tiptoe down the stairs. Once I've made my way into the kitchen, I head to the pantry for a package of Pop-Tarts before reaching inside the fridge for a lemon-lime sports drink.

Taking a seat on the island, I pull out my phone and open Instagram. The first picture I see damn near makes my heart stop. My Wildflower. She's laying on her side, body propped up by her elbow, dressed in a white tank top and short set with lace details and a slit separating her top in two underneath her breasts. She's reading a book with a mug and nail polish on the bed in front of her. Her long golden hair is tousled in messy curls that hang down her body. She's breathtaking.

As beautiful as she is, it's the quote underneath her photo that made me pause.

"My light illuminated in his presence because his soul was the one mine had been promised to." —Nicole Fiorina, *Stay With Me*

I knew it was a quote from one of her books. I've learned over the last couple of months that Chloe loves to annotate the words she reads. Luckily, I've witnessed this first hand from when I borrowed her book, but I've watched her whip out a soft case filled with highlighters and sticky tabs. When Chloe reads, she doesn't just skim the words. She absorbs the story and the message behind the black ink.

Chloe Mariano thinks I'm her soulmate. If you would've asked me six months ago if I believed in soulmates, I would've told you no. But now, after being reunited with the girl who stole my heart and got away, I'd say maybe. Maybe there's someone out there for all of us. A lost soul out in the universe searching for its mate.

For so long baseball has been my only love. It's the only love I thought I'd ever have, but something inside of me has changed. I love my pretty Wildflower. She's mine, and I'll stop at nothing to make sure she knows how much she truly means to me.

The squeaky sound of a wooden door opening above has me quickly hitting the like button on her photo. Hitting the lock button on the side of my phone, I reach down and gather up my bags, breakfast, and keys before sneaking out the door.

The boys are in for a real treat.

I guess we all are this morning.

I didn't realize I'd come to the realization that Chloe Mariano is my soul mate, much less surrounded by Pop-Tarts and a sports drink.

From my seat toward the back of the bus, I have the perfect vantage point to watch Chloe. Even though the two of us are dating, she still refuses to sit with me. Something about not wanting to be a distraction. She's probably right. I don't think I'd be able to keep my hands off her if she were sitting next to me, especially not on longer trips. Just the image of her sitting next to me in those tiny dresses I could so easily trail my fingers under has me squirming in my seat, trying not to get hard right here.

Yeah, the separation is a good idea. I still don't like that Billings sits with her, and she's constantly using his shoulder as a pillow. But I know nothing is going on between the two of them.

Speaking of Chloe, I can see the top of her blond hair as she climbs onto the bus. Since I was busy running around playing pranks this morning, I knew there was no way I'd have enough time to pick her up. She had Brynn drop her off, which ended up being perfect since the line at the coffee shop was longer than normal. Clearly, every student at CTU needed a caffeine fix this morning.

She effortlessly glides down the aisle, shoulders held back, with her mesmerizing smile spread across her face.

I can't help but appreciate how much she's changed in the last few months. She hasn't changed in a bad way, just in a way that makes her more confident. Her first time on the bus, Chloe's shoulders sunk forward as she fought to not draw any attention to herself.

Unfortunately for her, she had every guy on the bus watching her. Chloe just draws everyone to her with her sunny aura. It's impossible to ignore her.

Before she sits in her seat, her eyes find mine, and I give her a wink as she gives me the sweetest smile in return.

Chloe slides down in her leather seat, and I can only assume she's going through the little goodie bag which was left on her seat. I watch as her head turns back toward my direction; however, I'm pretending to be busy on my phone. I can see her out of the corner of my eye, and I take in the smile lines that are crinkled around her eyes as a bright smile fills her face.

Please don't hate me after this.

The sound of a bag rustling fills the near-empty bus as more guys continue to climb on. Hudson is next to step on, and I can't help the burst of laughter that erupts from my core.

"Are you fucking kidding me, Jacobs?" Hudson yells as he charges down the aisle. At the sound of his voice, the guys who were on the bus but not paying any attention all cackle at Hudson as he makes his way to my row. Chloe gasps at the sight of his blond hair now dyed bright vibrant pink. "You're dead, dickhead."

"But pink is your color."

"Fuck you and your April Fools' pranks. You nearly gave Niko a heart attack with the taped clown in the vanity."

Hudson's busy filling me in on the events at the house this morning which I avoided happily. He's mid-sentence when a shriek fills the bus and all heads—including the coaches—whip to Chloe's seat. Her arms are flailing as she stands, rushing up the aisle before spitting the contents of her mouth into the trash can.

She turns, wiping the corner of her mouth as her deadly glare finds mine. "Really?" she screams. "Toothpaste in the Oreos. Are you five?"

I watch as Chloe marches to her seat, reaching down and picking up the coffee that was waiting for her. She blows air through the small opening before taking a sip. Disgust mars her pretty face as she stomps her sweet ass toward me.

"And black coffee? Are you trying to piss me off?"

"You're not the only one he's trying to piss off," Hudson mumbles from beside me.

"April Fools," I say sheepishly, a smile spreading wide.

"I hate pranks." Chloe shoves the black coffee into my chest. I'm lucky the force didn't have the cardboard cup crumbling and spilling hot coffee down my chest.

Grabbing the takeaway cup from my tray, I hand it to her. "It's a honey lavender latte, I promise."

She eyes me skeptically, and I can't say I blame her. I pop the lid off so she can see that it is in fact her drink order, latte art included.

"Thanks," she grumbles, taking the drink from me and turning on her heels not sparing me another word.

Hudson's chuckle gains my attention. "What?"

"Pissing off your girlfriend, you are a dumb ass."

"Oh please, it was just a small prank."

"Yeah, well she holds the power of the pussy, and you just pissed her off. Guess you won't be getting laid anytime soon."

Oh fuck me, maybe he is right.

"Clowns! Out of all the things you could've pranked me with, you just had to choose CLOWNS!" Niko yells as he comes down the aisle. Ty is right behind him, but he's walking at a more leisurely pace. I shrug because his fear of clowns is absolutely ridiculous. So what? I taped a creepy *It*-style clown on the inside of the medicine cabinet so when he opened the door, he came face to face with his favorite creepy character.

Coach Weber is sitting in the front of the bus shaking his head as the guys freak out over the small, minor pranks they faced this morning. Bunch of babies. It's not like I shaved their eyebrows off or caused anyone harm.

Hudson actually pulls off the pink hair. Of course he does—the fucker pulls anything off.

Niko stomps past me before tossing his bag on the empty seat next to his. His frustration radiates off him, while Ty doesn't say anything. He simply sits next to Chloe. She says something to him, and he only shakes his head.

Sliding my headphones in place, I reach inside my pocket and pull out my phone. Thumbing through my apps, I find Spotify and click on my road trip playlist. It's the same playlist I listen to on every road trip. It's filled with classic rock anthems and 90s country. All the songs are made to put you in a good mood while being chill enough to sleep to on the bus. Before I lock my screen, I send Chloe a quick text.

Me: I'm sorry.

Chloe: Not as sorry as you're going to be.

Me: What's that supposed to mean?

Chloe: Guess you'll find out.

With a sigh, I lean my head back and settle in for our drive.

Another "W" was placed next to our name as we won another game. Super happy for the team, but it wasn't a game I was able to pitch. I hate the stupid pitch count rules. I mean, I totally get it and appreciate that the league wants to save our arms from throwing too many pitches in a week. It just sucks to be on the bench.

The only good thing that came from me being on the bench was that I was able to sit back and watch Chloe work her magic. The guys treat her like she's one of us. Some of them incorporate special handshakes with her. Or she heads out to the grass to celebrate awesome hits. She tries to hide behind the lens of her camera and say she's getting a shot for the paper, but we all know Chloe likes to be front and center in the action now.

Coach Weber even cracks jokes with her or makes fun of her so-called celebration dances.

The morale this season is like nothing I've ever seen before. I've never played for a team where the players gel together so seamlessly. I think our camaraderie is why we are playing so strongly and have a great chance of making it to Omaha—where the tournament ends with a national title game.

Coach gave us the night off, which is how all of us ended up at a local sports bar.

"Okay," Chloe starts, a pint glass in her hand as she points to where I'm sitting across from her. "We all know their walk-up songs, but since you don't get to hit, I've been curious what you would choose."

Baseball walk-up songs only last around thirty seconds before a batter takes home plate. It's a song that can get them hyped, calm them down, or just get the crowd entertained about what's to come. Some guys like to choose fun songs while others choose classics or even current hits.

Tapping my finger against my chin while holding my own pint of beer. I stare at the woman in front of me. Her pretty blue eyes are a little droopy from the alcohol consumption. She's still as pretty as ever.

"'Kickstart My Heart' by Motley Crue. Especially since I've got my girl. It'd be the perfect reminder as I walked up to the plate."

Her cheeks flame while Niko, Ty, and Hudson all make a gagging noise. It is just the five of us at a table while the rest of the guys filter around the space chatting up girls, throwing darts, or casually drinking.

"Oh, like your walk up is any better. Mine would be a classic!" I leaned forward, straightening my back as if I was preparing for battle...battle over the walk-up songs.

Hudson tsks as he folds his arms across his chest. "No, a classic is 'Party In the USA,' which is why I picked it."

My eyes roll as Niko laughs. "Nah bro, 'Party in the USA' is meant to be for batters who drop bombs."

"Fuck you, Niko." Hudson has been in a slump over the last couple of weeks, and we can't figure out what the problem is. Typically he's our number one hitter, but not right now. And Niko digging at him is just going to piss Hud off even more.

Niko raises his hand in defense before taking a pull out of his bottled Mexican beer.

"Yours is a song where no one understands the lyrics," Ty adds while he taps the table with his coaster. It's a habit he has. One that gets old after a while, especially in a quiet bar. Thankfully, this place is not quiet. At least it hasn't been since the baseball team showed up.

"It's not my fault you don't know good music when it's right in front of you."

Ty stops tapping the coaster and points it in Niko's direction. "Hey, I'm not saying it's not good, but not all of us grew up in Southern Cali."

I shake my head as the guys fight over who has the better song: Ty's "Boombastic," Niko's "Titi Me Pregunto," or Hud's "Party in the USA." My eyes find Chloe who's staring right back at me. A smirk is on her lips as she chews on her bottom lip. I watch as her eyes bounce from guy to guy.

She's enjoying the show. The show which she started. I squint my eyes as I observe her. If I didn't know any better, I'd say she knew her conversation would cause a fight between the guys.

"Wildflower?"

Her attention snaps my way as the guys stop talking.

"You knew this was going to happen, didn't you?"

Her shoulders shrug as my head shakes. Troublemaker.

"Alright." Bringing my elbows to the table, I rest my head on my hands as I steeple my fingers deep in thought. "What would your walk-up song be?"

She points to herself, and I quirk my eyebrow. It's funny how she's buying time as if she didn't know that this question was going to come back to her. The guys all take drinks of their beers filling the time.

A slow smile spreads across her face as she answers with a flip of her wrist, "'Fireman' by Lil Wayne, duh."

The table erupts in chortles. Hudson spews his beer across the table. I clutch my stomach as I watch my girl bring her hands up, placing one behind her head as she breaks out in the sprinkler dance moves.

Chloe raps a popular line from the chorus while she continues to do the sprinkler.

The heart that I thought would never love anything besides baseball, warms at the goofy blonde across from me. Gone is the shy girl, in her wake is a confident, adorable woman.

"God, I love you." The words slip out of my mouth with a laugh.

Silence falls over the table as three heads whip in my direction, while Chloe's eyes nearly bug out of her head. I cannot believe I chose this moment to let those words slip. Sure, I've been thinking of saying those three words, but the time has never felt right. Not that the timing is right in this dark sports bar surrounded by my teammates, but it happened.

"What did you say?" Her voice is barely above a whisper.

There are two options I can play. Either pretend those words didn't escape my mouth, which will be hard since I have three additional witnesses, or I can own the moment. Own the fact that I said I love you first because I've loved this girl since I walked into Marnie's Diner almost three years ago. She stood in a peach-colored waitressing uniform, as she tried to tamp down her nerves. She was—still is—the most beautiful girl I've ever laid my eyes on.

Chloe Mariano has owned my heart and soul for as long as I can remember. I was naïve in thinking that we'd never work out. That our past was too damaged for either of us to come back from. That baseball would be my only love. It turns out baseball was just a filler until we both were smart enough to see what's been in front of us this whole time.

"I said, 'I love you.'"

She tucks her plump bottom lip into her mouth as her teeth nibble on her lip in the nervous habit that I love so much. God, there goes that love word. Clearly, it's the only thing I have on my brain. Well, that and me being the one nibbling on her lip, down her neck, her perfect tits, and her—

The sound of a chair grating across the floor jerks my head out of my thoughts. My eyes follow Chloe as she slides off her seat, and slides behind Niko until she's standing right beside me. Her arms fly around my neck, her hand pulling my head toward hers. Our lips collide in a rush. Chloe flicks her tongue against my lips, and I grant her the access she's so desperate for. Our tongues tangle in the middle of the sports bar in front of my friends—our friends.

Pulling away breathlessly, our foreheads rest against each other as I watch Chloe's chest heave and her cheeks tinge my favorite shade of pink. "I love you, too."

Shouts and cheers ring out around us as our friends celebrate our love. Her smile is blinding as I pull her into my side—her standing next to me with my arm wrapped around her shoulders.

"I think it's time to head back to the hotel, boys." Hudson slides out of his chair while Niko and Ty chug the rest of their beers. All five of us have had more than we normally do the night before a game, but not too much.

The walk back to the hotel is a challenge. My Wildflower stumbles over her feet every few steps. It is like she has two left feet. Our grump, Niko, laughed like a schoolgirl the whole walk back. I don't even know what had him laughing so hard, but it caused the rest of us to lose it.

Stumbling into the lobby of the hotel, we make our way to the elevators. Tapping the button to call the car, I watch as Ty collapses onto the ground. His long, six-foot frame takes up most of the space. Niko's leaning against the wall. And somewhere along our journey home, I ended up with Chloe on my back. There's no way she would've made it home before sun up.

"Thanks for tonight, guys." Chloe's words mumble into my shoulder where she rests her head.

"Anytime, Chloe girl," Niko says from where he's leaning against the wall waiting for our elevator to open.

Tonight was a night full of love, laughter, selfies—thanks, Chloe—and memories. They say people come into your life when you need them the most, and I couldn't agree more. I didn't think the night could get any better.

"What the fuck?" I chuckle as I take in the hotel room I'm sharing with Hudson.

He steps in behind me.Chloe's still on my back. Everyone chuckles at the scene we are witnessing. "Dude, who did this?"

"I have no idea." I shake my head as Chloe slides down my back. She's like a newborn baby giraffe learning to balance on fresh legs. After a few stumbling steps, she finds Hudson's bed where she sprawls out watching me take in our room.

While we were out tonight, someone got into our room and wrapped all of my stuff in plastic wrap. The comforter was secured tightly to the bed with the pillows wrapped underneath the plastic. The black suitcase I had propped on a chair was now plastered to it. Hell, even my charger was wrapped to the nightstand. Whoever had done this had spent quite some time perfecting this prank. As the unofficial CTU prankster, I can't help but admire the handiwork.

Stepping over to my baseball bag, I unzipped the bag to find that my cleats and glove were individually wrapped in plastic. But that's not what made me pause. It was a note taped to my cleats.

Nice try, kid.

You better be rested and ready for tomorrow.

-CW, the OG CTU prankster

A laugh rumbles in my chest. Tucking the note back in my bag, I find a half-sleeping Chloe. Reaching down, I slide my hands underneath her as I fireman carry—which is oh so fitting for tonight—her to her room.

The mess can wait until tomorrow, tonight I'm curling up with the girl I love.

CHAPTER 28

Chloe

"**B**E PREPARED FOR OUR LAST EXAM ON MONDAY. We'll be covering all the chapters we've been discussing for the last six weeks. This is the last exam before finals. Some of you will need to do really well on this exam in order to make life easier come finals." The professor of my Seminar in Online Journalism class says from her podium.

Closing the cover of my iPad, I gather all of the items I used during class today and shove them in my backpack. Sighing out a deep breath, I make my way down the row and follow the line of students exiting the room.

This semester has been a challenge juggling coursework, the baseball schedule, writing and editing articles for The Eagle Gazette, and trying to maintain some kind of self-care routine.

Is the self-care necessary? For most, no. But for someone who enjoys her peace after a day filled with "peopling," taking time to myself to recharge is a must. It wasn't bad at the beginning of the semester since Cody and I weren't getting along. After games, I'd stay in with a book and take out, and depending on the hotel, a hot bath, while the team went out and did whatever they did.

But now my free time has been spent with Cody. I'm not complaining about it because I'd take my days with Cody over the last two years of pain and avoidance, but I miss time for myself.

Walking across the quad, I decide I need a latte to fuel me through the rest of my classes. It's only a little after nine, and I have a full day. The baseball team has an away game tonight, and the bus leaves at noon since it's a semi-local away game.

My mind is reeling with how I'm going to find time in the next couple of days to study for this exam. A road game tonight, nothing tomorrow, and another weekend full of baseball from Friday through Sunday. Thankfully we only have three more weeks of classes, but I need to pass all of my classes to stay on track for next year.

Scanning the crowd, I take in the groups of people making their way to the brick buildings where classes are held. Groups of girls are lying on blankets in the sun drawing attention from everyone passing by. Tulips are blooming in the flower beds. Their vibrant colors are a pretty contrast to the dark mulch that lies in the beds. Birds chirp and fly from branch to branch.

As I continue my perusal of people through the quad, my eyes snag on something—or someone—leaning against a large tree. Long legs stick out from under khaki shorts. A muscular chest is covered by a powder blue CTU tee. A baseball cap covers his face, but I know those legs and that chest anywhere.

Side-stepping a couple walking hand in hand, I beeline through the grass to the lone guy resting in the shade.

"Hey, handsome." I slide down the tree next to him and watch his face morph into his signature cocky smirk.

"Wildflower." His voice drawls sleepily as he fixes his hat which was covering his face.

Sitting next to him with my legs crossed in front of me to

keep the skirt of my dress from exposing the goods, Cody wraps his arm around me and pulls me into his chest. My back is to his front as his lips find the top of my head.

"What are you doing over here?"

"I needed some time to myself before the bus left."

Leaning up on my elbow, I look up and take in his face. His perfectly chiseled jawline has a light dusting of facial hair. Cody's face is always clean-shaven. I can count on one hand the times I've seen any hint of a five o'clock shadow. It's then I notice the dark circles hanging out under his eyes. "Everything okay?"

He smiles down at me. Only it's not his usual smile. This one doesn't reach his eyes. "Yeah, babe."

"Are we lying to each other now?"

"Everything's fine. My body is just feeling it right now. I have a meeting with Coach Weber tomorrow to talk about what's to come, and I'm just feeling the season on top of everything. Nothing for you to worry about." He leans down and kisses my forehead.

"I'm always here if you need anything."

He hums. "Have time to just sit with me?"

Glancing down at my watch, I nod at Cody with a small sigh. "I have some time."

"Are you okay?"

"Yeah, I just don't know how you balance everything. I'm feeling so overwhelmed with assignments, travel, and classes, and I feel like I haven't checked in with myself lately."

"It's a lot. If it weren't for the mandatory study tables, I probably would be way behind on assignments. There's nothing like being forced to do school work to give you the kick in the ass."

"Yeah, I bet that helps. I'm honestly thinking about skipping the game tonight. Would you be mad if I missed a game? I know you're supposed to be pitching tonight."

Cody moves so that he's facing me. I watch as he brings his hand to my face, tilting my chin until we are looking at each other. "I will never be mad at you for prioritizing yourself. Just because we are together doesn't mean you can't focus on yourself. I'll always be here, and I always want you around, but not at the expense of losing who you are."

"Thank you." My voice is quiet as embarrassment laces my face.

"You don't have to thank me. I love you, Wildflower. I love everything that makes you, you. Don't forget to take care of my girl."

"I love you too."

Leaning down he gives me a quick kiss. "Great. Now that we've got that out of the way, lay down here, make yourself comfortable, and pull out the book you have burning a hole in your bag. Read with me while I watch you."

My nose scrunches. "Ugh, I didn't mean for that to come out as creepy as it did. You read, and I'll rest my eyes."

That's exactly what we do for the next hour. When we both separated to go our own way—me to the newsroom and him to the bus—I felt like a weight had been lifted from my shoulders. I didn't know how badly I needed to hear the words that it was okay to prioritize myself. Of course, I know I didn't need Cody's approval on how I spend my time, but I know how important it is to have someone cheering for you. If he needs support in the stands, I want to know so I can be there for him. Especially knowing that his dad will text-bomb him leading up to the game.

I'll never understand how parents can be so cruel to their kids. How can someone fill their kid with negative thoughts? Let alone how can someone just abandon the child they helped create?

I don't know if kids are in my cards, but if I decide to have kids, I want to make sure they know how much they are loved.

How supported they are. How proud I am of them. I want to be their biggest cheerleader. Their shoulder to cry on. I want them to know that they are my reason and that everything I do in life is to better theirs. But that's a conversation for another day.

The alarm on my phone goes off, pulling me out of the mindless state of studying I've found myself in most of the evening. Tipping my head side to side, I welcome the pull of muscles and the small cracks of my neck as I ease some of the tension that has been building from the awkward position I'd been studying in.

Switching off my alarm, I reach for the remote and thumb through the channels until I find the baseball game. As much as I need my attention to be on the textbook in front of me as I prepare for my ethics exam, I want the distraction of the announcers as they call the baseball game. I might not be able to be in the stands, but I can root for the boys here at home.

Settling back onto the couch, I turn back to the textbook in front of me as I continue my reading while listening to the announcers talk. It's not until I hear Cody's name that I turn my full attention to the TV. A photo of him from the team picture flashes across the TV as the commentators discuss his stats and his projections for the pros.

Dread seeps into my stomach at the thought of him leaving college early. It's a selfish feeling and one that I shouldn't have, but I'm human. And I finally understand the nervous energy that radiates off Brynn when people discuss Quinton's future. Quinton has already announced he isn't coming back for his senior year and that he's entered the NFL draft. She has the answers for what her last year at CTU will look like, and it won't be with Quinton.

Will Cody choose the same journey?

Earlier today, he said he has a meeting with Coach Weber tomorrow about his future. As excited as I am for the two of us being together, I feel like we jumped straight into the deep end. Since I travel with the team, the two of us spend an obscene amount of time together, but neither one of us has had the harder conversations. Hell, I don't even know how much he wants to go to the big league. I know he's talked about it, but sometimes when he talks, it feels like it's just a requirement for him. Like it's the next step that he has to take.

Shaking the thoughts from my head, I promise myself that the next time the two of us are alone, we need to talk about what's next. It isn't me wanting to push the conversation of what's next in our relationship. I'm in no way ready for engagements or moving in together. I feel like the two of us just stopped hating each other. But what's next for each of us?

Next year I'll have to find an internship that could keep me local, or I could see myself finishing my semester remotely depending on where I get the chance to write. If I follow the path to where my dream career could lead me, my options would have me leaving Texas and going to someplace like New York.

Why do all the major corporations have to be in New York or California?

Why can't there be awesome opportunities in Texas or even the Midwest?

Tossing my textbook on the coffee table, I reach behind me and pull down the throw blanket which is resting on the top of the couch. My brain is too chaotic to focus on the words I'm supposed to be digesting. I'll just watch a few innings and get back to it.

Some time later, the incessant sound of buzzing on my chest has me fumbling for my phone. At some point during tonight's game, I must've dozed off. Clearly, my eyes had grown tired from the day of studying and worrying my brain found itself in.

Glancing at the screen, I see Cody's name and a candid picture I took of him at the Union. He's leaning back in his chair, arms in front of him, a black T-shirt stretched tight across his muscular chest and biceps, and of course, he's wearing his hat backward. Seeing him in his hat backward sends tingles down my body. My boyfriend is sexy.

Swiping the screen, I accept the call and hit the speaker button.

"He-hello?" My sleep-ridden voice cracks.

"Wildflower?" Cody's voice is riddled with concern. "Shit, baby. Are you okay?"

"Ye-yeah. I must've fallen asleep."

A deep exhale fills my ears. Leaning up from the awkward position I fell asleep in, I glance at the time on my phone and see that it's after 11:30. Shit, I must've been asleep for a couple of hours. The game started at 7, and I remember watching the first inning. Oh my gosh, was that all I saw?

"I'm just glad you're okay. I sent you a few texts, and you didn't respond. I uh-I got a little worried."

"Thanks for checking on me. I'm sorry, I think I only saw the first inning of your game."

He chuckles. "It's fine, Chloe. You weren't kidding when you said you were running on empty."

"No, I wasn't. How was your game?"

"It was good. We won five to one." There's a pause on his end of the phone, and I hear a door open as Hudson's voice starts. "Hey, Wildflower? I'm gonna go grab a shower."

"No problem. Text me after if you want?"

"Yeah, babe."

"Talk to you in a—"

"I love you, Chloe."

"I love you, too."

The call ends as my heart warms. How can three words pack

such a powerful punch? And how did Cody and I get here? It feels like yesterday we were avoiding each other, but at the same time, it feels like he's owned my heart for as long as I can remember.

Turning off the TV, I gather all of my textbooks before standing. Twisting my body from side to side, I welcome the cracks that erupt down my back as my body reacts to being in this weird position for the last three hours. Shutting off the lamp, I make my way up the stairs to my bedroom.

Those three little words keep ringing in my head as I drift up the stairs and step foot inside my room. The space inside our townhouse, which I've made into my own sanctuary, feels empty tonight. For so many weeks, Cody and I have spent days in between games together, nights curled up in each other's embrace, and even on those days before we were an us, he was just on the other side of the wall.

Slipping out of my clothes, I rummage through piles of clean laundry I've been meaning to put away until I find the oversized tee I've found myself wearing to bed on so many nights. Biting on the corner of my lip, I fight the smile that wants to break free and spread across my face.

Who am I kidding? I let the smile break free as I toss myself on top of my covers. Breaking out in a giddy dance, arms flying and legs kicking, I let the warmth spread throughout my veins.

Love is such a powerful feeling. It's a four-letter word filled with so many emotions.

Being in love is scary. It's trusting someone to guard your most powerful asset. To hold such a vital part of your being in the palm of their hand and hope to god they don't crush it along the way.

Love is joyful. It leaves you with this endless feeling of giddiness. Of kicking your feet together and squealing. Someone in this world loves you for who you are. The good, the bad, and the downright damaged.

Love is singing in the rain. When the world feels like too much weight is piling on your shoulders, love reaches in and gives you a hand to carry your burdens.

Love is the energy radiating from the sun, seeping into our souls. It's the energy our souls crave in order to allow us to flourish in this world full of challenges and struggles our inner demons possess us with.

A chime from my phone interrupts my inner ramblings.

Cody: What are you wearing? *wink*

Sitting up, I turn on my bedside lamp. Deciding to turn things up a notch, I lean up on my knees as I twist the long T-shirt in my opposite hand, working it up until more thigh is revealed. With my hand holding the phone, I raise it in the air before swiping the front-facing camera on. Biting down on my lip, I hope this pose is sexy. I snap the photo and send it to Cody before I give it too much thought. I've never been one to sext, and to be honest, I have no idea what the hell I'm doing.

Cody: Damn, baby. Is that my shirt?

Me: Yep! Wish you were here.

Cody: Me too. That shirt would be on the ground with you naked underneath me.

A small groan leaves my lips as I read over his message. Flashes of the last time we were naked in my bed came pouring back.

Me underneath Cody as he explored every inch of my body. His tongue licking my pussy.

Fingers pressing inside of me.

Curling just right until he hit that magic spot deep inside me.

My legs rub together, seeking out the friction to satiate the burning feeling pooling in my belly.

Cody: Where'd you go, baby? Thinking about the last time I got you alone and naked? My tongue skimming across your creamy skin. Tasting your sweetness.

Trailing my fingers down my body, I lift my shirt exposing my panties before sliding underneath the material. My fingers skim through my lips as I feel how wet I am. I'm needy for his touch, and his dirty words are only fueling the fire that's burning inside me.

Spreading my arousal, I coat my clit and begin rubbing soft circles building the sensation. With the hand that isn't working myself, I type out a quick reply, letting him know what his words are doing to me.

Me: God, Cody. Your words.

Cody: Mmm, I can almost taste you from here. Is my girl touching herself? Using her favorite purple friend?

Cody: Go ahead, baby. Reach inside your drawer and grab your purple vibrator. Turn it on, and put it on your clit. Work yourself up, and imagine it's for me.

Setting my phone aside, I do as he says and reach inside my drawer and grab my vibrator. Slipping my panties down, I kick them off as I spread my legs wide to give myself better access. With a click of a button, the soft whir of the vibrator fills the air as I bring it to my throbbing clit.

Me: Feels so good.

Cody: That's my good girl. Slide up and down, spread those pretty lips, and coat yourself in your slickness.

The sounds of my moans and the vibrator fill the room as I work myself with my toy. The sensation in my lower belly builds, and I need more. Before I have a chance to set my phone down, it buzzes in my hand.

Cody: Now let's have some more fun. Set the phone aside and play with those perfect nipples. Twist them, pull on them, pretend my lips are around you sucking and biting as you slide that vibrator inside that tight pussy of yours. Feel yourself suck the toy in as you fuck yourself.

Me: I could come from your words alone.

Cody: Good girl. Now set the phone down, and do as I say.

And that's exactly what I do. His words elicit an electric shock through my body which only fuels my bravery. Slipping the vibrating toy inside me, I moan at the sensation. Adjusting the toy, I make sure the little attachment is still vibrating against my clit while it works me from the inside.

It feels so fucking good.

Since the room is dark, I test the confidence I'm feeling by lifting the phone in the air as I raise my shirt higher. With my other hand, I slip it underneath the threadbare material and work my pebbled peaks.

That feeling coils in my stomach, and I'm almost to the point of release. Clicking the button on my phone as I record myself getting off from his dirty words and my hands.

Arching my back, I pinch my nipple harder, squirming on my soft sheets. The feeling pushes my senses, and I'm there. With one final twist, I'm coming.

Screaming out my release, I slip my hand from my breast and move it toward my purple toy. I work the vibrating plastic as I ride out my orgasm. Chest heaving, breaths heavy, I come down from one of the best orgasms I've given myself. Hitting the camera button, I end the video and send it before I have a chance to talk myself out of it.

A few minutes pass as I clean myself up and crawl back underneath my covers. Plugging my phone into the charger, it buzzes on my nightstand. I smile at the two words on my screen.

Cody: Fuck. Me.

Me: Goodnight.

Rolling over, I fall asleep with a satiated smile on my face.

CHAPTER 29

CODY

WAKING UP THIS MORNING, I'VE NEVER BEEN more eager to get back to CTU than I am right now. I've been wound up since last night's late-night texting session with Chloe. Images of her sprawled out on her bed, chest heaving, her favorite purple toy between her legs, had me desperate to get home and taste that sweet pussy I haven't been able to get out of my head. And that damn video she sent. *Fuck me.*

I never realized how hot it was to help get her off through words on a screen. The problem was I was unable to palm my rock-hard erection and rub one out with her. Hudson and I have grown very close over the years, but not close enough for me to jack off with him sleeping feet away.

Thankfully, he sleeps like the dead and had no idea what my thumbs were typing out to my girl miles away.

The bus pulls into campus later than we were expecting, which means half the team only has thirty minutes to get to the library for our mandatory weekly study tables. As much as my bed is calling my name, I'm behind on assignments, and with only three weeks of school left, I can't risk falling behind.

Rushing down the steps and off the bus, I head toward the side of the bus where the equipment team is unloading bags.

Thirty minutes later, I'm freshly showered and rushing into the Benjamin Liberty Library to get to my study session on time. Each player has a mandatory study session at the library that works in their schedules. The university enforces it to make sure that all student athletes are getting their assignments done in between games.

It was hard to not drop to my bed that was calling my name and take a nice long nap. But the quicker I get this session over with, the quicker I can be getting to see my girl.

Jogging up the stairs to the third floor where all of the private study rooms are located, my eyes scan to the open floor plan below the steps. Long rectangles are gathered in the center while rows of books span the border of the room. A large desk sits in the center, welcoming students. It's not the expansive woodwork that has my eyes bouncing back, it's the messy bun of honey-blond hair and a pastel purple sweater that has my eyes pausing.

Down below amid students is my Wildflower. Even in a room filled with people, it's like she calls out to me. My body is always aware of her presence. With one last glance, I finish climbing the flight of stairs.

Entering the beige room that feels more like a prison cell than a welcoming place to study, I take the last seat available.

"Cutting it a bit close, Mr. Jacobs," the library attendant addresses me. Each week a member of the library staff sits in our two-hour-long session to ensure we are all using the time block to our advantage. Nothing like being a junior in college and needing a babysitter.

Without acknowledging her, I sit down, pulling out my

textbooks. Hudson meets my gaze across the way. He raised an eyebrow asking me if everything was okay.

Giving him a tight nod, I start reading over the chapters for my psych class.

It's not long before my mind starts drifting to everything it can imagine besides the material I need to be learning.

Coach Weber moved our meeting to tomorrow since we got back too late to chat before study tables. I have a feeling he's going to give me an update on what the scouts are saying. I've been pitching exceptionally, especially after almost losing it all with the elbow injury last season. There's a chance I will be given an early offer.

But I don't think I want that. For years, the goal has always been to get to the major league. To prove to my dad that I could do it, even though he couldn't.

I placed so much pressure on myself with his constant mind games of telling me I'm not strong enough, talented enough, or good enough. Baseball has always been my way to get out of his house, to find something productive to do with my time so that I wasn't spending extra time under his roof with the drunken words he'd spew at us. I realized somewhere along the way that I had a natural talent for the game.

The natural progression was to aim for a scholarship at a university far enough away from Georgia. Once I was accepted at CTU, it only made sense to focus on a new goal. And that goal was playing professionally.

But now there's Chloe to factor into the equation.

Until this year, I was never a guy to consider changing the course of my life over a girl. But that was before Chloe. Because she stole my heart. And now I can't stand the thought of not getting to see her. It may not happen every day, but as often as I can.

There's a part of me that doesn't want to leave her behind. Not only with the idea of leaving college early, but there's also the training camps and traveling for away games where I'll be gone more often than not. And who knows where she will end up after she graduates? Chloe's talented with her words, her cooking, hell, everything she sets her mind to. She might end up needing to be in a big city where the large magazines are headquartered. While most major cities in the United States have a major league baseball team, who's to say I'll end up in the same one? I could be in LA while she's in NY. Or Toronto while she's in Chicago. Do I really want to spend the next however many years separated?

And I know I'm jumping the gun. This relationship is fresh, but I do not doubt that Chloe and I are endgame. I don't believe we were put in each other's path again without being destined for something bigger.

Chloe Mariano has stolen my heart, and one day, I hope she steals my last name.

I'm lost in thought when a balled-up piece of paper smacks me in the head. Glancing up, I find Hudson smirking back at me. Creases form between my eyes as I give him a quizzical expression. He chuckles. "Dude, the session is over. Where the hell were you for the last two hours?"

Looking around the room, I see that some of the guys have already cleared out. Where the hell was I? Did I seriously just space out for two hours?

"That two hours flew by."

"Well, yeah. Your head was in the clouds the entire session. Please tell me you were at least daydreaming about Chloe?"

"Yeah. I was thinking about her and the big leagues and everything in between."

"Bro, you're going to turn yourself gray with all that worrying. Stop stressing and let's just enjoy this season. You've shaped up to be a helluva captain. The underclassmen are thriving this year, and it has to do with you. Your energy is contagious on the field."

"Thanks, man."

"Now, go get your girl." His head nods in the direction of where Chloe is still sitting at the table. I have no idea how long she's been here, but knowing Chloe, she's due for a break. And I'm due for some one-on-one time with my girl.

Closing the distance between her and me, I sit down opposite her. She doesn't even acknowledge that someone is sitting across from her. Typical Chloe, lost in her head.

Clearing my throat, I try to get her attention. Her body flinches at the disruption. Slowly, she turns her head and faces me. Eyes widening, I watch as my favorite smile spreads across her beautiful face.

"Hey, beautiful."

"Hey, handsome."

"C'mon." I stand, rounding the table until I'm standing directly beside her. I watch her as her face scrunches in the adorable way that I've gotten used to watching over the years.

"Wh-what?"

"C'mon," I stretch my hand out and wait for her.

"Cody, I've got to study."

"I know, and you will, but right now I need my girl, and my mind is telling me that my girl needs a break."

She sighs, and I watch her shoulders deflate, some of that tension is leaving her body. "Yeah, I've been here since nine thirty."

My eyes widen at her admission. "Chloe, it's two o'clock. Have you at least stopped to eat?"

Sheepishly, she pulls her bottom lip in her mouth and nibbles on it. It's adorable and a habit she's had for years. The worrying of her bottom lip is the only answer I need.

"Alright, we are definitely leaving this library right now." I stand patiently while she gathers her notebook, textbooks, and iPad. Chloe will always look beautiful to me, but right now, my girl looks utterly exhausted. I knew she was pushing things too hard when she fell asleep after the first inning of our game last night. I should have let her go back to sleep once I knew she was okay, but I was selfish and wanted to keep texting her.

"Did you walk or drive?"

"I walked."

"Okay, I parked in the lot by the Union. Want to go back to your house?"

"Please."

With my arm wrapped around her shoulders, the two of us weave through bodies as we make our way to the parking lot. As soon as we get inside, Chloe's body sags in her seat, her head finds the window, and it stays there the whole way to her townhouse.

A second wind must have hit her somewhere along our walk from my truck to her front door because as soon as we cleared the threshold, Chloe's tossing her backpack and keys to the ground.

Her arms fling around my neck, nearly knocking me over, as her lips crash into mine. She laps at the seam of my lips, and I open allowing her tongue access. The two of us make out in front of her door like horny teenagers.

Hands roaming over every indent and curve. Her fingers slide underneath my shirt as her nails graze over the indents of my abs before she pushes my shirt up. Our lips separate long enough for her to rip my shirt over my head. My blood rushes to my dick, and I do not doubt that Chloe can feel how worked up I am against her stomach. My body is desperate for a release—one I didn't have enough time to give myself this morning in the shower. As tired as I am, my body is alive with the promise of what's to come.

"Take me to bed," Chloe murmurs against my lips.

Without hesitating, my hands slide down her back and below her ass. Gripping her, I lift her in the air as her legs wrap around my hips.

I carry her up the stairs, one hand hanging on to the railing, the other under her ass, our lips never separating. My girl is hungry. She's starving for my touch.

I don't stop until I'm laying her down on her perfectly made bed. Too bad for her, the crisp sheets are about to be wrecked.

Chloe relaxes underneath me, melting into my touch, her body molding into mine. Things between us have progressed slowly, which isn't something I'm used to. But for Chloe, I'll do anything she wants. This was a big step for her to admit her feelings and face some of her biggest insecurities, and I've not wanted to push her. I've been waiting for her to give me a sign that she's ready for more between us. And right now, she's giving me all the signals that she's ready to hit all the bases.

Breaking away from her lips, I trail kisses down her jaw, nipping her sweet flesh along her neck. My hands skim up her hips as I pull her sweater up and over her head exposing her white, sheer lace bra.

Sitting up on my knees, I take in my beautiful girl. Hair that resembles the sun is piled high on her head. Her sweet, creamy skin tinged pink from my nips and kisses. Ocean-blue eyes darkened to midnight sky. Chloe's stunning, and she's mine. And also wearing too many clothes.

"Fuck, Wildflower, you look beautiful." I watch as her cheeks flame my favorite shade of pink. Making her blush is my favorite hobby. Before she has a chance to say anything or hide herself from me, I'm leaning forward, my lips finding hers as my hand works the button on her white pants. Of all days she doesn't wear a dress.

As I work her pants and panties down her legs, my mouth finds her pebbled nipple, and I suck the sensitive flesh into my mouth. She groans as she kicks to help me free her from the confines of the pants.

Her legs are freed, and she tries to close the gap, hiding herself from me. My thighs spread to keep her spread for me. "Don't hide that pretty pussy from me, Wildflower. I've been dreaming of seeing her for days."

"Then fuck me already, Cody." Chloe groans from underneath me, her body writhing with my touch.

Pausing briefly, I'm thrown off by the vulgar words escaping my sweet, shy girl.

"So eager. Patience, baby." Her chest heaves from a deep inhale. "I'm not fucking you until you come twice—once on my mouth and once on my fingers."

Her body erupts in a shiver, and I smirk before sliding down her body trailing open mouth kisses in my wake, not stopping until I'm propping my body up on my elbows as my tongue sticks out licking up her wetness. I moan as my tongue finally tastes her again.

I had waited so long to taste her. To touch her. To bring her pleasure. And now that I have, it's all I crave. I'm starving for her. There's no doubt I'm going to savor every second of it. I won't be rushing this moment tonight. Even if my dick is pressing painfully hard against the zipper of my jeans.

A loud moan falls from her lips as I suck her clit into my mouth. Chloe bucks her hips against me, seeking more friction. I can feel how desperate she is to come as she rides my face causing her pleasure to drip down my jaw.

She's close. I can tell by the way her movements quicken as she seeks out her desperate release. I continue licking and lapping, sucking her swollen lips into my mouth as she rides my face, doing whatever I can to help her. With one final lap at her sensitive bud, Chloe is detonating beneath me. Her orgasm hits her hard as she screams out my name.

I don't care if she wakes the whole complex up. I've waited almost three years for this moment. I want the whole damn world to know that Chloe Mariano is mine.

Popping my head up from between her thighs, I find my

girl's eyes. Her chest is heaving, pupils blown wide, and a blissful expression pasted across her face.

"That's one," I say with a smirk before diving back down to my favorite meal.

My tongue licks up her come as she lets out another delicious moan. Sliding my two fingers inside her wet heat, I feel her pussy clench around the digits, greedily taking me. Already swollen from her last orgasm, it won't take her long to come again.

Selfishly, I'm ready for her to come again. I'm ready to slide inside her and feel her pussy wrapped around my dick. I've been desperate to feel her, and now that I've tasted her, I know it's going to feel even better with her molded around my cock.

I pull my fingers out as she lets out a whimper of protest. Pushing them back in, I pull them out again, over and over, until her cries are begging me to fuck her.

"Soon, baby. I need you to come one more time."

I continue pumping in and out of her. Her pussy is soaked, which helps me glide easily in and out of her. Curling my fingers up, I hit that special spot that has her screaming out my name. Her walls tighten around my fingers as she writhes underneath me, seeking out her release. I dive my face back down as I lick up her juices.

I'm starving for her.

Chloe's leg lands on my shoulder as she uses her heel to push me deeper. I moan as the movement presses me harder against her.

"Be a good girl and come for me, Chlo." Her hips quicken at my words. "That's it, Wildflower, ride my face and fuck my fingers."

Her hips buck against my tongue as my nose nuzzles against her clit. I pull away before sucking her bud into my mouth. My teeth bite down as I pump harder, curling my fingers to hit her G-spot.

"Cody!" Chloe screams in pleasure as the orgasm racks through her body. I feel her pussy grip my fingers as her walls pulsate against me.

"Goddamn," I say, licking her release one last time. "I need to be inside you."

My cock is hard as a rock and painfully pressed against my zipper. I'm desperate for her touch and feeling like a teenage boy about to come in my pants.

"What the hell are you waiting for?"

I chuckle, leaning back on my legs, I take her in. Her release coats the inside of her legs and my lips. I slide my fingers out of her before bringing them to my lips to suck clean. Her eyes widen at the gesture, and I smirk before standing to my feet. I make quick work of stripping out of my jeans as I stand before her in only my boxer briefs.

A sharp inhale has my eyes finding her widened ones. "You okay?" I ask as I dig in my wallet for a foil packet. Ripping the wrapper open with my teeth, I slide my boxers down my legs. My cock springs free as precum beads against the tip.

Glancing up, I find Chloe's eyes staring at my dick, and I could come from the attention she's giving me. I've wanted this with Chloe for so long that the little bit of attention she's giving my dick has me ready to explode.

"Yeah," she says, voice breathy from the orgasms. "I just forgot how huge you are."

Smirking up at her, I slide the condom down my shaft as I stroke my hand up and down. "You can take it."

And with a wink, I'm climbing back on top of her. My lips find hers, and she moans at the taste of herself on my tongue. My cock presses against her hot, swollen pussy as I nudge my head through her entrance.

Her legs wrap around my hips as her heels press into my ass cheeks. "Always so eager."

"Please, Cody," she begs as I gently begin rocking my hips, inching my way into her opening. I must be going too slow because she's pressing her heels harder against my ass, pushing me into her until I'm fully inside her.

Both of us moan at the contact.

"I feel so full," she says.

"Damn, Wildflower. You're so goddamn tight."

Fuck. It's never felt this good with anyone else. I knew the wait would be worth it. Chloe Mariano is my undoing. I'll never want anyone else besides this woman. This sweet, sexy, perfect woman. She's my everything.

Slowly, I pull out and slide back inside as I begin rocking my hips. Her walls grip my cock harder, desperate to keep me inside. "Wildflower, I'm not going to last."

"Then don't. Fuck me, Cody. Stop holding back."

Leaning forward, my lips find hers as our tongues tangle. Our hips rock against each other as we get lost in the kiss. I slide further inside her before I stop holding back.

Her legs shake as I begin thrusting inside of her. I can feel her stretch around my cock, and the feeling of her molding herself to me almost has me coming on the spot. There's a connection growing between us. It's the type of connection that she reads about in books. I wonder if she can feel it too. It's as if our hearts are weaving together, tethering ourselves to one another.

I thrust in and out of her, pushing deeper and deeper inside of her. My hands weave into her hair as I pull her face to mine. Needing to kiss her. To feel connected in every way possible.

"You feel so good," I mumble the words against her lips. "Be a good girl and come for me. Come all over my cock, Wildflower. I'm so close, but I need you to come again."

My fingers trail down her body until I'm rubbing tight circles against her already sensitive clit. I suck one of her pebbled peaks into my mouth. Sucking and nipping as I play with her clit.

Her hips rock faster against me as I thrust into her. Feeling my balls tighten as my impending orgasm builds. I need her to come before I detonate.

I feel her pussy tighten against my cock, and I know she's there. I press harder on her clit as I bite down on her nipple. The orgasm rips through her body, and I'm right there with her. Spilling inside the condom as stars explode as my vision blackens as her pussy milks every bit of my orgasm.

"Holy shit," I pant, resting my weight on top of her.

Her chest heaves beneath me. "That's what sex is supposed to feel like?"

"Nah, Wildflower. That's just sex with you. It's never been like that with anyone else."

Her lips find mine as she kisses me with everything she has left. This kiss feels like sunshine after a stormy day. It's fresh, crisp, and full of hope at what's to come.

Absolutely drained, I pull a naked Chloe into my chest and wrap her close to me. I want to spend every night with her curled next to me, creamy bare skin displayed and a sated glow to her skin. Savoring her warmth, I close my eyes and welcome the instant relief of sleep.

It's not long before I'm able to sleep that my body is begging me for hydration. Slipping out of bed is going to be a challenge. Gently, I lift Chloe's arm that is wrapped around my middle as I slide out from underneath her. Once standing, I slide my pillow underneath her arm so that it gives the illusion that I'm still next to her.

Glancing around the room, I find my boxers which are still in my pants from where I dropped them early. I step into my boxers before making my way down the stairs to the kitchen to search for water.

Leaning against their island, I'm chugging a bottle of water when a knock sounds on the door. Figuring it was one of our friends and not wanting to wake Chloe when I'm perfectly capable of answering the door, I unlock the bolt and swing the door open.

Fuck me.

Scott Mariano stands before me dressed in navy dress pants and a light blue button-up. I take in his full 6'3 height, dark auburn brown hair, and black wire-framed glasses, while he does the same to me, and it's in that moment that I wish I would have glanced through the peephole before swinging up the door in nothing but a pair of black boxers.

My heart plunges to my ass as I'm face to face with my girlfriend's dad—for the first time.

Stepping aside, I open the door wider. "Come on in."

"Thanks for inviting me into my daughter's home." His face is stoic as he gives nothing away, moving inside the front door and glancing around.

Clearing my throat, I step backward. My body feels like it's shaking. This is not how I planned on meeting Mr. Mariano. I wasn't sure if we were at the whole meet the parent step, but I definitely wasn't expecting to be meeting him practically naked after fucking his daughter into a post-orgasmic coma.

"Cody?" Chloe questions from the top of the stairs. The two of us break our stare off—well, his stare off and my fight not to cower from his intensity—and turn our heads toward her soft voice.

At the sight of her, my shoulders droop as my eyes snap shut, and my head falls. As beautiful as my girl looks right now in only my shirt, her gorgeous legs on full display, I doubt her dad appreciates her state of undress. It's clear what the two of us had been getting ourselves into.

"Amore Mia," her dad greets, and I hear Chloe gasp as her hands snap to the hem of my shirt, tugging it down trying to gain a few more inches. Unfortunately for her, stretching the material only causes it to tighten against her chest, exposing her nipples against the cotton.

"Hi, Daddy."

I fight to keep the groan which is building in my chest from erupting.

Fuck my life.

CHAPTER 30

Chloe

"A MORE MIA," I GASP AS MY DAD'S VOICE CLIMBS up the stairs which feels like a smack to the face. What the hell is he doing here? Not that I care he stopped by because it's been forever since the two of us have been in the same room at the same time, but of all times it has to be after Cody and I finally had sex.

Oh god, my shirt.

Glancing down, I remember what I'm wearing. Thinking that Cody was alone in the house, I grabbed the first thing I saw which was one of his shirts that I had slept in the night before, sans underwear. Snapping my hands to the hem of the shirt, I try tugging it down to gain a few more inches. While it gives me a couple more inches to make sure I'm not baring myself to my dad, it, unfortunately, stretches the material causing it to tighten against my chest exposing a very detailed image of my nipples pressed against the cotton.

"Hi, Daddy."

Scott's eyes snap to Cody where he takes in his half-dressed appearance, his lips pursing during his perusal before bouncing back to mine where he knows doubt is putting two and two together right now. "Would the two of you please put some clothes on, and we can all cook dinner together?"

Fuck my life.

Cody doesn't hesitate before he's bounding up the stairs. Taking them two at a time to quickly get away from my dad.

Scott Mariano is a fun guy. He loves to joke and make people smile. But he can also be an intimidating asshole. He has to be. In his line of business, being a head chef and restaurateur requires him to put his foot down, letting people know that he's in charge.

The same energy I've witnessed in his kitchen as he yells at chefs for providing mediocre food in his restaurant is the same energy he's directing at my boyfriend. I do not doubt that he's doing it on purpose. Dad knows what happens in college. I'm a testament to what college students do. If I had to guess, he's trying to challenge Cody to see if he can withstand the heat. He wants to make sure Cody's cut out for his favorite daughter. But it won't be long before he's cracking jokes and making Cody feel like he's a part of our little family.

Or I could be completely wrong.

After Cody and I quickly change into our clothes, and I smoothed down my sex-mussed hair by pulling it back up in a messy bun, the two of us enter the kitchen, nervous energy radiating from both of us. I've been wanting Cody to meet my dad but not under these circumstances

While we were changing, Dad set up the kitchen. He must've stopped at the store on his way over because my countertops are piled high with fresh ingredients. I know for a fact that our fridge was looking a little bare.

Standing at the opposite counter, I reach for a knife and begin dicing vegetables to add to the green leaf lettuce I've washed and spun dry. With each cut, I try to listen in to the conversation taking place behind me as Dad is trying to show Cody how to slowly incorporate the flour from the makeshift well where the egg yolks sit inside.

"Nice work, now take the dough and place it on the flour-covered counter," Dad instructs Cody. "The dough is going to feel pretty dry, but as you knead, it'll start to come together and feel smooth."

Glancing over my shoulder, I watch as Cody's strong back flexes and relaxes each time he presses into the dough.

He lets out a frustrated groan. "It's sticking to my fingers."

Poor Cody. I know he enjoys being in the kitchen, but that usually extends only to his Monday meal prepping before the busy week. Otherwise, he's all for ordering a greasy pizza from Cousin Jimmy's.

"That's okay, it happens. You simply need to add a little more flour to the surface." My chest warms as I hear Dad's calm, teaching voice instruct my boyfriend.

Forgetting about my task, I watch my two favorite guys. With a harsh exhale, Cody does as instructed, and I watch as a gleaming, prideful smile spreads across his face as he watches the dough form into the perfect consistency. Dad notices too, and the corner of his lips tip up.

"It's all about patience and staying calm while in the kitchen." Dad's attention turns my way. "Amore Mia, have you not had him in the kitchen with you while you cook?"

"We've been a little busy," I answer as I continue chopping vegetables. I'm not sure why Dad is having him even make pasta, I saw the bag of fresh pasta he must've brought with him.

I watch Dad's eyes squint, glaring daggers to his left where Cody stands wrapping the dough into the plastic wrap to chill. His beaming smile spreads across his face but quickly morphs into a neutral expression when he realizes Dad is eyeing him. "Yes, I see that the two of you have been busy."

Dumping the vegetables in the salad bowl with the leafy green mixture, I walk over to the fridge and find a bottle of chardonnay toward the back. Wine will fix everything. Pouring my dad a glass, I hand it to him, and he winks at me as he takes the glass from my hand.

I knew it.

"Yes, Dad, we've been very busy. What with all the traveling and hotel stays." I chuckle as Cody's head snaps in my direction, his eyes widening at my comment.

"Alright, Amore Mia, don't push it."

Dad turns to Cody and claps his hand on Cody's shoulder. "Thanks for being a good sport, but you can relax now son."

A deep exhale leaves Cody as we both watch as his body completely relaxes. His shoulders drop from the tense position up around his ears to a neutral, normal location.

"Thank God. I'm so sorry you met me under those circumstances."

"Don't sweat it. I was a twenty-year-old once upon a time. Although at twenty, I had a one-year-old." Dad pauses, finding me watching their interaction. With a wistful expression, he says, "I'm not ready to be a grandpa yet, just remember that."

Cody's eyes bug out, and I shake my head. "Yes, sir. We are uh—"

"I don't need details." Dad shivers. "Now the two of you go sit. I'm glad I brought a batch of my fresh pasta though."

Thirty minutes later, the three of us are sitting down at the kitchen table with lobster pasta in a cream sauce in front of us. Before I eat, I reach for my phone to snap a picture of my plate.

"Okay, everyone, squeeze together." Dad is holding his wineglass up, Cody is leaning forward, and I'm smiling from ear to ear. My two favorite people are together around my table, eating a home-cooked meal. I'm so happy that all feels right in the world.

Cody twirls the pasta on his fork before taking a huge bite. "This is delicious."

He moans, and I clench my thighs together because it's the same moan he makes when he goes down on me. And I should not be thinking about him eating something else right now with my dad sitting across from us.

"You two need to come to the restaurant sometime. Let me know what works in your schedule, and I'll make sure to have a table ready for you."

"Yes, sir. We'll definitely have to take you up on that offer."

Dad nods. "So, Cody, tell me a little more about yourself. What are your inten—"

"Dad!" I cut him off as Dad chuckles. He knows exactly what he's doing. And I know he's protective of me, it's only ever been just the two of us, but we don't need to do the whole "what are your intentions" convo.

"As you know, I'm a pitcher for the baseball team. I'm studying psychology with the idea of becoming a sports psychologist—someone who works with athletes and their inner workings. Most athletes when they struggle with their game are facing some kind of mental block, and I want to be the one to work with them to move past that blockade and get them back into their game."

Dad nods as he sips on his wine. "That's a really great career aspiration. Mental health is as important as physical health, and I think in today's society more and more people are starting to understand that connection."

"I completely agree. I know that when I'm in a good headspace, I can accomplish so much. Our bodies are temples, and we should treat them as such. That means starting with our mental health. With a strong mindset, nothing can keep us down."

I watch as my father sits back in his chair, fork in hand from when he took his last bite, as he stares at Cody with an inquisitive look creasing his forehead. Pointing his fork at Cody, Dad starts nodding his head before turning to look at me. "I *really* like this kid. Good work, Amore Mia."

Before there's a chance for me or Cody to say anything, our front door bursts open and in walks my roommate with Quinton right on her heels. The two of them stop, and I watch Brynn's nose point in the air before she's spinning on her heels as her eyes widen at the three of us at the table. "Daddy Mariano!"

Bringing my elbow to the table, I rest my shaking head in my hand with embarrassment. She did not just say that. Cody chuckles softly, and I remove my head from my hand in time to see my dad's cheeks reflect the same pink shade I get when I'm embarrassed.

He clears his throat, gathering his silverware onto his plate. "Brynn. Quinton."

"We're sorry to interrupt," Quinton says as he follows Brynn, who has an extra bounce in her step.

"You're not interrupting anything. Please, help yourselves to lobster pasta, we were just chatting."

And that's how I find myself on a Thursday evening having an unplanned dinner with family. We might not all be blood, but family doesn't have to come from blood. Family can be those who have your back no matter what. The people who pick you up on your hardest days. Or cheer the loudest on your best days.

Family stems from love, and when you love someone with your whole heart, you cherish each moment that you spend with them because you never know when the day may come when you find yourself alone.

I didn't know how accurate those words would feel.

CHAPTER 31

CODY

"Jacobs, got a minute?" Coach Weber asks from the doorway of the weight room where I'm busy pushing myself with weights to distract me from what's to come this weekend. The team has an away game series at Charleston Tech.

It's been a week since our impromptu dinner with Chloe's dad, and I'm still working off the extra calories

Placing the dumbbells back on the rack, I reach for my towel and wipe the sweat from my face before walking to where Coach is waiting. He turns as I approach, and I follow him, in silence, down the hallway toward his office. Coach rounds his desk, sitting in his chair as I take the seat across from him.

"We haven't had a chance to talk about your plans post-college. There have been a few scouts at our last handful of games, and your name has been tossed around. I wanted to take a minute to see where your head's at." Coach Weber steeples his fingers as he places weight on his elbows waiting for my response.

Sitting up in my chair, I readjust myself until I'm sitting

taller, more confident. "Honestly, Coach, I've been thinking about that very same question for a few weeks now." His brows quirk up at what I can only assume is the ominous tone in my voice. "I want to stay at CTU."

I watch as his lips purse together, the only reaction he gives me, and I'm stuck wondering if I've made the right decision. Or if he's going to be disappointed that I don't want to take my chances now.

"Does a certain blonde have anything to do with your decision?" he asks, again his face is stuck in a neutral reaction. If I hadn't seen the quick movement of his lips, I would have thought he hadn't moved at all.

Leaning forward, I straighten my spine. "No, sir. As much as I love how my relationship has evolved with Chloe, she didn't have anything to do with my decision. This is something that has been weighing on me for most of the season. As excited as I am that the league is sending scouts to watch me, I want to focus on completing my degree."

He nods. Nods. That's it. He stares me down for a few more minutes, and as much as I want to shrink under his intense gaze, I don't.

"Good," he says, leaning back in his chair, his arms relaxing, resting on his armrests before a smile spreads across his face softening his tough exterior. I relax along with him. "I wanted to make sure the decision was coming from you. I have no doubt in my mind Chloe wouldn't be the type of girl to hold you back, but this is a big decision. One I wanted to make sure you are most certain about. While I have no doubt you'll go far at the next level, selfishly, I'm glad you're staying for one more year. You've been an incredible asset to the baseball program and a tremendous guy to coach."

"Thank you, sir."

Bursting with pride I welcome the warm feeling it brings

that spreads through my veins. It's one thing to know that you are good at a sport, but there's something even more rewarding to know that at the end of the day, you are someone that a coach enjoys coaching. So many athletes are talented but have horrible egos. I'm glad to hear that while I do display a bit of a cocky behavior at the end of the day, I've been someone he doesn't want to see leave.

Coach Weber's desk phone rings interrupting our conversation. He glances at the screen before tipping his head back in my direction. "I've got to take this."

"No worries. Thanks, Coach." I stand, stepping out of his office. Once I've cleared the doorway, I let the smile I was fighting take over my face. With the admittance of my plans for the future, I feel a weight release from my shoulders. No longer do I have to worry about what comes next. For right now, I can focus on baseball and my girl, no more talks of the major leagues at this point.

My body feels lighter. My head is clearer.

Walking down the hallway toward the locker room, I stop to take in the photos on the wall. Looking at the previous team pictures, I can't wait to see this year's one beside them, only holding a trophy.

We've won over twenty games so far this season, and most of the sports commentators are predicting that come May, we'll be a real threat to any team we face. I have to agree with them. I know how bad I want it, and while not everyone on the team is on the same level as I am, they're close. Coach Weber can sense it too. It's why he's been pushing us so hard.

Pushing through the locker room doors, I find the rest of the team already inside. Most of the guys have showered from our light workout session and are gathered in the attached lounge room playing video games. Standing in front of my locker, I triple-check that I have all of my gear for our road game.

I'm almost done putting everything back inside my bag when I see Hudson from the corner of my eye.

"Everything good with you and Coach?" He crosses his arms while leaning back against the post separating the lockers. His game face is already starting to appear.

With a nod, I place my extra glove in my bag and zip it close before standing up and facing Hud. "Yeah, everything is good. We were having a follow-up on what's to come."

"Annnnd?" he draws out, spinning his finger in a circle. "Don't leave me in suspense."

With a shit-eating grin, I say, "I'll be back next year."

"Oh hell yeah!" Hudson shouts, his excitement bouncing off the walls, as he claps me on the shoulder. "The dynamic duo is coming back. They can't get rid of Larsen and Jacobs that easily."

Turning in the direction of the lounge room, I let out a soft chuckle as Hudson falls in step with me. "Bro, I don't think anyone has ever called us 'the dynamic duo.'"

"Wait, they don't? What the hell is up with that?"

Walking into the space, there's a group of guys on the leather couch playing a video game on the big screen while others are lounging on beanbags, cell phones in hand. This room is one of the only rooms where Coach permits cell phones.

Ty looks up from his spot on the couch, the game controller in his hand. "What's with you two?"

"Oh this dumb ass," I start, pointing my finger at Hud, "Thinks that everyone calls us 'the dynamic duo.'"

Ty stares at us from his spot on the bean bag as some of the other guys turn in our direction. His eyes squint, and the guys start laughing. "That's the douchiest thing I've ever heard."

"Right." Squeezing my way through the guys, I find an empty beanbag and plop down on it.

Closing his phone, Nolan leans up and looks at Ty. "No the 'douchiest,'" he says putting air quotes around douchiest, "thing I've heard is you saying douchiest. Who says that, and what does it even mean?"

"Like the most douchebag thing you can say."

Nolan shakes his head, turning his attention back to his phone. Whatever he's reading on his phone has him huffing his breath as a dark cloud dampens his mood.

"You good, Nolan?"

He grunts a response but doesn't take his eyes off his phone. I make a mental note to check in with him when we get to Charleston. Hopefully, by then he'll have his personal life sorted, but if not, it's my job as a captain—and friend—to make sure everyone's heads are in check.

A couple of hours later, the guys and I are walking across the pavement to board the bus which will take us to the airport where we'll board the university's jet to Charleston. Climbing up the three steps, my eyes immediately start searching for my Wildflower.

She's sitting in her usual row, a little before the halfway mark of the bus, the inside seat near the window. Her golden blond hair is pulled back in one of those clips she loves to wear as her head is tipped down, no doubt her nose is already glued in a book. I smile at the sight of my girl.

Slipping into the vacant seat beside her, I watch as she slowly turns her attention my way. Her eyes widen, and she startles slightly, no doubt she assumed I was Ty since they sit together every ride.

"Hey, handsome." She turns her whole body, smile spread wide, as she leans into me.

Wrapping my free hand around her shoulders, I pull her in

close to me. Our lips find each other in greeting. Her infamous scent of lilies and sandalwood envelopes my senses.

Humming against her lips, I reluctantly pull away. "How's my Wildflower?"

"Good. I just downloaded a new book to keep me company while we travel."

"Mmm, anything good?"

Her lips find mine again as she murmurs, "Wouldn't you like to know," against them. And yes, yes I'd like to fucking know.

She pulls away first, my favorite shade of pink is spread across her cheek. Hmm, looks like my girl is in the mood. As that thought flashes across my mind, I feel the blood rush south.

Reaching down I adjust myself underneath the team-issued travel sweatsuit. Her eyes track my movement as I watch her pull her bottom lip between her teeth. She bites down, and all I can think about is being the one to bite her lip, which isn't helping the situation in my pants.

"Looking forward to this weekend?"

She nods enthusiastically. "I am. I'm hoping to sneak away for a few hours to do a few tourist things. I've been wanting to explore Charleston's charm since I started watching that show on Bravo. I'll probably try to Uber to White Point Garden."

"You and your reality shows," I mutter. Chloe and Brynn are obsessed with reality TV. It's always playing on their TV, even if no one is sitting in the room watching. I swear they enjoy the drama as background noise. "Why there?"

She shrugs, a wistful expression sliding over her face. "I googled a couple of different things, and this was the farthest location, but I think I'll be able to see the most. Statues, historical architecture, the ocean, and everything in between."

"We'll have to try and sneak away."

A throat clears from behind us. "You sitting here, Jacobs?"

Pressing my lips tight against my girl's one last time, I pull away and stand to my feet. "Nah, man. Enjoy the ride."

Moving down the aisle, I slide past Hudson and take my empty seat next to the window.

I've no sooner sat down when my phone chimes in my pocket. I clearly forgot to put it on vibrate.

Dad: See you soon.

Dread instantly crawls up my spine. Not only am I dreading the fact that my parents will be at the game, but there's no way I want him to be in the same space as Chloe. Today there's a good chance that my two worlds are going to collide. I've tried everything to keep my dad away from my CTU family. He's like a leech who attaches to anyone in his path and tries to suck out their light.

It's for her own good.

I can't let Chloe get near him. I can't risk her being a victim of his torment. Of his abusive mind games. Especially after the game when he's had nine innings to sit and drink. The alcohol is like pouring lighter fluid on an open flame. It won't take him long before he's ready to combust. And as his favorite target, he'll seek me out immediately ready to spit his venom.

Will she understand if I start to distance myself from her?

Closing out the text and not wanting any more distractions, I flip my phone to "Do Not Disturb."

Hudson nudges my shoulder, his eyes bouncing from the phone in my hand back up to my face. "You good?"

With my lips pursed together, I give him a tight nod as I slip my phone back into my pocket. Closing my eyes, I take a minute to practice a few breathing exercises the yoga instructor was teaching us at the beginning.

Inhale the good shit. Exhale the bullshit.

Or whatever the saying she taught us was.

Slipping my Bluetooth headphones on over my head, I tune out for the drive to the airport and somehow our flight to Charleston.

Before long we are stepping off the plane, boarding another bus, and making our way to the hotel we are staying at. Even though Chloe and I aren't sitting together, I can still feel her positive energy vibrating around the bus. I wish I could contain a fraction of her excitement for this trip.

Unfortunately, I think I'm going to be on edge the entire time patiently waiting for the other shoe to drop.

CHAPTER 32

Chloe

PUSHING THROUGH THE DOORS THAT LEAD TO THE outside patio, I'm greeted with sunshine. There's just something about the sunshine in a coastal town that hits differently. I have spent the last fifteen minutes unpacking my suitcase and arranging my room so that I don't feel like I'm living out of my bags.

Scanning the space for a seat, I spot a familiar person sitting alone at one of the metal tables. Walking up next to him, I place my hands on the empty chair across from him. "Mind if I sit here?"

Bright blue eyes find mine, and his serious 'leave me alone' expression quickly morphs into warm and welcoming when he realizes who is bothering him. He gestures to the empty seat before speaking, "How's everything going, Chloe?"

Coach Callan Weber is nothing but intimidating. With his tan skin, piercing blue eyes, and dark—almost black—beard that is trimmed close to his face. Black ink peeks out above the neckline of his T-shirt before running down both arms and ending across his fingers. He screams rough and tough, unapproachable, but he's the farthest thing from that.

"Everything is going great. I just wanted to sit outside for a while. I love how the outside feels near the coast."

He chuckles. "I know what you mean. I grew up in a small coastal town, and I miss smelling the salt as it floats around me."

"Yes, the salt breezes through the air. It's the best. Candle companies are always trying to give you ocean breeze scents, but it's nothing like the real thing. Do you think you'll ever go back to your hometown?"

"Maybe someday. But right now my focus is on CTU. I love the culture the campus brings with it."

Callan leans back in his chair as he reaches up to remove his hat. Running his hand through his hair, which he keeps longer on the top and shorter on the sides, before returning his flat-billed hat to his head. There's a reason why Callan has been voted college baseball's sexiest coach and why he's the face of the sport. He oozes sex appeal from his chiseled jaw, model-like features, and fit muscular build which has his shirt stretching taut against his chest.

"Did you know you always wanted to coach?"

"Is this on or off the record, Ms. Mariano?" His eyes lower as he squints at me.

"Busted," I chuckle, and he returns my comment with a laugh. "Sorry, I thought I could ask you a few questions without it feeling like an interview."

"No worries. You're easy to talk to. That's what makes you a great journalist. You'll have people spilling all of their dirty secrets, and they won't even know they're being interviewed."

Blushing, I brush a loose piece of hair behind my ears. "Thank you, Coach."

"No, I wouldn't say that I always wanted to coach. Before my injury, I thought my future would revolve around playing in the majors. That at some point in my career, I'd settle down with a wife and kids before retiring from playing and picking up some kind of sports broadcasting job. But life had different plans. From the moment I went down on that ski slope, I knew my career was over. There was this overwhelming feeling that spread over my body. I decided that if I couldn't play, I'd coach. And that's what I've been doing."

"So is a wife and kids still in your future?"

"No comment," he says with a smirk. Smiling, I glance around at some of the other tables around us. Couples sit across from each other at a few tables while other tables are occupied by people working on their computers.

Returning my attention to Callan, I run through some thoughts in my head. Sitting down with him wasn't on my to-do list for the day which means my notebook with questions is currently sitting in my hotel room. I rack my brain with some things to ask him in the meantime.

"Is there anything you want your players to leave CTU with the knowledge of?"

"At the end of the day, baseball isn't everything. That might seem odd coming from a head coach at a prestigious university, but it's the truth. Life can flash before our eyes, and life-altering things can happen resulting in everything changing. The most important lesson to learn in life is how to adapt. It's okay to mourn the life you thought you'd have, but it shouldn't derail your entire future. Life is constantly evolving, and why shouldn't our dreams evolve with us? Take the time to process and say good-bye to what you thought your future would hold, but don't take too much time. Find something else that keeps you motivated. Set new goals, face new fears, but don't stop living."

Cody's dad should sit down and have a conversation with Coach. Maybe he'd get his head out of his ass and stop treating his son like a doormat.

"That's incredible advice. It not only applies to baseball, but to anyone who stares adversity in the face."

He nods before glancing down at his watch. "Exactly. I hate to cut this conversation short, but I have to get ready to head to the field for pregame press. We can sit down again and talk more, but I have a feeling you've been weaving things together over the last couple of weeks."

A sheepish grin lifts at the corner of my lips as I bring my arms out to the side, shrugging. "Guilty."

Laughing, Coach Weber slides his chair out from the table before standing to his full 6'2" frame. With a small nod, he walks away leaving me to sit alone in the South Carolina sun. Leaning my head back, I welcome the rays against my face. My skin absorbs the energy as the heat radiates, spreading warmth throughout my soul.

Yes, we have sun in Texas, but this sun just feels different. Maybe it's the refreshing aroma that when you smell it, you know you're near the sea. Or the change in humidity. Whatever it is, I welcome it like a desert cactus welcomes rain.

The sun is long gone as darkness surrounds the brightness of the stadium lights. Tonight's game was a late seven o'clock start. The guys just wrapped up the bottom of the seventh inning, and the Eagles are on top six to zero.

Cody is pitching another fantastic game. Honestly, I'm surprised he's been pitching as well as he has. I didn't see him much before the game started as he was busy with his pregame rituals, handling a few media interviews, and warming up for the game. But there was definitely a dark cloud following him around today.

I noticed it when we got off the bus to board the plane, but I didn't bring it up. I wasn't fueling the fire of whatever was sparking his poor attitude. I did spend the flight to Charleston combing my brain for any hints that I had done something wrong. When I came back with nothing, I was halfway through my book when I realized that his parents were coming to the game. He had mentioned it a while ago that they were planning on coming to South Carolina. That's the reason for the sour mood.

It was during the third inning that I noticed that his mood was starting to brighten. Maybe it had to do with the fact that his pitches were looking incredible. Ending the third inning with no hits, he found me waiting at the top of the stairs with my camera—something that I do every once in a while. Busy snapping photos, I didn't realize that Cody was making my way toward me. It wasn't until he stopped in front of my lens that I slid the camera down.

Lifting his hand in the air, Cody was waiting for me to give him a high-five. Hands smacking together, he gave me a small wink before brushing past me. And so the routine continued after every inning. He'd strike the third batter of the inning out, walk to wherever I was standing, wait for a high-five, and give me a wink before hopping down the steps that led into the dugout.

Now with only two innings to go, my anxiety is starting to rise. Cody's on his way to pitching another no-hitter—his third of the season.

There's a buzz in the dugout almost as if everyone is feeling the pressure to give Cody this win and to not cause any mistakes to jeopardize his no-hitter.

Making my way onto the field, I take advantage of the team throwing the ball around in between innings. The coaches have all been leaning against the railing in a relaxed manner. I was able to take a picture of their backs, but I knew that the picture would look really special if I was facing them. Glancing around at the guys on the field, I make sure that I'm not going to get hit with the ball before I'm quickly moving into position. Lining up the camera, I adjust the lens until I have the shot that I want. Hitting the button, I watch the shutter release before checking the picture on my screen. Happy with the shot, I glance up into the crowd.

Charleston's field isn't anywhere as big as ours, but it's still a nice facility with tan-painted brick buildings and green plastic chairs spread throughout the stadium. As I'm skimming our crowd—smaller than normal—my eyes catch on semi-familiar hazel eyes.

I have no doubt in my mind that I'm staring at Cody's father.

My breath stutters in my chest as I take in the man staring back at me. Not breaking eye contact, it's like he's sucking my soul from me. The sneer on his face is enough to make me shiver. Chills run down my spine, and I quickly stride back down into the dugout.

Not able to get the image of that man sneering at me out of my head, I make it a point to stay in the dugout and away from any camera, including the one that flashes images up to the screen in the outfield for the fans.

Thankfully, I don't have long to wait. The team pulls out a win as Cody pitches a phenomenal game. Without stepping out of the dugout, I'm able to capture the celebratory huddle from the top of the dugout steps.

My heart is bursting at the seams for Cody. I'm so proud of him for earning this accomplishment. We still have a month, if not longer, until the season ends, and there's a good chance he'll break the record for the most no-hitters thrown in a single season.

The guys all scramble into the dugout, heading straight for where the bat bags are kept. They're ready to pack up and head back to the hotel, no doubt exhausted from the day. The once quiet dugout is now thumping with an exciting energy that drums through the air. It's contagious, and the smile that breaks free across my face is unavoidable.

Cody's eyes find mine through the crowd, and the wink he gives me makes my panties wet. He's going to want to celebrate tonight, and there's nothing I'd like more than to be tangled in the sheets with the man who stole my heart.

Leaning against the opposite wall out of the way of the guys gathering their things, I wait until everyone is ready to leave the dugout. Coach Weber likes for the team to arrive and exit together. He says it makes the team look more serious, and I agree. There's nothing like a pack of athletes trudging through the stands with their metal cleats clanking against the concrete. They're like a pack of wolves hunting down their prey with determined energy and stoic faces.

Weber gives everyone twenty to thirty minutes after an away game before they have to report to the bus. This way everyone has a chance to meet up with anyone they know who came to watch the game, mingle with fans, or just a chance to unwind after a game.

The team makes their way out of the dugout as I slide in with the coaches and other members of the staff. We walk across the dirt path that leads to the gated steps up to the main level of the stadium. Keeping my focus on the person in front of me, I don't allow my eyes to stray. However, there's the niggling feeling deep in my soul that feels like eyes are burrowing into my skin.

Don't look up. Don't look up.

Once we reach the main level, most of the guys split up. Cody is one of them. Our eyes meet in the briefest of moments, but his hardened face has me walking right past him. I don't get too far before Ty sidles up beside me, wrapping his arm around my shoulder. He smells of sweat and grass stains from the diving catch he made late in the game behind third base. "Hey, Chloe girl."

Looking up at Ty, I give him a small smile. "Good game out there."

"Thanks! What'd you think about that diving catch in the eighth? I did that one for you."

I roll my eyes because no, he did not do that for me. "Uh-huh. I was so impressed."

"Impressed enough to leave Jacobs behind and take a ride on the Billings train?"

A laugh bursts from deep inside. Looking around ahead of us, I see Niko and Hudson waiting off to the side. I have a feeling these boys are distracting me from the mood Cody is in and the man who caused the mood.

"Oh my gosh, Ty," I say through laughter, hitting his stomach with my hand that isn't pressed against his side.

"Chloe?" a soft voice calls from behind us, interrupting our laughter.

The laughter slips away as Ty's and my heads turn toward each other. Brows quirked as confusion mars our faces. Looking over my shoulder, I'm doused in cold water as the feeling of paralysis shocks me still.

Her honey-blonde hair. The same as mine.

Her petite frame. The same as mine.

Her slightly upturned and slender nose. The same as mine.

I'm standing in the presence of the woman I thought I'd never see again.

"M-mo-mom?" As the words leave my lips, Ty's grip tightens as he pulls me in closer to him almost like a shield protecting me from a fire-breathing dragon. And she might as well be. Because the woman staring back at me, eyes wide and mouth slightly ajar, is definitely the villain in my story.

Bringing her trembling hand up to her mouth to cover the gasp. "Oh my god, it is you."

My eyes bug out of my head as the overwhelming feeling to

pass out washes over me. I can feel my knees buckle as Ty's grip is the only thing keeping me standing.

"Breathe," he whispers against my head. And I try to do just that as my mouth flounders, my mind forgetting every word in the English language.

"Wh-wh-what are you doing here?" I stammer the words out as my skill of speaking is clearly gone.

She steps forward, and I flinch at her movement like a scared deer who has just come face to face with a hunter. Camilla pauses. She has the decency to look hurt. As if.

"Mom." I turn my head as a guy approaches her. Dressed in a Charleston baseball uniform, he looks to be a little younger than me. My eyes track the movement from where the guy approaches my mom. I watch as her face morphs into a proud smile as she stares at the guy drawing near us.

I'm so goddamn confused.

My eyes flash back to the boy and over his shoulder I see two more kids following with an older guy holding the hand of a young girl. She couldn't be more than eight years old. Both look at each other smiling and giggling as they have no idea what shitstorm they are about to enter.

Four kids? Four *fucking* kids are making their way to *my* mother.

"Good game, honey," my mother greets the boy who wraps her in a hug.

"Mom, Jessi won't share her M&Ms," a younger boy whines as he makes his way up to them.

My mo—Camilla's eyes move past her children and find mine. I can't quite decipher the look in her eyes. Embarrassment? Pride? But the one thing I can read is how nervous she is.

"I never thought I'd run into you at a ballpark."

Scoffing, I step away from Ty who reluctantly lets me out from under his arm. Out of the corner of my eyes, I watch as

Niko and Hudson move toward us from where they were standing. "You *clearly* had no intention of running into me ever."

"Now wait—" she starts to protest, but I whip my hand in the air, cutting her off.

"You have four *fucking* kids!" I grit the words out, and they taste bitter on my tongue.

"Chloe Mariano, don't you dare speak to me that way." By now, the older man and young girl have joined. They look like one big happy, albeit confused, family. Nausea roils through my stomach with the overwhelming feeling of getting sick.

"You gave up the right to scold me when you abandoned me"

Hurt flashes over her features as her—husband?—slides in between her and her son, the baseball player. Her shoulders soften at his touch, and it makes me sick to watch her with her replacement family.

"Chloe, this is Heath, Maddox, Jessica, and Bria." She introduces me to her new family. I give a tight-lipped smile because what the hell else am I supposed to do when meeting my siblings I never knew about? She looks up at the guy next to her, and a dreamy smile lights up her face. "And this is my husband Charlie. Charlie and I met a couple of years after I—after I left—"

"*Abandoned*," I grumble.

"Heath is his son from his first marriage. Maddox and Jessi are ten, and Bria is eight." She pauses, glancing over my shoulder. "Would you like to get dinner with us?"

My jaw practically hits the ground. "Get dinner with you? What, like we're some kind of happy family?"

"Yeah, I'd like for my kids to meet their big sister."

"You've had fifteen years for your replacement family to meet your original daughter. The daughter you neglected and forgot about. The daughter who spent her whole childhood waiting for her mother to come back. The daughter who has never felt like enough in this world because if her *own* mother couldn't love her, why would *anyone* else?"

I don't recognize the woman spewing these words. All I know is that I'm pissed. I'm hurt. I'm devastated to see that I was right all along.

I wasn't good enough.

I wasn't good enough for her to stay. For her to love. For her to introduce to her kids.

A tight ball is forming in my chest as a burning sensation seeps into my eyes. I can feel the tears threatening and the sobs wanting to erupt. But I refuse to cry in front of this woman. I refuse to let her see how much she's cut me.

With one last look at the woman who birthed me, I will my feet to move. Taking off in a jog, I run past groups of people as my eyes scan the crowd looking for my favorite pair of hazel eyes. Tears burn and blur my vision. I see them up ahead, and I slow my pace to a walk. I've already caused enough of a scene, I don't need to run up on my boyfriend and his parents whom I've never met before.

I'm almost past a few lingering bystanders when more words slice through my body.

"Jesus, she's nothing. Nothing more than someone to help release the stress of the game. She's not the type you marry, so get off my back about it. I've told you that I don't have time for distractions, and I refuse to let a girl get in the way of my game."

Just a distraction?

Someone to help release the stress of the game?

She's not the type you marry?

Bile rises in my throat, and I turn around to see Ty standing right behind me. By the look on his face and his clenched jaw, it's obvious he heard everything I just did.

Walking straight into his arms, I let him lead me out of the stadium through a different entrance. Reaching into his pocket, he thumbs out something on his phone.

A few seconds pass, and he's leading us toward a line of cars. I spot the Uber and climb in the backseat next to him.

"What do you need from me?"

"Nothing. I just want to go home."

Ty pulls me into his side, and I rest my head against his shoulder. Digging out my cell phone, I pull up my dad's number.

After a few rings, he answers. The sound of his voice causes the floodgates to open. "Daddy?"

"Amore Mia, what happened?" concern is evident in his voice, and I fight the sobs so he can hear me.

"I need a flight home."

"Give me five minutes."

And with that, he hung up the phone, and I let my emotions win.

CHAPTER 33

CODY

CLIMBING THE STEPS UP TO THE BLEACHERS WITH THE team feels like it's taking forever. Dread feels like a bowling ball in my stomach. Not one ounce of me is looking forward to this encounter with my parents.

As great of a game I just pitched, I can't even be excited. I know that he's just going to ruin it, so why even celebrate?

Reaching the top of the stairs, I turn to the left. Placing one foot in front of the other, I steal my face in a hardened expression.

Never let him see you sweat.

And the thing is, I'm not scared of him. I quit being scared of him a long time ago. The longer this has gone on for, the more I've realized he's a coward. He hides behind his cruel words in his alcoholic haze. My dad is like a shark in the water. At the first scent of blood, he's attacking anyone in his path.

What makes me nervous is him causing a scene in front of everyone. I don't need the press catching wind that I'm the son of an emotionally abusive alcoholic father. I don't need the drama or the sympathy that comes with it. He doesn't matter. What matters is my performance on and off the field.

Honey-blonde hair catches my attention, but I keep my stoic expression neutral. It's killing me inside to remove myself from her. I want so badly to lift her in the air, spin her around, and plant my lips against her soft, rosy pink ones. She's the one I want to be celebrating with.

"Well, there's the golden boy," my dad slurs, wobbling a bit.

Great, how many beers deep is he? And why didn't they cut him off?

"Oh sweetie," my mom greets, wrapping her arms around my shoulders as she tries to pull me in for a hug. "Great game tonight."

With one arm, I return her hug. As I lean my head over her shoulders, I never take my eyes off my dad. "Thanks, Mom."

"Great game? Could've been better,' he grumbles from behind Mom. "It would have been better if he wasn't busy holding hands."

Pulling away from my mom, I steal my shoulders preparing for what's to come.

"Made arrangements and paid all this money to get here only to watch him play a mediocre game against a less than mediocre team."

The laugh that he emits is evil. It's filled with disdain.

Let's just get this over with.

"Oh Gary, he wasn't holding hands with anyone out there," my mom chastises, which only makes his sneer more venomous.

"I don't know how they expect you to win games when they have some tramp in the locker room.

"Gary," Mom scolds, but the look Dad cuts her with could crack ice. I watch as she cowers behind his glare, shoulders sagging. It's brief, but I notice the change in body language. She gives me a small smile as she steps to the side, moving so that she's behind him.

It pisses me off how much she lets him get away with it. But as I'm watching her for the first time, I see that she's been a victim of his words this whole time. I just don't understand why she didn't leave and take us away when we were younger.

"She's a part of the newspaper staff. She's covering our season and writing an article on Coach Weber."

He scoffs before he goes into a lecture on how women shouldn't be allowed in the dugout. The words keep pouring from his mouth. His speech is so slurred it's hard to understand some of the things he's saying. I know he's drunk. I know I should just ignore him but after what feels like hours, I finally have had enough. I can't listen to this shit any longer.

When I hear him talk about 'that girl' again, I lose it. The words tumble out of my mouth, and I don't even think about the repercussions of saying them. The only thing I can do is to shut him up. To get her out of his mouth. I can't handle listening to him spew venom about her.

This is what I was worried about.

This is why I told Leah to make sure she never says anything about Chloe at the house.

This is why I ghosted her that summer.

As soon as he had suspicions I was seeing someone that summer, he lost it.

For someone who was supposed to be staying calm after his heart attack, he used every opportunity to get under my skin about women and distractions. I'll never understand how someone can be so cruel.

"Before you know it, he's going to be pissing his future away because of some chick who's looking to wife him up."

It's why I don't think about how hurtful the words I say are. I just want him to shut the hell up.

"Jesus, she's nothing." The words feel bitter as soon as they escape my lips, and I want nothing more than to suck them back in, but my chest is vibrating with frustration and the need to shut him up.

The look he gives me shows me he doesn't believe what I say. With a haggard breath, I continue the lies that taste vile on my tongue. "Nothing more than someone to help release the stress of the game. She's not the type you marry, so get off my back about it. I've told you that I don't have time for distractions, and I refuse to let a girl get in the way of my game."

My mom's gasp is the only verbal response I receive as my dad just stares at me, eyes squinted, as if he's trying to get a read on me. It's then I see the edges of his lips curl in a smirk almost as if he sees something on my face, which I know is impossible. I've perfected the stoic look when it comes to talking to my dad.

Looking past my dad, I watch my mom's reaction as it morphs into pain. "I'm sorry, Mom, but I can't do this anymore. I can't be his punching bag."

With a deep inhale, I finally grow the confidence to stand up to my dad. "You know what? Fuck it. I've been so scared of you for *fucking* years, and all I've ever wanted is for you to be a dad to me. To tell me 'great job, son' or hell, that you're proud of me. It's been years of me wanting the approval of my dad, and it's never come. It's been years of slurred words and insults to the point where I can't even tell you about something—or someone—that makes me happy. You've got me downplaying a relationship over the woman I love, and enough is enough. This relationship, or whatever the hell you want to call it, is over. I'm done with you and your control. Don't call me. Don't text me. Don't come to my games. We're done."

Dad takes a step toward me, his leer more intense. His mouth starts to open just as someone yells my name from behind me.

Glancing over my shoulder, I find Hudson storming through the few remaining spectators. Anger radiates from him.

With one last look at my mom, I give her a tight-lipped smile before walking away.

From my parents.

From my bully.

From the years worth of pain.

Closing the gap between Hudson and myself, I can't help but feel the overwhelming weight of waiting for the next shoe to drop.

"What's up?" I ask, nodding my head at my pissed-off friend.

He shakes his head. "What the fuck is wrong with you?"

"Me?" I ask, pointing a finger at my chest. "What are you talking about?"

He turns and walks in the direction he came from as I fall in step beside him. Looking ahead, I see we are one of the last ones to get on the bus. Coach Weber stands outside the bus door, arms crossed, and a serious expression lines his face as he waits for us.

Hudson turns his head toward me, eyes me, before shaking his head. "She's nothing more than someone to help release the stress of the game. She's not the type you marry. Or how did it go?"

"How the fuck did you know I said that?" My pulse starts to rise as that feeling of dread courses through my veins. Bile starts to rise in my throat as I predict what he's going to say.

"Chloe heard everything you said."

"Fuck!" I roar, causing bystanders to look our way. Sheepishly I duck my head while my insides blaze alive. "She wasn't supposed to hear that. I didn't mean anything, I just wanted my dad to get off my back. He saw us together and..."

"And it doesn't matter. What matters is *that* girl has given you a second chance. She *gave* you her heart, and you *ripped* it apart before stomping on it. Not to mention she *ran into her mom* tonight."

My eyebrows hit my hairline as my eyes widened in shock. Of all the things he could've said, that was one thing I was not expecting. "What? Where is she?"

I take off at a faster pace, wanting to get on the bus and find my girl. "She took an Uber back to the hotel."

"Fuck. Fuck. Fuck." Walking past an angry coach, I climb the steps onto the bus. Everyone's eyes are on me as soon as I set foot in the aisle.

They all know. They know the words I said, and they're judging me for it. But what they don't know is that I did it to protect Chloe. She was never supposed to hear me say those things.

Tonight when she asked me how things with my parents went, I would've told her the truth. I would have told her that he saw us and knew from the look in my eyes that there was something more going on between the two of us. For me to protect her, I had to lie and tell him that nothing was going on between us. I couldn't risk him contacting her, and he would have found a way, he always finds a way. The words tasted like acid as they poured from my lips, and all I could think about was kissing her and telling her how much I love her. That she's it for me.

Instead, she heard the horrible things. She heard me say words that sparked her biggest fear. Not to mention it was on the night when she needed me. Never in a million years would I have guessed that we would run into her mom. Not at a baseball diamond in South Carolina of all places.

Pulling out my phone as I take a seat, I thumb through my contacts until I find her name. Hitting the call button, I listen as the ringtone plays in my ear before the automated voice of her voicemail picks up. Hitting the end button, I call her again.

Only this time, there isn't a ringtone. It goes straight to voice-mail. Running my hands through my still sweat-damp hair, I try again. And three more times for good measure.

After the fifth call, I open my messaging app and thumb out a message.

> Me: Wildflower, call me. I can explain everything. I love you.

The bus barely comes to a stop before I'm flying out of my seat and jogging down the aisle. Coach Weber's eyes find mine, and I can read everything he's not saying. He's telling me he's disappointed in me, and I think that's the worst thing he could ever say to me. I look up to the man, and his disappointment is soul-crushing.

Running into the lobby, I don't waste time with the elevator. I march straight to the door under the 'stairs' sign. Taking the steps two at a time, I don't stop until I'm reaching the fourth floor. Slightly out of breath, I burst through the door onto our floor. Even though I didn't see her before the game, I know which room is hers thanks to Coach's rule of alphabetical order.

Pounding on her door with my fist, I wait for her to open the door. "Chloe! Chloe, baby! Please open the door." I pause the knocking and wait a few seconds.

With each second that ticks by, the overwhelming feeling to throw up gets stronger and stronger. Reaching up, I knock a few more times. "Please let me explain. Open the door."

The elevator dings, and I turn my attention to the metal doors praying that my sweet, beautiful wildflower will step through the door and hear me out.

Only it's not her who walks out. It's Ty. He wasn't on the bus which means he was the one to console my girlfriend. It's evident how strong the bond between those two is.

He looks like he could punch his fist through my face as he

storms down the hall, straight for me. Putting my hands up, I try to back him down. "She wasn't supposed to hear it."

I feel his arms push me backward, and my feet stumble underneath me. In the next second, Hudson is standing between us. I don't even remember seeing him come up behind Ty. "Knock it off," he says through gritted teeth.

"Where is she," I ask, adjusting my stance until I'm standing upright.

"Gone."

"Gone? What do you mean 'gone?'"

"She called her dad and got a flight home," Niko answers. I roar a frustrated groan as I tug my hands through my hair knocking my hat off in the process.

Hudson unlocks our door with the key card before he grabs me by the crook of my elbow and ushers us into our room. He shuts the door on everyone else and pushes me toward the bed.

"Sit down and start explaining. I've dealt with a lot of your bullshit through the years. I know you would never purposefully hurt her, but you did. Tell me what the fuck happened tonight."

And for the next twenty minutes, the two of us recap what the hell happened after the game. I share the details of my conversation with my dad while he tries to give me some insight into the encounter with Chloe's mom. He wasn't close enough to get every detail, but he saw enough from where he and Niko were standing.

Sometime around midnight, I'm lying in my bed, freshly showered when I hear my phone buzz on the side table. Practically diving for it, I read the message that just popped in.

Brynn: You're an asshole.

Not wanting to deal with her tonight, I slide out of her message and pull up Chloe's thread of unanswered texts.

10:07 PM

Me: Wildflower, call me. I can explain everything. I love you.

10:32 PM

Me: Chloe, please. It wasn't what you thought.

11:02 PM

Me: I'm worried about you. Please call me.

Me: I don't even need a call, just let me know you got home safely.

11:23 PM

Me: I love you, Wildflower.

11:43 PM

Me: I'm so fucking sorry.

CHAPTER 34

Chloe

NUMB.

Broken.

Empty.

My heart feels like it's been ripped from my chest and stomped on by a herd of elephants.

It's been twelve hours since my life imploded, punching me straight in the gut. Last night I flew on a stranger's private jet—he was a friend of my dad's—-back to my empty townhouse. I'm sure Brynn was at Quinton's, and if I needed her, she would have been right over. But, much to my dad's dismay, I wanted to be alone. I had to beg him to stay home and not drive up from Dallas to get me.

Someone must have texted Brynn because at one point I had a missed call from her. I sent her a short text back letting her know I was fine, and I'd talk to her about it later.

I didn't want to talk about my feelings, I didn't want to re-play the night. I wanted to lie in my bed and let the tears pour from my soul.

I sobbed so much, I don't have any tears left to shed. After crying myself to sleep last night, my body woke me up at eight, even though I was exhausted.

Who knew bawling that hard could leave you feeling like you just ran a marathon?

Which is why I'm standing in my kitchen, 80s rock blaring from my Bluetooth speaker as I bake. Today calls for rage baking.

Flour coats the counter leaving a cloud in the air as I sort out my pain on the dough that needs to be worked. Being in the kitchen, focusing on recipes, it's my favorite way to escape. Only today, I'm struggling. Not even the blaring sounds of Twisted Sister can get me out of my head.

I reach for the scraper and cut the dough into eight triangles before brushing heavy cream on the tops. The smell of lemon and blueberry invades my nose. Lemon is such a calming fragrance.

Once the scones are in the oven, I feel a sharp pain rip through my chest. My brain is a whirlwind of emotions. I can't seem to shut out the noise. The chaos floods my system with visions of last night. I don't know what to grab onto first. Seeing my mom and knowing she's been living her best life without me. My boyfriend told his family I was nothing to him. There was a part of me that thought maybe someday they would be my family too—even with how fucked up his dad is.

The images of my mom and her four kids infiltrate my mind. I thought my eyes were dried out from all of the tears, but I guess there's more.

Sobs rip through my chest. I don't know how to handle these emotions. So much has happened in the last day. I went from being blissfully in love and watching my boyfriend pitch another phenomenal game to being devastated at what's become of my life. Who did I hurt in the past to warrant such horrible karma?

I don't get it.

I'm the type of girl who holds the door open for strangers.

Who lets drivers cut in front of her. I'm the girl who pays it forward in the drive-thru just to make someone's day. I stop into the local florist every week to support a woman who lost the love of her life by spending a few minutes with her and purchasing flowers to support her business.

Why do these things keep happening to me? Why does it all stem from not being enough for the people in my life? Am I that bad of a person?

The sound of the front door closing has me jerking my head in the direction of our front room.

"Babe." Brynn's soft voice fills the air as she rounds the counter and collapses on the floor next to me. Her arms wrap around my shoulders as I fall into her embrace. Sobs rack through my body as my tears soak her shirt.

For the longest time neither one of us says anything. I don't even know what can be said in a situation like this. It's only when the sound of the oven rings out that we separate. Standing from the ground, I grab the oven mitts and remove the lemon and blueberry scones.

"Do you want to talk about it?" Brynn asks hesitantly, as she leans against the counter. "Or should I break out the alcohol?"

I huff a breath through my nose. It's half a laugh and half an exasperated sigh. "Honestly, I don't even know where to begin. Which problem do I talk about first?"

"Are you asking because you want my two cents?"

Placing my hands on my hips, I huff the piece of loose hair from my face before shrugging. "You know, fuck it. Give me your thoughts."

My emotions have spun in a one-eighty from hurt to sad to plain pissed off.

"Well, first of all, fuck your mom. There, I'm just going to say it."

"She introduced me to her kids like I was an old acquaintance and then had the nerve to ask me if I wanted to have dinner with them."

"Yeah, fuck her. She doesn't get to take any credit for who you are as a person. She left. She screwed up. That's on her. She's missing out on one of the most incredible people in the world. One day she's going to come across your name in some fancy magazine, and she's going to be hit with the grief that she left you. You owe that woman nothing." I start to interrupt her, but Brynn's eyes give me a look that has me snapping my mouth shut. "I know it hurts, and I know it had to have triggered all of the pain from the past, but fuck her. You don't deserve to feel the turmoil anymore."

I nod because, at the end of the day, I know she's right. Everything that Brynn is saying is true, but it doesn't take the pain away. At least for the first time in my life, I feel like someone is giving me permission to forget about the woman who birthed me. I shouldn't have to dim my light to make her feel like what she did was okay.

Brynn moves from my side of the counter to the other side before she takes a seat on a stool. "Now the last part, I don't think you're going to like."

"If you defend him, our friendship is over."

She laughs. My so-called friend sits there and laughs. "First off, you're stuck with me, bitch. You're my ride or die until the end."

Giving her a tight-lipped smile, I hop on the counter, avoiding the flour mess, until we are faced to face. "Love you."

"Love you too. Now," she begins, her face squishing in a pained expression. "I think you need to hear him out. I talked to Hudson last night, and he gave me a brief recap. But I know Cody, and you know Cody. Deep down something doesn't add up. We both know he's in this with you, and it's so much for him than just a fling."

"But this isn't the first time he's pulled this shit. And I needed him last night and where was he? Telling his parents that I'm a nobody. That I'm nothing. I don't care what the reasoning is, that shit hurts."

Her shoulders sag as she lets out a long exhale. "I know. I'm not saying the two of you need to talk tonight, but just give him a chance to explain."

"Yeah, well it's going to have to wait. This week is finals prep, and I have a lot to focus on. This was not the week for my life to implode."

She drums her fingers on the counter, eyeing me. "What are you going to do when he shows up here today? You know you're going to be his first stop."

"Wanna tell him I'm not here?"

She lets out a sarcastic laugh. "Yeah, there's no way he's believing me when I say that."

Dammit, I didn't even think about him coming over here. Worrying on my bottom lip, I think of the potential places I could hide out. I guess I could try to reach out to Macy and see if she and Gregg would mind me crashing there. It won't take Cody long to figure out I'm there, but it might be long enough to let me figure out a better option.

"Hey, Chlo, why didn't you call me last night?" Her expression morphs into an almost hurt look as her eyes sadden. "You know I would've been here waiting, right?"

Sliding off the counter, I make my way over to her. Wrapping my arms around her shoulders, I rest my head on her. "Of course I know that. I just wanted to be alone."

"I get it," she replies, her hand squeezing my arm. "Just know I'm always here, and I'm always in your corner."

With one last squeeze, I release my arms and make my way back over to the counter to clean up my mess.

Thirty minutes later and the kitchen spotless, I reach for my phone. Closing out the messages from Cody and a few of the guys on the team, I scroll my contacts until I find Macy's name.

As great as it was to hash things out, I know our friendship isn't where it once was. The idea of calling her leaves me with an anxious feeling swimming around my stomach.

After the third ring, Macy answers, "Chlo?"

"Hey, Mace, I'm sorry to bother you."

She sighs. "You're never bothering me. Is everything okay?"

"Long answer, *absolutely* not. The short answer, it will be. But I was wondering if I could ask a favor?"

"Sure, girl, what's up?"

"Do you think I could stay with you and Gregg tonight? I can totally crash on your couch."

"Oh my gosh, girl. Of course, but you're not sleeping on the couch. Come over whenever, I'm home all day."

My shoulders sag with relief and a small part of the weight I'm carrying is released. "Thank you so much. I'll probably be there in an hour or so."

"That sounds great," Macy says before pausing. "Chloe, you never have to thank me. I'm always here."

The first smile I've had all day slides across my face as moisture gathers in my eyes, and the familiar lump in my throat grows.

Don't cry, Chloe.

"See you in a while."

"Oh my gosh, Chloe! I cannot believe she was there," Macy gasps, her jaw dropping open, from where she's sitting on the couch.

She and Gregg are wrapped up together on the couch while I'm sitting opposite them in a chair. Their Cavalier King Charles puppy, Boone, is curled up on my lap. And petting this sweet, brown and white puppy makes rehashing last night's events so much more bearable.

The two are disgustingly cute. And even though I'm in the midst of heartache, I'm so happy for them. Gregg suffered from a stroke in the fall, and while he was fine for the most part, he had to go through some physical therapy to regain strength in the left side of his body. The doctors wouldn't release him to live alone, which is why Macy moved in with him. The two weren't even seeing each other, just a casual fling. Turns out, they were both fighting feelings for each other.

I've been at their apartment for an hour, and I've been busy filling both of them in on the last twenty-four hours. Gregg was more than accommodating with my arrival. He went out and picked up Chinese for all of us—knowing it was our favorite. He even offered to make himself scarce while the two of us caught up. It was sweet but unnecessary. He can hear my dirty laundry.

"Oh yeah, nothing like fifteen years of trauma smacking you in the face the same night you hear your boyfriend say you're not wife material."

Gregg cringes at that, but he never gives his opinion on the matter, which I appreciate.

"I can't believe Cody of all people would say that."

"Yeah, join the club." Boone moves in my lap, and I run my hand down his soft fur. He nuzzles into my touch, and I'm instantly jealous that I don't have a sweet puppy of my own. "He's so cute."

Macy chuckles. "He really is. He's such a good boy."

"Only the best for my girl." Gregg leans down and kisses Macy's forehead.

Macy radiates joy. She loves traditions, especially at the holidays. And since Gregg was anti-holiday, she challenged him to one season with her to see what the Christmas spirit is. Needless to say, she won by making him fall in love with the holiday season while making him fall in love with her.

My romance-loving heart freaking swooned when I heard all the details. I mean who couldn't fall in love with someone after trips to the skating rink and Christmas light gazing? Not to mention a trip to a cozy cabin in the Midwest.

Snow, hot tubs, and charm—sign me up.

And now my heart hurts again.

Slumping in my chair, I turn my attention to the muted television where Gregg has a golf tournament playing. He's a member of the CTU golf team, but hasn't played since his stroke. He should be back on the green next fall, which is great for him.

It's not long before the screen blurs, and white noise fills my head as my mind drifts back off. My thoughts won't stop spinning as it replays the last couple of months.

He made sure my favorite latte was delivered to me.

He remembers how I take my pizza.

Sitting in the quiet while I read.

The tattoo of the wildflower.

There's no way our relationship was just a way to work out stress. Deep down I know I'm overreacting, but it doesn't ease the pain.

Sometime later, I stand up from my seat. Boone hops down from my lap, sitting at my feet. "Thanks for letting me crash here tonight."

"You're always welcome," Gregg replies with a smile.

"Seriously, Chloe. You can stay for as long as you need," Macy adds.

With a tight-lipped smile, I nod at them. "Thanks, guys, I appreciate it. I'll just stay for tonight. It won't be long, and my cover is blown."

"Love you, Chlo."

"Love you, too, Mace. Night." I move around the couch

toward the hallway that leads to the spare bedroom. There's a sweet little shadow at my feet. "Mind if I steal Boone for the night?"

"He's all yours!" Macy calls out from behind me. Boone and I continue down the hallway. Reaching down, I pick him up and set him on the bed where he spins around in a few circles before plopping down on the bed.

I fall asleep with the warmth of a puppy, a lump in my throat, and tears in my eyes.

Heartbreak fucking sucks.

CHAPTER 35

CODY

IFUCKED UP.

It's plain and simple. The acidic words burned the whole way out of my mouth, but I didn't stop saying them. I should have. I knew I shouldn't have let my dad bait me. But he did, and I lost the battle. In more ways than one.

It's been four days since I last heard from Chloe.

Four days of unanswered calls and texts.

Of her not being at her townhouse when I stop by.

Brynn is clearly in Chloe's corner, which she should be because of the whole girl code thing, but I'm her friend, too, dammit. She refuses to tell me where Chloe's staying, and it's really starting to piss me off.

I need to know she's with people who support her and not off someplace spiraling, her insecurities rearing their ugly heads. Especially since I couldn't show up and be the man she needed me to be.

Dammit. I need to find her. I need to be given the chance

to just fucking explain. I know we can move past this. At least I hope we can.

I know that my explanation won't take the pain away, but maybe it'll give her some insight on why I did what I did.

There is no excuse for it, but at the end of the day, I did do it to protect her. And I'm pissed that she won't just answer a text. Give me a 'leave me alone,' 'fuck off,' something. She won't even return Leah's messages, which yeah, she's digging around for information for me, but she's also in Chloe's corner.

"Bro, you look like shit," Hudson says as he enters our kitchen. I'm standing at our island with my hands resting on the cool surface, head draped down between my shoulders. There's no doubt that I look like shit. I haven't slept, and I've barely eaten. I've been abusing my body by pushing it to the limits in the weight room. If I'm not in class, attending mandatory practice, or visiting the girls' townhouse, I'm running through campus.

Lifting my head, I glare at him. "No shit, fucker."

"Hey, don't shoot the messenger," he says, raising his hands in defense. "Rumor on the street is a pretty blonde-haired girl is crashing at a sorority house."

My eyes snap in his direction. "Which one?"

"Whatever one Savannah Holycross is in."

"Delta Zeta."

He snaps his thumb and middle finger together before he's pointing his finger in my direction. "Yeah, that's the one."

I've spent four days trying to track her down. I've been to her townhouse. To Macy's apartment. To her friend from the newspaper staff's apartment. I never would have thought of the sorority house where Sav lives.

Savannah is new to the girls' friend group. She's been coming to more parties with the girls, and she completely slipped my mind. Honestly, I didn't see Chloe hiding out in a sorority house, but then again, I didn't expect her to overhear my bullshit and run into her estranged mom within fifteen minutes of each other.

Pushing off from the counter, I storm out of the kitchen.

"Might want to take a fucking shower!" Hudson yells after me. "You stink!"

Sniffing my armpit, I cringe. Shit, he's right.

Twenty minutes later I'm freshly showered with jeans and a gray threadbare T-shirt. The dark circles and bags are still under my eyes, but at least I don't smell like ass anymore. Running my fingers through my damp hair, I grab a hat and toss it on my head. Hopefully, the bill will help cover my stressed face.

The drive to the DZ house goes quicker than I want, even with a couple of quick stops along the way. I spent the whole drive running through different scenarios.

What if she slams the door in my face?

What if she's no longer living there? That seems to be her MO, not staying in one place for a long period.

It's smart, and if she wasn't running from me, I'd appreciate the clever trick. But I am the one she's hiding from, and I can't handle it anymore.

What if she's done with us? I've lived without her for four days, and I'm going crazy. Somewhere along the way, she's stolen my heart.

Hell, if I'm being honest with myself, she stole my heart two years ago. It hasn't been mine since I walked into that diner with the retro decor and laid eyes on the prettiest girl I've ever seen. She had a smile that made everyone's day brighter. Honey-blonde hair piled high on her head with pieces falling around her beautiful ocean-blue eyes.

Steeling my shoulders, I trek up the sidewalk that leads to the large colonial home. An oversized porch with columns welcomes you to the pink front door. Reaching for the gold knocker, I tap it a couple of times against the door.

Nerves swim in my system as I wait for one of the girls to answer the door. Hoping and wishing my girl is one of the many on the inside.

A brunette I've seen around campus answers the door. "Hey, Cody."

"Hey, is Sav or Chloe Mariano here?" Placing my hands in my pockets, I rock back and forth on my toes. My nerves are starting to weigh against me.

I watch as the brunette's face morphs into a pitying look, and it makes my skin crawl. "No, they're both out right now. I can let them know you stopped by."

"No, that's okay," I say with a frustrated sigh. "Do you mind if I just wait out here?"

"You can wait in the living room if you want."

Shaking my head, I step back. "I'm fine out here. Thanks."

"No problem. If it matters, I told her she should at least hear you out. In my experience, guys are idiots and don't realize half the shit they're saying when they say it."

"Thanks...I think?" She nods as if she just solved all of the problems in the world by announcing that guys are dumbasses who don't know how to think. In this situation, I think I can agree with her.

Moving backward until I reach the steps, I slide down on the first one and rest my back against the column. Adjusting until I'm comfortable, I wait.

And wait.

And wait some more.

Girls come and go, but it's never the one I'm searching for. Two hours pass, and I'm debating if I should give up when I spy golden blonde hair. She's dressed in an oversized sweatshirt with bike shorts peeking out below the hem. The light she always possesses is dimmed, and my heart aches at the pain I've caused her.

Savannah spots me first, her expression morphing into anger

like a mama bear preparing to protect her young. Chloe must feel the shift in Sav's body language because she bounces her eyes from her friend to where I'm sitting on the concrete step.

There's a brief look that passes through Chloe's eyes, and I can't tell if it's frustration she's been found or relief that I haven't given up.

She should know that I wouldn't give up. I've been leaving gifts at the townhouse, inside the newsroom, at Macy's, wherever I think she'll be. Honey lavender lattes, bouquets of wildflowers, I even went through her wishlist and purchased a couple of books she's been wanting to read. Every gift was accompanied by a note saying how sorry I am and what I love about her.

She tentatively approaches me, and I stand, reaching down and grabbing the large bouquet I picked up on the way. I stopped at Chloe's favorite florist, and she helped me pick out an arrangement she knew Chloe would love. The bouquet is a mixture of eucalyptus sprigs, a variety of white and peach garden roses, and babys'-breath—whatever that is—wrapped in brown craft paper and tied together with a pastel purple ribbon—Chloe's favorite.

"Hey, Wildflower."

Her feet carry her toward me, but she pauses at the bottom of the steps. Savannah is still firmly planted at her side.

"Cody. I see you finally tracked me down. I guess I can't expect a sorority house not to spread gossip." Her eyes bounce to Sav's, before saying, "No offense."

"None taken. Gossip is a requirement to be a member of the house."

"These are for you," I say, reaching the bouquet down to her. "Is there a place we can talk?"

She takes the bouquet from me, and I see a glimmer of sparkle in her eyes as a faint smile ghosts across her lips. She loves the flowers. Chloe's eyes glance around us, pausing off to the side where there's no doubt a group of girls watching from the window. Freaking nosy leeches.

"You two can talk in the dining room. I can shut the sliding doors. It's probably the only place where you'll get any privacy."

Stepping aside, I let the girls climb the rest of the way up the stairs and follow as Savannah leads us into the lion's den. Glancing to my right, I'm met with a group of girls scurrying away from the window as if they weren't just watching every second.

The dining room is off to the left and after following Chloe inside, Savannah steps away and shuts the door, sealing us into the space. Neither of us moves, both firmly rooted in place.

Flexing my fingers into fists, I relax them, repeating the motion. I'm fighting with every fiber of my being not to erase the gap between us and wrap my arms around my girl. I watch as Chloe's focus shifts around the room, avoiding me before her eyes rest on the bouquet in her hands. She leans down, smelling the floral aroma. I watch as her eyes widen when she notices the brown envelope sticking out of the blooms. Setting the bouquet down, she pulls the envelope out.

I watch as she reads the note. Moisture gathers in the corner of her beautiful eyes, and I fight like hell not to say anything. I'm hoping the words the florist helped me come up with are enough to spark the conversation we both so desperately need.

Words have never been my strong suit. Yeah, I might be able to flirt and joke around, but when it comes to using words to express deep feelings, I clam up. It's like I forget every word in the English language.

Thankfully, the florist was all too willing to help me capture my thoughts in a way that translated well to Chloe.

Chloe sits in the chair in front of her, her expression blank, as she plays with the card in front of her. I don't know what to do. I've never been in this position before with a girl who I can't imagine my life without.

"Your words *really* hurt," she starts, her gaze never leaving the deep brown table in front of her.

"Wildflower—" I start, but she's cutting me off before I have a chance to plead my case.

Her eyes find mine, and it kills me to see the tears that escape. I never want to make her cry, never want to be the cause of her pain.

"Let me say what I need to say." She pauses, inhaling a deep breath as she straightens her shoulders. "I know deep down you weren't trying to hurt me. In some twisted way, I see that you were trying to protect me from your dad, but it still hurts like hell to hear that I'm not enough. You know the baggage I've been carrying for years and to hear you use that against me, it felt like you reached inside my chest and ripped my heart out.

"I needed you, Cody. Never in a million years could I have imagined that I would run into my mom—especially the way that I did—but when I needed you most, you were shit-talking me to your family. And maybe this was presumptuous, and maybe I'm ahead of myself, but there was a part of me that thought someday, maybe, they'd be a part of my family too. And I know how insane that is, given your history with your father, but it's where my mind was."

Risking her fleeing like a skittish deer, I move closer. Reaching the chair beside her, I pull it out from the table and drop to my knees. With my thumb and finger, I find her chin and softly grip it, pulling her toward me.

"It wasn't presumptuous. The idea of making you mine, of being yours forever, it makes me feral. There's no way I picture my future, and it doesn't have you in it. You're my sun. My world orbits around you. You're my best friend and the person I want in my corner. You're the person I want in the stands cheering for me.

"You're the one I want to talk to first thing in the morning and the last person I talk to before I go to bed. It's always been you. Since that day in the diner when you fumbled through taking our orders, I knew then that it was going to be the two of us. Even when I was a childish moron and left you. A part of me deep down knew if two people could, we'd find our way back to each other. My story ends with you, Wildflower. You're my happily ever after."

Tears pour out of her eyes at the admission of my words. Somehow I was able to effectively communicate how I feel. I guess when my back's against the wall, my brain gets on the same wavelength as my heart. Leaning forward, I kiss the trail of tears, erasing them from her perfect skin.

Chloe Mariano is my endgame. If I have to beg until my last breath, then that's what I'll do. Because there's no way my story doesn't include her.

Her arms wrap around my neck, and she pulls me in close. Wrapping my arms around her, I tug her in close. Hoping and praying that my love for her is felt in this embrace. I need her to feel my love, feel how our souls connect. She might be the romantic, but I've learned a few things from her romance novels.

"I love you, Chloe. I love you so much." I whisper the words against her ear.

She sighs against my chest and hope soars through my heart. "I know you do, and I love you, too, Cody. But I still don't understand why you said what you said. Was it your way of protecting me?"

"In a sick and twisted way, yeah." Lifting my hat, I nervously play with it before settling it back on my head. "When he confronted me about you, I tried to play it off like you were just a member of the team, but he wasn't believing my bullshit, so I twisted it into something horrible hoping he'd drop it."

Chloe's face turns into pain as if she's reliving hearing those comments all over again. Before she can dwell on them for too long, I continue.

"The words felt like acid, and I wanted to take them back as soon as I said them, but I couldn't, the words were already out. As I watched his face turn into a twisted smirk as if he'd won, I decided enough was enough. The backbone I'd been slowly growing took shape, and I finally confronted him." Her head snaps in my direction as shock laces her pretty, albeit tear-stained, face. "I told him our relationship was done. I didn't want to hear from him, didn't want to see his name on my phone, and our twisted relationship had me downplaying my relationship with the women I love."

"I never should have said you weren't enough because the thing is, I don't feel like I'm enough when I'm in your presence. You're so good, Chloe. You have the purest heart, and I feel like I'm going to dim your light."

"Never, Cody Jacobs—" Her words are cut off as her lips find mine. Reaching my arms around her, I pull her to me, never wanting to let her go.

All too quickly she's pulling away from my arms. "Karma will get him. In the meantime, I hope he walks across Legos without shoes on and then stubs his toe on the stairs and then has hair in his food."

"Damn, feisty Chloe turns me on."

Her chuckle fills the space as she leans forward, her lips finding mine.

Damn, I've missed these lips.

"Take me home, Cody," she murmurs against my lips.

"Your place or mine?"

CHAPTER 36

Chloe

THE LATE AFTERNOON SUN STREAMS THROUGH THE library windows casting the space in a warm, golden hue. Tables are packed with students busy cramming for finals. That's exactly what I'm doing here. I've been living on a Red Bull and Twizzler diet all week as I try to cram any last-minute information into my brain. The baseball team has had two back-to-back away series, which hasn't allowed much time for final exam preparation.

Do I feel overwhelmed? Yes.

Am I panicking? A little.

Do I want this week to be over? Hell, yes.

It's been a week since Cody and I reunited. Well, we weren't really separated. Both of us just needed space to work our shit out. I knew deep down I was being a child by not giving him a chance to explain, but I needed to work out my childhood trauma.

Dad drove up one evening, and I told him everything about Camilla. It was hard for him to hear that she moved on and found a family of her own. Both of us have the overwhelming feeling of not being good enough. But he reassured me that there was nothing wrong with me. That Camilla's issues are solely on her. She decided to ignore the best person in the world—his words, not mine—and that's something she's going to have to live with for the rest of her life. With a big parting hug, my dad told me he'd see me soon as he departed for three months in Arizona where he'll be overseeing the completion of his new restaurant while getting it up and running.

While I was sorting through my trauma, Cody was busy working on his. He's officially cut ties with his dad. It wasn't an easy decision, but after a long conversation with his sister, one in which Leah assured Cody she could handle whatever came her way. Cody decided to block his dad's number.

It's like a weight was lifted from his shoulders. He's walking around with a lighter air. I think he's grown to love the game again. No longer does he carry the weight of waiting for the other shoe to drop. Now baseball can be his only focus.

Grabbing my planner from my book bag, a piece of paper falls out. Reaching down, I pick it up and flip it over. I smile at the words on the page.

There's no doubt in my mind that my favorite florist helped spruce up his words. And her little note on the bottom of the card was the perfect touch.

Wildflower,

The sun shines brighter with you in my life. I'm lost without you. Since the day I met you, I knew you were it for me. My world is trapped in your orbit, and it spins in chaos when you're not around. You're more than enough for me. You're my everything. I love you.

-Cody

PS—Put the boy out of his misery. Life's too short. Don't let love pass you by, sweet girl.

"Hey, Wildflower," Cody whispers in my ear, kissing my forehead.

I lean into him for a second, savoring his warmth. "Hey, babe. How was your exam?"

"Not bad," he says, dropping down into the empty chair next to me. "What time is your final?"

Hitting my phone screen, I check the time. "In an hour. I think I'm ready."

"I'd say." He laughs, reaching his arm around my shoulders. "You've been here for days, and you're starting to shake from all the energy drinks."

"Lattes weren't cutting it." My body involuntarily twitches. Maybe I've had too much caffeine. "I want to sleep for a week straight."

"You're lucky we're off all weekend. And we'll have the townhouse to ourselves since Brynn will be in Kansas City with Quinton."

This weekend is the NFL draft, the biggest weekend for college football players looking to play at the next level. Brynn finished her finals early so she could be with Quinton. We're all excited for Q as experts have predicted he'll go in the top five of the first round.

"Speaking of Q," Cody says, leaning in closer and kissing my neck. I blush because we aren't alone in the library, and I am still not one for PDA. "He needs me to do him a solid. Can I borrow your keys?"

I eye him skeptically. "Um, yeah, that's fine."

Pulling out my keys from my bag, I hand them over. Q must have some kind of surprise planned for Brynn, but I can't figure out why he wouldn't have asked me himself. Whatever.

"Thanks, babe. Good luck with your final." Cody stands, planting another kiss on my lips before he walks away.

"Hey," I hiss, trying not to disturb others. "How will I get back in?"

"I'll just wait for you." He smiles, making a heart gesture with his hands, and my heart melts.

I love him.

Three hours later I'm finally climbing the stairs to the front door. I'm exhausted. My brain feels like mush. I think my kidneys are failing from all of the caffeine. I just want to climb into the biggest pair of sweatpants I have and watch a movie.

I can tell from the windows that the lights are off, and I'm hoping Cody remembered he has my keys, and there's no way I can get in if he locked up and left. Pushing open the front door, I'm greeted with candles lit on the entryway table.

"Cody!" I call out, putting my bag on the hook and taking off my shoes.

I start toward the kitchen but catch movement out of the corner of my eyes. Cody walks into the front entryway from the living room. Athletic shorts hang off his slender hips, a CTU shirt stretches tight across his chest, and his CTU hat is on backward. But it's what he's holding that has me pausing.

"What's that?" I ask, closing the gap between us.

His famous smirk quirks the corner of his lips. "A DVD player. I thought we could watch a movie together."

Tilting my head to the side, I gaze up at him. "You know I have Netflix, right?"

"I know." He shrugs, stepping even closer until there's barely enough space for him to hold the DVD player between us. He peers down at me, a boyish grin appearing almost as if he's nervous for my response. "But I thought we could watch it on this. It reminds me of the time I came over and almost kissed you."

"During the ice storm," I whisper. "I knew you were going to kiss me."

"Well of course I was going to kiss you. Seriously, Chloe, you read romance books as a hobby. It was the perfect opportunity."

Leaning up on my toes, I wrap an arm around his neck, pulling him down to me. Our lips meet as I gently nip his bottom lip before pulling away. "Brynn said the same thing. I think her words were more like we should use each other to keep warm."

"I knew she was a good wingwoman." His laugh vibrates his chest as the two of us separate. He takes my hand and leads me into the kitchen, which only has candles lighting the room.

On the counter sits a pizza box, a bowl of salad, what looks like lemon bars, and paper plates. Dropping my hand, he heads to the fridge. Popping the door open, he reaches inside and pulls out a can of hard seltzer. "You've really made yourself at home while I was gone."

"Only the best for my girl." Setting the cans of hard seltzer down, he gestures for me to step around the island. "Fill your plate, babe."

Lifting the pizza lid, I smile down at the pepperoni and pineapple pie. Cody Jacobs left nothing out of his plans for tonight. If I didn't love him already, I would now.

"Thank you for doing this."

Wrapping his arms around my waist, he slides his chest against my back before trailing kisses up my neck. "I love you."

"I love you too," I say, tilting my neck so he can get a better angle. With one last hard nip, he backs away, leaving me a wet, needy mess. "Forget the pizza, let's go make out."

He chuckles. "There'll be plenty of time for that."

"Oops, I didn't mean to say that out loud."

Cody spins me until my back is pressed against the counter as his front presses into me. I can feel his hard length against my stomach. I'm glad I'm not the only one who's worked up.

"I think you did mean to say it. I think my sweet, shy, quiet girl wants to be loud and demanding about what she wants."

I hum at his words because yes, yes I do. Cody Jacobs turns me into a sexual deviant. Years I've gone without sex, but he makes me never want to go without it again.

Placing my plate on the counter, I look up at him. His darkened eyes find mine as I lower to the ground, taking his pants down with me.

"Fuck. I'll never get tired of seeing you on your knees."

Releasing his hard length from his boxers, I watch as it bobs in front of my face. Licking my lips, I take in all of him. And I mean all of him. I've never been one to think dicks look good, but Cody's cock is gorgeous. It's long and thick, veiny in all the right places.

Leaning forward, I flatten my tongue, running it from root to tip. Cody lets out a groan of approval, which only fuels me. Licking around the tip like it's my favorite flavor of lollipop, I lap at the bead of moisture on his tip before I swallow him whole. He hits the back of my throat, and I let out a small gag. I get in a rhythm of working him with my hand as I bob my head.

"Fuck, Wildflower. I love the way you suck my cock. Such a good girl. So needy for me." I hum around his shaft at his praise. Never would have guessed I was such a ho for the praise, but damn does it light up my insides. My mouth moves higher up his cock until my lips are wrapped around his tip while my hand circles his thick shaft.

Cody groans deep in his chest, and I feel the vibration run through his body. My head bobs faster to keep up with the pace of my hand that is working him. "Damn, baby. Keep sucking me like that, and I'm going to come quick."

Sitting backward, I let his dick slide out of my mouth with a pop. Looking up at him with a devilish smirk, I tell him what I want him to do. "So, fuck my face, and then you can fuck me."

"Who are you, and what have you done with my sweet Wildflower?" he says as I suck him deeper, swallowing around his tip. I feel the sharp tug as his grip tightens around my hair causing tears to form in my eyes.

His hips thrust harder, faster, as he uses my mouth to seek out his release. With one deep-throated suck, Cody is spilling his hot cum, and it slides down my throat. I moan as the saltiness hits my tongue, and my head continues bobbing until I've milked every last drop.

"Fuck." His words drawl out in a raspy tone as I let his cock slide out from between my lips. Leaning back on my knees, I wipe the corner of my lips with my thumb.

"Mmm, my favorite appetizer."

Reaching down, Cody helps me to my feet before his hand cups the nape of my neck as he pulls my mouth to him. His tongue plunges inside my mouth as he flicks my tongue. Within minutes, his dick is hard again and pressing against me.

His hands slide down my back as he trails kissing down my neck. Grabbing the backs of my thighs, he lifts me in the air before he's moving. Gently, he lays me down on the counter.

I'm so worked up, he could blow on my clit, and I'd come from that alone.

His fingers grab a hold of the waistband of my leggings as he peels them down my legs, taking my panties with him.

"Damn, baby, I can see how wet you are from here." A sly grin spreads across his face before he reaches behind him and pulls his shirt over his head as he drops to his knees. A soft sigh escapes me as I look down at my favorite set of hazel eyes. "I plan on being a messy eater."

Oh for fuck's sake.

He blows on my throbbing clit, and I let out a deep moan. A fire sets off at the base of my spine. "Greedy, girl."

"Cody, I'm so close."

As if those were the words he was waiting for, his mouth closes over my pussy as a full-body shiver erupts over me. Cody laps up my arousal like I'm his favorite meal. He's starving for me. A man obsessed who's stumbled across his favorite feast. With his hands behind my knees, he pulls me closer to the edge before he's pushing my legs further apart.

He shifts his mouth to my clit, sucking the swollen bud between his lips. His teeth bite down on the sensitive button as his fingers dive into my throbbing pussy. I can feel my orgasm coil in the pit of my stomach.

"I'm so close. God, Cody," I scream out his name.

His fingers work me as he pushes them in and out. "That's it, baby, scream out my name. Let the neighbors know who's tongue fucking you tonight."

I moan deeper, feeling it vibrate through my body as I curl my toes. "That's it, baby. Let go. Drown me in your pussy, like a good girl."

My legs close around his ears, trapping him where I want him, as my fingers pull his dark hair. In mere seconds, I am screaming through my orgasm.

Cody never lets up. He keeps pumping his fingers rough and hard through my throbbing pussy before biting down on my already sensitive clit as I ride out the waves of my orgasm.

Chest heaving, I watch as he pops to his feet, bending down to grab his wallet from his abandoned shorts. Pulling out a foil packet, he rips it open with his teeth before sliding the rubber down his thick, hard cock. The sight alone had my orgasm building again.

"Hop down and turn over." His voice demands, and I do exactly that. I rest my shirt-covered chest against the counter where I am bent over, legs spread, exposing my wet and needy pussy.

I feel his heat from behind as his dick notches at my sensitive entrance. His hands skim up my thighs, over my ass where he kneads my cheeks in his hands, before climbing higher up my back. He takes my shirt with him before he's lifting it over my head. His fingers flick the clasp of my bra where I slump forward, letting the lace material slide down my arms.

"That's better. You had too many clothes on," Cody says, as he's pushing my back down. The coolness from the counter bites into my skin causing goose bumps to break free. Leaning forward, I feel his lips graze my skin. "I love you."

"I love yo—" My words are cut off as Cody thrusts inside of me, causing me to lose my breath before a loud moan ricochets off the walls. He slams inside of me without giving me a chance to adjust to his size. But the slight burning sensation only helps build the pleasure. "Cody!"

"That's it, baby." He begins pounding into me from behind. His hips hit my ass as my hips hit the edge of the counter. I whimper at the first contact, and Cody's hands immediately rest on my hip bones, protecting me from the counter. I arch my back as I try to get him deeper. Cody understands the assignment and starts fucking me without abandon. He pumps into me faster and faster, both of us on the brink of another orgasm.

"Be a good girl and touch yourself for me."

Sliding my hand down my stomach, I find the sensitive flesh swollen and throbbing. I rub in tight circles as Cody fucks me from behind. "I'm so close."

"Me too," he grits the words between his teeth. One of his hands leaves my hips and finds my nipple. Pulling and tweaking with the mixture of everything else happening, my senses overwhelm. My vision starts to darken with every tug on my nipple and circle of my clit.

Another orgasm rips through me, and I feel my pussy grip his cock as he pulsates inside of me, spilling his cum in the condom.

When I come back down, it's with Cody's forehead resting against my back. Chest heaving as both of us are completely spent.

"That's one way to work off post-finals stress," I say, spinning around and trying to catch my breath.

He slides out of me and walks over to the trash can where he discards the used condom. Erasing the gap between us, he grabs my face in both of his hands before stealing another kiss. "I fucking love you."

"I love you, too. Now can we eat? I'm starving." Bending down, I grab my discarded panties and pull them up my legs before tossing on his shirt. I grab us both plates of cold pizza while Cody swaps out the room-temperature seltzers.

We make our way into the living room where Cody has more candles lit. He quickly hooks up the DVD player while I settle into the couch.

The opening credit of *Neighbors* fills the screen. I smile over at Cody as he takes a large bite of pizza. His eyes find mine as a smile spreads across his face.

I love how he can make the simplest things feel like the most romantic. Neither one of us needs glitz and glamour. We just need each other.

In the midst of all the chaos this semester has brought up, one thing is for certain, I never would have gotten to this point without the change up that I thought was ruining my life.

Cody Jacobs is the change up I never saw coming.

EPILOGUE

Chloe

Post Season

"**H**EY, HANDSOME." I WATCH AS CODY STARTLES AT the sound of my voice. He's sitting inside the dugout at Charles Schwab Stadium dressed in joggers and a black hoodie, his hands clasped and hanging between his legs as he stares out over the field. His signature backward hat sits on top of his head. Smiling, I take a second to take in my boyfriend on the eve of his biggest game.

The Eagles made it to Omaha, home of the College World Series. To say that I'm proud of him—and the team—would be an understatement.

Tomorrow, well today, will be the biggest game of their lives. It's the final game of the College World Series. The winner goes home with the hardware. It's been a very long postseason run over the last four-and-a-half weeks. Seventeen games have been played in multiple locations. With an early loss during the conference tournament, The Eagles were able to walk away champs.

That only fueled their fire. Since then, they've dominated

the Regionals, Super Regionals, and so far, the College World Series. Thankfully, the series is the best out of three because the boys suffered a tight two-to-one loss yesterday.

But today is a new day.

The atmosphere around the team feels like the pressure change of an incoming storm. Energy radiates in the air. Restlessness is taking over. This is why when I rolled over in my bed and felt a cold spot where my boyfriend should be lying, I sat up concerned. When Cody wasn't in our room, I had an idea or two where he might be. My first thought was to check the hotel gym. It felt like a poetic moment since that's where he found me so many weeks ago. Cody seems to be creating a lot of full-circle moments since we had a *moment* in Charleston. When the gym was empty, I knew he'd be at the stadium visualizing.

And I was right.

Cody's face lights up. "Hey, beautiful. How'd you get in here?"

His eyes track my movement as I make my way closer to him. Lifting my press badge, he nods. "Makes sense."

"I also bribed the security guard with an Oreo blizzard. I figured everyone likes Oreos and ice cream." He chuckles, and the sound warms my soul. For the past two weeks, I've watched the man I love pour every ounce of his energy into the game that he loves.

As I go to walk past him, his hand reaches out and pulls me down onto my lap. Seated on his thigh, my hands rest in between his spread ones as his arm wraps around me. I melt against his side and the feeling of being wrapped in his embrace.

"Are you doing okay?" The words are hushed against his neck as I press my lips to his pulse point.

Cody leans down, kissing the top of my head. "Just nervous."

"For the game? Cody, you're going to be amazing. You always are. Just shut the noise out and throw your pitches."

He hums at my response. "It's not just that. My mom is going to be at the game. I saw her text when I got up to pee, and then I couldn't go back to sleep. It'll be the first time I've seen her since..." The words trail off.

Since Charleston.

Since the day I overheard him saying horrible things about me after running into my mom for the first time in fifteen years.

But that was then, and this is now. We've pushed most of the events from that day from our minds. It was a moment neither one of us wanted to relive.

In the time that has passed, Cody has cut off all communication with his father. Leah moved in with the boys four weeks ago so now the pressure of keeping his dad away from her has eased.

His mom took his dad's side, which we both figured, and he hasn't spoken with her since he returned from Charleston, and she tried to come up with excuses for his dad's behavior. He drew a line in the sand and told her that if she couldn't see past the bullshit, Cody didn't want her in his life either. It's been messy, but we've had each other to help ease some of the stress.

While he's had a stressful few weeks, my life has been just as chaotic. The article I wrote on Coach Weber for The Eagles Gazette went viral and went national. It's baffling to me that an article I wrote—about sports, nonetheless—was picked up by a reputable sports broadcast company. Professor Weaver has insisted I stay on as a reporter through the rest of the season, which is why I have a press badge for the College World Series. She also insisted I apply for sports journalism internships, as well as lifestyle options.

I'm still not sure if sports journalism is the direction I want to go, but it doesn't hurt to weigh out all of my options, especially since we have no idea where Cody will be a year from now. While I'm an independent female, I still want to add him into the equation of what I do post-graduation. But that's a worry for next year.

"She wants to meet you." His words interrupt my thoughts as my breath stutters in my chest.

"Sh-she does?" I fumble the words as anxiety creeps in.

He hums his response as his hand coasts up my inner thigh beneath the hem of the T-shirt dress I slipped on. Warmth spreads, licking my body with flames. "But I don't want to talk about her."

"What do you want to talk about?" My voice is raspy with desire. Cody Jacobs has turned me from a shy little bookworm to a fiend who can't get enough of him.

"How about we don't do any talking at all?" His fingers reach the apex of my thighs; in about a second, he's going to discover...

"Chloe Mariano, where are your panties?" Cody says as his finger grazes the outside of my sex.

Breath stuttering, I push the words out as he continues running his finger up and down my slit, drawing out my wetness. "I was in a hurry to get out the door to find you."

He groans at my admission, and I feel him start to rise beneath me. The feeling of him getting aroused because of me will never get old.

His voice drops to a deep, husky whisper as he leans in closer to my ear. "Can you be a good girl and be quiet for me?"

As soon as I nod my head in reply, Cody is plunging two fingers inside me. I gasp and fight the moan that is desperate to escape. Working his fingers in and out, he builds that pleasure deep inside me.

Soft moans escape my lips as I whisper his name. His thumb grazes my clit, and my stomach tightens as my orgasm builds. My walls clench around his fingers as my lips find his neck, needing to occupy my lips before I cry out.

Cody Jacobs is a god on and off the field, and the way he strokes my pussy like he's lining his fingers against the laces of a baseball is otherworldly. The man knows how to use his fingers. His thumb strokes across my clit, applying just enough pressure that has me biting down on the soft, tan flesh of his neck.

A soft chuckle rumbles against my lips as my impending orgasm continues to climb higher and higher. "Bite marks on national television, you're really making sure everyone knows that I'm taken, huh, Wildflower?"

I feel his cock twitch underneath me as I release his skin with a pop. "Shit, I'm sorry."

Sheepishly, I glance up only to find wild, untamed eyes staring back down at me. "Don't. It turns me on that you want to mark me for everyone to see."

He removes his fingers from my soaked sex, and I groan at the loss of his fingers.

"Stand up and turn around," he demands with a light slap on my ass. Quirking my head, I eye him skeptically. "Up, Chlo."

I do as he commands and stand in between his spread legs while Cody reaches into his pocket and removes his wallet, plucking out a foil wrapper in the process. In one swift motion, I watch in admiration as he frees himself from the confines of his sweats as his thick erection bobs free.

Before he has a chance to sheathe himself, I'm dropping to my knees. My eyes find him, and even in the dim light of the dugout, I can see that arrogant smirk quirk across his lips as his eyes darken even more in desire. Reaching forward, I lick him from root to tip before my lips pull everything he has to offer into my greedy mouth.

His approval vibrates throughout his body. "Damn, my Wildflower looks pretty with a mouthful of my cock."

The dirty words only spur me on as I suck on his head before pulling him as deep as I can down my throat, using my hand to pump what I'm unable to. He thrusts harder, hitting me deeper, and I fight the urge to gag. In all our time together, Cody has always made sure that I'm well taken care of. Now on the precipice of one of his biggest games, it's my turn to make my man melt before me.

Continuing my assault, I alternate between licking and sucking while pumping and laving up his taste.

"Wildflower," he grits out the words, thrusting against my face as I hum around his shaft. His cock hits the back of my throat again, and this time it forces me to come up for air. With a deep inhale, I descend back down only to be stopped. Quirking my eyebrow, I look up at the mess of a man before me.

His thumb skates across my swollen lips. "As much as I love these pretty lips wrapped around my cock, I need to be inside you."

Standing to my feet, I watch as Cody slips the condom on. He looks up at me with desire across his face and love in his eyes. There's no doubt in my mind that after all the hell we've been through, the two of us are going to make it through whatever life throws at us.

"C'mere, baby." His voice softens as he reaches his hand out for me to hold while I straddle his lap—in a dugout.

Placing my hands on his shoulder, he lines himself up with my needy entrance. I slowly sink down on his waiting cock. We both moan at the contact as my pussy swallows his erection until I'm fully seated. Our lips find each other, and in that kiss, we pour everything we have into it.

Love. Desire. Lust. Hope. The future.

With his hands gripping my hips, I begin to ride him. Euphoria and white-hot desire spur me on. Rocking my hips slowly, I build the pressure between us knowing that it won't take either of us long to get to the finish line. In this position, Cody fills me up and hits that spot inside me that has me ready to come. Tightness coils in my stomach, and I chase the high. My clit knocks against his pelvis bone, and I have to crash my lips to his to keep from screaming out.

Slipping his hands under my dress, his rough, calloused fingers kiss my skin until he reaches my tight pebbled nips. Twisting and tweaking my peaks between his fingers, my back arches, pushing my boobs closer to him. The action causes me to sink even more on his cock as my head flies back.

"Cody," I grit between my teeth. "It feels so good. Oh my god."

"I know, baby," he pants. "Touch yourself. I'm so close."

Reaching between us, my finger massages my bundle of nerves, and it's seconds before I'm detonating. I continue riding out my orgasm as I feel Cody pump his release into the condom. Chests heaving, we stay like that until both of us have come down from the euphoric, earth-shattering orgasm.

"I love you, Wildflower."

"I love you, too, Cody Jacobs. Now let's go get you a championship."

Hands cup around my face as my knees bounce up and down. The anticipation and stress of this game has me wound tight.

It's the top of the ninth inning; Cody is on the mound with a three-to-one lead over Oklahoma Central University. This game has been a battle of strikes as both pitchers have been throwing their best games. Even though we've given up a run, Nolan and Cody have been in sync all evening with their pitch calls.

Speaking of Nolan, today has been a remarkable game for him. Not only has he manned behind the plate with excellence, but he's hit not one, but two home runs. And even though they were home runs and not grand slams, I still stood at the top of the stairs that led out to the field and did my celebratory dance.

The crowd has been insane this whole game. Beer showers have rung out from the stands after each shut-out inning, or home run, coating the fans around them in warm, sticky beer. The feeling has to be getting quite gross considering it's been in the mid-80s all day with the sun beating down on us. Nothing like caked-on amber liquid coating your already sweaty skin. Hard pass.

The crack of the bat has me snapping my head back to the game before me. I watch with bated breath as the ball sails in the air down the left field side. Exhaling a deep sigh of relief, I watch as the ball lands foul in the stands.

"Shake it off, Jacobs," Coach Weber yells from where he's leaning on the dugout fence. Cody's gaze finds Weber's, and he gives a quick nod, his face hidden behind his glove. I watch as Cody's shoulders lift and lower as if he's physically shaking off the pitch.

"Come on, Cody," I whisper the words out loud for only myself to hear. But it's like the words flew through the air and straight into Cody's ears. His head turns back toward the dugout, and I swear our eyes lock. With a wink, he turns his attention back to home plate where the batter is waiting.

Shaking off the pitch Nolan called, he finally shakes his head yes at a pitch. This could be it. One more strike will give us the last out in the inning, and since we are the home team with the lead, we won't need to bat again. One more pitch could end the game.

From my position in the dugout, I see a slight tweak of his lips into his favorite smirk, the one I love so much, and I know what he's going to throw.

With his feet lined up on rubber atop the pitcher's mound,

I watch with my breath caught in my lungs as Cody's feet stride forward. His arm cocks backward as he releases the ball at the same trajectory he always does; however, the velocity of the pitch is much slower than normal.

The batter doesn't see it coming. In one big swing, the bat slices through the air as the ball sails after his swing.

A perfect change up.

The umpire's arm flies out to the side before coming back into position in the signature movement of calling a strike.

A strike.

Strike three, and the batter's out.

That's it.

Holy shit! We just won the College World Series.

Chills break out over my skin as I watch Nolan throw his catcher's helmet and his glove in the air. Cody's shoulders sag in relief as a wide grin spreads across his gorgeous face. Arms fly in the air from the other guys on the field as those left in the dugout are hopping the fence and rushing the stairs fighting to get onto the dirt to celebrate.

Chaos ensues as my eyes fill with tears. Shock has me paralyzed as I watch the team I've grown to love this season celebrate a hard-earned victory. They did it. Snapping myself out of my stupor, I jog out onto the field and soak it all in. Spinning in a circle, I watch as liquid flies into the air, celebratory yelling echoes around the stadium as cheers of "E-A-G L-E-S" start from the crowd.

I'm stuck watching the celebrations when I feel hands grip my waist, and I'm being spun around. Cody's sweat-soaked and red-rimmed eyes fill my line of sight as I throw my arms around his neck, welcoming the sweaty feeling of his skin.

"You did it, baby!" I yell in his ear.

"We fucking did it!"

Yeah, we fucking did it.

This season I got the boy, he got the hardware, I got my self-confidence, and the journalism break. I think it's safe to say that I, Chloe Mariano, got her happily ever after.

Bring it on, universe.

I'm ready for you.

THE END

Not Ready to Leave CTU?

Want to watch sparks fly between a football player and his teammate's sister? Check out ***The Pass Protection***, a forced proximity, forbidden romance releasing Fall 2024!

Preorder and Add to Goodreads Today!
https://mybook.to/passprotection

Have you read book one in the CTU Eagles series? If you want banter, plenty of sexual tension, feeling all the feels, and a twist you don't see coming, check out Brynn and Quinton's story in *The Late Hit.*

https://mybook.to/latehit

Want to learn more about Macy and her decision to abruptly move out of the townhouse? Check out *The Christmas Scramble*, an emotional holiday novella.

https://mybook.to/christmasscramble

Acknowledgments

And that's a wrap! Cody and Chloe's story is finally finished and it is very bittersweet. To say this book was a labor of love is an understatement. It's no secret that I struggled to write this book. I wanted Cody's book to be perfect which led to me constantly second guessing his story. But after typing 'the end', I couldn't be happier with Cody and Chloe's love story.

First and foremost, to my incredible husband, thank you for constantly listening to my meltdowns and struggles. You literally kept me from breaking down and throwing in the towel. Thank you for keeping the kids busy on days I needed to lock myself away. I love you endlessly.

To my kids, I love you both so much. Seeing you both pick up books and constantly want to read them makes my heart melt. I hope you both continue to love reading as much as you do now.

To Amy, thank you for listening to my endless voice messages of me working through plot holes, venting my frustrations, and everything in between. I couldn't do this without you.

My incredible Alpha and Beta readers—Allie, Amy, Brianna, Brooklyn, Carlene, Chelsea, and Natalie, thank you ladies for everything! These stories wouldn't be possible without your help. You see each draft at the roughest and help me work through my thoughts and projections on how I want the story to end. I hope you guys never leave because I want to keep you forever.

To Mel, I don't even know where to start. Your eye for design never falls short. Seeing you bring my story to life on the cover was magical. The warm and fuzzies hit hard. Thank you for your patience as I worked through what I wanted. I love and appreciate you so much!

My editing and proofreading team—Brittni at Running Bookworm and Ellie and her team at My Brother's Editor, thank you is never enough. Brittni, you helped me work through what felt like a literal dumpster fire. Our conversations and video chats were greatly appreciated. You saw what I was trying to write and helped me get there. Ellie, you always pretty up my words and help me fix my terrible grammar mistakes. I appreciate everything you do to make sure my books get published.

Last and certainly not least, to the entire reading community. THANK YOU! Thank you for picking up my books and for reading my stories. Your constant excitement over the CTU universe keeps me writing. This wouldn't be possible without you. Every share, every comment, and every message warms my heart and I'm so incredibly grateful for you.

All my love,

Alexis

About the Author

Alexis Buxton is an avid reader turned author. A lover of all things love, Alexis enjoys reading all varieties of romance novels – the steamier, the better. Writing has always been a passion of hers and with the encouragement of friends and family, Alexis decided it was time to follow a childhood dream. She enjoys writing romance novels with damaged characters who need a little extra love and leave you *feeling all the feels*.

Born and raised in Ohio, Alexis currently resides in a small, lake town in Ohio with her husband and two small kiddos. Alexis is a small-town girl, through and through.

An avid sports fan, when she doesn't have a book in her hand, you can find Alexis watching sports. She prides herself on being a Cleveland Browns fan, even on the hardest days (or years). She also enjoys adventures with her family, visiting breweries, attending races at her local dirt track, and supporting local businesses and restaurants.

Alexis runs on coffee, craft beers, and chaos, but she wouldn't have it any other way.

Stay in touch!

facebook.com/authoralexisbuxton
instagram.com/author_alexisbuxton
goodreads.com/alexisbuxton
tiktok.com/@authoralexisbuxton